ADVANCE PRAISE FOR *THE SIXTH CONSPIRATOR*

"Taking us through the hideaways and haunts of European capitals in the mid-nineteenth century, this intriguing historical mystery—the search for Lincoln's 'Sixth Conspirator'—keeps us guessing right up to the last page. As in his highly acclaimed novels, *Jefferson, Jackson,* and *Grant,* Max Byrd tells the tale with witty and fast-paced writing that kept me turning pages, eager to know more about the 'real' men and women of the era along with the fictional characters of his creation."

—Cokie Roberts, Emmy-winning political commentator and author of *Capital Dames: The Civil War and the Women of Washington, 1848-1868*

"From its brilliant and devastating opening scene to its surprising and breakneck conclusion, *The Sixth Conspirator* takes the last tendril of the Lincoln assassination and weaves it into a compelling, erudite, witty, and wise novel that should secure Max Byrd's place among the premier writers of historical fiction working today. Not to be missed!"

—John Lescroart, bestselling author of *The 13th Juror* and *Betrayal*

"I absolutely love this novel! I think it's one of the most interesting books I've read in a long time."

—Diane Johnson, *New York Times* bestselling author of *Le Divorce*

The SIXTH CONSPIRATOR

A NOVEL

MAX BYRD

PERMUTED PRESS

A PERMUTED PRESS BOOK
ISBN: 978-1-68261-878-3
ISBN (eBook): 978-1-68261-879-0

The Sixth Conspirator:
A Novel
© 2019 by Max Byrd
All Rights Reserved

Cover art by Cody Corcoran
Interior design and layout by Honeylette Pino and Sarah Heneghan

PERMUTED
PRESS

Permuted Press, LLC
New York • Nashville
permutedpress.com

Published in the United States of America

For Haley, Abby, Noelle, and Toby, with Love

"Mr. Lincoln is, I think, the ugliest man I ever put my eyes on; there is also an expression of plebian vulgarity in his face that is offensive (you recognize the recounter of coarse stories). On the other hand, he has the look of sense and wonderful shrewdness, while the heavy eyelids give him a mark, almost, of genius. He strikes me, too, as a very honest and kindly man; and with all his vulgarity, I see no trace of low passions in his face. On the whole, he is such a mixture of all sorts, as only America brings forth. He is as much like a highly intellectual and benevolent Satyr as anything I can think of. I never wish to see him again, but, as humanity runs, I am well content to have him at the head of affairs."

—Lt. Colonel Theodore Lyman

"It may be doubted whether we should be more benefitted by the art of Memory or the art of Forgetfulness."

—Samuel Johnson

CONTENTS

PROLOGUE

Washington, D.C.

July 7, 1865

THE YOUNGEST SOLDIERS GOT UP EARLY for the hangings.

The corporals and sergeants came out into the courtyard later, yawning and blinking at the heat and slowly buttoning their tunics.

The prison carpenter and three assistants were already there, having worked by torchlight through the night to construct a scaffold and frame. Just after eight o'clock the captain in charge, a former sheriff and hangman, arrived and began to prepare four ropes and nooses from the ninety feet of two-thirds inch-thick Boston hemp that the Navy Yard had supplied the previous evening.

Close observers up along the penitentiary walls could count seven knots for each noose except the last, which the captain put aside, unfinished. But most eyes were fixed, not on the courtyard where there was only the hangman and scaffold to see, but on the open road that led north from the Old Arsenal Penitentiary gate to the end of Delaware Avenue. All the way up the road, and presumably up Delaware Avenue as far as the distant white dome of the Capitol, soldiers had been posted in loose formation, keeping the crowds of sightseers off to the sides and leaving a clear path through the center in case a messenger would come galloping down from the White House with a pardon in his satchel.

Because nobody in the prison, nobody in Washington City, nobody in Maryland or Virginia or the Eastern Seaboard or the whole vast green inland space of the thirty-five United States, now growing still and hot under the rising sun, nobody in the civilized world thought that the American government would hang a woman.

Back down in the courtyard, the carpenter had completed the scaffold and started to hammer rough, unpainted pine into coffins. In the northeast corner of the yard, a detail of soldiers had set about digging four new graves in the hard-baked ground. But it was the scaffold, forty feet away from the high south wall, that dominated the scene, a "great machine of death" according to the single newspaper reporter who was allowed to approach the structure.

Including its massive oak crossbeam, it stood at least twenty feet high, almost reaching the guards' walkway on top of the brick walls. The reporter counted and held up his fingers. The prisoners would have to climb thirteen steps from the ground to the platform, the traditional number since the days of Oliver Cromwell. Toward the front of the platform were two wide trapdoors, attached by iron hinges. Each trapdoor was held up by a single, surprisingly thin wooden pole. When the signal was given, someone would have to knock the two poles aside so that the traps would fall open, and the prisoners would drop.

The executions had been ordered to take place between ten o'clock and two o'clock—though, shockingly, the prisoners themselves had only learned of it the night before, when letters were delivered to their cells along with their suppers. Almost at once their lawyers had begun frantic steps to stay the order, and at midnight a civilian judge had actually issued a writ of habeas corpus for Mrs. Mary Surratt, commanding the government to bring her to his courtroom by ten o'clock that morning. Just as his predecessor had done, President Andrew Johnson had written his own counter-order, suspending habeas corpus, and sent it to the judge.

At eleven twenty-five a few soldiers came into the courtyard with a pair of cannon balls. They mounted the scaffold, placed a cannon ball on each of the trapdoors, and proceeded to test the mechanism. For some reason the trapdoor nearer the prison, the one that would hold Mary Surratt and Lewis Payne, failed to open when its prop was kicked away. The soldiers tested it six or seven times until it functioned properly. Each time they tested, the door slammed downward with a loud, violent bang that could be heard in the cells and out in the road.

By noon, although the government had printed only one hundred official tickets of admission, at least a thousand spectators had jammed into the rooms, windows, and walkways of the two adjoining prison buildings. One window in the center was reserved for the photographer Alexander Gardner, whose bulky stereopticon camera poked its glossy black snout into the stifling heat like a miniature cannon.

At twelve-fifteen three nooses were tied to the crossbeam.

In the northwest corner of the courtyard, in the shade, two bored soldiers built a miniature gallows out of scrap wood and with mock solemnity took off their caps and hanged a rat.

Off to one side, watching them and wearing an expression of unreadable blankness, stood Major Mary Edwards Walker, an army surgeon, the first woman ever to hold such a position, an outspoken supporter of women's rights, and known, when out of uniform, to wear the bloomer costume.

At twelve-thirty a carriage came rolling down the penitentiary road at high speed and every soldier around the perimeter was shouted to attention, sparking the sudden, excited rumor that a rescue attempt was underway—Confederate soldiers would spring out of the ground, reborn—an escape ship was planning to enter Greenleaf Point with its guns blazing. Some said artillery fire could distinctly be heard across the Potomac.

In fact, the carriage contained only General Winfield Scott Hancock, who walked quickly through the main gate and disappeared. Soldiers and spectators alike turned back toward Delaware Avenue and the Capitol.

At twelve forty-five soldiers placed four wooden chairs on the platform, two behind each trapdoor.

At one o'clock, even as more rumors of an imminent pardon or rescue swept through the crowd, a new detail of soldiers took their places around the base of the scaffold. Then General Hancock pushed open the heavy wooden prison door and ordered them to parade rest. The crowd went silent. Those closest to the prison door heard a brief, almost whispered exchange between Hancock and the captain.

"You may proceed, captain."

"Her too?"

"Her too."

The captain picked up the unfinished fourth noose and hastily tied it.

A moment later Mary Surratt emerged from the same door, arms supported by two soldiers. She wore a black dress and a black veil and bonnet, and at the sight of the graves and the huge scaffold fifty feet away she staggered and tried to turn back. The soldiers gripped her tightly and half carried, half dragged her up the steps to the platform. Behind her came two Roman Catholic priests with crucifixes, murmuring the Church's last rites.

After she was seated in the first chair, the three male prisoners filed out, each guarded by soldiers, and took their chairs. In front of them the four nooses swayed back and forth in what little breeze there was. An officious sergeant brought black silk umbrellas to hold over the prisoners' heads and ward off the sun while they sat and listened to an officer read the charges and sentences.

Then the hangman approached the chairs. He looked at Mary Surratt and at Hancock. With visible reluctance, he tied her hands behind her back. After a long pause, he muttered something to the general, and finally, with much fumbling, knelt and wrapped two white cotton ties around her billowing skirt.

With another, stronger show of reluctance, he removed her veil and bonnet and slipped the noose around her neck.

In the back of the courtyard one man whirled around to the crowd and threw his hands into the air.

"Gentlemen, I tell you this is murder! Can you stand and see it done?"

When no one spoke, he lowered his hands and turned back, breathing rapidly, to the scaffold.

The hangman pulled the knot of the noose down against the trembling Mary Surratt's left ear. One of the soldiers on the platform handed him a white cotton hood and he slid it over her head, so that her stark, bone-white face disappeared.

To her left, the other three prisoners were bound and hooded in the same way. All four were ordered to stand and move forward onto the trapdoors. The huge, powerful Lewis Payne took his place next to Mary Surratt. On his left were the smaller figures of David Herold, formerly a clerk and errand boy for Thompson's Drug Store on New York Avenue, and the hapless German immigrant, George Atzerodt.

The hangman came down the steps and stood before the platform. He looked at the four soldiers underneath, holding the props. Then he looked up at Hancock, who nodded.

He clapped his hands once, twice, and on the third clap the soldiers butted away the poles and the trapdoors dropped with a heavy slam. The cross beam creaked and groaned with the weight, and the crowd of spectators let out a long, soft, collective sigh like the rustle of dry leaves.

Suspended in mid-air, Mary Surratt slowly drew her knees up until she seemed to be sitting in an imaginary chair. Then she began to shake from head to toe. Lewis Payne kicked once and was still. John Wilkes Booth, shot to death two months ago in a Maryland barn, already lay buried in a secret grave underneath a storage room floor in the prison. When Mary Surratt, sheathed in her black dress, at last stopped twitching, all of the conspirators who had plotted to murder Abraham Lincoln were dead.

All but one.

PART ONE

Washington City

January 1867

1

ALL BUT JOHN H. SURRATT, JR.

"The Fifth Conspirator," as the newspapers, monotonous as sheep, invariably called him.

The hanged Mary Surratt's fugitive son was known to have been a secret Confederate courier for the last two years of the war, and a close friend of the assassin Booth. He was the only one of Booth's coterie who was allegedly not in Washington the night Lincoln was shot. Allegedly. But because nobody saw Surratt that night, it had taken almost forty-eight hours before he was tied to the plot, and by then it was much too late.

He was last reliably seen, in fact, two days after the assassination, buying clothes in a shabby dry goods store near the train station in Elmira, New York. And after that, though Federal detectives rushed to Elmira and fanned out across the whole northeast, Surratt simply disappeared from view, gone to ground like a burrowing animal.

It was a full year and a half after Lincoln's murder—on November 23, 1866—before the War Department could announce that the Fifth Conspirator had finally been captured in, of all the unexpected places in the world, Alexandria, Egypt.

"And now that we've got him, we'll hang him, just like his mother," Daniel Keach said with his usual sneer. "Hang him till he shits his pants just like her."

"Shut up, Keach." Quintus Oakes glowered at his former colleague. "Watch your mouth."

Nobody else, however, seemed to mind Keach's language. On Oakes's left, as if indifferent to boys quarreling, General George H. Sharpe studied a blue cardboard State Department file with his name on it and dated that very day: January 4, 1867. He murmured, "Quint, Quint," but didn't look up. Behind an enormous many-paneled desk, lighting what was, by Oakes's count, the third cigar since they had sat down in his office, Secretary of State William Seward was intently watching Oakes.

"It says here," General Sharpe read, "that when the Marines caught him, he was wearing the uniform of the Papal Zouaves. I didn't know that.'"

Seward flapped away smoke with his left hand. "He was, indeed. He was wearing a red turban and gray canvas leggings, and he had a long blue sash for a belt, the very picture of a Papal Zouave. He came strutting off the mail boat from Malta and our consul in Alexandria was on the docks and recognized him and clapped him in the brig. I remember that just about the first casualty of the war I ever saw was Colonel Elmer Ellsworth, killed across the river over there, in Alexandria, Virginia, as it happens, and *he* was dressed in the Zouave uniform, his whole regiment was—a bunch of former New York firemen. They thought it looked martial and distinguished. He was shot trying to haul down a Confederate flag somebody had run up on a hotel roof. Before that he'd been a clerk in the President's law office."

When Seward referred to the *President*, Oakes thought, pulling his mind away from Keach and his unhealthy nature, there was no need for a name. Vice President Andrew Johnson might have taken the oath of office, but for men like Seward and General Sharpe the only President who counted now lay in his tomb half a continent away, in Springfield, Illinois.

"Apparently," Sharpe said, still reading, "Surratt enlisted in the Zouaves last December."

Seward nodded. "But we only found out in August, and then we asked the Vatican to arrest him, which they ultimately did around the first of November. Then he somehow escaped—*somehow*—and got away to Naples, and from there to Malta, and from Malta on, of course, we were looking for him."

"*Somehow*," Keach repeated with the same sneer. "The Vatican *let* him go. They knew who he was, they just never liked Lincoln, that's all. They were glad to see him dead. The Catholic Church favored the South, and they let him go. Plain fact."

"Where's Surratt now?" Sharpe asked.

"He's in irons in a locked and guarded cabin on the U.S.S. *Swatara*," Seward said. "That's one of our new sloops. He's heading home from Egypt. It took almost a month to get all the paperwork done in Cairo or he'd already be here. I had a telegram yesterday that they'll reach Baltimore on February eighteenth. We'll put him on trial June first."

"Well, if you already have him, Mister Seward," Keach said, "and the trial date is set, why on earth did you and the General call us here?"

Seward leaned forward and peered over his cigar. "You don't say much, do you, Captain Oakes?"

"Captain Oakes didn't want to come," Sharpe said. "I had to drag him down from New York."

"A brigadier general can be very persuasive," Oakes said drily, "even if you're out of the army."

Seward gave a soft, gravelly-voiced chuckle, but he didn't, Oakes noted, answer Keach's question. Instead he got up from his smoke-obscured desk and walked over to the big double-framed window beyond their chairs.

The Secretary of State, it was obvious, dressed with a politician's flair for capturing attention. He wore yellow pantaloons, a yellow waistcoat, and a contrasting old-fashioned black frock coat. He was about sixty years old, Oakes guessed, ten years older than General Sharpe, with thin white hair that might have been auburn in his youth, and a hooked nose big enough and sharp enough for most people to say he looked like a parrot or a red-beaked macaw. But few people looked at his nose anymore.

The reason was even more obvious than his yellow waistcoat. The same night that Abraham Lincoln was shot, Booth's co-conspirator Lewis Payne had forced his way into Seward's bedroom and slashed his face and neck so terribly with a knife that for weeks Seward's life hung in the balance. A specialist dentist had made a jaw splint for him out of vulcanized rubber that was fastened by screws driven into the teeth—which must have been an incredibly painful process, Oakes thought. Even now, General Sharpe had warned them, the Secretary sometimes had to hawk loudly and drain saliva out of his cheek with a tube, and the best policy was to look away while this operation went on. But in the cold afternoon light of the window, it was hard to avoid seeing the long, loose flap of discolored skin on his right cheek, or not to notice that Seward made a special effort to keep his profile turned the other way. The Fifth Conspirator, Oakes thought, ought not expect much mercy from Seward's quarter.

And none at all from Daniel Keach, who was staring openly at Seward's scars. During the war, Keach, the son of an impoverished Irish immigrant, had never risen higher than sergeant, though he petitioned regularly for a field commission. After the war, thanks to his cleverness with numbers, he had found a job in a New York City bank, but dealing with widows and orphans' savings hadn't changed one atom of his innately violent nature. "I wouldn't bother bringing him back," Keach said, "if it was up to me. I'd drop him overboard in the middle of the Atlantic and feed him to the sharks."

"And what about due process?" Seward asked without looking around. "Trial by jury? Habeas corpus?"

"I would appeal to a higher law," Keach said, and smirked.

Seward gave his raspy chuckle again and turned back from the window, and Oakes had to nod in grudging admiration of Keach's nerve. If William Seward was famous for anything among the general populace of the United States, he was famous as the author of two remarkable phrases. The first was his prophetic description in 1858 of the coming "irrepressible conflict" between the North and the South, and the second was his claim nine years earlier that, although the Constitution sanctioned slavery, there was nonetheless an appeal open to a "higher law."

"Stupidest damn speech I ever made," he said now, and settled back behind the elaborate custom-built desk chair that they had spent the first five minutes of their visit admiring. It contained, they had been shown in detail, special hidden compartments for cigars, ashes, pens, ink, all linked and concealed by hidden panels.

Not a bad image, Oakes had begun to think, for Seward's own secretive and compartmentalized mind.

There was also a small swiveling writing board carpentered onto the right armrest of the chair, which the Secretary began to work thoughtfully back and forth as if pondering a decision.

General Sharpe didn't care for silences.

"When they shot Lincoln on April fourteenth," he said, slapping the cardboard folder closed, "Surratt went straight to Canada, with that one stop in Elmira." He began tapping the folder with his index finger, in a slow, maddening, unstoppable rhythm Oakes remembered from the war, when Sharpe's temper would begin to rise. "It says here he traveled from New York to Montreal on the train, and he stayed in some kind of convent or monastery there, then took a ship to Liverpool. Then he went to London and stayed some months. Then he went to Paris and Rome and finally godforsaken Egypt. Where the hell were the British police? Or the French?"

Seward stopped fiddling with his special chair. He planted his elbows on his desk and stared straight ahead at Oakes.

"What do you make of all that, Captain Oakes?"

"He had to have help," Keach answered for him. "Surratt was an unemployed, penniless clerk. He couldn't possibly have traveled to all those places without somebody helping."

"Captain Oakes?"

"There was money and there was help," Oakes said. "There was a Sixth Conspirator, and that's why you called us here."

THERE ARE SOME PEOPLE you just love.

Quintus Horatius Flaccus Oakes, whose Latin-besotted father had much to answer for in giving him that knotted kite's tail of a name, put down his second glass of mediocre claret and allowed himself a small but thoroughly genuine smile. Out in the lobby he could see General Sharpe briskly making his way between the reception desk and a row of sickly yellow palms that the management of the Willard Hotel mistook for ornamentation.

It was 10:15 p.m. by the big round railroad clock over the bar, nearly five hours after their meeting with Secretary Seward had ended—ended with some acrimony—and Sharpe was half an hour late, which was unlike him in the extreme. The shoulders of his elegant black civilian overcoat, Oakes could see, were dusted with snow where, two years ago, the epaulets and stars would have been. His gray slouch hat was turning dark in spots. For a small man, Oakes remembered, the general somehow always cut a broad swath through a crowd. On either side of him, people were stepping back quickly to let him pass. Two Negro porters bowed in unison. The white assistant manager behind the desk called out a greeting.

"You're going to have to change your mind, Quint," Sharpe grunted as he pulled out a chair and sat down. "And get your hair cut, too." He twirled his finger in the general direction of the hair that, since the war, Oakes had let grow down to his collar.

Oakes let his smile fade. He loved General Sharpe, but he often thought that some men are born to gruffness, some have gruffness thrust upon them, and some just go way the hell out of their way to achieve it.

"The effect aimed at is rhapsodic and sublime, General, like Lord George Byron, one of your favorite poets."

"Well, you look like Lord George Custer, the jackass."

Sharpe tossed a small brown paper sack on the table, and Oakes picked it up and found that it contained several dozen palm-sized pasteboard cards. Each card had a photograph printed on one side, with a caption at the bottom. He turned over one of John Wilkes Booth in a formal black coat and ribbon necktie, posed with his gaze tilted theatrically to the sky, his right hand on a bust of Shakespeare. There was a more prosaic one of Lewis Payne in the hat and coat he had worn on the night of the assassination. Yet another showed a youthful Mary Surratt in a striped dress, and on the reverse side, Alexander Gardner's photograph of her shrouded body hanging from the gallows.

"They sell this filth down the street," Sharpe said, "as 'souvenirs.' I bought every one they had."

He leaned back while Mike, the Willard's strangely famous headwaiter, deposited a brandy smash on the table in front of him and another glass of wine for Oakes.

"You still have that old wood stove back in your cloakroom, Mike?"

"Yes, sir, General."

"Take this sack and burn it."

Although everybody in Washington knew he had been born and reared in Bethesda, Maryland, the famous headwaiter affected a thick Irish brogue. "In the fee'er, sir," he said. "Right away, faith."

Sharpe watched his retreating back and then turned in his chair to study the row of faces lined up in the mirror behind the long bar. Oakes leaned back and studied Sharpe's own face.

Not that there was any need to. He had seen it almost every day for the last two years of the war. For weeks at a time he had sat opposite Sharpe—when Sharpe was still a colonel—at a folding table in a big, leaky, remarkably foul-smelling tent that accompanied the headquarters brigade of the Army of the Potomac wherever it went, down the muddy back roads and alongside the slow, melancholy blood-stained rivers of Virginia, from the Rapidan at Fredericksburg, all the way to the stately James, where it dropped south toward Appomattox. He also had in his rooms in New York two photographs of the General left over from the feature story he had once helped a reporter named Dana cobble together for the *New-York Times*. Oddly enough, they were also on pasteboard cards.

In the first one, taken early in the war, Sharpe stood with his hands in his pockets, long European-style moustaches curving down to a clean-shaven chin. His eyes glared imperiously from beneath his garrison cap. He looked every inch a swashbuckling warrior, the beau ideal of a modern soldier. This was the photograph the *Times* had used as a model for their engraver to sketch. The other one showed Sharpe hatless, nearly bald. It had been taken two years later, and in it his moustaches drooped, without the virile curve of the first picture. His eyes were not fierce, but gentle, thoughtful. He was still in his colonel's uniform, but now he looked like the chaplain of the regiment, not the commander, certainly not the ruthless, superbly effective, and much-feared founder and spymaster of Ulysses S. Grant's Bureau of Military Information. When Oakes had briefly studied painting in Paris— one of his several misadventures in trying to find a path in life— he had been shown a novelty drawing of a rabbit that flickered back and forth as you looked and mysteriously became, if you stared long enough, a snarling bear. Which picture was Sharpe? Whichever one you chose, he thought.

"Seward," the actual man in front of him said as he turned back from the bar, "was not very happy with you, Quint."

"For a diplomat he made that pretty plain."

"Two months is what he's asking," Sharpe said. "Three at the most. People don't tell Seward 'no.'"

"It'll take six months to do what he wants and you know it, General. And if they delay Surratt's trial, that's another six months. Too long, much too long." Oakes pushed his wine glass to one side in as obvious a gesture of impatience as he could permit himself. "I have plans, anyway."

"Seward said he knew your father years ago, back in Connecticut." Sharpe took a sip of his brandy smash and wiped his moustache carefully. Now he looked like a cat, Oakes thought, and remembered that yet another complication of Sharpe's character was the rugged spymaster's incongruous love of cats. In his home in Kingston, New York, he and his wife kept a regiment of them underfoot, in the dining room, in the guest room. Oakes hated cats.

"Everybody knew my father," he said shortly. He pulled his wine glass back and brought it up to his mouth, then put it down again without drinking. "And as everybody reminds me, he was the best lawyer in New England, except maybe for you, and the best governor in the history of Connecticut. If he hadn't been too old to join up, he would have undoubtedly been the best general in the army. And the stubbornest, just like you."

Sharpe smiled. Oakes expected to see him bring up his paw and lick his whiskers.

"I learned one thing from my father, General, and one thing only. The first time I went to law school, or maybe the second, he took me aside for a serious father-son talk, and he told me that the secret of his success as a lawyer was very simple. He never let a client leave his office without figuring out the answer to the only question that mattered—*what does he want?* Not what he *says* he wants—what does he *really* want?"

"This is leading somewhere," Sharpe said, "I trust."

"Vengeance," Oakes said. "What Seward wants is vengeance. You heard him talk—that rug in his office he brought from his house because it reminded him of how Lincoln would wander over to visit him in the evenings, and Seward would drink brandy and Lincoln would eat apples, core and all, just like a horse. And the photograph of Lincoln on the desk, and the funny stories about Lincoln's funny stories—Booth killed Seward's hero, and almost killed him too, and Seward hasn't had enough blood yet. What he really wants is more vengeance." Oakes leaned back to avoid any swipe of the paw. "And that's what you want too."

There was a clatter behind them, angry murmurs and a general scraping of chairs. At the long bar, under the twelve gas-lit globes of light, every head was turned toward the door. A woman about thirty years old stood at the entrance, of medium height and possessed, Oakes would have said if he were still trying to be a painter, of a slim, perfect, Botticelli-like figure. She wore a black fur-collared coat and a pale blue dress that set off her blonde hair, and her lips were curled in a kind of teasing smile. The very tall, beautifully dressed older man beside her had an expression of disdain that was turned not on the woman, but on the roomful of muttering men.

"No ladies in the bar!" The famous Mike was hurrying forward, wringing his white towel between his hands. "Ladies served in the lobby, please, or the dining room, not here."

The woman took two more steps inside the barroom and looked slowly around, from table to table, amused and defiant. Mike crossed his arms over his chest as if to stop her. Her companion said something sharp that Oakes couldn't hear, and the old headwaiter visibly deflated.

"Bring us," the woman said quite clearly, "a bottle of champagne, please." She smiled and patted his crossed arms. "In the lobby."

When she turned to walk away, every man was still watching. Oakes found he was straining to follow her figure until it disappeared behind one of the disreputable potted palms.

"Kate Chase," said General Sharpe. "Or rather, Kate Sprague. She's married to William Sprague of Providence."

"Ah." Oakes had seen William Sprague several times during the war, when he was known as the boy general. Before that he had been known as the boy governor of Rhode Island. Before that, he supposed, the boy boy. As an act of patriotism, but also because his cotton mills were running out of raw cotton from the South, Sprague had raised one of the first volunteer infantry regiments in the Union Army and as a reward Lincoln had made him a brigadier general. He was known to be a heavy drinker, extremely near-sighted, and, as Oakes could attest from personal observation, very short and slight of build. He had once watched

Sprague review his troops outside Richmond and he had thought Sprague looked like a mouse in a yellow-plumed hat.

"And no, that's not Sprague," Sharpe said. "That's Roscoe Conklin, Congressman from your adopted city of New York, and nobody in Washington is much scandalized anymore by their"—Sharpe hesitated and circled around to find the right word—"dalliance."

Oakes nodded and continued to watch the door. Sharpe wasn't scandalized, but he didn't approve. Sharpe was happily married to a woman his own age from his own hometown, and though during the war Oakes had seen women practically throw themselves at him, or his uniform, the general had been thoroughly self-disciplined and chaste. The general had always been, Oakes thought, something of a Puritan.

"Then Sprague is going to want vengeance too," he said and added, just to be saying something, just to be avoiding the subject of the Sixth Conspirator, "*Cherchez la femme.*"

"*Qui cherche, trouve.*" Before the war Sharpe had lived three years in Europe, one of them in Paris. He folded a dollar bill under his brandy glass and stood up. "Come outside," he said.

3

THE MAIN ENTRANCE TO THE WILLARD HOTEL was at the corner where Pennsylvania Avenue met Fourteenth Street, just two hundred yards down and on the opposite side of the street from the President's Mansion. Back in the dim, distant administration of James Monroe, the Willard had been little more than a modest boarding house for commercial travelers, but over the decades it had added five new floors and sprawled rapaciously outward until, having swallowed every other building on the block, it had become Washington's largest, ugliest, and most important hotel. Few Washingtonians could cross its celebrated lobby without stopping two or three times to murmur a word to one of the influential but unelected men seated in the big leather chairs by the fireplace or next to the potted palms.

Sharpe certainly couldn't. Oakes waited by the front door, beside a mountain of travelers' luggage, while the general paused at one chair for a laugh and a handshake, paused at another for a fraternal squeeze of the shoulder, and made a third stop at the marble registration counter, where a clerk handed him a fistful of letters.

"Did you hear the name Grant gave those people back there?" They stepped out onto the Pennsylvania Avenue sidewalk and Sharpe slapped on his gray slouch hat again. "'Lobbyists,' he calls them. I thought that was pretty good for somebody the newspapers are always calling illiterate and stupid."

"We never thought he was stupid," Oakes said.

"No."

The snow had stopped falling, but the streets were covered with an inch or so of white carpet. A horse-drawn streetcar went by, jingling madly. The wind whipped up a pair of ghostly, spinning miniature vortexes coming along the sidewalk toward them. Sharpe turned right and started walking in the direction of the President's Mansion.

"You never knew him," he said as they reached Fifteenth Street and the Mansion came into view. As before, Oakes didn't need to ask who "he" was. Lincoln.

"I saw him," he told Sharpe. "And spoke to him. At least twice. I saw him when he came down to talk with you after Cold Harbor, and one other time."

"Richmond, April fifth, 1865," Sharpe said with his near-perfect lawyer's memory, which was of course correct. After the fall of Richmond, Oakes had followed Abraham Lincoln down the main street of the Confederate capital—for the life of him he couldn't remember the name of the street—while up ahead, guarded by twelve very anxious sailors with carbines, calmly walked the President in his tall stovepipe hat, holding the hand of his young son Tad and inspecting the bombarded city. For the first few minutes the street had been empty, practically deserted, though from the windows of the office buildings still left standing you could hear the faint buzz of voices. Then slowly the sidewalks had begun to fill with faces, white as well as black. By the time they reached the end of the street, the crowd was enormous, men and boys were clinging to every telegraph pole, eager to get a glimpse of Old Abe or to curse him, and the jubilant blacks were cheering and singing. And just as Lincoln turned to go into the Capitol, a strong wind came out of nowhere and blew thousands and thousands of sheets of paper, government documents, out of a ruined warehouse, so that briefly it looked as though, in the month of April, Lincoln was already a ghost walking in a snowstorm.

The other time—

"Where are you staying, Quint?"

"The National, just down the Avenue. And I have a train back to New York in the morning, General, which I do mean to be on."

Sharpe nodded and led them across Sixteenth Street and into the President's Park—a dark, open rectangle of sycamores and oaks about a city block square, facing the President's Mansion. For some reason people had taken to calling it Lafayette Square, though for as long as Oakes could remember the center of the park had been not a statue of the great Gallic "Friend of the Nation," but a big equestrian statue of that most un-French of all the presidents, Andrew Jackson. Tonight, even under a crust of frozen snow, the old Tennessean looked ferociously hot and angry, an ancestral figure eternally prophesying war.

"Curious thing," Sharpe said, halting before the statue. Oakes looked around at the houses on three sides and the deserted park itself and realized that Sharpe had, characteristically, led him to a place in the middle of the city where, of course, there was nobody at all to overhear their conversation.

"I'm staying there"—Sharpe pointed toward windows on the southeast corner—"as Seward's guest. He was telling me this morning that before he bought it the place was called the Old Club House, but the club disbanded after Dan Sickles shot Frank Key"—Sharpe waved a gloved hand in front of the statue—"right about here, and the neighbors carried him into the Club House to die. It was over a woman."

"Sickles's wife," Oakes said. "They were having what you call a dalliance and Sickles's lawyers got him acquitted on something new they dreamed up and called 'temporary insanity.' We studied that in the law school."

"Did you know one of Sickles's lawyers was Stanton?"

"No." Oakes turned his heel on the slick snow and looked over toward the President's Mansion, where gas lights flickered in the living quarters and downstairs in what he knew was the Blue Room and which was, he now remembered, the third place he had ever seen the President, stretched out in his coffin with the blue-gray bullet wound and bruise on the left side of his head still visible, despite the undertaker's art. Edwin Stanton was Lincoln's Secretary of War, and now Andrew Johnson's, though Johnson was trying to throw him out for being too harsh on the unreconstructed rebels.

"Stanton and Grant," Sharpe said, "those are the only people who know about Seward's plan."

"And us," Oakes said, "and I told you, General, I don't have time and I don't think the plan makes any sense—you and Seward want to retrace every step Surratt took from the day the President was shot till the day they picked him up in Egypt. And you want to do it right now, while you think the trail is hot. But that trail is long cold, long dead. And the other problem is, you don't really know exactly where Surratt went after Booth was caught—Canada, England, Rome. I was listening when Seward read us those reports and laid out all those papers. You really don't know where he went or who was hiding him, much less how he paid for any of it."

"We know he went to Liverpool, then London. Maybe Paris. Paris was riddled with Confederate agents."

"And if he went from there to Rome and the Vatican helped him, then Keach, I hate to say it, is right and you're going to be shadow-boxing with the Pope, and my irreverent father used to say they should have a sign over the Vatican door, *'Lasciate ogni speranza, voi ch'entrate.'*"

"'Abandon all hope, ye who enter here,'" Sharpe translated. He had also lived in Rome. "And keep your damn voice down."

The snarling bear was definitely in the ascendant, Oakes thought, remembering the novelty drawing. He started to circle the big equestrian statue slowly. Sharpe stayed just where he was, like the fixed foot of a drawing compass, erect military posture, slouch hat low over his forehead against the wind.

Oakes reached the other side of the statue and looked up at its grim, cast-iron features. Somebody had tried to assassinate Jackson too, he remembered—the first president that anybody ever tried to murder. In 1835 a man named Lawrence had fired two pistols at Jackson as he was walking out of the Capitol and missed both times. They had locked him away in an insane asylum. No conspiracy talk back then, no dead trail, no Vatican. Surratt, he remembered, was Catholic. Surratt's mother was Catholic.

"I'm sorry, General," Oakes said. "But—"

"I'm not going to argue with you, Quint," Sharpe said. "I want you to do this."

Oakes felt anger flash across his face. *And if I don't,* he thought, *what are you going to do? Have Daniel Keach grab my fingers with his pliers, or fill a bucket with water and shove my head in it?* Which was what George H. Sharpe did, did cruelly and ruthlessly, when the bear was ascendant, in the war. Even if you loved him, George H. Sharpe could be a hard, hard man.

He swallowed the disloyal thought, but not the anger. "Not even for you, General."

Lincoln used to keep official letters and papers of all kinds tucked away inside his stovepipe hat—it was one of the things everybody knew about him. Sharpe, on the other hand, kept all his letters and papers tucked neatly away inside his specially tailored overcoat, in a series of hidden pockets not unlike the compartments in Seward's desk. He was clearly angry in his turn now. He turned on his heel and walked away from Oakes toward the nearest gas street lamp. When Oakes caught up to him, the general had pulled two sheets of paper from the coat. Instinctively they both waited until another horse-drawn streetcar clopped past on Pennsylvania Avenue, churning up a little cloud of floating snow.

Then Sharpe handed him the papers. The first one was simply a long list of dates, cities, and hotels, beginning with the Grand Hotel du Nord on Parker Street in Montreal, April 15, 1865. Each entry was followed by different capital letters of the alphabet.

The second sheet of paper was a short list of names. Oakes held it up to the light. Snowflakes were drifting over from the street, and he brushed them away from the paper with a gloved finger.

"Read the third name," Sharpe said.

Oakes read it and closed his eyes.

In the blankness of his mind he could hear Sharpe's footsteps crunch on the snow, and he knew the general had turned his back on him and started to walk away. The crunching sound grew fainter, but he kept his eyes closed. The wind pushed his long, unmilitary hair against his neck and collar. He let his hand find and crumple the now useless train ticket for tomorrow in his own coat pocket. When he opened his eyes, he saw Sharpe's back on the other side of the park, across the street from the Old Club House, where somebody had been killed over a woman. The general paused for a moment under a street lamp and then, like the tick of a clock or the beat of a pulse, he disappeared into the shadows.

4

SOME EIGHT HUNDRED MILES to the north, a person known in certain State Department documents only as "S" was standing at a window watching the snow come down in winding sheets across the dreary, deserted expanse of what was, in Montreal's brief and excited summer, the flowery rue Saint Jacques.

Sarah Slater disliked snow. She sometimes joked to the nuns down the road in Saint Liboire that snow, in her opinion, wasn't really *natural*. To which joke the nuns, although they understood her Parisian-accented French perfectly well, always lifted their puzzled faces and frowned like tranced cows.

She had disliked snow in Connecticut, too, where she and her mother would also stand at the window of the little house on Sachem's Head and peer at the sugar-powdered road down which, eventually, her father would come trudging home from Guilford. She had disliked it less in North Carolina, where she had stood at yet another window and watched her boy-husband play with his sled and the neighbor's children; but of course, she told herself, there had been less snow in the South to dislike.

She had just turned to go to her writing table by the fireplace when there were three soft raps on the door. She opened it to find the little boy from the porter's cloakroom downstairs, grinning up at her. He had his cloth cap in his hands and his thumbs on a tiny square of paper spread across the cap, and he read the few words printed on the paper in a slow, careful monotone.

"Come to desk when received." He folded the paper and added in much more natural voice, "Signed, Lee."

Sarah grinned back at him. He was nine years old—a nine-year old boy, her father had once told her, was the height of human felicity—and she liked little boys very much—no doubt the reason she had married Rowan Slater.

"Tell him that I'll be there in five minutes." She placed a coin on the cap. "*Et pour toi, merci, cher monsieur*," and was rewarded with a bow.

But it took her much longer than five minutes to put away her writing material, damp down the fire, and change into clothes warm enough for the short walk down the rue Saint Jacques to the Saint Lawrence Hall Hotel. And if part of her was surprised and tense at the thought that a message that came so late at night, and from Benedict Lee, must portend difficulties, another part of her was simply glad to be stirring, to be doing something, *anything*.

Benedict Lee, she thought, studying her figure in the wardrobe mirror. One of the South's apparently inexhaustible supply of Lees, a second or third cousin of the revered General Robert E. He could easily have written a longer message for the boy to carry. But of course, he wanted to see her in person.

Despite the cold and the snow, she thought, she would wear the green silk dress with the very low *décolleté*. She wasn't as blonde and apple-bottomed as most of the women Lee notoriously, comically pursued. But at thirty she was still slender, lithe.

Heads still turned as she walked by. If her belly was a shade too prominent, she told herself, that was only the result of poor posture—she smoothed down the silk and almost laughed. Married to the son of a dancing master, and she had indisputably the worst posture in the county. One way or another, she thought, still smiling, picking up her heavy wrap, always a rebel.

On the street she walked briskly, purposefully. The snow was falling in great fat flakes that plopped against the street lamps like frozen moths. As usual, the breeze from the Saint Lawrence River carried just a hint, just the faintest tang of salt from the seaway. She could smell it from half a mile away, salt water flowing east and north toward Quebec City, past Quebec City, toward vaunted Europe.

At the corner of rue de Lille she waited for a pair of big lumber wagons to lurch by, on their way even at this time of night to the warehouses by the docks. There were a few other people on the sidewalks, hurrying home, hunched against the weather. When she used to come here during the war, when she would arrive carrying her valises full of letters and "greenback" dollars, in those days the streets, day and night, would have been teeming with people she knew, men, women. In those days General Edwin Lee—another Lee!—ran the Montreal Bureau of the Confederacy, and agents, bankers, refugees, detectives, every kind of person who could be of use to Richmond, swarmed around him. A whole great Roman circus of scheming humanity had made Montreal buzz. In those days she never stood and looked for hours out a window, alone. She touched her chest. She thought of Guilford, Connecticut. *I am here,* she thought. *Come find me.*

At the lighted portico of the Lawrence Hall Hotel, the snow seemed to draw back for a moment and the night slipped into a deep silence. Farther down the block a cobweb of telegraph lines stiffened overhead in the cold. The idea came suddenly to her that Lee's message was almost certainly relayed from Washington City.

THE NEXT DAY WAS TUESDAY, January 3. At eight o'clock, Oakes came out of the absurdly elaborate marble-pillared front doors of the National Hotel and started to walk up Pennsylvania Avenue. The snow had stopped falling about midnight and now, in clear, brittle sunshine, he could see all the way across the Potomac to the blue hills of Virginia, where a distant flash of white marked the stately columns, not marble but painted brick, of Robert E. Lee's old family home.

No escaping the past, he thought, ever. In Washington City the past was a flashing light, bright enough to blind.

At Seventh Street, while he waited for a horse car to navigate the slushy turn from Louisiana Avenue, he glanced back at the Capitol, the new dome towering over everything at this end of the Avenue. Proximity to the Capitol was the main reason, apart from its low prices, that the National Hotel had always been more popular than the Willard with Congressmen, especially with Southerners. Before the war the sidewalk in front of the National had been a customary gathering place for their slaves, who loitered outside while their masters, in their wide-brimmed planters' hats, loitered inside at the bar.

Then its popularity plummeted, Oakes remembered, because in 1859 a sewer pipe leaked into the kitchen storeroom and before the leak was found, hundreds of guests became violently ill, among them President Buchanan's nephew, who actually died of the National Hotel disease. Naturally, the Southerners had blamed the epidemic on a Republican plot to poison their leaders. Plots—and leaks—were the order of the day in 1859.

1859, Oakes thought, not even ten years ago. At the corner of Fourteenth Street, he met Sharpe, who was just coming up the block, elegant and pink-cheeked in his fur-collared overcoat and neatly brushed gray slouch hat. He carried six or seven morning newspapers under his arm, and automatically Oakes glanced down Fourteenth Street, where the massed sidewalk hoardings and a great latticework of telegraph wires announced the start of Newspaper Row.

"Stanton can see us at nine," the General said. "Did you have breakfast?"

"Buttermilk cakes and honey, and sausage and hominy grits with two kinds of red-eye gravy. The National still specializes in fine Southern cuisine."

Sharpe shook his head in feigned Yankee incomprehension.

At Fifteenth Street the mud and slush were so deep that Negro boys stood on each corner with wide, unpainted boards in their hands and, for a small coin, either carried pedestrians across or skillfully constructed a kind of moving duckboard. At Sixteenth Street they passed the President's Mansion opposite the park, and then at the next block turned and walked up to the offices of the War Department.

The State Department, where they had met Seward yesterday, was located in temporary quarters far out on S Street, in the old Protestant Orphan Asylum building—a sure sign, Washington savants said, of Seward's fall from favor with the new President. But Stanton's War Department—and Stanton was so far out of favor with Andrew Johnson that the two were said not even to speak to each other—Stanton's War Department still occupied the same building Oakes had known in the war—a four-story brick structure with yet more marble columns and a third-story balcony that mimicked the portico of the President's Mansion.

"You came here before, I think," Sharpe said as they walked up three steps to the porch, "for some of Stanton's mornings."

"Once."

"Once was probably enough."

Oakes almost smiled, but he was still furious with Sharpe, he reminded himself, still there in Washington City against his will, still back in the army against his will.

Stanton's office was on the third floor, in a corner looking down on the President's House. The suspicious and harried-looking secretary in the ante-room told them they were early and would have to wait next door in the reception room. As they entered, Oakes recognized it as the same room where Stanton had held his notorious mornings.

Oakes had come up from Grant's headquarters in late 1864 on some now-forgotten and pointless errand. But he remembered with shocked clarity the room and the scene. Every week-day morning during the war, Secretary of War Edwin Stanton had given over an hour to the public. He was a short, portly man, whose rudeness to all and sundry was legendary. At nine o'clock precisely the Secretary materialized through a side door and took his stand behind a high writing desk that reached all the way to his shoulders, so that the various petitioners and clerks crowded into the room saw little more than his enormous gray beard and his flashing steel-rimmed spectacles.

He looked, Oakes had thought, like either a perpetually irritated schoolmaster, or a mottled gnome.

The room fell silent. Orderlies moved among the crowd, whispering names and taking notes, and one by one Stanton summoned the politicians, job-seekers, army officers, widows, and contractors to his desk. There, in a brusque moment or two, he disposed of their cases. Oakes remembered nothing of what the Secretary had said to him, only that the woman in front of him, clutching a handful of official-looking papers, had left the writing desk in tears. Stanton was reputed to be a particularly devout Christian, who had been so undone by the death of his first wife that he had dug up her body from her grave with his own hands, to see her face again. After that, so far as anybody knew, Stanton had never loved anybody else in his life except Lincoln, and even Lincoln Stanton had once famously called the "original gorilla." It was Stanton who stood over Lincoln's corpse in the house across from Ford's Theater and pronounced the remarkable words, "Now he belongs to the ages."

Except, Oakes knew from a fellow army officer present in the room, what the pious Stanton actually said was, "Now he belongs to the angels," a phrase the calculating and much less pious Seward later revised for the newspapers.

At two minutes to nine Daniel Keach, the former sergeant turned bank clerk, sauntered into the room and gave them both a mock salute. And at nine, just as the reception room clock began to chime, the Secretary's secretary poked his head through the door.

At his desk, Stanton continued writing in a notebook for about half a minute, then he stood up, offered his hand to Sharpe, and pointed to three straight-backed chairs. He nodded once to each to Keach and Oakes and that, Oakes realized, was going to be the extent of their introduction.

"Booth had help," Stanton said abruptly, back in his chair and looking down again at his notebook. He tugged at his enormous beard, faintly violet in color, and Oakes thought he caught a whiff of apple pomade. "Seward thinks the ultimate authorization came from that Hebrew traitor Judah Benjamin, but of course he would think that, since Benjamin was the rebel Secretary of State, his counterpart, and Seward, as you doubtless observed, lives in a hall of mirrors. I think otherwise. I think the whole vile conspiracy was dreamed up in Canada and then authorized in Richmond, probably by Davis himself. Benjamin would have been a major part of it, of course. Benjamin probably set it in motion. Now we have Davis in custody, but Benjamin is living in plain sight in London, protected by his fellow Jew Disraeli. We can look at him, but so far, without evidence, we can't touch him. In any case, that still leaves open the question of who financed Booth and who else was part of the plot."

"Which is where we come in," Keach said.

Stanton stared at him through the imposing steel-rimmed glasses. Then he twisted in his chair and studied the corner of the President's Mansion that was visible through his window. Below the window was a rickety wooden turnstile that marked the path between the two buildings, as if you had to pay a toll to go back and forth. "The President," he said, "had a big pigeon hole cabinet over his desk that was always stuffed with papers, in no particular order." Stanton squared the sheets of paper on his own desk.

"They were reports of assassination plots. At any given time there were about eighty reports in that pigeonhole. I had twice that many over here, in a special file that I kept."

"Good Lord," Keach said, "eighty."

"Did you know, General," Stanton said, turning to Sharpe, "that after the election of 1860 some Secessionists sent jars of poisoned fruit to him? I saw them myself."

"I had heard it."

"You may believe it. There were plots abounding. I was a target, too. The night before the murder a man in a black cloak came to my door, then ran when my servant opened it. Grant was supposedly a target along with the President at the theater, but by some malevolent trick of Providence Grant didn't go that night and the President did."

Stanton paused to flip a page in his notebook and Oakes recalled that by Stanton's orders, Ford's Theater had been shut down immediately after the assassination. When the owner, Ford, obviously innocent of anything, had complained he was losing business, Stanton had threatened to clap him in jail along with the other conspirators, and Ford was now reputedly bankrupt, living on a farm in Silver Springs and selling eggs by the side of the road. Oakes had walked past the theater yesterday afternoon and its doors were still locked and barred and the interior gutted.

"There was, for instance," Stanton said, "the case of Doctor Luke P. Blackburn. He was in Toronto. He wanted to infect northern cities with yellow fever. He gathered clothes from victims in Canada and sent them to various garment distributors in New York and Chicago, and he actually sent a valise full of infected shirts to Lincoln." He pointed at the window. "Right over there. Hired a shipping agent to deliver the valise, but our people stopped him before he reached the door. I arrested four hundred people after the murder, and I still didn't get them all."

"Well, Mister Stanton." Sharpe shifted impatiently. "We have copies of your files with some of that unnerving material, and the files of Ward Lamon as well, and also Judge Baker. Mister Seward briefed us pretty thoroughly. We're off to New York tomorrow, to start tracing Surratt's movements. Then to Canada, then to Liverpool and London and Rome. If anybody else helped Surratt, we intend to find them. These were two of my best men in the Bureau of Military Information, all through the war. I just wanted you to meet them and impress on them, as you have, the importance of finding out the truth."

"The rebel South did this, and that is the truth, General. And the South, as the Scripture says, should 'beware of the people weeping.'" He pulled a bell rope behind his chair. "This assignment of yours, gentlemen, is completely secret. No one knows of it except Seward, Grant, and myself, which is how I want it to remain, even when you're abroad."

Keach, who had himself, Oakes thought, a capacity for rudeness almost Stantonian, had been obviously chafing under the Secretary of War's curt manner. Now he gave one of his snorts.

"Not much of a secret, in my opinion, sir. People saw us come into the office, some secretary wrote up our letters, somebody else copied out our orders and God knows how many people saw General Sharpe walk in here this morning. You can't keep a secret in Washington City, sir."

Stanton inflated his torso slowly, like a squat gray bearded frog, and leaned across the desk. "You would be Sergeant Keach, I assume."

"Yes, sir."

"You would be the banker from New York who's going to assist in tracking the money Surratt got."

"I work in Ward, Hilliard in New York, yes sir, but I wouldn't call myself a banker."

"Nor would I call you a member of the President's Cabinet, with executive responsibilities. You will pass your reports—and opinions—to the General, not me."

Keach smirked. Sharpe sighed. At the door, as he waited to let the other two go in front of him, Oakes heard Stanton call his name.

"Stay here, Oakes. You can catch up to them later."

6

IN THE CORNER OF HIS OFFICE nearest the big window, Stanton had an eight-foot-long library table covered, in the latest fashion, with a garishly red and blue Turkish carpet. Unlike Seward, who kept his reports and files out of sight in hidden compartments, Stanton evidently piled them helter-skelter along the table, in the kind of conspicuous disorder that suggested its creator knew exactly where to find each and every individual scrap of paper.

Now he closed the outer door firmly and walked over to the table. Oakes hesitated, then sat back down, uninvited, in what had been Sharpe's chair. Stanton pulled a blue cardboard folder from the stack. He placed it on his desk and returned to the table.

"I don't like Mister Keach," Stanton said, with his back still turned.

"I don't like him either, sir. But he was a very effective member of the Bureau."

"The Bureau of Military Information," Stanton said in a flat voice and continued shuffling through papers at the table. "You went to Harvard College, Mister Oakes, and you belong, I understand, to an old and influential New England family. Governor Urian Oakes was your father. Keach is the son of an Irish immigrant who attended no college and who has had to work his way up in life without family or, I should imagine, given his manners, friends. It would be surprising"—Stanton turned and went to his own chair behind the desk—"if you liked him. Or he liked you."

Oakes felt his face begin to burn. Stanton took no notice. He opened the folder and spread it on the desk.

"In any case, what we are about to discuss is not to be divulged to Mister Keach. He is to be kept, as General Sharpe requests, in the dark. For what will be obvious reasons. There is enough tension between you two already."

"Yes, sir."

"You are acquainted with one Sarah Antoinette Gilbert, I believe?"

Oakes took a deep and, he thought, inaudible breath. "No, sir."

Stanton lifted his head and peered over the steel rimmed spectacles. He looked like a man made out of ice.

"Sarah Slater then," he said.

"I wouldn't use the word 'acquainted,' Mister Stanton."

Stanton bared his teeth in an astonishingly unfriendly smile. "Are you, Mister Oakes, like Shakespeare, to whom Doctor Johnson said a quibble was like a luminous, irresistible vapor?"

"No, sir."

"You went to Harvard College Law School"—Stanton rapped the folder—"twice. You left both times without a degree. Do not, Mister Oakes, attempt to play the lawyer with me. Do not quibble. You grew up in the town of Guilford, Connecticut, as did she. You knew Sarah Gilbert very well. Some sources claim that you were sweethearts, very serious sweethearts, but the difference in your stations—her father gave dancing lessons—prevented that from going further. Your father sent you off to Europe to put a stop to it."

"It was a long time ago," Oakes said. "I haven't seen Sarah Gilbert in years."

The smile grew even colder. "A pity you left law school, Mister Oakes. The ability to lie in a forthright and honest manner is the hallmark of a good lawyer."

Stanton rose and walked to the window and frowned down at the President's Mansion. "Or perhaps," he said, "you were so well trained in the Bureau of Military Information that deceit is second nature now?"

Oakes decided to say nothing.

Stanton turned from the window and walked up to Oakes's chair, and Oakes, looking up at him, remembered that according to rumor, Stanton had once made George Custer, a two-star general, stand at attention in his office while he inspected the general's posture.

"You were present at the Washington Navy Yard on April eleventh, 1865," Stanton said in a nearly conversational tone of voice.

That didn't seem to require an answer either.

"Just come up from Appomattox, right after Lee surrendered," Stanton said.

"I was bringing confidential messages from General Sharpe to General Halleck."

"And because of the confusion and excitement of Lee's surrender, you were filling in that afternoon for the duty officer, who was, I gather, profoundly drunk."

"Profoundly."

"Two enlisted men brought in a prisoner they thought was a Confederate courier, and since you were the duty officer they turned her over to you and presumably went off to get profoundly drunk themselves."

Oakes rose abruptly from his chair, without permission, and walked over to the window himself and stared down at the President's handsome mansion. He didn't see what was so god-damned interesting down there.

"She was traveling then under the name 'Kate Thompson,'" Stanton said, "to take care of your quibble about her name, and she was alone when she was arrested. She told the two enlisted men she was going from southern Maryland to New York, but she had a large steamer trunk and a smaller traveling bag. The traveling bag had a newspaper from Richmond and an envelope with Missus Mary Surratt's name and address on it—Sixth and H Street, Washington City."

"I didn't open her bag, Mister Stanton."

Stanton gave his frosty smile again and Oakes found himself wondering why the older man's face and beard didn't freeze and shatter like ice.

"No," Stanton said. "You let her go."

In the long silence that followed, Oakes remained just where he was, leaning against the windowsill, arms folded across his chest.

"Sarah Antoinette Gilbert married one Rowan Slater in May, 1858, in Salisbury, North Carolina. Neither family approved." Stanton looked up from the folder on his desk. "Her husband appears to have been a remarkably charming and incompetent young man. He got himself killed at Ball's Bluff, early in the war, one of the few Confederates to have suffered even a scratch in that wretched little skirmish. After that, his widow was at loose ends, without much money, disliked by her late husband's family as both a Northerner and a foreigner. She was not a political person, that is, she held no particular views about the war. But because her father was French and she evidently speaks the language perfectly, she somehow drifted into working as a courier between Richmond and Montreal, a very well-paid occupation."

Oakes thought of General Sharpe. "This is leading somewhere," he said, "I trust."

"As best I can establish,"—in an exaggerated, leisurely manner, Stanton turned another page in the folder—"Sarah Slater or Kate Thompson is said to be a very attractive woman, though it's hard to be sure because she always wore a veil or some kind of disguise, in the North. People knew her as the 'Lady in the Black Veil,' which sounds like trashy fiction but is true. She would be a little over thirty now, about your age, no doubt less attractive than before, older. But in late 1863, if not before, she caught the eye of Booth. Twice she traveled with him from Montreal to New York and stayed at the same hotel. At least half a dozen times she came to this city with Surratt."

"I went over this with General Sharpe, yesterday."

Stanton slammed his fist on the desk and shot straight up. His face was no longer icy cold, but burning red, furious as Mars. "She knew what Booth was doing! You stupid, stupid man! She *had* to know what was happening, she could have *told* us—and you let her go!"

Oakes studied the floor.

Stanton came around the desk. "And you let her go." He planted his feet in front of Oakes. "She traveled with Booth, she lodged at the Surratt house, she was in Washington exactly two days before the murder. She must have known what Booth and Surratt were planning, and she knows who else in the South helped him do it, and you let her go."

Stanton wheeled and returned to his desk. "General Sharpe says you are a highly intelligent, highly intuitive person, and—this is his word, which I find sentimental and vague—'lost.'"

Oakes looked up and frowned. "Lost?"

"Lost. You leave law school without a degree. You change employment. You're in New York City with no visible plans to work at anything. Lost. I think you let Sarah Slater go in a moment of romantic or sexual weakness—I don't use vague or sentimental language—and I find nothing so far to persuade me that you're intelligent. But the two enlisted men who arrested her have long since disappeared, nobody has a photograph of her, or if her family in North Carolina does, they refuse to cooperate. That leaves you. You are actually the only person I can command who knows what she looks like."

"You can't command me."

Stanton looked up from the desk, and there was a look of surprise on his face that made him seem almost vulnerable. "But *guilt* can," he said, with the tone, Oakes thought, of someone who knows all about guilt. "You might have prevented the murder of the greatest human being this nation has ever seen, but you were weak and you let Sarah Slater go, and if you hadn't done that we might have stopped Booth. Now you can at least help bring Jefferson Davis and Judah Benjamin and all the other filth to justice."

"I told General Sharpe I would help him for three months."

Stanton began to leaf through the papers on his desk again. "You're dismissed."

Oakes walked to the door and stopped. "What if we find her and she won't talk?"

Stanton continued to leaf through his papers. "Your friend Keach and the General have experience in making rebels talk." He paused. "Keach especially."

Oakes felt his own face turn to ice. "What will you do with her, after that?"

"Hang her," Edwin Stanton said, and turned a page.

7

In 1867 trains from Washington City to New York still terminated at a waterfront station in Hoboken, New Jersey. Passengers who wanted to go on to the city had to take a ferry across the Hudson River to lower Manhattan and disembark at the Battery Depot, near Christopher Street.

It was a little past eleven that same night when Oakes, Sharpe, and Keach slung their bags over their shoulders and hurried through the Hoboken station and out onto the docks and into a cold, steady January drizzle. Twenty minutes later, still ducking under the rain, they clattered down the ferry's gangplank and shoved through a crowd of passengers stampeding, as usual in New York, the other way.

Oakes stuck out an elbow, clamped his hat down with one hand, and followed Sharpe's squared shoulders out to a waiting line of miserable wet horses and rain-soaked cabs. Keach muttered good night and set off north toward Broadway, to disappear under whatever rock he was using these days. Sharpe climbed into a hansom. And Oakes switched hands on his hat and headed toward Vesey Street.

No visible plans to work at anything, Stanton had said, *you are perfectly free, Mr. Oakes, to do exactly what I tell you.*

Oakes's father the governor had been a non-drinker the last ten years of his life. Oakes could still remember the big white "T" on his vest for "Teetotaler," the official insignia of the Connecticut Temperance Union. But Oakes had no particular reverence for filial loyalty. He liked to drink. He liked bars.

Just before Vesey Street he pushed open the double doors of a dreary, almost empty saloon and ordered a "razzle-dazzle," a brandy and seltzer decoctum he had first tasted a few months ago with a *Harper's Magazine* editor when he was half-heartedly trying to find a job.

Not much razzle or dazzle. He gulped it down and wiped his mouth on the moustache towel and ordered another. At the other end of the bar a man about his age was drinking beer from a tomato can, which was the usual crockery in this kind of establishment because it was cheap and not dangerous in a fight. His right arm stopped at the shoulder. A veteran.

Oakes turned the other way to look between the curtains at the rain coming down. A little thunder and lightening now, to complete the atmosphere; everything, he thought, except "Enter three witches." War amputees like the man at the bar were a daily sight in New York, on the streets, on the sidewalks, begging usually; human detritus, mutilated glory.

But there were other kinds of physical reminders of the war as well. Across from the saloon, behind a gas streetlamp, loomed the dark burned-out shell of one of the Lottery Centers set on fire in the Anti-Draft Riots of early July, 1863—ironically enough, only days after the great Union victory at Gettysburg.

And a few steps down Vesey Street, he knew, was another reminder, the ruins of the old Lenox Hotel, where Confederate agents had crept down from Canada in late November 1864 and planted a phosphorus bomb in one of the rooms. They had planted such firebombs all over the city, in fact, sixty of them. Most of them simply fizzled harmlessly and died out, but a few had done spectacular damage, including one at a hotel next to the Winter Garden Theater where, in one of the Muse of History's smug little japes, John Wilkes Booth was playing Brutus in *Julius Caesar*, the perfect incarnation of treachery and assassination.

Julius Caesar. Oakes thought of the stone-faced Stanton, frozen in Puritanical paranoia—What did Shakespeare have Julius Caesar say about somebody like Stanton? "He loves no play, / As thou dost, Antony; he hears no music; seldom he smiles." Just before midnight, unsmiling, Oakes pulled out his key at Number 20 and began to climb to his room on the fourth floor.

The first two floors of the building were rented out to a group of recently hatched Harvard graduates who, with the sublime overconfidence of their class, were putting together a new political weekly called, modestly, *The Nation*. Their objective, according to their masthead, was to "Move the Reunited Country Forward." Once in a while Oakes stopped in and listened to them argue about which way was "Forward."

On the third floor, the single big triple-spaced office was dark, though that was by no means a sign that it was unoccupied, because two of the rooms inside the office were darkrooms used for developing photographs. The incongruous Gothic script on the glass door said "Ingersol and O'Sullivan, Commercial Photography."

Ingersol and O'Sullivan were acquaintances of his, a little older, not army veterans but what might be called civilian-veterans. Oakes had met them both, when they were photographing battlefields for Matthew Brady's archives. Now they were in business for themselves, taking "society" portraits of New York worthies and saving their money to undertake, one of these days, a much discussed, long-planned expedition west, to the Wind River Mountains of Wyoming, the last true American wilderness, they said, before civilization washed over it and finished its job of plowing up the continent. They wanted to preserve—for the historical record—the way the forests and the mountains and the Indians looked, just as Brady had wanted to make the war into a history book of photographs, black and white and everlasting. And Oakes thought he would give just about anything to go with them.

He paused on the landing. Ernest Ingersol was very likely to be inside even now, working on something. He kept late hours and he was always ready to drop what he was doing and talk about the technical side of photography—exposures, shadows, "points of light," his favorite phrase. He also liked to reminisce about the war.

Oakes climbed one more flight of stairs and put the key in his lock. It had been a grim, largely silent railroad trip up from Washington City. He'd had about all of remembering the war he could stand.

Since mid-summer, when he decided to leave Boston and try New York, Oakes had rented two rooms on the fourth floor of Number 20—a bedroom and a sitting room with two wooden chairs, a bookcase from his father's Guilford house, and a cheap desk where he spent long hours writing business plans and ideas on tablet sheets, then wadding them into balls of trash. At the window by the desk he could see that the rain was turning into a driving sleet. Farther north, in Canada, it would certainly be snow.

There are some people you just love.

You recognized her at once, Stanton had remarked drily, I suppose? Mrs. Slater? When they brought her into your office in Washington?

Oakes watched the sleet swing back and forth in the wind, like a white curtain in front of a closed door.

A foolish question, utterly foolish. He had recognized her in a heartbeat, even before the drunken sergeant had thrust her rudely forward, wrists manacled, and stood back to read his arrest report. He had known her walk when her face was still in shadow. He had known the cut of her shoulders and the swell of her bust and the sway of her hips. He had known her hair, though it was darker now, her cheeks, lips, all, all exactly the same. He had bent over his desk to sign the release, blushing like a schoolgirl, trying furiously to think of something to say, and when he had looked up again there was only the sergeant's back and the top of her head going down the corridor again. But her face was an image long ago burned into his mind, a perpetual point of light. Next to her, other women were plain as cabbages.

Why were they coming after her now?

8

"MONEY," KEACH SAID.

Sharpe stopped in mid-sentence and turned to stare at him.

"Money," Keach repeated. "We haven't talked about it yet. But I have to take time off from the bank to do this, General, and the bank won't pay me for not working. I have a mother and two homely unmarried sisters in Rockaway to support. I'm not rich like friend Oakes here—I need to be paid."

Oakes started to open his mouth, but Sharpe waved him down. "Secretary Seward agreed to pay your salary, I thought I told you. The State Department will pay you seven dollars a day and your travel expenses, for as long as you're gone. Quint will receive exactly the same."

"He doesn't need it," Keach muttered. "But *I* do, I need much more than that. I wish I had Jefferson Davis's gold." Then he sniffed loudly and looked toward the lobby. "Who," he said, "is that?"

The Astor Hotel had two bars, one that opened onto Fifth Avenue, the other onto Sixteenth Street. Both of them were closed to women, partly because of tradition, partly because both bars were lavishly decorated with alternating nude plaster statues of Venus and Diana, peering lasciviously out between pots of yellowing palms; in the case of the Fifth Avenue room, the bar and the statues were also overlooked by a very large and badly executed painting of a Greek nymph reclining, as European women were widely thought to do, naked in a forest.

Coming out of the Fifth Avenue bar now, in front of an indignant bartender, was a red-haired American woman in her early thirties, clearly not Greek, wearing a duck green dress, no bonnet, and a grim smile. She headed across the lobby toward the lounge corridor.

Sharpe rose, Oakes rose, Keach twisted in his chair.

"Miss Lawton, welcome." Sharpe extended a hand, which Maggie Gail Lawton shook once, firmly. "I thought you had gotten lost."

"And I thought you would be in the Louvre Museum over there," Maggie Lawton said, "restoring your tissues and enjoying the fine arts." She sat down in the fourth chair around the table and signaled to a lounging waiter. "Long hair. Boyish eyes," she said briskly. "You would be Captain Oakes." She turned to her left. "And you would be Sergeant Keach. Sandy hair, not that much of it, unfriendly smirk. A pot of your best black tea," she told the waiter. "Sugar, no cream. I see it brewing over there."

"This is Miss Maggie Lawton," Sharpe said. "Her bark is worse than her bite."

"No, it isn't," Maggie Lawton said.

"*Miss* Lawton," Keach said. "You're not married."

"Not even remotely." She patted his sleeve. "So hard to choose."

"Miss Lawton worked for Pinkerton during the war," Sharpe said. "I've asked her to join us."

"On our trip?" Keach bent forward across the table. "You don't mean it. A woman?"

"To Montreal and London, certainly." Sharpe began the ominous tapping of his index finger on the table that was a sign of his temper. "There are a number of names to investigate on the list that Seward gave me. Many of the men escaped with their wives. And there was one unmarried woman. We don't think she was accompanied by a man."

"Sarah Slater, also known as Kate Thompson." Maggie Lawton craned her neck to track the waiter's progress with her tea. "The lady courier in the Black Veil. She traveled with Booth and occasionally with John Surratt, sometimes staying in the same hotel. Quite the little hussy. I wonder how she paid for her escape? Perhaps flat on her back, in the usual female way."

"*Maggie*," Sharpe said, almost primly.

"We don't need a woman," Keach again.

"We need Miss Lawton's help," Sharpe said. "In England there are certainly going to be doors that are closed to men."

"It's bad luck."

"One woman to do the work of three men," Maggie said. The waiter slid a silver tray with a Chinese porcelain pot and cup onto the table beside her. "About the right ratio."

Oakes laughed, Sharpe's finger stopped tapping. "Miss Lawton—Maggie—left Pinkerton's six months ago. She came to me to ask for advice, since we had worked together on several missions in Richmond in '64."

"I didn't know that," Oakes said.

"He doesn't tell us everything," Keach grumbled. "He never did."

"*Pauvre petit.*" Maggie spoke to Keach but looked over the top of her teacup at Oakes.

Margaret Gail Lawton was thirty-five years old, tall, thin, no beauty but something more than plain. Her left cheek was faintly scoured with tiny pockmarks, the result, Oakes guessed, of a flawed smallpox vaccination. She had indeed, Sharpe explained, served as a secret courier for him and for Alan Pinkerton's Detective Agency, sometimes as a spy, and toward the end of the war, thanks to a slip-up on Sharpe's part, she had spent four very difficult weeks in Richmond's notorious Libby Prison before the Army of the Potomac marched in.

It was a tribute to the complexity and reach of Sharpe's mind—his *deviousness*, Keach would say later—that neither Oakes nor Keach, Sharpe's two closest aides, had ever heard her name or known of her presence behind Confederate lines. But as Sharpe began to lay out the details of their journey and slip their passports and train schedules across the table, it was clear that she and the general had gone over everything before, and clear as well that her mind was as sharp as her tongue.

"I had my office telegraph ahead to Montreal." Maggie opened her passport and made a face at Seward's enormous swirling signature. "Good grief. Jupiter Pluvius wouldn't write his name this big." She creased it closed and shook her head. "Seward," she said. "Stanton, Surratt, and Slater, and Sharpe, of course. All these names that start with 'S.'"

"Another conspiracy," Oakes said.

Maggie raised one eyebrow and a corner of her mouth. "I reserved three rooms at the Brainard House Hotel, General, one for you, one for me, and one to be shared by the young gentlemen."

Keach made no effort to keep the sneer out of his voice. "Your office?"

"Miss Lawton owns a female detective bureau."

"Open six months," Maggie said. "Two clients. That's why I need the General's money. My office is the front room of my apartment. And besides, unlike the strong, silent Captain Oakes here, I've never traveled outside of this country, unless you count the South."

"I've never traveled either," Keach said.

Maggie Lawton's not quite plain face became animate with mischief. "We'll be comrades in arms, Friend Keach, two peas in a pod."

9

THERE WERE, IN FACT, TWENTY-FOUR NAMES to investigate on the list Sharpe now began to pass around the table. Most of them were American citizens currently living abroad, some of them had been officially named by President Andrew Johnson as co-conspirators. Two of them stood out, Maggie Lawton said, like spiders on an angel food cake.

The first, the most notorious, perhaps the most hated Rebel of all, was the Confederate Secretary of State, Judah Phillip Benjamin—a Jew and oddly enough, a British subject by birth. As part of his official duties, Benjamin had directed all Confederate clandestine operations. Among his links to Booth, quickly uncovered by Stanton's detectives, was a $200 payment in Montreal for "unspecified purposes." And at the bottom of Booth's trunk in the National Hotel in Washington City, searchers had found a cipher code identical to the cipher codes used in Benjamin's office in Richmond. And more, John Surratt himself had been personally hired by Benjamin as a courier to Canada and reported directly to him, though all correspondence between them had apparently been lost in the siege of Richmond, or cannily destroyed. No one doubted that John Wilkes Booth himself had also reported directly to Judah Benjamin.

And no one doubted that every incriminating slip of paper linking them had long ago been burned to cinders by "Mister Davis's pet Jew." For millions of God-fearing Americans, Judah Benjamin, the "Mephistopheles of the Rebellion," as the *New-York Times* called him, was without doubt the sinister, murdering puppeteer behind the crazed, fanatical actor.

To blacken his infamy, Benjamin also was widely believed to have made off with a very large sum of Confederate treasure. Certainly, as he was fleeing Richmond, Davis had loaded the second car of his escape train with, according to the manifest, a "special cargo"—gold ingots, gold double eagle coins, silver coins, silver bricks, and Mexican silver dollars—virtually all the capital of the doomed Confederacy. Benjamin was on the train. When it reached Danville, Virginia, chaos and Union cavalry overtook it. Some of the treasure was hidden in sugar barrels and steamer trunks and spirited away into Georgia. But the bulk of the gold mysteriously vanished—along with Benjamin. Who more likely to have stolen it than the Jewish banker?

Oakes had given a certain amount of thought to Judah P. Benjamin.

By one of history's more mischievous coincidences, Lincoln had been assassinated on Good Friday, 1865. On the following Easter Sunday, ten thousand northern preachers proclaimed to their congregations that the dead president had been *martyred, crucified*, slain by the forces of Satan. Lincoln's death was like the death of Christ. He had given his blood for his country, just as the Savior had given his blood for the world.

The Jews had carried out that first murder. Now, the churches announced, they had done it again, thanks to the black arts of "Judas Iscariot Benjamin," who had betrayed the President, not for thirty pieces of silver, but for a boxcar of gold.

In the last month before his own death in early 1866, Oakes's father had written him a long letter about the assassination, and though the senior Oakes was a Lincoln supporter and a devout and abrasive Protestant, even he expressed misgivings about the comparisons of Lincoln to Christ. He had nothing but contempt for Andrew Johnson's repeated attacks on "that miserable Jew, Benjamin." The whole country, his father wrote Oakes, in a phrase Oakes had never forgotten, was "Christ-haunted."

On the other hand, his father said, it was impossible to believe that one man, acting alone, had killed the president.

* * *

The other outstanding name on Sharpe's list, though not a Jew, had been Benjamin's protégé.

At the beginning of 1864 Secretary of State Benjamin had signed over $900,000 in gold and bonds to one Jacob Thompson, a former governor of Mississippi, who was to settle in Toronto and use the money to launch aggressive, subversive operations across the border of neutral Canada. His assignment was to weaken and destroy Northern morale, and thereby sabotage the re-election of President Lincoln.

To that end Thompson planned a number of attacks on Union prisoner of war camps in New York and Illinois, and on various federal arsenals, where weapons and ammunition could be found and carried off somehow to the South. From there he proceeded to what Sharpe always called "black warfare." He underwrote the infamous scheme to spread yellow fever in the North through dirty linen. He tried to introduce smallpox into several small border cities. He twice sent agents to poison the drinking water in New York City's Croton Reservoir.

Then "black warfare" seemed to turn into comic opera. In August 1864 Thompson authorized a special railway shipment to Confederate sympathizers in Chicago, where Federal agents duly found and captured four thousand revolvers in hundreds of boxes marked "Sunday School Books." Later that month he underwrote a spectacularly inept and unsuccessful plan to storm the *USS Michigan* on Lake Erie with a fleet of rowboats. (The ship's captain was to be given drugged champagne.)

After that, to replenish his coffers, Thompson launched a raid on the little town of St. Albans, Vermont, where his raiders robbed three banks of almost $200,000 and set fire to a hotel. But the gold proved too heavy for their horses to carry in saddlebags, the Confedeerates had brought no wagons to transport it, and in a matter of hours, volunteers from Vermont had dashed across the border and seized them.

Judah Benjamin now lived comfortably in London, openly practicing law. No matter what Stanton thought about the brotherhood of Jews, Benjamin, whose parents were British and who was born in Saint Croix in the British West Indies, was still a British subject. The ties to Booth and Surratt that Stanton's men had so far untangled were far from strong enough to make the British government yield such a person up to extradition. Sharpe's orders were to circle him, quiz him, harass him, turn him upside down and shake out his pockets in the hope of finding something. Gold, maybe.

As for Jacob Thompson, he had left Canada in April 1865, only a few days after the assassination, using a passport signed by Benjamin. Where he was today, no one knew.

The other names on the list, apart from Sarah Slater, meant nothing to Oakes. Keach recognized someone named Thomas Courtenay, but couldn't remember why. Maggie Lawton knew the name George Nicholson Sanders and had once seen him when she was in prison in Richmond, but that was all.

Sharpe cleared his throat to signal that the meeting was almost over. Then he put away his brisk, efficient spymaster's face and put on a sober professorial mask. "I have a somewhat philosophical view of this mission," he said quietly. Something in his voice made Oakes stiffen in his chair. Maggie Lawton paused her cup of tea halfway to her lips.

"After great, unthinkable Providential events like the assassination of the President," he said, "it's human nature to search for explanations that make it less mysterious, that bring it back to the human scale."

"Conspiracies, in other words," Oakes said.

"Conspiracies."

"I remember," Keach said with one of his unhealthy laughs, "while they were hunting Booth, all over the country they were arresting anybody with pale skin and a long moustache. One fellow in Massachusetts was arrested four times in a week, till he finally just locked himself in his house. It was all a farce then and it may be a farce now. I told you and I told Stanton, if there were any more conspirators—and probably there weren't—they're long gone now."

"Some days," Sharpe said, rising from the table, "I completely agree with you." He held out his hand for his hat and coat, and a waiter came hurrying toward him at a trot. "But I was in the Old Arsenal Penitentiary before they hanged Lewis Payne. He was an oaf and a lug, but he had a certain presence. When he heard who I was, he looked hard at me and said, 'All I can tell you, friend, is that you haven't got the one-half of them.'"

He took his hat and coat. And in the gesture that Oakes thought he would always consider Sharpe's characteristic movement, he turned on his heel and walked away.

10

LIKE SO MANY RAILWAY JOURNEYS IN 1867, the trip from New York to Montreal was complicated by the anarchic competitiveness of the seventeen different train companies that served the city.

In the first place, each company used a different time setting for their schedules, so that in the main Spring Street Depot there were seventeen different clocks, each showing a different time, arranged in two ranks across the platform gates—a bizarre situation repeated in train stations all over the country.

And in the second place, to cover a distance of not quite four hundred miles, Sharpe's party had to take three separate railroad lines, two of which used different gauge tracks. At the Spring Street Depot they clambered into a stubby Metropolitan Central second-class carriage, comprised of two parallel rows of unpainted wooden benches, an undersized but sulphurous pot-bellied stove in the center, and brass spittoons on both sides of the aisle. At the end of the carriage the railroad had fixed a line of poster advertisements, one for "Sozodont," which cleaned teeth like a giant foaming broom, to judge from the drawing. In a gesture toward modern elegance, the Metropolitan Central had also laid down a garish blue and yellow floor of slippery new English linoleum.

During the war, because of what Sharpe regarded as his cool New England competence with schedules and baggage, Oakes had served as Sharpe's de facto transportation officer. On Sunday, January 13, as if nothing at all had changed since his army days, he supervised the loading and tagging of their valises and boxes, including one oversized trunk that Maggie Lawton cheerfully announced contained her lady's "unmentionables."

Keach and Sharpe sat together on a bench close to the moody little stove. Maggie Lawton gestured to Oakes and brushed her skirt aside to offer him a place beside her on a bench near the front. For seven or eight minutes they sat in silence as the train rattled slowly northward. Then Maggie cleared her throat. "This part of New York," she said, as they crossed Sixth Avenue for the second time, "is called the Tenderloin."

Like Sharpe, Oakes disliked being told things he already knew. He looked past her pointing finger and grunted.

"It's called that," Maggie said, "thanks to a police captain named Clubber Williams. I met him before the war, when I first started working for Pinkerton. He was the crookedest old sack of guts in New York, and when he was transferred to the Sixth Avenue Precinct, he thought he had landed in whore and payoff heaven. He told the newspapers, 'I've been living on chuck steak, boys, but now I'm going to get a little tenderloin.'"

Oakes nodded and sat back and thought that Miss Maggie Lawton's conversation was...unorthodox.

"So, what did you and the dapper general find out in Elmira?" she asked.

Oakes almost smiled. Sharpe *was* dapper. He was also a great believer in keeping his troops busy, whether usefully or not. On Friday, while Keach had closed down his desk at his bank and

Maggie Lawton met with her two clients, he and Oakes had taken yet another train line—the Erie-North Central—to Elmira, a few hours northwest of the city. The idea had been to poke around the city where Surratt had last been seen, two days after the assassination.

According to Stanton's detectives, Surratt's assignment was to plan a prison break *en masse* from the huge prisoner-of war-camp there and send the liberated soldiers south to join Lee's army—another of Jacob Thompson's hair-brained snow-ad-dled schemes, Stanton had said. Elmira was four hundred miles north of Richmond. What were thousands of ragged, starving Southerners going to do, suddenly let loose to wander the New York countryside? And besides, anybody who could read a news-paper could see that in April 1865, the Confederate States of America were finished, were going to pieces, bit by bit, like a wreck in the sea.

"Well, we learned that somebody had torn out the pages in the hotel register where Surratt stayed."

Maggie made a dismissive snorting sound. "Very sinister."

"And we found out Surratt had been buying a twenty-dollar tweed overcoat when the clerk told him Lincoln was dead, and he threw down the overcoat and bolted out the door."

"He probably ran all the way to Montreal."

By the stove Keach suddenly raised his voice and they could hear him clearly, arguing for more money. He had responsibilities, he said, the government was rich, the government *owed* him.

"*Radix malorum cupiditas est,*" Maggie said.

Oates looked up, surprised.

"Don't make that face," Maggie said. "A woman can know Latin. I learned it at school, with my brother."

"Your brother?" Oates didn't know when he had sounded so stupid.

"He was killed at Antietam, which in turn killed my father. My mother was already dead."

"I'm sorry."

Maggie shifted on the bench and looked at him steadily. Hunter's eyes, Oakes remembered somebody saying about the implacable U.S. Grant. "So, former Captain Oakes," she said, "do you think he had help? John Surratt? Or are we all wasting our time?"

On that subject, Oakes's thoughts had not changed at all. "Well, somebody helped him, nobody disputes that. He went from Elmira to Montreal and after three or four months, it seems, to Liverpool and then London and Rome, finally Egypt, all without visible funds. We know that at least one Catholic priest gave him shelter in Montreal, and another one in Liverpool—so Seward's probably right that Confederate sympathizers knew who he was and took him in and hid him anyway, and paid his bills. But that just makes them sympathizers, not conspirators or assassins."

"I wake up every morning," Maggie Lawton said, "furious at Abraham Lincoln."

Oakes stared at her.

"It was," she said slowly and firmly, "a senseless, unnecessary war. I wake up every morning *furious* at him. He should have let those godforsaken secessionists go. I would have let them go."

She turned and looked out the window. "*Dulce bellum inexpertis,*" she said.

Oates started to object, then stopped. What about slavery? He would have asked. What about *treason*? But he had no taste for political argument, no taste at all for arguing with Maggie

Lawton, who had lost a brother and been in prison. And in any case, some deep hidden part of him knew that he would have been on shaky ground.

"War is sweet for those not in it," she translated. "Like Congressmen and Presidents." She nodded cryptically to herself. The cityscape, blanketed with dirty snow, unrolled outside like a spool of canvas on a stage.

At Peekskill they crossed the Hudson and changed to the New York Central line. And at Saratoga Springs, as night came on, they switched to yet another railroad company, the Delaware and Hudson, and settled into a comfortable parlor car where food was served and a pale, lanky Ichabod Crane lookalike sat folded in a corner and played waltzes on a violin.

A little past eight that evening they stopped at Champlain for a perfunctory Customs inspection, and ten minutes later they crossed over the border and entered what was technically still known as British North America.

11

Or Canada, as everybody now called it.

Or Our Lady of the Snows, as Sarah Slater called it, the eternally frostbitten end of the world. "'The ice was here, the ice was there,'" she muttered, looking at the gray metallic sky, "'the ice was all around.'" Whoever wrote that old poem, she thought, had grown up in Canada.

As she moved off the porch and into the courtyard, the cold air struck her face like a slap. It was like living at the North Pole. Why hadn't the powers in Richmond set up their foreign bureau in someplace warm, like Mexico? If she never saw another red plaid lumberjack jacket in her life, she told herself, she would be content.

"Be *careful* with that," she said sharply in French to one of the two bearded giants upending her steamer trunk. The equally gigantic horses in front of the wagon shivered under their blankets and bobbed their heads.

The nearer giant said something impatient back to her, in the strange Canadian French that her father used to say reminded him of a woodchuck gnawing a sausage. Over by the convent gates she could see Sister Marie-Thérèse waddling out into the snow toward her. Sister Marie-Thérèse had been crippled since birth and heaved her bad left leg along with the help of a thorn crutch. Another of her father's sayings came back to her—"she was so fat that she was taller lying down than standing up." Sarah arranged her face in suitably humorless Canadian piety.

John Surratt's first hideout after fleeing Elmira had been in the private home of one John Porterfield, a Nashville banker who was part of the Confederacy's loose organization of schemers and saboteurs planted in and around Montreal by Jacob Thompson. Sarah had seen Surratt once at Porterfield's house, when she was invited for tea, and she had heard him curse Stanton and Seward and especially Booth, whose wretched ineptness, he whined, was going to send his mother to prison—no one believed they would have the nerve to hang her.

But then Surratt's own ineptness in repeatedly showing his face around town had forced him suddenly to abandon Porterfield's comfortable guest rooms and scuttle some thirty miles east to a monastery where the pro-Southern monks, knowing full well who he was, had kept him hidden another two months.

"That is a very big trunk," Sister Marie-Thérèse said suspiciously. "Quite heavy. What do you have in it, guns?"

Sarah placed herself carefully between the old woman and the trunk. "I left a purse in your office," she told the old woman. "The money in it should more than pay for the time you kept my things."

"Fifteen months. Over a year's storage. A big trunk. That's a long time." A significant pursing of the lips.

"The money should be plenty." Sarah was no longer much surprised by clerical greed. It was clearly a substitute for more carnal appetites, suppressed by their ungodly godly vows.

"It's not Confederate money, because that's worthless."

"It's coins, double eagles."

"Because the Americans are coming back."

"I didn't say that, Sister."

"You don't need to. Why else would you come out here for your trunk in January, after all this time? Why else would you leave your hotel and hire these galoots to carry you up to Quebec? They're coming back for you, the Americans."

The old woman pivoted on her crutch and glared south in the general direction of the border. When the war started, Sarah remembered, most Canadians were vaguely sympathetic to the North. But little by little they had come to believe that once the Union had subjugated the South, its murderous, perfidious gaze would turn north. Seward had talked openly of annexing Canada. One chuckleheaded senator from Michigan had introduced a bill to send two hundred thousand troops into Quebec to exact "reparations" for the cost of the war, and thirty fellow senators had signed on to it, a plan that may or may not have died with Lincoln.

The other reason for their hostility was, of course, the Church. Canada was inflexibly Catholic. After he left Porterfield's house, Surratt had been passed along from monastery to monastery by what amounted to an underground railroad of Catholic priests—droll thought, an underground railroad for a rebel—who all considered the militant Protestantism of the North far more distasteful than slavery. Then too, Surratt was Catholic, like his mother, and had once studied to take holy orders. A nice joke, that, Sarah thought, considering his ruttish behavior when she had been forced to travel with him.

The galoots had finished strapping the trunk onto the wagon, and the slightly less mountainous one had taken a seat behind the great golden Clydesdale horses, who began to snort and stomp their readiness to jingle out into the open highway.

She walked a few steps out into the road and sighted up and down, as if to judge its condition. A solitary figure, visible for half a mile in either direction. *I am here. Find me if you can.*

"No river boat service to Quebec in January," Sister Marie-Thérèse, still looking south, told her. "Too much ice in the water in January."

"I didn't say I was going to Quebec, Sister."

"Didn't have to. After Quebec, are you going to Paris?"

Sister Marie-Thérèse kept a large printed map of Paris on the wall of her classroom and often taught her girls by having them memorize its street names and neighborhoods and monuments. People said she could have gone around the city blindfolded, so well and so long had she studied it. But Sister Marie-Thérèse, Sarah thought, looking at the old woman's crutch and withered leg, would never have that chance. Paris would remain her distant, unreachable Celestial City. Some people she knew would have had witty thoughts about the sad irony of the Sister's life, or about the strong likelihood that Paris would have turned out to be more Vanity Fair than Celestial City.

Sarah had lied so easily and so often during her three years as Confederate courier that she scarcely heard herself saying, "No, not Paris. Nowhere near Paris."

At the Saint Lawrence Hall Hotel, she stopped by to gather her much smaller and lighter trunk of clothes and papers. As usual, Benedict Lee was behind the reception desk, and as usual he made a slow, leering inspection of her bodice as she approached, though she was bundled like an Eskimo against the arctic cold and still, she assumed, radiating apple-cheeked wholesomeness from her visit to the convent. "*Uomo es sempre cacciatore*," her father used to say in Italian. "Man is always a hunter." Then he would laugh and add in French, "And woman is always an actress."

Sister Marie-Thérèse had been right, of course. She was going to Quebec, and not by the river. The trunk on the wagon was much too heavy to risk on a boat in the middle of a black, ice-cluttered river. Her two giants were going to drive her all the way to the Quebec City docks, where big, anonymous ocean-going steamers now braved the Atlantic crossing every month of the year.

"We are all very sorry to see you go," Lee said with syrupy gallantry. "Very sorry indeed, a lovely person like yourself." He made an exaggerated moue and then motioned her toward the alcove a few steps away from his desk. There, glancing around furtively enough to catch the attention of everyone in the lobby, he stood very close to her shoulder and murmured down into his gloved hand. "They arrived late last night. They're at the Brainard House, four of them."

"All right, good."

"Don't you want to know their names?"

Sarah was already turning away, peering through the windows at her waiting wagon. "I'm leaving Montreal," she said. "Forever and for good. I really don't care who they are."

12

IN THE WAR KEACH HAD BEEN the cruel interrogator—prisoners of war, spies, hapless civilians, young, old, it made no difference to Keach. In the war at least, Keach had an unhealthy nature. He stood, his prisoners sat. He lowered his face to theirs and screamed till they were covered with spittle. He ordered wounded, frightened, thirsty men—boys, really—tied to trees with their arms pinned over their heads or had them splayed against a spare wagon wheel, where they baked bareheaded for hours in the unforgiving Virginia sun. He had men strung up by their thumbs. He brought out big oak tubs of filthy water for head dunking, which could go on for an hour or more. And not often, but sometimes…Once, outside Richmond…

Sharpe, on the other hand, was a lawyer. He gave Keach his orders. He turned his back and left the room. Sometimes, when he permitted himself the question, Oakes wondered who really had the unhealthy nature.

At their first breakfast in Montreal, Sharpe assembled them in a private room and marched them methodically, in his meticulous lawyer's way, through the names on Seward's list. Individually or in pairs, they were to visit hotels where Confederate agents like Jacob Thompson had stayed. They were to talk with friendly Canadian passport clerks and look over passenger shipping manifests. Oakes was to go to the nearby village of Saint Liboire, where a truculent pro-southern Catholic priest had sheltered Surratt for ten weeks, knowing full well who he was. Keach, the banking expert, on a tight leash now, was to burrow about in Canadian banks that had handled Confederate funds.

On the third day, Oakes and Sharpe traveled together to the home of one Clement Claiborne Clay, in the town of Lac Saint Louis just south of the city. Clay—a third cousin of the great Kentuckian, Henry Clay—had been a United States Senator from Alabama, but resigned with a flourish from the Senate in 1861 when Alabama seceded. He was reportedly a charismatic, highly-competent person, and at first Jefferson Davis wanted him to serve as his Secretary of War, but Clay, talkative as well as competent, decided he had rather be a senator in the Confederate Congress. In 1864 his portrait would be engraved on the Confederate one-dollar bill.

In 1864 he also came to Montreal to work with Jacob Thompson, and subsequently—here was his interest for Sharpe— his signature appeared on one of the checks that Booth received when the kidnap plot was in the planning stage.

Because of that one signature, Clay had spent a year in Fortress Monroe Prison in Hampton, Virginia, until his wife, Virginia, browbeat President Johnson into conceding that Clay had nothing to do with the assassination. Now the Clays were in Canada again, looking to restart their lives. But still furious at his vindictive, humiliating year in prison, the erstwhile senator refused to speak with Sharpe, and his wife spat on their boots as they left. Two other former Confederates refused even to answer the door.

Early on the final morning, Sharpe assembled everyone in the half-empty hotel lobby and handed out their last assignments.

Keach had one more banker to interview. Maggie Lawton was to arrange their railroad travel next day to Portland, Maine, where a transatlantic steamer would set out on February 24 for Liverpool. And after breakfast, Oakes and Sharpe were to take a hired carriage to the Convent of the Sainted Mother some dozen miles west of Montreal.

"That would be about Sarah Slater," Maggie Lawton said.

The hotel cat had inevitably found Sharpe as soon as they had arrived. Now it scampered across the carpet and wrapped itself like a vine around his trouser leg. The former chief of U.S. Grant's much-feared Bureau of Military Information bent down and scooped it up, then cradled it in his arms, belly side up, and scratched. "Sarah Slater," he agreed.

"Why not send her?" Keach jerked his head in Maggie's direction. "If I know nuns they might not even speak to a man."

"Quint speaks good French."

"She speaks French." Keach put on his interrogator's frowning face. "I've heard her."

"I thought I had mentioned," Sharpe said. He put down the cat and peered out the lobby window. It was not yet seven in the morning, but the dark streets were already crowded with shadowy commercial wagons and, under the street lamps, puffing men stacking crates. "I thought I had mentioned," he said casually, "Quint is the only person we have who knows what Sarah Slater looks like. We have photographs for everyone else, but not her. You remember Stanton's notes; she always wore a black veil in the North. But by good luck Quint actually grew up in the same town in Connecticut. He saw her a number of times before the war."

"My, my," Maggie said. "What other tidbit did you just happen to forget to mention, General Secret, sir?"

Sharpe made his face blank as a plate.

"Guilford, Connecticut," Keach said. "That's where he grew up." Keach had long made it a point to know all he could about Oakes's background.

Maggie Lawton flipped through her dog-eared folder of papers. "She was only a low-level courier, between Richmond and here. I never quite saw why she was on the list."

"She made half a dozen trips with Booth to New York," Sharpe said. "She stayed at Missus Surratt's boarding house once. We know she came here after Richmond and she stayed at the convent for one summer. After that, Stanton's people lost track. I thought the Sisters at the convent might know something."

"She traveled with Booth," Maggie Lawton said.

"In the same room probably." Keach snorted.

"She speaks fluent French," Sharpe said, as if that settled any question about Sarah Slater's morals.

Oakes had opened his own folder and was studiously decoding Sharpe's miniscule handwriting. He didn't look up.

"She also traveled with a big steamer trunk and another smaller one." Maggie Lawton snapped the folder shut. "I wonder why so much baggage for somebody running away?"

"I had the same question," Keach said.

"Seward thought she might have carried off some of Booth's letters, records," Sharpe said briskly. "Now we need to move on. They're laying the breakfast out."

Maggie studied Oakes with her sharp, disconcertingly intelligent eyes. "Did you know her well?"

The ability to lie in a forthright and honest manner was the hallmark of a good lawyer, Stanton had said. Oakes shook his head with a rueful expression.

"Talkative Captain Oakes," she said, and after a moment added, "What did she look like?"

But Oakes pretended not to hear and turned away toward the dining room, where white-coated waiters had just flung open the folding doors.

PART TWO

Liverpool and London

February and March 1867

1

"On my first sail across the Atlantic," Chester said, "I saved the whole ship."

Thomas Morris Chester was the blackest man Oakes had ever seen, and one of the tallest. Maggie Lawton was grinning up at him like a child about to open a Christmas present. "How did you do that?"

"I shot the cook!" Chester roared, and he laughed and patted a startled Liverpudlian on the shoulder as they walked past. Chester looked back at the Englishman and roared again, "I shot the cook!"

At this point they were just crossing Standish Street, in the nearly geographic center of Liverpool. It had taken sixteen blustery days to cross the Atlantic—four more than usual—and another two days for Maggie Lawton and Keach, first-time European travelers, to adjust to the hundreds of little differences in architecture, food, and clothes that made this a foreign city. Sharpe had been patient and then, of course, impatient.

"Now," Chester announced, "take that big white building." As they reached the opposite curb, he pointed to the great colonnaded bulk of St. George's Concert and Courthouse, which was far and away the most imposing building in Liverpool, visible even from their ship as they had steamed up the Merseyside estuary.

"Now," Chester repeated, "you could pick up a rock and throw it from that old rich white man's temple and hit the most miserable slums in Europe—worse than anything in Africa—and that's where I'm going to take you. Hang on to your money!"

He wheeled on the sidewalk, slipped Maggie's arm inside his, and gave another of his great booming laughs.

Oakes trailed a few feet behind them, shivering in the wind and marveling at the ease with which Chester moved through the crowded streets, the crowded *white* streets, where pale English faces turned and swayed like blanched sunflowers toward him as he passed. It had been that way all day. He had met them at their hotel at ten a.m., and while Sharpe and Keach went off on their rounds of visits to banks and consuls, Thomas Chester Morris had taken them in hand and more or less swept them away for a personal whirlwind tour of the city. Theme: John Surratt on the run.

They had just left the *oratoire* of the Church of the Holy Cross, where two years earlier yet another Catholic priest, one Charles Jolivet, had taken Surratt in and given him shelter, fully aware that Surratt was wanted worldwide for the assassination of Abraham Lincoln. But in heavily Catholic, violently pro-Southern Liverpool, that was almost a recommendation. From the start of the war, Liverpool, as the main English port of entrance for all Southern cotton, had lent its moral support to the Confederacy, and often more than just its moral support. A "charity" auction in St. George's Hall raised a hundred thousand dollars for Jeff Davis's armies. At least three new armored warships for the South had been built right there on the Mersey docks—illegal under British neutrality laws, but an open secret in Liverpool—and launched against the Union. Before the trip, Oakes understood abstractly that Liverpool depended for its jobs and shipping on "King Cotton," but he had been completely unprepared for the snarling insults, the turned backs, the muttered curses that greeted all four of them when they started to ask their questions.

"Now *when*," Maggie Lawton said almost girlishly, "were you in Africa?"

Another great rippling laugh, a flash of white teeth in a black, cold-puckered face. "Bless your innocence, child. I lived five years in Liberia. I was born in Philadelphia, but that was no place for"—he drew out the word to mock it—"a *Nee-gro*. I've been to Africa, France, Germany—now I live in England. If you're black enough you can be anywhere in the world, because you're invisible, like a ghost."

Oakes thought that was the most untruthful thing he had heard yet. It was impossible to imagine the six-foot five-inch tall, enormously forceful Chester invisible. Energy somehow baked off of him. It was sometimes as if, Sharpe had said, waxing Shakespearean, Falstaff had somehow metamorphosed into Othello.

"I even saw our slowpoke little puppy Captain Oakes back there," Chester said over his shoulder, "in Richmond, when Lincoln came strolling in."

They stood about two hundred yards north of St. George's Hall now, and just as Chester had said, the handsome red brick offices and shops had disappeared. They were now entering a kind of urban wilderness of tiny three-story wooden hovels and amazingly narrow, arthritically twisted alleys.

"You saw me?"

"I came back from Liberia in late 1863, right after Gettysburg, and the editor of the Philadelphia *Courier*—a good abolitionist— hired me on as a newspaper reporter. I can read and write like a white man—dat I'se can. I went with Grant's headquarters right through Virginia in '64. When Jeff Davis took his French leave of that fine city, I wrote the story for my paper *and* for the *New-York Times*. Captain Oakes has a distinctive look, a handsome look."

"He was younger then," Maggie Lawton said sardonically.

"And I saw him about fifty yards behind the President, worried to death and running back and forth with his pistol out."

Oakes nodded. He barely noticed that Chester had brought them through one of the stinking alleys and up to what must have been a tavern, though there was no sign above the door and the windows were too filthy to see through. He had indeed walked behind the President that day in Richmond—it was the same scene Sharpe had reminded him of back in Washington City. He was following with a squad of Marines, feverishly watching the shattered buildings and side streets for stalkers, gunmen, assassins. Up ahead Lincoln, wearing his usual black suit and stovepipe hat, his back to Oakes, was walking hand in hand with his obnoxious little son Tad. Tall and short shadows going down a bombarded street toward a sunset, toward the end of the war. If he had been a photographer, if he had had a camera, it would have been the image of a lifetime. Once or twice he had tried to write about it.

"Now this," Chester said, "is what I wanted you to see."

Two boys in rags, "street Arabs" as they were called in Liverpool, stared up at him. Chester patted them absently on the head, ducked his own head and led them into the tavern.

"Dear Savior and figs," Maggie Lawton murmured. "The Astor Hotel this is not."

The tavern with no sign was in fact "The Spotted Horse." Oakes read the name on a long white plank hanging behind the bar, which consisted of two long greasy planks supported by wooden barrels. As his eyes adjusted to the gloom, he could see a crude drawing of a horse on the sign, two rickety tiers of glasses and brown bottles, and the single glowering bloodshot eye of the barkeep leaning toward them with both knotted fists on the bar.

They had been in Liverpool for three days now, but even though the language was in theory English, Oakes understood very little of the rapid, high-pitched local dialect, "Scouse," which Maggie Lawton said sounded like somebody's nasal plumbing in the morning.

"He says," Chester translated, "get the hell out." A few streaks of pale sunlight found their way through the front windows. The black man grinned and spun a gold sovereign on the plank, in a little circle of light. "I gentled his exact words a little, for the lady." Two ancient wraiths in sailor's gear and a fine alcoholic stupor watched the coin spin.

"We're not going to drink anything here," Oakes said and rubbed his nose against the caustic mixed smell of urine and stale beer and unwashed bodies.

Behind Chester, the barkeep had stiffened. He watched the coin spin, too, but made no move to reach for a bottle.

"Cholera," Chester nodded, "typhus. Runs through these sorry warrens three or four times a year. Kills half the people off, but the next wave pours in from Ireland or wherever and you don't even know it happened. I wouldn't drink anything here either. But I wanted you to see what kind of man old Thomas Dudley is."

Maggie Lawton was studying the claustrophobic little room with what Oakes recognized as one of Pinkerton's search routines, High to Low in quadrants, Left to Right, repeat. "You mean Dudley the consul?"

In a far corner two knobby shadows sat slumped over a table, an emaciated hound sprawled on what seemed to be a dirt floor. A black curtain slid aside and a woman stepped out, rubbing her hands on a cloth.

"Thomas Haines Dudley, I do mean him." One of the old sailors tugged at Chester's elbow. "Give them both a drink," Chester told the barkeep, who still didn't move. "One brave man, one brave man."

"He came here?"

"That little New Jersey Quaker used to slip out of his nice paneled office on Water Street and come in these awful back streets and wander around from bar to bar talking to sailors. He was looking for people to sign up, people that would ship out with the rebels and spy for him. So he had to go where the sailors were. Not many people would."

Oakes nodded, less surprised than he might have been. Thomas Dudley had been the American consul in Liverpool throughout the war—still was—and according to Sharpe he had recruited more spies, hired more detectives, broken up more Confederate schemes than anybody else in Europe. He was a wan, sickly-looking man in his fifties, still carrying horrible scars on one side of his face from a steamship explosion before the war, and by any measure he should have been wasting away in some rural sanitarium.

But he was still at his desk today, still sending long weekly reports to Seward about Liverpool shipping. When he had welcomed them to his office three days ago, he had coughed until they thought his lungs would burst. Yet, like many Quakers that Oakes had known, Dudley possessed an iron core, impressive and determined and unstoppable. He had instantly reminded Oakes of U. S. Grant.

"I was here for a little while," Chester said. He turned slowly and looked hard at the barkeep. After a long moment, the barkeep slid a pair of glasses in front of the sailors.

"I passed through on one my trips." Chester turned back to them. "This town was one big nasty nest of Southerners, you know, all of them trying to persuade the British to sell them a ship or build them a ship or lend them a ship, and they kept throwing bricks through Dudley's windows and writing him threatening notes. Somebody took a shot at him. I was here when three hired rebels of the genteel class broke into his office and grabbed the housekeeper, and little Dudley drove them back down the steps with an axe handle." He boomed out a laugh and the sprawling dog sat up and barked. "My kind of Quaker!"

"He was an abolitionist," Maggie Lawton said.

"He did everything a white man could do to help the black man," Chester said. "I just wanted you to see. If somebody in Liverpool, besides that god-forsaken priest, helped Surratt get away, Dudley can find him. He knows this city like a hawk."

"There are people on our list," Oakes said, "who had nothing to do with Surratt."

"I saw your list."

"Sharpe is talking to bankers, ship owners, sympathizers who might have financed Booth."

"Dudley is some kind of tenacious beast," Chester said. "I wouldn't want him after me." He slapped his big palm down with a bang and left the coin on the bar. Then he hitched his shoulders and started toward the door. "But General Sharpe," he said, "that man scares me."

"The mildest-mannered little man," Maggie said, "that ever cut a throat."

The Liverpool docks stretched more than five miles along the tidal estuary of the Mersey River. The city itself lay almost entirely on the eastern side of the river, but the crowded wet docks lined both sides of it, north and south, until the river curved out of sight and disappeared into the green, always-cloudy distance. There was a double-track railroad line from the southern end of the docks to London. Around them, sprung up like weeds, crowded innumerable small export houses, cordwainers' shops, carpenters' shops, sail makers, coal merchants, beer shops, sailors' flops—a frenetic Babel of nations swarmed up and down its muddy, foul-smelling wharves. As for recreation, the disapproving Dudley had told them that there were more than a hundred brothels along the docks alone.

It was four-fifteen in the afternoon of the following day, a cold, bright blue English afternoon, and the sailors were milling about the docked ships and clambering up the riggings, while the ladies of the brothels were lounging in their doorways or, in one or two instances, in the front windows of their places of business.

Sharpe paid no attention to any of it. He emerged from Dudley's consulate office on Water Street and snapped his watch shut. Then he strode purposefully past the Prince's pier-head ferry landing, made an abrupt turn east on, as far as Oakes could tell, a completely anonymous street and abruptly right again down an alley called, rather grandly, Rumford Place. He stopped in front of a tidy two-story office building, constructed of the ubiquitous red Liverpool brick, and pushed open the ground-floor door.

Gordon Hulse's secretary was expecting them. He ushered them up the stairs to Hulse's office, which had a certain nautical bareness and tidiness, and behind a fine polished oak desk, Gordon Hulse himself, rising to extend a hand.

Preliminaries out of way, cigars and port offered and refused, Hulse leaned back in his chair and smiled like an alligator.

"So I understand from your letter that you—and your associate here—" He looked inquiringly at Oakes, who said nothing. "You're interested in having Fraser, Trenholm build a merchant steamer, something, you said, over four hundred tons."

"I haven't the least interest in buying a ship, Mister Hulse." Sharpe slid over the desk one of his official letters of introduction from Seward. "I want to ask you about John Surratt and George Trenholm."

The crocodilian smiled vanished. Hulse picked up the letter between thumb and forefinger, as if it were on fire. While he read, Sharpe straightened the model ship on the corner of Hulse's desk.

"You lied to me, sir." Hulse started to crumple the letter, thought better of it, and slid it back to Sharpe. Then he rose from his chair and towered over the general. "You wrote me a complete and utter falsehood. Kindly leave my office at once."

There is nothing quite so deflating, Oakes thought, as giving a stern and pompous command and having its object simply continue to sit and stare back thoughtfully.

After a moment Hulse sank back into his chair. "I will have someone come and force you to leave, sir. I'm not impressed by"—he jerked his chin at the letter—"the exigencies of a foreign government." He reached for a small copper bell next to his ink-well. "I'm going to call my secretary to show you out."

"Well as to that, Mister Hulse, of course you wouldn't have received us if I had written the truth."

Oakes thought he should do something useful, so he picked up Seward's letter, noticed in passing the fine bold seal of the United States Department of State, and folded it into his coat pocket.

"And as to throwing us out, let me just observe that your company Fraser, Trenholm does some eighty percent of its construction and shipping with American businesses. Those businesses require all kinds of paperwork and permissions from our Treasury Department, who control our customs offices, and from the Department of State, who oversee commercial treaties. I have another letter from our Secretary of the Treasury, if you'd care to see it."

Oakes cleared his throat, but neither man looked at him. There was no such letter, he knew, from the Secretary of the Treasury. Seward and Stanton had insisted that Sharpe report only to them.

Hulse said nothing. He rapped his knuckles three or four times against the edge of the desk.

"You would find the delays and permit refusals infinitely frustrating," Sharpe said calmly. "As would your bankers, as would your creditors."

Hulse exhaled loudly, scornfully. But he pulled his fingers away from the bell. "Trenholm," he said, "left this company in early 1864. He went back to Virginia where he served your late opponents in President Davis's cabinet. I know nothing about his activities after that."

Oakes had seen Sharpe explode in anger when someone referred to "President" Davis, but this time he simply nodded calmly. "George Trenholm is at the moment in the Fortress Monroe Prison in Virginia," he said. "He's in extremely bad health, and in any case, he refuses to talk with us."

"Good for him," Hulse said.

"We would like to go over Trenholm's letter files. We know that they're still here, no doubt in this building. He left a great many personal effects—he thought he would be returning—and I want to know if he corresponded with the assassin Booth or any of the other conspirators."

"You ought to be talking to Bulloch, not me." James Dunwoody Bulloch had been the chief Confederate agent in Great Britain—Thomas Dudley had been eloquent on the subject of his deviousness in purchasing ships and supplies—and Oakes and Sharpe had already gone to his offices the very day they landed in Liverpool. Bulloch was now a Liverpool cotton speculator. He had no more desire to cross the United States Treasury Department than Hulse did.

Sharpe didn't bother to explain that. He glanced at Oakes and said, "Go downstairs and tell them Mister Hulse requires all of the Trenholm files. Mister Dudley will return them after we've left."

Hulse barked out a curse that, "Scouse" or no "Scouse," Oakes had no trouble at all understanding. When he came back, the two men were sitting in the same positions, staring at each other.

"A young American woman named Sarah Slater—or perhaps Sarah Thompson or Kate Thompson—came here a short time ago," Sharpe said. "We know she traveled on a Canadian passport. Did she come to see you, Mister Hulse?"

Hulse swiveled in his chair and glowered out the window on his right, which looked over a row of chimneys toward the innumerable cranes and riggings of the docks beyond. Liverpool was a sea town, nothing but a sea town, and in the chilly late afternoon sun its spires and masts looked faint but sharp, like silvery lines in an old etching.

Oakes started to say something, closed his mouth. George Sharpe was a great admirer of his former commanding general, U.S. Grant, after Lincoln the man he revered most in the world. But Lincoln was a famous talker, whereas *Grant*—to say that Grant was *taciturn* would be a wild understatement. Grant was perfectly capable of listening to someone's question and then sitting silently, motionless, with a face as expressionless as slate, and simply not answer. Simply not say a word. Oakes had seen him sit mute like that for as long as four minutes, an incredibly long and awkward time. Oakes had witnessed questioners who waited for as long as they could stand it, then abruptly left the room. Invariably the other person broke first.

Hulse watched one of the tall loading cranes dip like a praying mantis below the rooftops. He moved his inkwell. The brass ship's clock on the wall ticked loudly. Hulse took a deep breath.

"She wanted to know the name of a banker."

Sharpe said nothing.

After a pause, Hulse added, "She wanted a banker who had dealt with Confederate funds, someone friendly to the South. She apparently had funds to exchange."

"Nobody would take Confederate money," Oakes said.

Hulse shifted in his chair, plainly relieved to speak to him rather than Sharpe. "Actually, there are still some Confederate bonds and cotton invoices that can be negotiated, at a steep discount, of course."

"Is that what she had?"

"She didn't tell me what she had." Hulse stopped. Oakes did his best imitation of the silent Sharpe. Hulse sighed. "She had a purse full of gold coins. They looked to be worth three or four hundred of your dollars. They were United States mint coins, so she could exchange them for pounds anywhere, except I gathered there might be some history to them."

"Which bank did you send her to? Can you give me the names?" Sharpe handed a pocket-sized notebook to Hulse, who picked up his pen and started to write.

"There were three or four."

"What name did she use?"

"Sarah Slater."

"What," Oakes found himself clearing his throat again, "was she wearing? As to clothes? To help us find her."

Sharpe stood and turned toward the door. "I'm going down to see about Trenholm's files. Kindly give Captain Oakes here the names and addresses of the banks and any description of Sarah Slater you can."

A smile, not pleasant to see, crept across Hulse's lips. "She was," he said, "quite sensual-looking."

2

UNLIKE MOST AMERICAN HOTELS, the Royal Mersey Hotel in Liverpool had no great central dining room. Instead, there was a warren of alcoves and booths so dimly lit and labyrinthine that it seemed to Oakes as if, seated in a high-walled booth under a watery gas lamp, they were tucked away in their own private snuggery. He could hear rain spattering on the windows and the voices of other diners somewhere behind a partition, but the only thing he could see clearly was the crown of Sharpe's head. The rest of him was hidden behind a pasteboard menu the size of a newspaper. They had already ordered their dinner—lamb and potatoes and mint jelly and some soggy green entities the menu insisted were vegetables. But Sharpe had explained, a slightly risqué joke for once, that in dining as in marriage, even if you had ordered, you could still look at the menu.

His right hand emerged from behind the pasteboard to pick up his wine glass. And at the same moment, in a fuss of wet clothes and curses, Maggie Lawton arrived like a redheaded tornado.

The two men stood up. A pair of waiters appeared behind her, wringing their aprons. Sharpe handed her into their booth next to him and signaled something to the waiters, who hesitated, conferred, muttered indecipherable Scousian protests, then backed away into the gloom.

"England!" said Maggie Lawton. "Just as bad as America. They weren't going to let me in. 'There's a Ladies' Lounge, Madame,' the little man simpered with that awful accent, 'in our other building.' It's a miracle I understood him."

"Yet here you are," Oakes said.

"I told them I was armed."

"'Tempestuous petticoats,'" Sharpe said and smiled, doubtless quoting somebody. Sharpe had a son that he rarely spoke about. Oakes thought he was a man who would much rather have had a daughter. Which would explain Maggie's presence and his evident affection for her. Sharpe offered her the giant menu but she waved it away, saying, "I'll have what you're having." She poured some of Oakes's claret into a wine glass of her own. "I passed our ever-cheerful Sergeant Keach as I was coming in. Is he still mousing about with bank records? I thought the banks were closed by now."

"Keach has his ways," Sharpe said.

"Well, I spent the day with Mister Dudley and his chief detective." Maggie leaned against the back of the booth and sighed. "I hadn't met him before, and I was impressed by *his* ways. Pinkerton's could learn a lot from him."

"A force of nature," Oakes agreed. Ignatius Pollaky was a retired London police detective, of murky reputation, hired by Dudley during the war to coordinate his network of spies and informers. He and Sharpe had met him earlier, an energetic, nearly bald little Cockney whose remaining hair sprang out over his ears like puffs of gray smoke from a locomotive. In 1863, he claimed, he had agents in every shipyard in Liverpool, he had pretty women, he had hardened thugs, he had a budget of three thousand dollars a month. He had paid Bulloch's postman a pound a week to write down the dates and return addresses of every letter the Southerner received.

"Pollaky told me that at the Liverpool charity auction for the South somebody bought Robert E. Lee's pipe for a hundred pounds. A fool and his money.... Imagine paying so much for a souvenir."

Oakes lowered his eyes to the plate of grayish lamb and greenish jelly a waiter now slid in front of him. Sharpe cleared his throat. Sharpe had been in the room of the house in Appomattox when Robert E. Lee surrendered his army to Grant, and Oakes knew that Sharpe paid the owner of the house ten dollars for a pair of souvenir candlesticks.

"Surratt," Sharpe said, "stayed in Liverpool only about two weeks. We have one more day to interview Confederate sympathizers here, but I don't have the feeling we'll find out much more. Day after tomorrow we go to London."

"Maybe there," said Maggie Lawton, "they'll speak English."

Oakes went back to his room in the hotel after dinner. At a few minutes before ten, while he was writing notes for his folders, there was a knock and Maggie Lawton swung the door open.

"You're still awake," she said, and walked in. "Good."

Oakes went to the door and looked up and down the corridor. "You really shouldn't come in here," he said, feeling foolish as he said it.

"Oh, for heaven's sakes. People have cursed me and hand-cuffed me, and I enjoyed the southern hospitality of that godawful Libby Prison for a month. I can bear up under some disapproving glances. Besides. The English," she added enigmatically. She walked past the bed and pulled the curtains aside to peer out. Reluctantly Oakes closed the door. "I imagine you have a better view than I do," she said, "when the English sun decides to shine."

"Just the mews."

"I like horses. My mother always said that if I ever joined a church it would be the Church of the Horse. Our dapper general keeps telling me about a horse he had in the army named 'Babe.' He wants me to meet her."

Oakes was tired and wanted to sit down, but there was only the chair by the little writing desk and the bed. The bed wouldn't do. "Where is the general?"

"He's in his room, going over letters and writing reports and sipping brandy. You know he really didn't need the three of us to come on this hunt. He could do all of it by himself, except maybe for Keach's banking experience, and then again, the General's family runs a bank, back in New York, not in the city."

"In the war he always said he didn't like the perpendicular pronoun."

"I." She sat down on the chair beside the desk. "The perpendicular pronoun. I wish I had seen the two of you in the war, you and Sharpe. You and I must have just missed each other in Richmond, when you liberated it and I got out of prison. I would remember you, like Thomas Chester." She glanced at the open folder. "Sharpe has a photograph of his wife on his bureau, you know. He takes it with him everywhere and puts it out as soon as he unpacks. Makes me jealous."

"A very uxorious man."

Maggie Lawton grinned her unsettling grin and shook her red hair. Oakes's room had only one weak gas lamp on the wall and a brass whale oil lamp on the desk. In the dim light her tiny smallpox scars were invisible, her feminine vitality almost palpable. "Don't use a fat three-dollar Harvard word like that around our skinny Keach," she said. "Did you know he brought a pistol with him?"

"Where is Keach?" Oakes had no idea why Maggie had come to pay him a visit so late at night. Slowly he lowered himself onto the edge of the bed.

"Whenever my father bought a new pen," she said. She squared his notes and inspected the nib of the new-fangled metal pen on the desk. "Whenever he got a new pen, the first thing he would write was 'Hamilton, Butler County, Ohio,' because that was where he grew up as a boy and he said it was the happiest time of his life. Did you also know that Keach was fired from his first job in New York? It was at another bank. Suspected embezzler. Such is the rumor."

Oakes stiffened. "I didn't know. Do you believe it?"

"I think it's possible. Money seems to be his 'Ruling Passion,' as the poet says. He talks about money as much as the English talk about the weather. Remember, Harvard former Captain Oakes, when I'm not making the Grand Tour of Europe, I earn my living as a detective. I detect like nobody's business. Pinkerton trains his people well, even the ladies."

"Did you tell the general?"

Maggie Lawton shook her head. "Why would I? He's not embezzling anything now. And nothing was proved. Besides, I had an uncle who used to say *all* bankers were crookeder than cat shit. In any case, Keach's not that bad. You have to put yourself in his place—an aged mother to support and all those sisters, and his Irish bad manners. Besides, he's very useful. He came back about an hour ago, not long after we finished in the dining room. He found Sarah Slater."

Oakes felt his throat turn to ice. He crossed his arms to hide his clenched fists. "Where is she?"

"Not here." Maggie Lawton watched him carefully. "She's not in Liverpool *now*. She *was* here. She left two days ago. Before that, she stayed ten days in a hotel near St. George's Hall—registered as 'Kate Thompson.' Evidently, she has several passports, all Canadian, some likely forged."

Oakes nodded. For all the grandness of the name, a passport was usually just one sheet of paper with a florid signature by someone like Seward. Some countries numbered and stamped them. Others didn't bother. Not a difficult thing to forge. "One of her aliases," he agreed, "'Kate Thompson.'"

"I thought you would want to know."

Oakes stood up and walked to the window and peered out at the rainy darkness just as Maggie had done. It was too wet to smell the stables. The oil lamp flickered under some invisible push of English air, foreign air. "Well, if she's not in Liverpool, I suppose we still don't know where she is."

"Exactly how well did you know her, Quintus?"

Oakes was surprised to hear his first name. He turned and frowned.

"Guilford, Connecticut," Maggie Lawton said, "has a population of just over three thousand. I looked it up. It might have been even smaller when you lived there." She tilted her head and raised one eyebrow in an expression as indecipherable as Scouse. "You're the same age."

"Well, I knew her, yes, that's true. But then I went off to college and she went off and became a Rebel and a courier for Booth. A traitor," he added lamely. "Maybe even an assassination conspirator."

"And so now you want to catch her?"

"Of course, I do."

Maggie Lawton shook her head again. "I wonder."

3

JOHN SURRATT HAD STAYED THREE WEEKS in Liverpool. No one knew how long he had stayed in London.

His presence in Liverpool, of course, had been no secret. Stanton's investigators had early on traced him to the Church of the Holy Cross on Standish Street, where he openly enjoyed the hospitality of the unrepentant and still defiantly pro-Southern Abbé Charles Jolivet. And soon after he landed in Liverpool, one of his fellow passengers on the Atlantic crossing from Canada, rightly suspicious, had filed an affidavit with the American consulate office, describing a supposed drunken confession in the ship's mess.

The great Consul Dudley was unfortunately away on leave at the time. His assistant, a classically bureaucratic Ohioan named Henry Wilding, tracked down Surratt and actually interviewed him in Jolivet's rectory. And yet, despite the affidavit and a furious cable from Stanton's Washington office, Wilding was unwilling to arrest an American citizen without an official warrant. After waiting a few days, he took a train to London to meet with the one person who could give it to him, Ambassador Charles Francis Adams—a Bostonian, the son of a former president, and a distant cousin of Oakes, whose ancestral New England family ties included both Adamses and even Cabots. Cousin Ambassador Adams thought the affidavit too flimsy to support a warrant and made plans to come to Liverpool himself.

But before that could happen, some unknown Confederate sympathizer advanced Surratt seventy pounds in cash—a small fortune—and on October 8, 1865, the Fifth Conspirator simply carried his valise to the Great Western Railway terminus beside the docks, climbed into a first-class carriage, and disappeared in the direction of London, flower of cities all.

There, even more money probably awaited him, and possibly Judah Benjamin, and certainly the welcoming assistance of a score of influential English partisans, who still thought the martyred Lincoln an incompetent fool and also (illogically) a vicious tyrant.

Around eight o'clock in the morning on March 17, a Sunday, Sharpe led his little band along the Mersey docks to the same Great Western Railway terminus Surratt had used. They gave their tickets to a conductor dressed as an English major general and clambered into a compartment in a first-class carriage. At quarter past eight, the train shuddered and bucked like the iron horse it was and began to roll away from the clean ocean air of Liverpool toward the brown and yellow stench of London, which was then, if someone had looked down from the moon, far and away the largest man-made thing on Earth.

It took its time showing up. Miles before their train crept and chattered its way into the cavernous iron maw of Euston Station, outlying signs of the enormous city began to appear—rows of squalid, soot-coated tenement houses built so close to the tracks that Oakes thought he could reach out and touch the filthy bricks. Great towering smokestacks and endless, windowless warehouses announced the factory districts. Then streets so twisted and haphazard that, after the geometrical grid of Manhattan, they seemed misshapen and freakish. Then more soot, more smoke, walls, terraces, chimneys, behind windowpanes dirty white petals that metamorphosed at the last minute into faces.

Somewhere near the Edgeware district, Sharpe, always the most surprising man Oakes had ever known, suddenly sat up straight and began to loudly chant a poem to them—"And did the Countenance Divine/Shine forth upon our clouded hills?/ And was Jerusalem builded here,/Among these dark Satanic Mills?" After which he clamped his mouth shut and stared wordlessly at the encroaching city. Maggie looked across at Oakes with either amusement or sadness, he couldn't say.

From the muted uproar of the Euston Station platforms they pushed their way out into a cold gloomy late afternoon, already dark, and took their places in a queue for hansom cabs. Oakes, once again the transportation officer, bellowed and bribed them along the line, settled the trunks and valises in one cab, the four of them in another, pulled by the saddest specimen of horseflesh, Sharpe said, he had ever seen.

At five-fifteen they were creeping down crowded Drummond Street, behind the northernmost buildings of the University of London, where, a lifetime ago, Oakes had actually passed two or three months in what he assured his father was the serious study of political economy. In another ten minutes they had traveled about half a mile through the densest, most chaotic traffic in the world and were pulling up in the middle of the block on a wide, mostly residential, dingy black macadamized street.

The United States Embassy stood at 147 Great Portland Street, in a handsome modern building constructed, like every other building on the block, of gray Portland limestone. It lay some six or seven blocks south of Regent's Park—one of London's famous "green lungs"—and about the same distance north of its busiest, brownest commercial artery, western Oxford Street. Ordinarily the Embassy offices would have been closed on a Sunday, but thanks to the efficiency of the British telegraph system, not the Ambassador but his Assistant Secretary, a middle-aged Philadelphian named Benjamin Moran, was waiting on the steps to receive them.

"Himself," Moran explained, "is doubtless at a coin show. Mister Adams is an inveterate collector of coins, you see."

Moran sniffed loudly to show his opinion of godless Mammon, especially on a Sunday afternoon. "Or else, he's visiting someone in the country. He rarely informs me of his precise movements. Possibly he's on one of his long walks to 'study the city.' It is I who am to greet you."

Moran sniffed again to show his opinion of studying the city. Oakes thought he had never actually heard anyone use the word "inveterate" in conversation, not to mention "I who am." Nor had he ever seen anyone who looked quite like Moran—short, bald, a complexion so extraordinarily pasty-faced as to suggest a lady's cosmetic cream. He looked, Oakes thought, changing the metaphor, like a boiled egg in a cut-away coat.

Greeted, they stood in awkward silence on the steps, leaning into a cold north wind, next to their pyramid of trunks and valises. All around them like a swampy miasma was the peculiar rank London smell of horse dung and damp straw. At the end of the street, in the smoke and wind, London seemed like a city of a million silhouettes. Then Moran flicked an invisible particle of dirt from a sleeve, frowned thoughtfully at Maggie Lawton, and informed them that General Sharpe—the eggshell inclined like Humpty Dumpty toward Sharpe—would of course be a guest in the Ambassador's residence around the corner on Upper Portland Street. The rest of them would be housed in a hotel on Langham Place a few blocks away.

Maggie Lawton pulled a repeater watch as big as a turnip out of her traveling cloak and announced that the young gentlemen could see to her room in the hotel. Meanwhile she, as a new visitor to this cousinly island, was off to visit the world-celebrated London theater. To be precise, the Olympic Theatre in Piccadilly where, she had read, something called "The Ticket of Leave" was playing to packed houses. "According to the *Times*," she told a frowning Moran, "it promises 'an evening saturated in crime.'"

And in the end, Keach and Sharpe both went to the theater with her, leaving Oakes to install their baggage in the Langham Arms, while Moran busied himself, with the maximum of bustle, with the General's things. After which, and despite the hour and the cold, Oakes set out on foot toward the great black-green open space of Regent's Park.

He had come to London for the first time in the late spring of 1852, sent by his father to stay with elderly cousins (on his mother's side, for once). Sent, to be precise, as Maggie Lawton would say, to be an ocean away from the French dancing master's daughter—the belle of Guilford, the tall, enchanting Sarah Antoinette Gilbert. Maggie was actually wrong about their ages. Sarah was two years younger than he was, and she was the first girl Oakes ever kissed—an event witnessed, as it happened, by one of his father's law partners and subsequently described to him in what Oakes supposed was imaginative and salacious lawyerly detail. His father seemed to think it was much more than a kiss, and in fact it was—in fact she was not quite Beatrice to his Dante, in fact she was more Eloise to his Abelard, and the first pleasures of youth, he thought, never left the deep heart's core.

"No French bastards in our family," the *pater familias* had pronounced with his best New England chilliness, and letters had promptly gone out to cousins in London, to the shipping companies in Boston, to his friend Ebenezer Hoare, President of Harvard, to assure a place for the wayward boy when he returned, far away from the charms of Guilford.

Oakes crossed aimlessly into the park, dodging between carts and wagons in the apparently perpetual flow of London traffic. The park itself was nearly empty. On the left, he thought, would be the boating lake, where Londoners skated when the water froze. Directly ahead would be the Inner Circle, an oval, not a circle in fact, outlined now by a series of yellow-bright gas lamps. On all sides, shadows, shrubs, low, leafless tree branches, scraping their bony fingers together. It had been one of his favorite walks, even at night, fifteen years ago, but that was in bright and leafy summer. He had never been here in winter. Left and right, the shadows detached from the background, and swayed and dipped and muttered to themselves.

As he reached a better-lit path and started uphill, he suddenly remembered the night he had crawled back through Confederate lines near Cold Harbor, across a farmer's ruined meadow. To fool the Rebels, he had worn a cowbell around his neck—Sharpe's suggestion—and crept past sentry after sentry, with scarcely a glance in his clanking direction. Now he paused to listen to sharp-edged sounds coming through the shrubs, over the dead leaves. Ducks, he diagnosed, not Confederate sentries.

At the crest of Primrose Hill, he could look northeast toward the zoo, closed now of course, long past nine o'clock at night, all the animals inside their winter housing. In the other direction much of the city spread out under him in a formless pattern of dots of light, steeples, chimneys, headless black bulks of foreign space. Under his feet, Oakes could almost feel the earth rolling eastward, toward home. Lincoln had once told Sharpe that the great sight he truly hoped to see before he died was the Pacific Ocean, off the coast of California. Sharpe had asked if he wouldn't rather see Europe, but Lincoln had been American, nothing but American, deep down into his Western bones. Oakes guessed that, having brought his country to so bloody a rebirth, he would never have been able to leave it.

Abraham Lincoln in London—impossible to picture.

On the other hand, Lincoln's mad wife Mary spoke fluent French, they said, and had caused one of her numerous Washington scandals by flirting with the French Ambassador in that most logical and erotic language. Mary Lincoln, Sharpe had once muttered in a nearly unique moment of disloyalty, was as charming as a toothache.

The very last time Oakes had seen Abraham Lincoln was on April 17, 1865, not quite two years ago, as his body lay in its open coffin on the high catafalque under the Capitol dome—a tall, gangly figure, utterly motionless as only the dead can be. His long, unbeautiful face had been caked white with some funereal cosmetic, but the expression of endlessly weary kindness was still there. What had Lincoln told Sharpe once, when toward the end of the war the general complimented him on his good health? "Yes, Sharpe," he said, "I feel well enough. But nothing can touch the tired spot." A line of mourners had wound out of the Capitol doors and down through the streets, as far as you could see—men, women, blacks, even some former Rebels.

Where was Sarah Slater now?

Somewhere off to the right, deep in the city, a gas lamp flared bright orange, then fierce yellow, then blinked and went out.

4

"I saw Abraham Lincoln exactly once," Henry Adams said the next morning at breakfast. "It was at that melancholy function called an 'Inaugural Ball.' He was quite awkward. He had a plain, plowed face"—Adams paused as if to admire his metaphor—"and he seemed not to know what to do with his white kid gloves. A typical country bumpkin. I thought he was in need of an education. As, of course," Adams added gracefully and insincerely, "was I."

"This is my cousin, Henry," Oakes said, rising and pulling back a chair for Maggie Lawton. "He's the Ambassador's son."

"And private secretary." Henry Adams also stood politely, but the effect was hardly noticeable. Oakes was just under six feet tall. His cousin was barely five feet tall and though only a year or two younger, already balding and almost as high-domed as the middle-aged Benjamin Moran. His face, however, was serenely smooth. He was dressed in a beautifully tailored formal morning coat and black silk cravate, and his little bow and gesture of welcome had the self-mocking precision of a courtier. His eyes turned from Maggie to Oakes, one eyebrow rising (Oakes admired his own metaphor) like a question mark.

"Miss Lawton is traveling with us."

"Ah. How...unusual. Well, we're only *just* cousins." Adams sat back down and reached for his coffee. "Quintus and I. Perhaps third or fourth cousins. It would take an Old Testament genealogist to sort out the begats and begots of the New England Adamses."

"I read some of your articles in the *New-York Tribune*, about the English diplomatic scene," Maggie said. "During the war. Very impressive. You must have learned a lot from living here all these years."

Oakes would have bet that his cousin would lean back and preen at this, but Adams only nodded gravely and said, "All an author ever asks is constant, unconditional praise."

But there was no more unconditional praise from Maggie. She gestured to a hovering waiter and then turned to Oakes. "The General has a full day planned for you—he wants you at the Embassy by ten. You're to start at the top of the list."

"Benjamin?"

To the waiter's visible consternation, Maggie reached down the table for an empty cup and began to pour her own coffee from the pot. "Eggs," she told the waiter, "scrambled. Toast, jam, everything you can carry. And tea. I don't like coffee. Yes, Judah P. Benjamin, British Citizen, Member of the Sacred English Bar. Sharpe wants to surprise him."

"I know Judah Benjamin," Adams said. Delicately, he buttered a slice of his own toast, placed it on a saucer, and offered it to Maggie. "Or at least, I've seen him around the Inns of Court." He smiled at her. She bit into the toast with strong white teeth. "When I was preparing some little articles after the peace. The Hebrew of Hebrews he is, a greasy little man, not to be trusted, of course. A typical Jew. He had to leave Yale, you know, after two years, for petty thievery. Always a little knowing smile on his face."

"Where else would it be?" Maggie said, and smiled sweetly herself.

"How was the play?" Oakes asked quickly.

"Excellent. It was about a bank embezzler. Keach enjoyed it enormously."

* * *

Henry Adams lingered until half past nine, evidently trying to draw Maggie into further discussion (or praise) of his "little articles," but Maggie Lawton was all business that morning and hurried off. At ten minutes past ten, Oakes and General Sharpe were in the Embassy's own official carriage, rolling southeastward toward the Thames, toward the ancient and honorable Inns of Court, where London's best barristers and solicitors had their rooms, and where Judah P. Benjamin, a member of Jefferson Davis's Cabinet for the whole four years of the doomed Confederacy, was, after all, expecting them.

"In fact," Benjamin said as they were shown into his study, "friends told me of your arrival in Liverpool. I thought you would be here much sooner."

Sharpe was fond of saying that no plan of battle survives first contact with the enemy. If he was surprised or disconcerted by Benjamin's greeting, it was impossible to read it on his face.

"This is Captain Oakes," he said with a nod toward Oakes. Judah Benjamin was far too sensitive and poised to make the mistake of offering his hand to either of them. He merely smiled a tight, pleasant little smile, just as Henry Adams had said, and gestured expansively toward the two comfortable chairs in front of his elaborately carved, Seward-worthy mahogany desk.

"Captain Quintus Oakes," Benjamin said as he took his own seat behind the desk. "Late of the Army of the Potomac. Son of Governor Urian Oakes of Connecticut. Highly intelligent, according to my friends in Liverpool, and the very soul of honor. Named, I suppose, after the poet Horace. I think we were on opposite sides in our education as well." He shifted his smile to Sharpe. "Captain Oakes went to Harvard, I went to Yale."

"Well, probably those talkative friends told you why we're here," Sharpe said. Benjamin said nothing.

"Let me put it bluntly, no lawyer's jargon," Sharpe said. "Secretary Seward and Secretary Stanton believe Booth didn't act alone. Given your position in the Secession Cabinet—given your role in supervising clandestine operations—they believe you aided and instructed Booth in the assassination of the President. They believe you were part of the conspiracy, maybe even instigated it. And they want me to find proof."

"Is that what you believe too, General Sharpe?"

Outside the high mullioned window to Benjamin's right, a judiciary flock of black silk gowns and preposterous white wigs drifted by, chattering. For no reason at all Oakes remembered that the original meaning of the word "jargon" was "the noise of song birds."

Sharpe's eyes stayed fixed on Benjamin. "What I believe," he said, "doesn't matter."

Benjamin leaned forward on his elbows. He had, Oakes thought, a striking face. From his Portuguese-English father he had inherited an olive complexion and a broad, even Sephardic forehead, a wide fleshy nose, and extremely dark eyes. His cheeks were as plump as a cherub's. He wore a closely trimmed beard, but no moustache. His hair, almost ginger colored, was curly. Among the race-conscious Southerners of Jefferson Davis's cabinet, he must have stood out like something exotic and untrustworthy, something Mediterranean.

"When I was in the United States Senate from Louisiana," Benjamin said, "possibly the only other Senator I actively disliked was then-Senator Seward. A highly secretive man, given to imagining that other people are equally secretive. Or perhaps," he turned the smile toward Oakes, "that was a *failure* of imagination on his part, not an example of it. He's a crafty manipulator of everyone and everything around him. He really doesn't see that not everyone is like that."

He turned back to Sharpe. "I was born on the island of St. Croix, as you know, when it was a British possession. That makes me de facto a British citizen. There is no legal authority here that can force me to answer any questions you have. It would probably take an act of Parliament for you to arrest me. But in the war you had a reputation as a fair man, if hard. I am speaking to you now only because it would be useful for me, in my present profession, to clear my name from this…" The perpetual smile flickered. "This 'misapprehension,' I started to say."

Calmly he pulled an elegant gold watch from his vest and rose. "I must go before one of the judges to plead a routine motion. I won't be back until perhaps three o'clock. You're welcome to come back then. I'm afraid I don't choose to offer you the hospitality of the Inns, but not far away, up the Strand, you will find the old Mitre Tavern where Doctor Johnson used to toss and gore poor Boswell in conversation. I can recommend the beer."

He passed to the door and held it open. "If you're interested, my assistant can give you something to read during your meal. I've written a book on Property Law, to be published at the end of the year. Most of the manuscript is ready. You might consult," he smiled at Sharpe, "the chapter on Evidence."

"No wonder his goddam wife left him!" Sharpe slammed his palm on the table and all eyes in the room turned toward him. "That goddam condescending smile."

"I don't know about his wife," Oakes said, to pacify him. "Tell me."

Sharpe had decided to pass up Dr. Johnson's favorite tavern, as recommended by Benjamin. He had chosen instead a nondescript public house a few hundred yards from the Inns of Court. It was raining now—it was always raining in England, Oakes thought; no wonder they were all Druids at heart—and to add to Sharpe's anger, their table was in a cold draft beside a dirty window, regularly shaken with icy, bad-tempered gusts.

"A sad story." Sharpe rarely drank beer, but the pub keeper had told them beer or nothing. He poured a third and final glass from the pitcher, then changed his mind and pushed the glass aside. "Apparently a remarkable woman, very attractive, some-what French in her morals. After a few years of marriage in Louisiana, she was bored, so she simply up and left him one fine day—this was long before the war—and moved to Paris, where I think she still lives. He used to visit her there, but that was a long time ago. Maybe he still does. It's a peculiar arrangement. I know she joined him in Washington once when he was a Senator, and the Congressional wives got all in a dither about the wicked Frenchwoman living in sin and wouldn't call on her, so back to Paris she went."

"And are we going to Paris? After this?"

But Sharpe had a faraway look and didn't answer. "I wonder how he supports her in that ruinously expensive Babylon-on-the-Seine. With old Jeff Davis's stolen gold? You cross the Channel, you know, and your money literally flies out of your pocket, bevies of banknotes all over the sky."

He shook his head at nothing in particular. Then he started for the door, and just as they had in the Willard Hotel lobby, or in the headquarters tents around Richmond, or in the filthy bivouacs before Cold Harbor, people stood aside, parted to let the small, dapper man with the marble countenance pass by.

Judah Benjamin's study had a Lilliputian fireplace opposite his enormous desk. When they were shown in this time, he was stooped and feeding bits of sea coal onto the grate.

"I'm sorry you didn't choose to go to the Mitre," he said as they all resumed places. "I always enjoy the thought of the great Johnson's ghost hovering over the patrons, silently correcting their grammar, clearing their minds, as Sir Joshua Reynolds said, of rubbish."

Oakes was impressed and amused. How did he know where they had eaten? Obviously, the former Chief of the Confederate clandestine services was spying on U.S. Grant's former spy. A hall of mirrors. Sharpe's world. His world, too, once. Sharpe made no acknowledgement of this at all. He had brought his notes with him in a neat brown oilskin wrap, as protection against the daily insults, he said, of the English climate. Now he pulled a small tripod table next to his chair and laid out his papers.

"I give you this much credit," Sharpe said. "We know that originally your people intended to kidnap President Lincoln, not assassinate him."

Oakes had heard this before, but never so starkly put. He leaned forward to study Benjamin's reaction.

There was nothing to study. "That," Benjamin said mildly, "is true."

"In fact, at one time you undeniably had three separate plots to do just that, kidnap Mister Lincoln and imprison him, not kill him. Two of the plots were directed by Confederate army officers in the clandestine service. They would have been under your orders."

Benjamin made a little tent of his fingers and looked at the weary rain outside the window.

"The third kidnapping plot was Booth's alone. When Grant took Richmond, the Confederate army in effect no longer existed, the first two plans no longer existed. Then Booth stepped in. You had been in touch with Booth in Canada—you had written him a large check of money. Undoubtedly you stayed in touch with him after he came back to the United States. But at some point you dropped the idea of kidnapping. In your desperation, you and Jefferson Davis decided to kill the President. Either you knew that Booth was planning to do it on his own, or else you put him up to it. But make no mistake, you helped him. Judah Benjamin was a central part of the plot."

"No."

Sharpe took out a sheet of paper from his case. "On March twenty-fifth, 1865, Booth traveled from New York City to

Washington City on the overnight train. He had as his companion a young woman named Sarah Slater. One of your couriers." Sharpe smoothed the paper with one hand. "She was carrying letters and other documents from Montreal to the confederate Secretary of State. You. The train reached Washington at 7:30 a.m. the next morning. Booth went directly to his hotel. The Slater person was picked up by John Surratt at the station—you see, sir, we had spies as well—and they went to his mother's house on H Street. Mary Surratt came out the door and off they went in a rented carriage to a country tavern the Surratt family owned. From there Slater and Surratt moved on together to Richmond."

"In other words, General Sharpe, I received a letter from Canada, contents unknown. How very damning. How very pointless."

"There's more. In Booth's trunk in his Washington hotel we found a cipher book *identical to a cipher book we later found in your personal Richmond office.*"

Sharpe sat back as if he had delivered a crushing blow. Benjamin unfolded his little finger tent.

"You're a lawyer, General Sharpe," he said slowly. "Would you really go into a court with that as your evidence, your *only* evidence? I received a letter from Canada? My dear friend, I received *hundreds* of letters from Canada. None of them concerned assassination. And let me point out that in the last year of the war perhaps a dozen different cipher books were used in my office by perhaps a dozen different staff members. The one you allegedly found could have been stolen, lost, copied by one of your very able spies, looted when the city of Richmond fell—any number of plausible explanations could put it in Booth's hands. It could even have been 'planted,' as they say here, in Booth's trunk, perhaps by your monomaniacal friend, Seward. Or by your mad, bloodthirsty comrade, Edwin Stanton."

He turned slightly and smiled at Oakes. "I should explain myself. Here in London we hear all kinds of rumors about Stanton. We even hear that he is thought by not a few people in Washington to have ordered the assassination *himself*, out of fear that Lincoln was going to be too soft and forgiving to the 'rebels.' It's no secret that Stanton wanted to crush the Southern states under the iron heel of the army for a thousand years." Benjamin shook his handsome head. "You both know as well as I do that Stanton is a mentally unbalanced person."

Oakes made an effort not to remember Stanton's bullying face, his thick glasses and cruel eyes, his hysterical grief for the martyred Lincoln. But he hadn't heard that particular rumor before. Kill the President? "Unbalanced" was maybe too kind a word for the strange, death-obsessed Secretary of War. It was well known in Washington that when Stanton was a young lawyer in Ohio, his landlady's daughter had died suddenly from cholera, and Stanton, weeping and howling like a man possessed, actually ran to the graveyard and personally dug up her body, to make sure she hadn't been buried alive.

"You hired John Surratt." Sharpe looked at his notes again. "A known assassination conspirator."

"I did. I hired him and I sent him off to Canada to help keep track of Jacob Thompson's foolishness. To the best of my knowledge, Surratt was not involved in Booth's plot."

"In the beginning of June he'll be on trial in Washington. He'll testify about you. I think you should be deeply worried about what he'll say, under oath, with the threat of the noose in front of him."

"But I'm *not* worried." Judah P. Benjamin studied the rain at his window as if he were sizing up a jury. A handsome man, a charming man, Oakes thought. What had gone wrong between him and his wife? How had he let her go? Lost her? How did a man turn his back on a woman he loved?

Benjamin pulled his gaze back to Sharpe and sighed. "Let me summarize the case once and for all, dear General Sharpe. In November 1864, our people captured your Colonel Ulric Dahlgren in a skirmish near the Mattapony River, not far from Richmond. Your own Union soldier. He was carrying orders, *written* orders from Edwin Stanton, to burn Richmond to the ground, liberate as many prisoners as he could from Libby Prison, and—here I quote from memory, because I saw the note—'kill Jeff Davis and cabinet on the spot.' As the schoolboys say, you started it. In fact, at our subsequent Cabinet meeting almost every person present wanted to assassinate Mister Lincoln in revenge, in return for this proposed murder. But President Davis said no. He ordered, *ordered* each and every one of us never"—Benjamin bent forward, smile gone, face white—"*never* to raise the question of assassination again. He said we were Christian soldiers and would abide by all the rules of honorable warfare."

"You're not a Christian," Sharpe said bluntly, cruelly.

An unseen clock ticked in a corner. The rain drummed its fingers against the window. Coals stirred in the fire.

Then the smile returned, small and unreadable. "And if you prick us, General Sharpe, do we not bleed?" Benjamin said softly. "When you hang us, do we not die?"

Oakes felt his face flush. He lowered his eyes and examined the carpet.

"Do you imagine, my friend," Benjamin said in the same soft voice, "for one instant, that if I came back to the United States to plead my innocence, I would receive a fair trial? Benjamin the Jew? Benjamin the Jew who killed Lincoln?"

Sharpe held his gaze but said nothing. His face was immobile, stony and unhealthy as Keach's.

Finally, Benjamin rose. "I directed our operations from Canada," he said with a kind of controlled intensity that Oakes thought would have swayed any jury. "Yes. Certainly. Though Jacob Thompson took on grandiose notions and soon decided to ignore every order I sent. I also hired John Surratt, but only as a courier. He was very good in escorting certain female agents we employed. I paid Booth two hundred dollars once, and once only, but that was to settle his debts in Canada, and that was a full year before the assassination, and it is not really the same as thirty pieces of silver. I did not especially admire Abraham Lincoln, but I had nothing to do with his death."

He let the intensity subside like a retreating wave. He smiled at Oakes and walked to the door and pulled it open. "Nothing," he said. "Nothing. Nothing. Nothing."

6

LAMBETH, A LOW, SPRAWLING DISTRICT south of the Thames River, was easily the nastiest part of London that Sarah Slater had yet seen, though someone had assured her that the East End was even more squalid.

She stopped at the door to her building. "Belvedere Road" had an elegant sound to it, but she could see nothing elegant about the narrow, treeless, dirty black little street. She pulled out her key and wrinkled her nose at the trash that was piled knee-high beside the front steps and spilling over onto the sidewalk. "Dust" was what the English called trash. Sarah thought the English were a very peculiar race.

Down at the end of the block, leaning against a miserable, ill-built plank house, a man she knew only as Huggins stared at her. When he caught her eye, he touched the brim of his hat in a salute.

Sarah ignored him. She cleared her mind, just as a dancer does before she takes her first step. Deliberately, calmly, she looked the other way.

It had stopped raining an hour or so ago. She made herself observe that now the air was heavy again with the sweet, sticky smell of yeast and hops that the wind carried down from the huge Red Lion brewery half a mile to the north, just over Hungerford

Bridge. Dust and beer, welcome to London. Her hair and clothes smelled like beer. Her throat scratched constantly from whatever else was in the smoky air. "Darkness visible" had been a favorite phrase of her bookish North Carolina father-in-law, who said it was an "oxymoron," a self-contradictory saying. "Air visible" described what you breathed in London.

She turned the key and entered the boarding house, pulling up her skirts as she always did, to avoid catching the cloth on one of the numerous nails that seemed to be slowly lifting their heads and shoulders out of the staircase, readying themselves like everybody and everything else in Lambeth to make a run for it.

"Visitor, Miss Thompson."

Sarah turned slowly and looked at her landlady. There should be no visitors whatsoever.

"Waiting in the lounge, isn't he?" The landlady was shaped low and wide like a squashed London postal box. She had evidently been born—and would doubtless be buried—wearing a disapproving look. That, and a white apron and a long and aggressively modest dark blue dress that completely concealed her feet. She probably had, Sarah thought, as many chins as toes. "I'm not having any trouble, Miss Thompson. You Canandians and Americans, I know you. First and last warning."

The "lounge" was actually the dining room, a dingy, gray, claustrophobic space dominated by a long table and eight chairs, one for each of the women who boarded here. They all worked in some capacity or other in the warehouses or tanneries or soap boilers that, besides theft and brothels, made up most of Lambeth's commerce. In the one week she had been here, Sarah had been careful to keep to herself. Nonetheless, she had learned that one of her fellow boarders, a sickly young woman from Kent, worked as a laundress for something called the London Necropolis Railway—an institution that really and truly existed, a special railroad line that took corpses, and only corpses, from the center of the city to a network of cemeteries out in Woking. Quietest passengers in the world, she had said. The English were undoubtedly a peculiar race. Another woman in the boarding house worked gathering "pures" for a tannery. "Pures" was the tanners' word for dog turds, used to polish leather.

"I wasn't certain," said Colin McRae, rising politely from the far end of the table, "that I should use your name. I just asked for the young American woman."

Sarah looked over her shoulder at the half-open door to the hallway.

"We could go up to your room," Colin McRae suggested.

Sarah smiled—so as not to offend him—but shook her head. When she had come to London from Liverpool nine days ago, she had gone directly to Colin McRae's quite handsome townhouse on Upper Seymour Street, because McRae had been the Confederacy's chief financial agent in Europe and McRae knew everything there was to know about London banks. But McRae's unlovely and extremely jealous wife had taken one look at Sarah and banished her from Upper Seymour Street.

"When I said you should find inconspicuous lodgings," he said, "I never imagined—" He paused and looked around the lounge.

"I did go to the Strand Hotel the first night." Sarah took a seat at her end of the table and McRae came and sat down beside her, close enough that their arms brushed and she could smell the pomatum or whatever odd grease he put on his hair. Or maybe he had just walked by the Red Lion brewery. "I went to the Strand Hotel and the next morning that little man Ignatius Pollaky was around asking for me."

"The detective."

"He asked for me by name."

"As Sarah Slater?"

"As Sarah Slater or Kate Thompson or Sarah Gilbert."

McRae looked startled. "Three names?"

"He left men posted around the lobby. I went out by the servants' door, and I had to hire a very rough-looking man to carry my trunk. Unfortunately, he's taken some kind of interest in me and appointed himself my unofficial bodyguard. You probably passed him out on the street."

McRae used one finger to push a chipped ceramic teacup into the center of the table. "Yes," he said. "But still…"

"He thought I would be all right here. He said the law couldn't touch me in Lambeth."

"Yes, well. Lambeth in fact lies outside the legal jurisdiction of London proper. It belongs to the county of Surrey. Things," he said with the idiotic smile of a middle-aged man who had a certain taste for the laxness of Lambeth, "things are less strict here." He looked around the grim room. "It was originally a swamp," he added inconsequentially. "They called it Lambeth Marsh. There's still a wretched little creek somewhere."

Sarah had stayed in hotels with John Surratt, as part of being a courier. She had stayed in hotels with Booth, for that matter. She understood one side of men very well. Even during her extremely short stay in his house, McRae had made himself plain. His wife was no fool. Disliking herself intensely, Sarah now placed her warm hand on his and leaned in to let their shoulders touch.

"Your note said you'd found a banker for me."

McRae put his left hand on top of hers. "Can't we talk upstairs, in your room?"

"When I have a house of my own," Sarah promised. "When I buy a house in the West End."

McRae cleared his throat. He reached in a coat pocket and pulled out an envelope. "There are two names here, both bankers in the City. When I—" he paused and studied the half-open door. "When I worked for my government, these were the two most reliable. The first is very discreet. The second will give you a better rate. The first is a Jew, if that matters to you."

Sarah shook her head. "No."

"I also had a message from Hulse, in Liverpool."

Sarah opened the envelope and began to read the names.

"He said that madman Seward has sent some people to arrest alleged conspirators—*assassination* conspirators—in England. They went around to his office and took away all sorts of papers, and he thinks they're coming to London. He thinks they're probably already here. They would go to the Ambassador first, of course— much good he'll do them. One is a retired army general, one is a woman."

Sarah looked up. "A woman?"

"Another is some kind of bank specialist. The fourth, he says, is a young man who gives off, he says rather prettily, an air of 'shaken competence.'"

"An oxymoron," Sarah said automatically.

"With an odd name, Quintus something."

Sarah slowly withdrew her hand. McRae put his arm around her waist and tried to squeeze, but she rose abruptly and thrust the envelope into the folds of her dress. "I'll see the first name tomorrow," she said, "the Jew."

7

IN THE WAR, THE TWO GREAT DISCIPLINARY PROBLEMS for the Union had been drunkenness and desertion.

In Oakes's experience most commanders were tolerant of the first, so that the punishment was usually light. Sharpe's practice was simply to make the offender stand on a box for a day holding a heavy chunk of firewood, subject to the jeers and catcalls of anybody who passed by. Sometimes he ordered an extra day or two of hard labor, and once he had flown into a genuine rage when one of his New York recruits complained—whined, really—that he wasn't drunk, he was just following General Grant's example. Now and then, after the carnage of battle had been especially horrific—Chancellorsville was one time—Sharpe only shrugged and turned a blind eye and quoted Dr. Johnson to the effect that who wouldn't drink in order to rid himself of the pain of being a man?

But desertion was another matter. In the spring of 1864, as Grant put his grand strategy into action and the Army of the Potomac began its long drive south toward Richmond, the fighting reached an intense and unbearable pitch, worse even than Gettysburg. In the month of May—the month of the battles of the Wilderness and Spotsylvania Courthouse—in that month alone, well over five thousand Union soldiers deserted. As Grant pressed brutally on, the numbers kept climbing and climbing, until by early summer almost two hundred Federal soldiers a day were slipping away from the ranks and disappearing.

On this matter the army regulation was clear: "Desertion is a crime punishable by death."

But few officers—and fewer enlisted men—could bring themselves to shoot a comrade in cold blood. Instead, and despite regulations, other punishments were used when a deserter was caught—prison, flogging, solitary confinement. Many commanders ignored even those. Instead, some men simply had half their beards shaved off, as public humiliation, or were forced to wear boards with the inscription "Coward."

But far and away the most barbaric punishment—Oakes witnessed it only once—was *branding*.

Here the letter "D" would be cut by a razor on the deserter's cheek and then the wound smeared with black gunpowder to make a permanent scar. In many cases, the letter would be cut and then an officer—customarily a regimental doctor—would approach the kneeling figure with a red-hot iron and *sear* the letter into the flesh. Some doctors refused to do it.

Oakes put down his folder of notes and stared out the window at the London sky. One lonely cloud hung motionless above Regents Park, like a fugitive from Wordsworth's poem. He was sitting in the third floor of the Embassy, in a borrowed room, going over reports from Keach about Confederate bank accounts that were still in use, lists of possible names to interview from Sharpe, and a marked-up map of central London that the little Cockney ex-detective Ignatius Pollacky had left for him, since one particular fugitive was his particular responsibility, for the moment his responsibility alone.

It was possible, Pollacky's accompanying note said, that Kate Thompson was staying in a Bedford Square Hotel. His men were watching; they would need Captain Oakes's help in identifying her. There was also a young American in Lambeth, and a Sarah Gilbert they had their eyes on. Sarah Gilbert had just rented a flat off the Strand, near the Inns of Court, near Judah Benjamin's chambers. "Closing in!" Pollacky had written cheerfully at the bottom of the map.

Oakes folded the map in two, then folded it again, then stuffed all the papers angrily into the desk drawer. No mystery at all. He thought that his mind had turned to desertion.

What were they going to do when they found her? Would they rush forward at his signal in a crimmage and surround her? *Snatch* her? When he nodded *yes, that's Sarah Slater*, would Pollacky's men seize her by the arms, wrench her around, screaming, frog march her into a waiting carriage? Could they *do* that in London?

Could he nod yes when he saw her?

He looked at his watch. Two o'clock. He was supposed to find the Ambassador's Assistant Secretary, that malcontent penguin Benjamin Moran, at two o'clock. He locked the desk, left the room, descended two flights of stairs, turned left in the corridor, and passed from military savagery into drawing room comedy.

* * *

"Well," Moran was saying with a kind of bloodthirsty primness, "I pray that you apprehend him *soon*." The little man turned from Sharpe to Charles Francis Adams. "I told General Sharpe that

Mister Judah Benjamin's extraordinary success at the Bar is meant to be a deliberate mockery of us, of the United States. I have even heard a rumor"—he lowered his voice and his chin—"that he will soon 'take silk.' That is, actually become a *Queen's Counsel*."

But Charles Francis Adams, the United States Ambassador to the Court of St. James, paid no attention whatsoever to his Second Assistant Secretary. They were all three gathered for some reason in the anteroom to the Ambassador's private office, a pleasant, well-lit little space whose walls were crowded with patriotic-themed American paintings and miniature busts of the Founders, including the Ambassador's own father and grandfather. The Ambassador turned on his heel, pulled open his private door, took Sharpe courteously by the elbow and led him in. When the door closed, Moran sighed operatically and nodded a greeting to Oakes.

"You see how he treats me, Captain Oakes. He ignores everything I do. He never invites me to diplomatic functions. Other ambassadors invite *their* secretaries. He never has me to dine at his home. His wife doesn't speak to me. And as for his son Henry…"

Moran turned on his heel, much as the Ambassador had done, and motioned for Oakes to follow him downstairs.

In Moran's office there were two desks—the First Assistant Secretary had resigned at the end of the war and never been replaced. A long, high slit of a window gave a view of Great Portland Street's passing heels and ankles. Two damp-looking walls were lined with filing cabinets and document boxes.

"I have several addresses for you." Moran took his seat behind his desk and waved his hand at a leather club chair beside it. "Colin McRae, for one. William Yancey, though I don't think that address is good any more. And Mister Ambrose Mann. He was the Confederate agent in Belgium, but keeps a *pied-à-terre* in London. These are all pretty small fry," Moran added with a sniff. "Benjamin is the one you want. I told that to General Sharpe. May I offer you, Captain Oakes, a small glass of fairly good sherry?"

He broke off abruptly and stood. "Please don't trouble yourselves to knock," Moran said icily, as Maggie Lawton walked in, followed by Henry Adams.

"We've come to take away your prisoner," Maggie said. She looked around the office and made a face. "This is a terrible little room, Moran. Do they keep you chained and manacled down here all the time?"

Henry Adams ran one finger along a dirty molding. "Quintus."

"Henricus."

"I'm afraid," Moran said, "that you'll have to wait. Captain Oakes and I were about to go over some addresses I've managed to find for him. Without," he informed Adams, "neglecting my Secretarial duties, you may tell your father."

"I spent some time in this office," Adams told Maggie. "When we first came here, this was like a military outpost. I wrote those dispatches you mentioned at that desk over there, for the *New-York Tribune*. In the beginning, you know, we Northerners were completely ostracized by London society. We were the enemies, we were told, of those aristocratic Southerner cavaliers who had so much better manners than we did. I used to writhe with torture at some of their insults."

It was a day, Oakes decided, for everyone to ignore everyone else. Maggie Lawton put her hands on his shoulders and turned him around to face the stairs. "March, *mon Capitain*." Over her shoulder she apologized to Moran. "We need this grizzled old soldier to interview somebody wicked. You can hang on to Mister Adams."

Adams and Moran watched in silence as they mounted the stairs and the door closed behind them.

"High-spirited young woman." Moran sat down again. "Pity about those little scars. I believe," he made a show of being busy with his papers. "I believe Captain Oakes is the only person who can identify one of their fugitives. He's their indispensable man."

Adams tugged at the points of his vest. "What about photographs to identify somebody?"

"I asked the same question, but as usual no one bothered to answer. You will recall that last year I proposed attaching photographs to all the passports I *vise* here, so that we would have a gallery of questionable persons for reference. Your father said it was impractical."

"He was right."

"I think," Moran said with a certain expression of malicious pleasure, "Miss Lawton is rather taken with our Captain Oakes."

Henry Adams walked to the door without answering.

8

IN LATE 1863 A MIDDLE-AGED ST. LOUIS MAN named Thomas Courtenay invented something called the "coal bomb," which would eventually take a certain number of Northern lives in the war and destroy many dozens of Northern railroad locomotives.

After his invention was demonstrated to Jefferson Davis, Courtenay was authorized to form a special rogue "bomb squad," as the Confederate army called it, and he was allowed his pick of twenty-five skilled assistants to perform, as the authorization put it, "secret service against the enemy." Courtenay, however, negotiated one special provision: he was paid a commission on the monetary damage he did to the Union troops—he was to receive four percent bonds on cotton warehouse stock, up to fifty percent of the value of whatever he bombed into splinters. By the time the war ended, he was a wealthy man, and a hunted man, and by early 1867 he was a happily settled man, an exiled man, the owner of a handsome Georgian townhouse at an *addresse de prestige*, number 5, Cheyne Walk, in the very best part of Kensington.

"Where you have absolutely no authority over me," he told Oakes and Maggie Lawton cheerfully. "I've never taken the oath of repatriation or whatever you people call it. I live here in London now, but I'm a citizen of no country whatsoever. A very advanced concept. I recommend it to you."

He stepped aside and made a low, sweeping bow to usher them in. "That said, I'm always happy to see my former adversaries—although, my dear, I don't recall glimpsing your attractive smiling face across the thin red line. So charming to see you in any case."

Courtenay was one of those men, Oakes noticed, who cannot resist touching himself. He straightened, fingered his moustache, and gestured toward a side table furnished with a sherry decanter, plates of biscuits, and a set of beautifully filigreed goblets.

"I live here, but I can't adopt all of their customs—afternoon tea, for example. Can't stomach the muck. 'Cat-lap,' the cockneys call it. So I compromise with a drop or two of old Jerez." He pulled out a chair for Maggie Lawton, nodded toward another for Oakes, and rang a little silver bell on the table, which instantly produced a short, dapper little butler who bore some passing resemblance (Maggie said later) to General Sharpe. Sherry poured, biscuits offered and declined, Courtenay leaned back on his great red velvet sofa and stroked his chin.

"I would say you're much too young to be General Sharpe, my friend. Or you would have been too young in our army anyway."

Oakes handed him an envelope and a personal card. "General Sharpe," Maggie said, "can't come today. Perhaps you can meet him another day. I'm Maggie Lawton. We work for him."

"I sincerely doubt there will be another day." Courtenay opened the envelope and read the letter. Against the fading sunlight from a window behind the sofa, Oakes could make out Seward's huge swirling signature on the translucent paper.

Courtenay glanced at the official letter, studied more closely the card.

"So, 'Captain Oakes, of the Bureau of Military Information.' I commanded a division in President Davis's Secret Services corps, but we never had calling cards like this. I remember that many, many of your private soldiers carried these things, with their photographs printed on them. I never understood why. Northern *vanitas*, no doubt. Did we ever have direct dealings with each other, Captain?"

"I saw one or two of your bombs."

"Unexploded ones, of course!" Courtenay laughed and caressed the back of his left hand with his right thumb. "Or you wouldn't be here!"

"I never did," Maggie said. "Tell me about that." Over the past weeks she and Oakes had, more or less unconsciously, worked out a technique for interviewing these ex-Confederate tricksters, as she thought of them. Aggression didn't work, appeals to justice or reconciliation didn't work. But most of them, like so many Southerners she knew, were gregarious individuals. They liked social chatter; defeated, humiliated, they liked to reminisce about their victories.

"What did *you* do in the war, little Miss?"

"I spied on you," she said sweetly. "I spied on you every chance I got. In 1864 I stayed in the same hotel in Richmond as Timothy Webster, and when you caught me there I enjoyed the hospitality of Libby Prison."

"We hanged Webster," Courtenay said.

"You did, very efficiently."

"Were you the young woman staying in his room, posing as his wife?"

Maggie glanced at Oakes. The same fading sunlight just brushed the tiny pockmarks on her left cheek. It left her expression momentarily stiff and frozen. Then she smiled sweetly again. "Tell me about your bombs, Mister Courtenay."

Courtenay grinned and sharpened his profile against the sunlight. "My most effective bomb," he said, "was made out of thin cast iron, very irregular in shape. It was coated with a mixture of broken coal and pitch, and the hollow interior was stuffed, absolutely stuffed, with high-grade powder. We used it mainly against Union shipping on the Mississippi, where my men would slip them into bins of real coal. Eventually those little black bombs would make their way into a ship's furnace or boiler, where the heat would do the rest, with most gratifying results, I should say. We tried them on railroad locomotives too, but they tended to be better guarded."

"We found one of them on Jefferson Davis's desk," Oakes said, "when we took over his office in Richmond."

"I gave that to him myself. It was a dummy, naturally. President Davis liked unusual weapons. He once tried to recruit camels for our people in the desert west, but with not much success. Nasty animals, camels. They spit like a bandit."

Courtenay switched thumbs. "They gave me an idea, though. Before the war ended I was just about on the point of making a bomb that looked like a mule turd—pardon my French, Miss—or even a camel turd, but I couldn't figure how to set one off, except with a timer of some kind sticking out, and that wouldn't have fooled anybody."

"You tried to blow up the President's Mansion with a timer," Maggie said.

Courtenay held up the sherry decanter. Maggie and Oakes shook their heads. "So now we arrive by stages at the assassination," he said. "A smooth team you make, you two. Now let me save you some time. Here's what you really want to know. Did I aid the actor Booth? Did I aid John Surratt, the unfortunate fellow you've just captured over in Egypt? Short answer to both questions: No. I never met Booth in my life. Surratt I knew, because I was sometimes in Mister Benjamin's office when Surratt and his other couriers would come in to receive their orders. But aid him in the assassination plot? No."

"Did you know a Sarah Slater?" Maggie asked. "She was close to Booth and John Surratt and she came through this city very recently, a fugitive too."

Courtenay pulled gently at the hound-like dewlaps under his chin. "London. Sarah Slater."

"Perhaps you gave her money?"

"I don't give anybody money!" Courtenay laughed a big, self-satisfied laugh. "Not even pretty ladies."

"How do you know she's—"

Oakes interrupted. "The bomb you invented," he said. "Maybe you didn't help Booth or Surratt. But you tried to kill the President. Your man Thomas Harney tried to set a bomb off just outside Lincoln's office in Washington. Isn't that right?"

Courtenay looked from one to the other.

"It was one of your 'horological' bombs," Oakes said, reading from his notes. "It had a fuse and a clock timer, and after the plan to kidnap Lincoln fell apart, Sergeant Thomas F. Harney of your Bomb Squad met with Surratt on March twenty-ninth, 1865. Harney was ordered to plant the mine in the grounds next to the Mansion, on the War Department side. Those were your orders. Isn't that right?"

Courtenay shrugged.

"I *know* it's right," Oakes said, "because after the cavalry captured Harney on April tenth, I went to Lincoln personally to show him the bomb, but he refused to meet me."

Oakes felt an unexpected, reckless anger building. He could still remember his shock when the cavalry brought the bomb to the Bureau. The wires had been pulled safely loose, but a timer clock on top of the explosives was stopped at nine forty-five. At nine forty-five in the morning, in his office, the Confederates, in the most cowardly way possible, would have blown Abraham Lincoln to eternity. Every man in the office had stared in disbelief. There were codes of conduct and decency, even in war. Bombs and assassination were what they did in Europe, not America. This is a *sneak's* way, Sharpe had hissed between clenched teeth— it was wretched, desperate, *pusillanimous*.

In a matter of moments, he had ordered Keach to go to Harney's cell and interrogate him—"*strenuously.*" Then he told Oakes to find the President, who happened to be on a Navy warship that day on the James River, not in the Mansion at all. Idiot rebels, Sharpe said, can't even get their information right. But when Oates sent in Sharpe's note, Lincoln had simply sent it back, saying he was too busy to talk. The Navy lieutenant who told this to Oakes said that after he read the message, Lincoln had just looked up and smiled that tired smile of his and said he couldn't believe that anybody really wanted to harm him.

Maggie watched in alarm as Oakes's cheeks grew stony pale. "Set a bomb and run away," Oakes said. "Very gallant soldiering. Are you proud of that?"

Courtenay stared at him. "I don't find myself much amused any more by talking about the war," he said finally.

"Did you help John Surratt last year?" Maggie asked, trying to push her way back into the conversation. "When he came through London?"

"I don't actually believe Surratt had anything to do with killing Lincoln," Courtenay said and stood up.

"That's not an answer to my question."

"No," Courtenay said. He rang the bell for the butler and turned on his heel and left the room.

"You interrupted me in there," Maggie Lawton said brusquely. They were outside on Courtenay's stoop. She slapped her bonnet open with a fist and jammed it back on her head. Cheyne Walk was only a few blocks from the Thames, and a cold breath of river air was flowing steadily up the narrow street, through the plane trees on the sidewalks, toward the great parks farther north. Off in the west the cold, gray afternoon light had given way to a dark, bruised sky, full of waiting rain. "You *interrupted* me when I was about to find out something about your famous Sarah Slater."

"I hate bombs. Sharpe hates them too."

"And you lost control of yourself. Courtenay's clearly seen that woman here—he said she was pretty—and he looked like the kind of man who would talk about a pretty woman. Sharpe told us to stay calm, unprovocative."

"Those coal bombs were craven, *cowardly*."

"Does it *matter?* So he was underhanded and treacherous and set bombs for people—you *all* did terrible things in that stupid, unnecessary war. *I* did terrible things, for that matter."

"All right." Oakes ran his hand through his hair. "All right. I'll ask Pollacky to set a watch on him. Maybe he did see her. Maybe he'll try to see her again."

"Give me tea," she said. "And explain something."

Oakes pulled out his watch. "I should go back to Moran."

"No, you shouldn't. You've made me mad, and I'm hungry." She put her left arm through his and signaled for a passing hansom cab with her right. "And an army travels on its stomach."

The cab rolled up, drawn by yet another mournful, skeletal specimen of London horseflesh, and Maggie Lawton looked down at something in the gutter and made a face. "Horse turds," she said. "Mule turds. Camel turds. What an awful little man."

Opposite the South Kensington Museum they found a hotel with a refreshments room, and settled into uncomfortable chairs in a far corner, out of sight of the reception desk. As usual, Maggie Lawton ordered strong black tea. Oakes, who largely shared Thomas Courtenay's views on tea, ordered coffee. When it had arrived, supplemented by a tray of chalky, sclerotic English pastry, Maggie leaned forward, pushed her bulky skirt to one side, and placed both elbows on her knees like a man. "Before the war," she said in a matter-of-fact tone, "I worked six months as a reporter for a Philadelphia newspaper."

"Like Thomas Chester."

"Much like Thomas Chester. Neither of us cares for the rules of the world we were born into. My father sent me to an excellent school for girls where I learned Latin and a little French and a little chemistry, of all things—he thought I should be the first woman doctor in Ohio—but I discovered that I was a better writer than chemist. Or speaker of French, for that matter."

She sipped her tea and cocked her head at him. "'Why is she telling me this?' Captain Oakes asks himself. She is telling you this because the editor at my little weekly gazette didn't care at all about my chemistry or my imperishable prose. He wanted me to learn how to interview people. He said there is always and only one question to keep in mind when you interview somebody, whether it's the new mayor or the new captain of industry— always men, of course," she added, "always men. It applied just as well when I went to work for Pinkerton."

"One question?"

"One question. What does he *want*? Deep down what does he *really* want?"

"Motive, in other words. Oddly enough, that's exactly what my father the lawyer always said, too."

"Two minds in the same rut. Motive, it is. And you, former Captain Oakes, have two contradictory ones. First, you want to find Sarah Slater because Sharpe wants you to, and you would march off a cliff if Sharpe told you to. You probably did in the war. You likely have some feelings about the Martyred One, too, and duty and justice. And second, just possibly you *don't* really want to find Sarah Slater—or whatever her name is—because in your mis- spent youth you were closer to her than village schoolmates. Much closer. The 'Lady in the Black Veil,' very romantic. Keach said your father sent you off suddenly on the Grand Tour and then installed you in Harvard Yard two years early for a freshman. Keach knows all about you. Keach is very jealous of your money."

Oakes decided that coffee was not what he wanted, not what he *really* wanted, and he called a waiter over and ordered a glass of whisky.

"Everybody says she was beautiful." Maggie watched a woman walk past them, toward the lobby. "Sarah Slater. She must have been bitter, being abandoned like that, by her husband's people after he was killed. Or maybe she was used to being abandoned." The woman in the lobby had blonde hair piled in two high buns, according to the latest London fashion. She was wearing a handsome green overcoat, elegantly trimmed with silky brown fur, and she was leading two children, red-cheeked and blond, a boy and a girl, who might have skipped off the pages of an English nursery rhyme.

"Jack and Jill," Maggie said, looking after them. "This whole city's like a book. Even the street names sound like books— Gloucester this, Gloucester that, Primrose Hill, Lambeth. I certainly don't find London a disappointment, not after Liverpool. They still talk funny here, but I can understand them. Usually."

She watched Oakes take a swallow of his whisky. "So you don't want to catch Sarah Slater, because if you did, they would put her in prison at the least, or hang her if that toad Stanton had his way." She reached over and picked up his glass and took a sniff, then replaced it on the table. "Or maybe, because men are like that, you *do* want to catch her, for old times' sake, whatever those were. But then what? Could you live happily ever after with a fugitive?"

She leaned back in the uncomfortable chair and watched the woman in the handsome overcoat disappear around a column. "Maybe she doesn't want you now."

It was not a new thought to him. Oakes said nothing.

"Or maybe *she* has two contradictory motives too. She wants to run away and vanish into messy old Europe. Or else she *wants* you to find her, in the perverse way a woman would. Some women would."

Oakes pushed one of the terrible pieces of pasty with his finger. Camel turd.

"So what would you do if you *did* find her, friend Quintus? Would you truly hand her over to Sharpe and Stanton?"

To clear the mind, Sharpe had often instructed them, choose a single object, something banal, and stare at it, concentrate on it. Oakes chose a badly carved lion's head on a wooden upright behind her head.

"Would you turn her in if you saw her?" In answer to her own question Maggie shook her head from side to side, as if to say maybe *yes*, maybe *no*. She looked past him with heavy-lidded hunter's eyes. To Oakes she seemed to be reading her own thoughts, spread out invisibly in the air in front of her face. Her voice took on an abstracted, ruminative quality. "And what would you do if our Sergeant *Keach* found her first? The *strenuous* interrogator?"

He stood up, fumbling in his pocket for coins.

"There's a third motive," Maggie Lawton said.

Oakes looked down at her.

"You're lonely," she said.

Oakes turned his head sharply away, in the direction of the vanished nursery rhyme family. Nothing people said or did, he thought, surprised him any more.

"I am, too," Maggie said.

9

ALTHOUGH IT WAS NOW LATE MARCH, London had yet to hear of spring.

Sharpe, in particular, seemed to be stranded in a wintry doldrums, icy and becalmed. Much of the time he spent amassing evidence—none of it satisfactory—most of it hearsay, rumors, vendettas—against Judah Benjamin. Most days he spent in the Embassy, filing notes and writing lengthy reports to Seward, for the diplomatic courier's bag.

Keach, meanwhile, was making slow headway against the mulish courtesy of the London bankers, none of whom apparently had ever heard of the Confederate States of America, much less dealt in loans and cotton bonds with such an obscure entity. Or if they had, it was certainly no business of a faintly shabby, certainly unimpressive-looking American clerk with no official title or standing. Their best weapon, he complained to Sharpe, was the lifted chin, the glacial silence. If the London banks ever went to war, he said, no guns needed, they would just ignore the enemy to death.

As for Maggie Lawton, she met much the same wall of implacable formality. There were at least half a dozen British women of high social standing who had involved themselves in various societies that supported the Southern cause. Some had made speeches, some had written pamphlets. The most enterprising had organized citywide raffles and auctions to send money to Richmond. None of them would receive her, even with the handsomely written and impressively stamped letters of request that Charles Francis Adams (actually, Moran) supplied her.

The only exception was the magnificently named Harriet Sutherland-Leveson-Gower, Duchess of Sutherland, who had early on established herself as a leading abolitionist and perpetual gadfly to the British government. But she had no real information to give, only heated anecdotes about the notorious (and notoriously attractive) Confederate spy, Rose O'Neal Greenhow, who had come to London for a few months to raise money for the Cause, then subsequently drowned off the coast of North Carolina, while returning to the South. When her ship foundered, she was evidently dragged down in the sea by the gold sovereigns in her pockets. The curse of Jeff Davis's gold, the Duchess opined.

Which left only Ignatius Pollacky and his team of watchers. But here too the doldrums persisted. The possible Sarah Gilbert in the Strand turned out to be, when Oakes saw her in person, the youngest daughter of a Yorkshire parson, in London seeking work as a governess. Up close, the Kate Thompson in Bedford Square was at least forty-five years old. And the Sarah Slater in Lambeth had not been seen for at least five days. Probably she'd moved on to somewhere else, Pollacky thought, possibly the Continent.

It was into this vacuum that Henry Adams stepped with an unexpected proposition.

"It is going to be," he announced, with a tone that suggested it was either by his order or for his personal pleasure, "quite fair tomorrow. No rain. The *Times* goes so far as to predict 'sunny spells,' which always sounds to me," he turned toward Maggie Lawton, "as if some 'weather wizard' has waved his magic wand."

"'Sunny spells.'" She waved one hand in a more or less wizardly way at the rain-streaked window. "Abracadabra."

"So I rather think," Adams said, "one could risk a little excursion."

"Risk away, Mister Adams."

"I had thought"—he found something of compelling interest on the corner of her desk—"of Cambridge."

They were in yet another of the Embassy's seemingly inexhaustible supply of unused offices, this one on the ground floor looking out on sodden and deserted Great Portland Street. In one corner, facing the main window, was a small desk that Maggie had moved in. There was a club chair of cracked red leather, a bookcase with somebody's leather-bound set of Henry Fielding, and two very badly engraved views of Wordsworth's Tintern Abbey. According to a mysterious system of her own, Maggie had arranged her notes in three separate piles and appeared to be ready to shuffle two of them together, like a card player. Now she turned slightly in her desk chair and smiled at Oakes as he came through the door.

"Your cousin has invited us all to go to Cambridge."

Adams opened and closed his mouth. Opened it again. "Unless you're too busy," he said, hopefully.

In a few years all trains from London to East Anglia would be leaving from a new and imposing terminal at Liverpool Street, as part of a vast expansion and modernization of London's seemingly endless railroad web (the Necropolis Railway would, Adams said with witty solemnity, expire). But for now, he explained, they had to make do with the ancient Bishopsgate terminus, a great sooty black pile located on the eastern side of Shoreditch

High Street—Maggie Lawton had purchased a little notebook in which she was entering London street names that amused her—just inside the slums of Hackney, slums, she announced, that made the Tenderloin of New York seem genteel by comparison.

Henry Adams led them through a maze of carriages eponymously called—to Maggie's delight—"hackneys" and then through a phalanx of out-of-work London laborers who were milling around the station entrance, from time to time listlessly waving signboards and placards in support of Disraeli's newest Reform Bill. This was a scheme to extend voting rights to all male heads of households, and it was inspired, Sharpe had lectured them at dinner one night, by the North's victory at Appomattox, generally seen in England less as a military victory than a mandate for more and more democracy. After all, if even blacks could vote in America…

"Horse evidence," Adams warned primly, pointing down at the pavement, as he piloted them between carriages toward the station entrance.

"London," Maggie quoted Sharpe quoting the poet Spenser, lifting her skirts, "'Flower of cities all.'"

Inside, insisting that they were his guests, Adams bought first-class seats on the eight forty-five train to Cambridge, and when they were installed in their compartment, bought coffee and buns from a cart on the quai.

"Such luxury!" Maggie sat back with an ironic, theatrical sigh. "A private compartment, leather cushions, undrinkable coffee, inedible buns, England in a nutshell. Why didn't you spoil me like this, Captain Oakes, on our hajj to Canada?" She turned to Adams. "He's a rich man, you know, but tight."

Adams and the locomotive both seemed to snort at the same time. "He's not rich. Who told you that?"

Maggie dropped her theatrical irony and looked curiously at Oakes.

"None of us Adamses are rich," Adams said. "Quintus's father made a number of quite bad investments. Then I believe our Captain here gave most of what little he had inherited to—what was it, Cousin mine, an orphanage in the South?"

"A photography studio." Which was partly true. Oakes took one of the buns from Maggie's tray and rapped it with his knuckles.

"Inspect it for a bomb," she reminded him.

"Ingersol and Sullivan, Photographers," he said. "I met them in the war, when they were working for Matthew Brady. They're working in New York until they have enough money to go to Wyoming, and I've invested in them. They want to make a photographic history of the frontier and publish it in a book the way Brady did with his war pictures. It's possible that I can go west with them next year, if they save enough." He looked at Maggie. "That's what I *really* want."

"Photography," Adams said, "is not history."

They reached Cambridge well before noon and began a slow, informal tour of the ancient colleges. Because the university was still in term, an occasional black-gowned student flitted like a bat out of a shop or alleyway. Some of them, on new-fangled front-pedal bicycles or French velocipedes, cheerfully banged away on warning bells as they wove their way through the streets. Under the first warming sun of late March, the city was a green, sleepy, bucolic retreat, as unlike the lunatic bustle and marketplace noise of London as possible.

He loved it here, Adams explained to Maggie as he introduced her with a mock bow to Emmanuel College (John Harvard, he explained, had gone there; he always made a little reverence to the Founder). He had often taken the train up to Cambridge during the war simply to escape the "lacerating" social ostracism he had endured as an American loyalist in London. He loved the medieval spires that punctuated the low East Anglian sky. He loved the sense that here he was surrounded, as a person should be, by books and scholars, not snobs and politicians.

Maggie made a grimace of distaste—for what Oakes wasn't sure—and picked up her pace.

"This was Lord Byron's college," Adams informed them in front of Trinity College. "Byron's personal rooms," he added as they stepped inside the courtyard, "were up on the second floor, by those bay windows. He kept a pet bear, of all things, tethered over there"—Adams pointed to another, smaller doorway in a far corner of the courtyard. "This was apparently an annoyance to his tutors. But then, Byron was a peer of the realm, and a genius, and what were they? He's supposed to have returned home late one night with guests, none of them strictly sober, and asked if they would like to see the Master. Whereupon he picked up a rock and threw it through one of the windows, and when the Master's outraged face appeared, the great poet simply nodded with satisfaction and said, 'There he is.'"

In the chapel he showed them the statue of Isaac Newton and quoted some lines from Wordsworth, and then led them round the various stained-glass windows, gesturing, rising on his toes to indicate this or that remarkable pane or figure. Oakes listened with half an ear. He was used to his cousin's precocious pompousness—it was a well-known failing, his father used to say of the Boston Adamses. Maggie's reaction was harder to gauge. From time to time, when Adams pulled up some arcane fact or anecdote, like a magician conjuring a sunny spell from a hat, she would laugh. Once, when he read aloud a Latin obituary on a burial stone, she crossed her arms and said it was all Greek to her. But when he tried to take her arm or elbow to guide her over a curb, she pulled away and frowned.

At King's College she clapped her hands in admiration of the famous Chapel—a fifteenth-century miracle of stone and glass sailing apparently lighter than air across the immaculate lawn—until Adams's long lecture on Late Perpendicular Gothic architecture made her turn away with impatience.

At lunch he grew increasingly attentive to her. "Did your pack of hunters capture any fugitives of interest yesterday?" he asked with his usual faintly derisory tone. "Anyone I know?"

Maggie sniffed and signaled the waiter for more claret.

"At least people speak to you, when you go for your interviews," Adams persisted. "The advantage of an attractive woman. I had no clubs to go to in those dire days of the war. I had in fact nobody to talk to except Moran, so you can imagine my ordeal. It was terrible beyond anything I had known in Boston. One lived, but one was flayed alive, socially. London was really like a military outpost."

They had found a student café on Great Trumpington Street—a name Maggie had instantly entered in her notebook—and a kindly mutton-chopped waiter had seated them by the window, to watch the sunlight glint off the gray and brown limestone of the colleges. She finished her wine and, with an unreadable face, turned slowly toward him.

"At one point I actually thought of leaving here and joining the army back in Virginia," Adams said. "My brother was there. I thought it would be a much pleasanter life than the severe trial that London had become. But then I really couldn't desert Father, could I? But it was hard, every morning over my muffins, reading of yet another Northern defeat."

"Was this," Maggie said in a slow, deliberate tone that made Oakes sit up, on his guard. "Was this after the 'crushing' satire the *Times* ran about your newspaper articles?"

"You remember that?" Adams was pleased. "People said the *Times* only showed how good the articles were. My brother thinks I should make a little book of them. My philosophy of writing is quite simple—I just toss my sentences up in the air and they land on their feet, like cats."

"It's nice that you should think of the war as a pleasanter life than your London clubs," Maggie said pleasantly. "I remember other things besides your articles. I wasn't in actual fighting, like our big, silent friend here, who rarely, I notice, talks about his 'ordeal' or being 'flayed alive' or 'crushing' satires. I don't think he—or Sharpe or even Sergeant Keach—talk much about what they saw. Once or twice I did have occasion to walk over a battlefield just after the fighting had stopped, before the ambulance wagons came. I recall seeing a soldier propped against a fence, near a cannon that had split open when it fired. His right arm had been blown off by some flying metal, so his artery was severed. I remember noticing that the blood actually gushed higher than his head. Two days before Appomattox, when that whole unspeakable war should have come to a complete halt, the men-boys were still playing their games. I saw a Federal officer shot behind the bridge of his nose. He walked directly toward me. He kept blinking at me, though both eyes were gone and the blood came out of the sockets in little pumped spurts."

Adams pushed his chair back. "I had no intention," he began, "of making light—"

"I cannot," Maggie said, "stand the way you talk." She reached over and took Oakes's glass of claret and swallowed it down in gulps.

"Maggie—"

"You be quiet, you Quintus. You just keep quiet, as usual."

"I think," Adams said, "we should go." He stood and looked around for the waiter.

"Once, early in the war," Maggie said, "I was between assignments for Pinkerton, so I volunteered to be a nurse in a hospital in the old Union Hotel in Georgetown. I saw a good deal of the 'pleasanter life' then. I saw corpses that were burned black as charcoal, I saw blisters the size of your fist on a man's neck and face."

Adams had pulled out his coin purse and was hurriedly scattering money across the table. Oakes started to stand as well, but Maggie caught his wrist. Other customers, students in their gowns, their waiter were staring. Dishes rattled nearby, then none.

"One boy was dying while I sponged his face," Maggie said loudly. "He was nineteen years old and he'd been shot in the belly—a vulgar word, I know, not fit for Harvardian ears. He was breathing in great terrible rasps and crying, and he reached out his hand and touched my breast and then he pulled my hand down to the middle of the blanket and I reached under it and bent over and kissed him and gave the last bit of pleasure he ever knew in this life."

Henry Adams gave a little cry and turned and fled. Maggie picked up his wine glass and drained it as well and sat watching the street with a face that looked as if it had been chipped from the whitest, saddest stone on earth.

When they reached London, Isaac Pollacky was waiting for Oakes.

10

Oakes and Maggie walked into the Ambassador's anteroom, having lingered in Cambridge on their own until late afternoon, well after eight o'clock that evening. The sunny spell was over. Sharpe and Charles Francis Adams were sitting in red leather chairs, sipping whiskey and declaiming poetry at each other. The theme apparently was the city of London, and Sharpe, in full flow, had just launched into some gloomy lines (he later explained) from Jonathan Swift on what washed through the streets in a London rainstorm—"*Dung*," he pronounced with relish, "guts and blood, /Drowned puppies, stinking sprats, all drenched in mud, /Dead cats and turnip tops, come tumbling down the flood."

Charles Francis Adams chuckled. Sharpe nodded to the two of them but said nothing. Isaac Pollacky appeared at the opposite doorway.

"Now, no one writes like that about New York," Sharpe said, "or Philadelphia, or your Boston, Adams, the 'Hub of the Wheeled Universe.' But *London* brings out some deep black chord in a poet. Do you remember the one about the 'mind forg'd manacles?'"

"The mad poet Blake," Maggie said from the doorway. "One of your favorites."

"Supposedly mad," Sharpe corrected her. "As sane as you and me, actually. Although it's true he used to sunbathe nude in his garden."

"In this climate?" Maggie said. "Clearly out of his mind."

Sharpe waved her silent and began solemnly to intone still gloomier verses about harlots in London's "midnight streets."

"Sir—" Pollacky's voice was barely a whisper. It was clear that he had something to say, but didn't dare interrupt. Lincoln's secretary John Hay once told Oakes that he and his colleagues used an unofficial code for Lincoln's various moods—in moments of wartime stress he became "the Ancient," after the old word for Ensign; in moments of Congressional intrigue the "Tycoon," after that most formidable and scheming emissary from Japan. For Sharpe in one of his irrepressible fits of erudition, Oakes had long ago decided on the word "Pundit," a Hindu wise man who preached in Sanskrit.

"We were just talking about various metaphors people have used for London." The Pundit finally turned in his chair and acknowledged them. "The poet Spenser called it a flower. Smollett called it a head too big for the body of England. Somebody else called it—"

"Bedlam," Pollacky said quickly. He came into room. "Begging your pardon, all, but Captain Oakes and I have some business. You too, General, if you like. It's about that young lady Slater-Thompson."

"You've found her?"

Pollacky tilted his head. "Well, that's for the Captain to say, isn't it?"

In the ground-floor room that Sharpe was using as an office, Pollacky came to a rough form of attention. "You remember our three earlier sightings, sir? The young lady in Bedford Square, the one on the Strand, the Lambeth girl? Kate Thompson?"

"None of them fit," Sharpe said. The Pundit was still carrying his whiskey glass and looking wistfully back toward the door to the Ambassador's suite, as if the poetry were still rolling on inside it without him.

"Well, we did eliminate the first two as not your person. But the Lambeth girl seemed to disappear before I could get the Captain here down to see her. Nothing skilamalink about that, sir—means 'shady' or doubtful, Miss, pardon my London French—people go, people come. Landlady thought she'd moved to the Continent."

Maggie Lawton had the kind of impatient mind that skipped intermediate steps of logic. "She's back," she said.

"Well, we think so. I sent a man around this morning, just to be checking, in case. Being thorough."

"She's back," Maggie said and looked directly at Oakes.

Pollacky's hair had long ago gone missing, except for two reddish steam puffs over his ear. Nobody had yet seen him in anything except a black wool overcoat and a dark blue scarf and a shapeless green hat with, improbably, a little yellow canary feather pinned to its crown. He had a nearly round face like a pink and white moon and the dogged, plodding attitude of the Metropolitan policeman he had once been.

"So, early on," he said, "there was a big ramper been hang-ing about her lodging house, the first time we went down there. Ugly, heavy-set chap, salt and pepper beard. We don't think he knows her. We think he may be stuck on her, like. Watches her, clears a path on the street for her, all your riff-raff doing their hus-tle, she gives him a bob or two—Lambeth's not your West End crowd, sir. *He* disappeared for a while, too, when she did. Now my man says he's back. Lurks about half a block down from her drum—what you call your boarding house, Miss—watching for her, I should think, back at his post."

"How," Maggie asked, "does this 'ramper' know her?"

"Carried her trunk and such for her three weeks ago, didn't he? When she moved in."

"The lady does travel with a good deal of baggage," Maggie said.

Sharpe looked at his watch. "Should we go there now?"

Pollacky shook his head. "No, sir. Fog's coming in, coming in thick. Besides, my men are off now—I've only two now anyway, one of 'em out sick—and the lady'd be in her room at this time of night, wouldn't she? Can't just go barging in a private house, got no warrant. What we can do, sir, we can go with the Captain first light tomorrow morning, if the fog lifts, and watch till she comes out, *if* she's there. Or simpler, if he will just bang the knocker and ask to see her. Then, on his word, you can approach her how you like." A faint note of reproach crept into Pollacky's voice. "I can bribe a little and bully a little for you, sir, all in a day's work. But I can't go into a private house and *enleve* a young lady. Not without the law behind me."

Keach had evidently arrived at some point in the conversation. Now he stepped out of the shadowy doorway. "What does she look like? Redhead? Blonde? Nice figure?" He smirked at Maggie.

"That's for the Captain to say," she said, and turned away.

The Captain had nothing to say, in fact. The Captain took a note card from Pollacky with the Lambeth address, refused a glass of whisky with the Pundit, and went soberly off to the Langham

Place Hotel, as expressionless and unexcited, Maggie remarked, as a block of wood.

But at half past eleven, when the hotel had settled into a creaky somnolence, he came quietly downstairs, turned left from the Reception desk toward the empty kitchen and stepped outside into an alley. He paused for a long moment until the squeak of the door hinges died away. The lamp in Maggie's room had still been burning when he passed by in the corridor. He had heard the rustle of her skirts as she paced back and forth. Maggie Lawton was capable of almost any surprise, he thought, but not even Maggie Lawton was going to venture out at this time of night alone into a strange city, into a thick, greasy fog that Pollacky, taking his leave of them, had described, with some pride, as looking like a "genuine London particular."

Oakes didn't mind fog. In Connecticut, the waters of Long Island Sound had often thrown up a summertime bluish-green lingering fog that crept along the coastal rocks, up the hillsides, and then shredded itself into flags in the trees. Outside Richmond in the war, mist from the James had sometimes thickened and settled in the trenches and transformed that filthy and besodden maze into a mysterious and even haunting landscape of ghosts and flares and shadows, Elsinore Castle, Hamlet in the tidelands. This London fog, he guessed, would sooner rather than later give way to rain.

He turned left down the delivery alley and emerged on Langham Place. From there, guiding himself by the dim orange match heads of the gas street lamps and the omnipresent growl of the city, he made his way to the Euston Street Railroad Station, where a few wet and discouraged drivers stood around a little fire in a barrel, stamping their feet in unconscious echo of their horses' hoofs. Sometimes London, to use his father's expression, was as crowded as an egg. At other times as empty as air. Oakes patted the flank of the nearest horse and swung himself up into the hackney. One of the shadows detached itself from the fire and rose noiselessly onto the bench.

It took almost half an hour to reach Lambeth and then another ten minutes to find the address—19, Belvedere Road—that Pollacky had scrawled on the card. Oakes tried to pass the time as he used to in the army—scrubbing his mind clear, erasing images, painting its walls white and gray, like the fog. Tried, failed. *Redhead? Blonde? Nice figure? You can't just waltz in and 'enleve' her,* Pollacky had said. *'Enleve' was a bizarre French word coming from a Cockney detective—you can't just waltz in and kidnap her,* he meant. *Grab her and run.*

And what would you do if you did *find her? Maggie had wanted to know.*

And what do you *really* want?

In one corner of his mind, impossible to scrub away, was the image of Maggie Lawton bending over the dying soldier's bed, lowering her face…The carriage slowed and rolled to a stop.

Oakes slipped down to the street and peered into the fog, which was shifting restlessly under the push of a river breeze, though there was no river to be seen, nothing to be seen on Belvedere Road, in fact, except the dim guttering candle that was the single street lamp visible. And shadows. And mud. The pavement here was not the fashionable new tar macadam of the central city. Lambeth pavement was ancient, slick filmy cobblestones with hunched and rounded shoulders, lifting slowly out of the mud. A scared cat flitted by. The air felt cold and heavy.

"Found it by smell." The driver bent over and took Oakes's coins.

"Wait here."

The driver looked doubtfully around. One or two lamps winked and floated high in the fog, a distant voice, no face, no faces.

Oakes gripped the driver's heavy sleeve in a fist and jerked him violently forward. "*Wait*," he said between gritted teeth. "*Here.*" He held a gold sovereign up to the light and put it on the bench. Then he hunched his shoulders too and turned away.

The front steps at Number 19 were littered with trash, blown there by the wind or simply washed up by the tides of city life— *dung, turnip tops, stinking sprats, and guts and blood*. Eight steps up, a door shrouded in gray fog, with a crescent of light over the lintel. There was no knocker or bell pull, or if there was Oakes couldn't see it. He hammered twice on the door, hard, on Sharpe's theory that a soft knock was somehow more alarming than a loud one, and then waited.

Half a block away the carriage horse's back glistened like black oilskin in the muttering fog. He thought he saw a wheel half turn, but he couldn't be sure. The air was dripping, soaking his coat, plastering down the wet hair on his bare head. The rain felt closer, cold.

And what would you do if Keach found her first?

He hammered again, twice, and scraped his feet loudly on the wooden stoop and just as he raised his fist one more time he heard a woman's voice and he stood up straight, took one step back, and stiffened his face.

The muffled word "Nancy." Then "bloody keys again." Then the door pulled open an inch and a single eye appeared. Then the door swung half open.

"I thought you were Nancy," the woman said. She poked her head out into the fog, like someone peering through a curtain. "Lost her key again, I thought. Bloody cow. You look lost too. Go away, no visitors this time of night, gentlemen or not."

Oakes gripped the edge of the door with one hand and held it open. "I know it's late."

The woman was short and stout and wore some kind of lace nightcap on her head and she pushed back at the door, puffed, pushed again. Then she fell back a step into the hallway. "I can call the rozzers," she threatened and stretched one hand toward the wall. "Bell cord right here that goes straight to the station. You turn around and go home, go home and drink yourself daft before I call Billy."

From the threshold Oakes had a clear view of the hallway, narrow brown carpet, stairs, some kind of dark wallpapered room to the left. In the clinging, encircling fog the I of the boarding house looked white as a sail. But inside, except for one gas lamp on a sconce by the stairs, the house was unrelievedly dark. Oakes said something—he scarcely heard his own voice—while the part of himself that sometimes seemed only to be a spectator of the rest watched intensely as, into the cone of light spilled by the little lamp, a white hand appeared, then an arm and shoulder, a wisp of blonde hair and then, like a bursting star, her face.

11

"Is there something wrong, Missus Owen?"

Mrs. Owen snapped her head around and gave a sharp look to Sarah Slater. Then she switched back to Oakes.

"I must have the wrong address," he said.

"You're a bloody American, aren't you?"

"My cab is just down the corner, under the light. I'll go look at the address again. It may take some time."

The door slammed in his face like the crack of a pistol.

There is more order in life than you think, Oakes believed. Deep down, he told himself, life has patterns, life has direction. In the geometry of desire, the perfect figure is a circle. His pulse was jumping in his throat, despite the freezing cold air his face was swimming in sweat. There was no direction in the thick gray fog, however, none at all, except straight along the filmy slick cobblestones of Belvedere Road, right through its scraps of trash, its unseen obstacles and noisy moving shadows, straight toward the single poor candle of a street lamp and the blackish oilskin shiny outline of the hackney's horse and cariole.

"Back now, sir? Later than I like, down this way it is. Euston Street again?"

Oakes handed him two more coins and wrapped one hard fist around the horse's reins where they looped up toward the driver on the bench. "Five minutes," he said in the iron tone of command he had learned from Sharpe. "You wait five minutes."

The driver studied the coins in his open palm. "A young lady is it?"

"Five minutes."

Whether it was the menace in Oakes's voice, the clink of the coins in the fog, or some vague and enlivening sense of romantic liason and fraternity, the driver twisted his end of the reins around the brake handle and dropped heavily to the pavement. "Five minutes," he said. "I'll stand back here."

It was nine past one o'clock—four minutes later than the five-minute deadline he had set—before she appeared.

She glanced quickly at the driver and peered into the shadows. Two drunks emerged from an alley singing an Irish song. They shouted obscenities and laughed as they passed the hackney. Doors slammed, a dog. The driver shuffled back to the hackney and slipped up onto the wet bench. Oakes stepped into the frayed cone of light cast by the streetlamp.

And suddenly his thoughts went mute. He must have rehearsed this meeting a thousand times in his mind, imagined every possible word, every possible gesture—and now the words fought and tangled and fell apart and he had nothing at all to say.

"It *is* you," she said and her voice was older, harder, but he would have known it in a chorus of millions. "Quint, Quintus Oakes—I didn't believe them, but it's *you!*"

He reached for her arm and pulled them both into the shadows, but even there he could see the light on her face. "The *police* are coming, Sarah. They're hunting you, they mean to arrest you."

She shook his arm away and her face went tight. "How do you know that?"

"For helping Booth—Seward's people are here looking for you—General Sharpe from the army, others. I can't stop them. And they will *absolutely* be here in the morning. Today."

"They don't know what I look like," she said. "Nobody knows."

He said nothing and her eyes widened in disbelief. "But *you* know." She clutched her throat. "*You* know."

He framed her face in his hands, an oval of light. "Sarah," he said, so softly that he scarcely knew what he was betraying. "I lied for you in Washington. Even if I lied for you here, they don't trust me now. There's a man—"

Her face was a theater of anger, panic. She shook her head furiously and backed away. "I *can't* leave London yet. I need money."

"I can find money."

"No, you can't—and where? *Where* would I go?"

He started to say Paris, Amsterdam, anywhere at all, but she suddenly stepped toward him again and touched his cheek with her fingers, skin against skin, and it was as if an inside charge had met an outside charge and sparked. His left hand curled around the back of her neck and he drew her toward him roughly, urgently— the driver coughed and looked away. Doors slammed down the street again, one after the other, and the long-awaited London rain began to fall, slowly, pattering to the ground through the gray, uneasy fog. When Oakes stepped back he was still gripping her waist with his right hand, his breath could be heard even over the dull tap and click of the rain.

"Quintus." One white hand touched his lips. "Quintus. Sweet, crazy Quintus. Why in the world should I trust you?"

The rain fell harder. It began to tear away the fog in strips. Belvedere Road began to take on weight, bulk.

"What happened with Booth—" she started to say.

"Hey now! You!" Two London constables emerged out of the rain, in the middle of the street, helmets shiny, clubs swinging at the waist. The hackney driver sat up straight and untwisted his reins. The Irish singers went silent.

"You by the lamp!"

Sarah Slater melted into the darkness. Oakes turned toward them.

"Go along now," the nearer constable said. He squinted at Oakes through the rain. "Back where you belong, sir. There's nothing here for you."

12

"SOMEONE TOLD ME," SHARPE SAID, "or I read it somewhere. The Eskimos have a hundred different words for snow, different kinds of snow." He let the curtain drop back across the window and sighed. "There must be twice that many words for London rain."

Nobody spoke. Everyone listened to the rain hammering loudly on the eaves, enough like gunshots to make Oakes wince.

"After today it's supposed to be clear for weeks." Daniel Keach sat in a corner, in a straight-backed chair, knees pulled up to his chest, and, although it was only nine o'clock in the morning, he took another gulp of sherry or scotch whiskey or whatever he had in the green cut-glass tumbler he had brought in from the Ambassador's kitchen. Keach had one of the worst colds Oakes had ever seen, a red-eyed, honking, gravel-throated demon's grip of a cold. There must be a hundred different words for London colds, too, Oakes thought.

Keach raised the glass and a defiant eye to Maggie Lawton. "I'm drinking myself back to health, Miss Prue," he said unpleasantly.

On the other side of what Moran had rather grandly called the Embassy Conference Room—in reality just another office with a long oak table and scattered chairs—Isaac Pollacky was fussing with a small, polished mahogany gun case. They had been supposed to go this morning—Oakes, Sharpe, and Pollacky—to Belvedere Road and ask for the woman Pollacky persisted in calling the "target." But the rain that had come on around midnight had swollen through the morning to a nasty Atlantic storm, with high, shifting winds near gale force and occasional window-rattling, rolling, and tumbling booms of thunder, and Sharpe, whose attention was still obsessively focused on Judah Benjamin, had rather offhandedly decreed a postponement for the Sarah Slater project. Let it rain, Oakes thought, let it storm for a year.

"It's a French rain," Pollacky said, studying the catch lock on the case. "Comes right across the Channel blustering and talking, like your Frenchman, talks itself to death by sundown. Always does. We can go tonight, General Sharpe, sir. Catch her when she's come back from wherever. Damn this lock!" He pulled a tiny L-shaped wire from his vest pocket and bent over the gun case.

After Gettysburg, Oakes remembered, pulling his mind away from any thought of Lambeth, after the battle of Gettysburg, Sharpe had made a detailed, scientific study of how men were killed.

No one had ordered him to make the study, and no one, it turned out, was much interested in its conclusions. But Sharpe, only a colonel then, had gone to considerable trouble nonetheless. He ordered his Bureau of Military Information staff to pull death records from every regiment in the battle. He went himself to all the field hospitals and interviewed every sober doctor he could find. (By no means an easy task, finding a sober doctor.)

How had the men died? He wanted to know—by gunshot wound? By bayonet? Artillery? Infection? In what proportions?

Damn little use the medics were, he later told Oakes. The first resort of military medicine, he said, the first and apparently *only* resort, was amputation, amputation and nothing else. Shot in the arm? Chop it off. Shot in the leg? Hack away. And in the chaos of an army field surgery, as ambulances and littermen dumped out their bodies and hurried off for more, in that particular butcher's circle of hell, nobody had time to take notes or write reports on how their patients died. There were far too many of them, far too much alike in their mutilation and pain.

The embalmers were better, Sharpe discovered. Early on in the war some enterprising Massachusetts businessman had devised a method of embalming bodies right on the battlefield itself, so that recovered corpses could be shipped home to their families for a proper church burial. The idea was so popular that at many camps there were special tents where a soldier could sign up for personal embalming insurance. And the embalmers, as it happened, kept far better records than the army.

Most of the casualties, Sharpe finally decided, were the result of artillery fire. Nothing in the war was as deadly as cannon balls or the exploding hollow shells, as improved by the Englishman Henry Shrapnel. In tribute to his genius, its deadly fragments were universally called, "shrapnel," and shrapnel evidently killed even more people than the doctors. In contrast, almost nobody was killed by a bayonet blade, but many were clubbed to death by the blunt end or knob handle of one—Based on my personal experience, Sharpe wrote in his report, people can hardly ever bring themselves to stab or rip or cut into the flesh of a living person, even a *stranger*, standing right in front of them. Hammering or smashing a skull doesn't seem to bother people as much.

Most interesting of all, he determined, after Gettysburg the Union army recovered from the field over twelve thousand rifles and muskets that were still fully loaded. They had, in fact, never been fired. They were startling evidence that even in the midst of a savage modern battle, soldiers were strangely reluctant to kill. Those who *were* shot, were most often shot in the *back*.

Oakes had puzzled over that. What kind of person shot retreating soldiers in the back? Then his mind swiveled over to Keach, who had once in a fury emptied his entire revolver at a fleeing pack of Rebels. But the war had unearthed Keach's violent character. In the war, Keach's first impulse had been to settle something by force. Sharpe took a larger view. It was simply human nature to kill something that was running away. That way you don't have to see the face of the man you were shooting.

"There." Pollacky unlatched the wooden case and turned it around to display two black, short-barreled revolver pistols nestled on a green felt base.

"I think it was a Deringer that killed your poor president?" he said.

Oakes nodded and picked up one of the pistols. Keach uncoiled himself from his chair and came over to the table. Sharpe and Maggie Lawton stood back.

"Lightweight." Keach was unimpressed. He wiped his nose with a handkerchief and took the pistol from Oakes's hands. "We used Navy revolvers ourselves, in the war, didn't we, Captain Oakes? Stop a buffalo with one of those. Anyway, Mister Pollacky, I brought my own pistol with me, straight from America's golden shores. But I'll want some extra ammunition."

Quint listened to the howl of the wind outside. They were called Navy revolvers, he thought irrelevantly, because for some reason they always came with naval battle scenes etched on the barrels. He had never seen a naval officer carry one. He tried to remember how many times he had actually fired his own gun at someone whose face he could see.

"Well, this is no Deringer, Sergeant Keach, and it doesn't have what I call your intemperate Yank firepower." Pollacky was amused. "This is a William Tanter special, manufactured here in Sheffield, nice, quiet no fuss little model. You Americans do tend to overdo things a bit, we think." He flashed a quick smile at Sharpe, who remained stone-faced. "No buffalo to shoot in London, are there? I'm not expecting to have any use for this little beauty tonight. Just a precaution."

"And my extra bullets?" Keach was sighting the pistol at one of the engravings of Tintern Abbey on the wall.

"I mean, the young lady is not likely to shoot at us, is she?" Pollacky said with a deprecating laugh. "The ladies like another method—your poison usually. Suits the maternal instinct, feed him something, you know, like your mum. Or a knife sometimes, from the kitchen, same idea. But from what the general says, this is just a look around to identify the lady. Knock on the door, tip your hat, hello Miss." Gently but firmly he gripped Keach's wrist with one hand and replaced the pistol in the case. There was more to Pollacky than you might guess, Oakes suddenly thought. Behind the Cockney performance, sir, was a shrewd, uncluttered, unsentimental intelligence.

"Still, you know, Sergeant Keach. There's that bruiser that lurks around her building. I'll bring another box of your cartridges tonight, if you want, but no need for them sir, not really, not tonight."

Just as Pollacky had predicted, around half past four the rain began to ease, pushing away to the northeast and pulling in behind it a world of soft warm air and the first green stirrings of an English spring. It was going to be clear as a mother's conscience for weeks, he said.

"'Lhude sing Cuckoo,'" muttered Sharpe as he went briskly down the Embassy steps on some errand or another. Despite the change of weather, occasional showers still made little dancing pimples of white rain on the sidewalk, and he pulled his hat down tight.

Watching from the top of the steps, Keach blew his nose and twisted to look at Oakes. "Going tonight, after all?" he said.

"As soon as the general gets back."

"He used to do that," Keach said. "Do you remember? Sneak off without a word to us, no telling what for." He blew his nose again, a violent skreak of nasal plumbing that made Oakes edge away a step. "He wouldn't let us have umbrellas in the field. Do you remember that?"

"I remember."

"You're going to have to see the Consolidators Bank tomorrow. If those snob mi'lord bankers hear this cold I have, I won't get in the door. Besides, they'll like your proper old Harvard College manners. I'll write out the questions for you."

Oakes looked at his watch. The macadamized pavement was slick and ebony black from the rain, and water could still be heard running down drainpipes and dripping thickly from the Embassy roof. The carriages that splashed by in both directions looked miserably wet. The horses' heads bobbed and shook and sprayed water in an unhappy rhythm. Great Portland Street was a busy street and already knots of people were coming out onto the sidewalk. At the far corner on the left a beggar woman, had settled down in her usual spot and begun rolling up her sleeves so that passers-by could see the terrible sores and eruptions on her arm, the result Oakes suspected of rubbing bloody lamb shanks and vinegar on the skin, an old gypsy trick. On the opposite corner... he took a step down and heard his name.

Henry Adams was walking up the sidewalk, making a little twirling gesture of greeting with one finger. Keach snorted. Oakes nodded. Adams started to say something—the Massachusetts Adamses *always* say *something*, his father used to grumble—but the front doors of the Embassy swung open and Maggie Lawton stepped out and Adams, smiling tightly and insincerely, continued on up the steps and into the building.

"Going with us boys, Miss Lawton, sir?" Keach asked.

"The General said I could."

"Know what Pollacky told me they call these?" Keach asked Oakes. He put both hands up to his chest and made a lewd bouncing gesture, looking all the while out of the corner of his eye at Maggie. Oakes watched a big man at the corner detach himself from a milling group of laborers and start to stroll in their direction. "'Cats' heads,'" Keach said, "is what the Brits call them. I thought I'd go along too and see what her cats' heads look like."

Maggie was unruffled. "I just want to see our Quintus here identify the lady."

"Hah." Keach rose to new heights of unpleasantness. "I told the General if she looks good enough, our bachelor 'Quintus' here might tell a fib and run off with her himself. Run off, disappear in darkest London like a rabbit down a hole."

Oakes made himself turn and speak in a calm, modulated voice. "Shut up, Keach."

But Maggie was interested. She looked at Keach, then at Oakes, then at Keach again. "What did the General say to that?" she asked.

Keach made his nasal plumbing noises again. "He said Quintus won't help her. He said his Quintus is an honorable man. He said Sarah Slater helped kill Lincoln. He said Quintus knows she's the Sixth Conspirator."

13

Whether or not she had helped kill Abraham Lincoln was of no serious consequence to Thomas Courtenay. He poured himself a second glass of Scotch whiskey at the side table and waved the cut-glass decanter vaguely in the direction of his guests. Colin McRae held out his own empty glass. Sarah Slater smiled and shook her head.

"I have always thought it a nice irony," Courtenay said. He came over and sat down in what seemed to be his usual spot on a long, red velvet-covered sofa. "A nice irony," he said, "that John Wilkes Booth's father was named Junius Brutus Booth, for the assassin of Julius Caesar."

"Another tyrant," McRae said automatically. "Like Lincoln."

"Like father, like son," Courtenay agreed with a little barking laugh at his wit. "Now you knew *our* Booth pretty well, I think"—he hesitated long enough to make plain that Sarah's status as a gentlewoman was not quite settled—"Miss Slater."

"Sarah doesn't like to talk about that," McRae interjected. The "Sarah" to establish his proprietary interest, the interruption because, Sarah thought, the whole question of her relationship to Booth made Colin McRae uneasy.

He shifted his legs in the leather chair by the window, which was oversized enough to make him look small. Courtenay's butler had installed him there, doubtless on Courtenay's orders, doubtless for that reason. "What'd I like to know," McRae said, "is how their faces looked this morning when this General Sharpe person came trooping through Lambeth. I wasn't there, of course"—he grinned without quite baring his teeth at Courtenay—"but neither was Sarah!"

Courtenay grinned back. They looked like a pair of old alligators, Sarah thought.

"I understand from this Huggins"—McRae nodded at Sarah for confirmation—"this English laborer she uses—he says that three or four of them came to the door. This was about six-thirty last night. One of them, tall fellow, long hair, knocked and went in while the rest of them waited in the street. Then he comes out, shaking his head, and they trooped out again, egg on their faces."

"He was supposed to identify our friend here," Courtenay said. "He's an ex-soldier named Oakes, some kind of relative of their idiot ambassador. He lives in New York and his father was governor of Connecticut."

"How would you know all that?" McRae was skeptical and impressed.

"How would *he* know to identify *you*, Miss Slater?"

Sarah had gotten up from her chair during this and gone to the window behind McRae. There was no sign at all now of the furious rainstorm that had swept across London yesterday. From Courtenay's window you could see through the trees straight down Cheyne Walk, almost to the Thames. She imagined that she could see the racing water of the river, flowing east toward the Channel, toward the Continent. She imagined she could see the little fleet of tidy white houseboats the hansom cab had passed as they turned off the riverfront. She imagined she could see Quint Oakes walking into the shabby little anteroom on Belvedere Road, and Mrs. Owen squawking in indignant, unintelligible Lambethese, wringing her apron in protest. Quint was tall, he had a quiet manner at first…

"I knew him some years back, when we both lived in the same town in Connecticut," she said over her shoulder. The Georgian brick house directly across the street, McRae had told her, belonged to a famous English savant named James Clerk Maxwell who had strung all kind of wires and connectors along his iron rail fence for electrical experiments, though the effect was less of a scientific experiment than of a shiny metal spider's web.

"You're very cool about this," Courtenay said. "Being followed, pursued all over England."

Sarah continued to look at Clerk Maxwell's ingenious wires. Really, they resembled the skeleton of some unearthly arachnid. Though of course, any kind of spider's web was still a trap. She was very cool about being hunted because people had been hunting her, pursuing her for nearly four years now. Booth used to say she was cold, not cool.

"Don't they have a photograph of you?" Courtenay said. For all his fatuousness and disgusting habit of constantly rubbing his body in private places, Courtenay was no fool, she thought.

She turned around and smiled at him over the back of McRae's chair. "No one has a photograph of me," she said.

"A waste," Courtenay said, and it was clear he didn't believe a word of it, "a pity with someone who is so remarkably attractive, who still has the figure of a young girl, if I may say so."

McRae stood up and held out his glass. "I think I would have just one more, old man," he said.

"Are you sure?" Courtenay rose and went to the sideboard. "I always say strong drink is like a woman's breasts." He lifted his chin and smiled at Sarah. "One isn't enough and three are too many."

Sarah was only mildly surprised and not at all alarmed. In view of his very careful coiffure, his tightly tailored frock coat, his general air of overly fastidious good taste, she had guessed that his interest in women might be secondary to his interest in men. But she had long experience in dealing with all categories of men— the metamorphic actor Booth alone covered most of them—and she could certainly, if she wanted to, fend off a pair of paunchy middle-aged alligators.

"Well." Colin McRae had no idea what to say. He made a sniffing sound that would pass for indignation perhaps. He twisted the other way in the oversized chair and stole a glance at her torso, as if counting.

Sarah walked around the chair and proceeded slowly, smiling, unoffended, to the far corner of the room where the not-very-lit-erary Courtenay—his taste, she thought, ran to fragile glassware and gewgaws—had nonethess placed eight or nine books and pamphlets on an eye-level shelf otherwise given over to Venetian brandy snifters. "This is," she said, running one finger along their spines, "quite a library, Mister Courtenay."

"Thomas, please."

"Thomas." She had developed sometime in the last two years an occasional problem with her vision. Things far away were per-fectly clear. Up close—she bent forward and read the nearest title aloud. "*The Great Conspiracy: A Book of Absorbing Interest! Startling Developments, and the Life and Extraordinary Adventures of John H.*

Surrat, the Conspirator. I see he spelled his own name wrong," she said dryly. "And published it last year in Philadelphia while he was a fugitive in Canada."

"A little joke," Courtenay said. "Dozens of books like that around, you know. I have one that proves Booth was really the illegitimate son of Jeff Davis. Another one says he escaped from Washington in a balloon. Another one is his missing Diary, right in front of you."

Sarah put out her hand and read aloud the title of a lurid red cardboard-covered pamphlet: *Confessions de John Wilkes Booth, Assassin du President Lincoln.* "Actually," she said, "Booth didn't speak a word of French. He had a terrible Baltimore accent."

"You were going to tell us about Booth."

"No, she wasn't," McRae said.

"I remember one of his actor's tricks," Sarah said. "I forget the name of the play, but he was playing Cardinal Richelieu. Booth carried a sponge that was soaked in red dye on stage, and when the good Cardinal expired, he squeezed the sponge and blood squirted out of his mouth."

"He broke his ankle when he jumped out of Lincoln's box," Courtenay said.

He didn't, in fact, Sarah thought. He broke it later, when he fell from his horse. She replaced the pamphlet and walked restlessly to the last window in the room, which had a view of two rows of leafless ash trees—stick figures that looked as if they had been drawn by children. Her mind wandered from children to Quintus Oakes to a future otherwise bare as the trees. She pinched the back of her hand hard and turned back around.

Courtenay was little more than an old gossip, she thought, smiling at him. But he asked too many questions about Booth.

There were more toys and baubles along the windowsill. She picked up a jeweled snuffbox and opened the lid to see a tiny, quite pornographic painting of a naked couple engaged in what she could only describe as hydraulic maneuvers.

"You didn't write any memoirs, did you, Sarah?"

"Sarah is entirely un-political," McRae said in her defense.

"But you were the last person to see Booth, I understand, before he went to Washington, yes?"

Sarah had long ago learned that it was not necessary to answer a question just because it was asked. You don't have to respond, or reply, or react in any way. Besides, she trusted no one, not even Quintus Oakes of the long hair and soft eyes—after all, he had come to Belvedere Road anyway, hadn't he? With all his promises, he had still come to find her with his lynching posse.

She put down the rather fascinating snuff box and turned to smile across the room, first at Courtenay, who was amoral enough, she thought, to hand her over to the authorities just for spite, or for profit. She transferred the smile, a touch warmer, lips a little more open, to McRae, who was weak-chinned and besotted but also perfectly capable of giving her up if he felt at risk.

Despite his abstemious philosophy, Courtenay had now poured himself a third tumbler of whiskey, and his voice had grown much coarser. "There are stories about Booth's private parts," he said with a leer.

"His penis," Sarah said.

McRae came to his feet. "This is really too much, Courtenay."

Courtenay raised one palm. "Just repeating—They say, too, too plain was Signor Gonorrhea."

Sarah had left her bonnet on a hook in the entryway, along with her new spring coat. In her pocket she had the hundred pounds she had come for. There was no reason to stay and listen to donkeys braying. "I'm staying at Mauguy's Hotel," she said, "on Regent Street, under the name of Foreman."

"Foreman?"

"Susanna Foreman. My new passport. The banker you sent me to, Mister McRae—Colin—was not very helpful."

"Your trunks and things—?"

"Quite safe. When Huggins moved me out yesterday he took care of them. His strength," she told Courtenay with an unreadable smile, "is as the strength of ten, because his heart is pure."

"What are you going to do?" McRae asked.

"I'm going to see the other banker you named."

"Where are these interesting trunks?" Courtenay asked, sober again. "At your hotel?"

Not necessary to answer a question. Not necessary to trust. She smiled the same indecipherable smile. With a decisive gesture that would have reminded Oakes of General Sharpe, she turned on her heel and walked toward the door.

14

TWO DAYS AFTER THE ANTI-CLIMACTIC VISIT to Sarah Slater's boarding house in Lambeth, Sharpe summoned Oakes to his rooms in the Embassy. It was well past nine o'clock in the evening. Sharpe had evidently dined privately with the ambassador and his son and then taken early leave of them, with the ever-useful excuse that he had papers to go over. When Oakes knocked, he was just setting out a bottle of brandy and three glasses.

"I saw Keach before dinner today." Sharpe gestured to a leather sofa in front of the little coal fireplace and poured an inch of brandy into two of the glasses.

"I saw him this afternoon," Oakes said. "He was spraying germs and groans on all and sundry."

"Then the ambassador's personal physician came while we were eating. He says Keach has 'attraped'—I don't know why all these Englishmen use bastardized French—'a pneumonia' and has to stay in bed for at least a week, probably more." Sharpe held his snifter to the firelight and studied it the way one might study a painting. "Silly man."

This, Oakes thought, was ambiguous. "Is Keach really that sick?"

There was another knock on the door and Sharpe rose to answer it. "Well, he's been moved to a hospital at least. The embassy will pay his medical expenses. Ambassador Adams said the important thing is for us to continue."

He opened the door and bowed Maggie Lawton in. "I'm not going to offer you tea," he told her.

"That's all right. It's started to rain again." She took off her bonnet and warned Oakes. "You should move over. I might shake myself like a wet dog." She pulled and tugged at her skirt. "Men," she said. "Women. I wish I could wear trousers and a coat like you two ruffians, instead of crinoline and wool. General, if you're going to ply me with brandy you'll have to pour more than that in the glass."

"Keach is sick," Oakes said.

"Of course, he is."

"Pneumonia," Sharpe said. "We've sent him to Charing Cross Hospital."

Maggie shuddered and looked at the spits of flame in the coal fire. "I'm not going to any hospital again, ever." She turned her gaze briefly to Oakes. "Ever."

Always efficient, never wasting a moment, the Pundit had been reading before they came in. Often it was poetry. Tonight... Oakes squinted at the book's spine.

"Johnson," Sharpe said. "*Lives of the Poets*. The ambassador said he'd been reading Milton and his squirt of a son confessed he'd never finished reading *Paradise Lost*."

"I stand amazed," Maggie Lawton murmured. "Something Henry Adams hasn't read."

"So I was looking it up in Johnson. He says, 'No man ever wished the poem longer.'"

This, Oakes recognized, was a habit Sharpe had picked up from Grant, who always began a meeting with a minute or two of informal chatter while he studied the faces in front of him. Sharpe's hero—What was Colonel Lyman's famous description of him over lunch one day? "Grant habitually wears an expression as if he had determined to drive his head through a brick wall." If there had been a brick wall handy, Sharpe would have tried the same thing.

"General." Maggie Lawton shifted impatiently. "Get to the point."

"Well, I've written Seward that I can find nothing culpatory about Benjamin." He looked at Oakes. "I still think he knew what was coming, I think he knew exactly what Booth was going to do."

"General."

Sharpe sighed. "In any case, that said, and Sarah Slater a dead end, I've now turned my attention to William Lindsay."

"Another little squirt," Maggie said. William Lindsay was a prominent English ship owner and Member of Parliament. In the early days of the war, a self-appointed diplomatic agent, he had shuttled back and forth between Paris and London, trying to persuade France to recognize the Confederacy. When that failed, he introduced resolutions of recognition repeatedly in the House of Commons, never quite mentioning that he himself was deeply involved in speculative purchases of Confederate bonds.

"So, I plan to devote two more days to Lindsay and also to the Reverend Kensey Johns Stewart," Sharpe said, "and then, with or without Sergeant Keach, we leave for the Continent."

"The many-named Reverend Stewart left London," Maggie Lawton said, "in 1864. He's not here. He went to Richmond, then Toronto, then came back to Richmond for the end."

As always, Sharpe disliked being told things he already knew. He drummed his fingers on the little table beside the fireplace. "Yes, and he revised the Book of Common Prayer for Confederate services, so as to include a blessing on the institution of slavery, and in a fit of godliness he objected to Doctor Blackburn's plan to spread yellow fever in Washington. I read the files, too, Miss Lawton."

Unabashed, Maggie grinned and poured herself more brandy.

"Stewart also became involved in the earliest scheme to abduct the President. He talked openly about it here. I have him in my notes." He started to thumb through a pocket notebook.

Oakes stood up and walked to the window. Sharpe had been given a suite of rooms on the second floor of the ambassador's residence, looking down on Upper Portland Street. Oakes pushed one corner of the heavy curtain aside and listened to rain hammer loudly on the eaves, enough like musket fire to make him wince.

"I want you and Captain Oakes over there—Quint, come back here where I can see you—I want the two of you to go to the last three banks on Keach's list. He left a good memorandum. Quint, you've already seen one bank for him."

"Go together?" Maggie's grin had vanished. She shook her wet red hair from side to side. "I would much prefer to go alone. The Captain can keep chasing Sarah Slater."

Sharpe shifted his gaze and stared at Oakes. "Pollacky thinks Sarah Slater has left London," he said slowly, "and so do I."

"That's just a guess," Maggie said.

Sharpe said nothing.

"Well, there's still," Oakes said, running through his mental file of names, "Sir William Gregory." Gregory had been a loud-mouthed, largely ineffective pro- Southern Member of Parliament. No one, British or American, had ever taken him seriously.

Sharpe had stopped drumming his fingers and, which was worse, had begun slowly to tap the table with one finger only. "Were my instructions unclear somehow, Mister Oakes? Miss Lawton? Were they too long and complex for your attention?"

"No man ever wished them longer," Maggie said, but the witticism fell flat.

"Is there some personal tension I should be aware of?"

"No, sir," Oakes said.

"Then on your way out, take those folders on the chair by the door and start first thing in the morning. Moran is going to make our travel arrangements. This is Tuesday. I want to leave for Rome on Friday."

Sharpe rose and watched as they gathered their coats and hats and went to the door. As soon as Maggie had stepped through it, he called Oakes back.

"Quintus." He stopped. "Quintus. Can you be kinder to her?"

"Sir?"

"Maggie. I value her. You should too. As for your pursuit of Sarah Slater—do you remember the story of Achilles and Penthesilea?"

"No, sir."

"Look it up. It's in Smyrnaeus. He nodded once and turned his back and walked away, toward the fireplace.

15

COUTTS & COMPANY—FOUNDED IN 1692—was one of the oldest banks in England, admired and celebrated across the Empire for its untold wealth and its Olympian arrogance toward one and all. From the cultivated disdain of the doorman, to the high-collared rudeness of the Gentleman's Assistant, to the Foreign Transactions Department, every gesture, every curl of the lip was calculated to impress upon unimpressive Americans that British discretion, not to say snobbery, ruled out the very possibility of discussing any client or former client, however disreputable, with mere renegade colonials.

But Sharpe had supplied Oakes and Maggie Lawton not only with official recommendations from Ambassador Adams and Secretary Stanton, but also with a personal letter from Seward, who, in the small, linked world of speculators and statesmen, on an ante-bellum English holiday in 1859 had actually dined several times with the present Director of Coutts & Company. So it happened that at half past two the next afternoon they were ceremoniously ushered into the office of the great man himself, where they found him rising from behind an enormous and magnificent oak desk—once the personal property, they were quickly to learn, of Admiral Lord Horatio Nelson himself. Sir Frederick Cridland was a taller, unsmiling version of Benjamin Moran, equally bald and egg-shaped, equally pasty-white in color, but dressed far less formally in a green tweed jacket and comfortable-looking old brown trousers.

"I didn't know you wanted to bring your wife, Mister Oakes," Sir Frederick said, shaking his hand and looking aside toward Maggie.

"Miss Margaret Lawton," Maggie said. She extended her hand to the startled banker. "I'm nobody's wife. I'm one of Mister Seward's investigators."

Sir Frederick had not achieved his high rank by doing business with forward-pushing, red-haired, young American women. Cautiously, as if testing a bath, he extended two fingers to Maggie. "I was going to propose coffee," he said.

"I like tea." Maggie sat down uninvited in one of the visitor's chairs in front of the enormous desk.

Sir Frederick decided to be amused. "Then tea it is, my lady." He nodded to the assistant (male) hovering at the door and with an amiable nod took one of the other chairs. There followed then several Sharpe-like minutes of exploratory chat—inquiries after poor Seward's health, comparisons of their two desks—a tour of several of the bullet holes and sword cuts on his own desk, which had seen service on the *HMS Victory* at Trafalgar, where regrettably Lord Nelson had been mortally struck down. Finally, with tea, coffee, and a very meager plate of chocolate-coated biscuits before them, he brought out Seward's letter to read again.

"Well." He placed a modest gold repeater watch beside the biscuit plate. "I can give you a bit of time, for Secretary Seward's sake. Say, twenty minutes."

They needed half that. Sir Frederick knew very little about Confederate finances. True to the Banker's Credo, in fact—"Give Nothing Away"—he knew very little about anything. Yes, Coutts & Company had underwritten some of the bond sales for the London Confederate Bank, while it was in existence. But Sir Frederick left such things to subordinates. He himself was not personally acquainted with any Confederate sympathizers at all. He had scarcely even *seen* a Rebel. The one exception was a fellow helping manage the London Confederate Bank for a time, John Slidell, who had even been proposed for the Athenaeum Club. He thought Slidell extremely able—a little elderly, but tall, well-built, rather *feline* in manner. His French was excellent, as was his taste in wine.

"He's in France now," Maggie said.

Sir Frederick looked down at his watch. "Paris, yes. He's written me once or twice. An excellent salesman, you know. He even persuaded me to invest some of my own money in Confederate bonds, not the bank's money."

"Worthless now," Maggie said with a touch of disdain.

"*Actually*," Sir Frederick shook his head, pleased to correct her. "Actually, Miss Lawton, some of them are still quite valuable. The bonds were backed by Confederate cotton, which was stored all over the South in warehouses. Your pyrophilic General Sherman burned a great many things, but enough of those warehouses survived to repay some of the bondholders. It depends on what bonds you bought." The banker's smile widened. "I bought rather good ones, from Arkansas."

"We're particularly interested," Oakes said, "to learn about your bank's Canadian transactions during the war."

Sir Frederick glanced again at Seward's letter. "Yes, I can see that you might be."

"Coutts & Company did a great deal of business with the Ontario Bank."

"Did we?"

"Over a short period of time the assassin Wilkes Booth deposited about twelve thousand dollars in the Ontario Bank, in various sums. I have the details here." Oakes nudged a large brown envelope across the table, toward the biscuits. "That money was highly instrumental in supporting his plot. We found Ontario Bank receipts in his hotel room, but we don't know where the money came from. If it came from you…"

With one delicate finger Sir Frederick nudged the envelope back toward Oakes. "I direct the Bank, Mister Oakes. But I don't involve myself in details of that kind."

The gold watch ticked loudly. Oakes folded his arms across his chest. Crookeder than cat shit. "Secretary Seward will be delighted to hear how much you could help," he said, and pushed back his chair.

Sir Frederick sighed. "I suppose I could ask our Mister O'Beare to look into those particular transactions." He rose and gave an unmistakable nod of dismissal to each of them. "If you come back at this time tomorrow, you can speak with him."

"Did you," Maggie said, turning back at the door, "have occasion to meet with a young American woman named Sarah Slater—in connection with all this?"

Sir Frederick had already taken up his position behind the nautical desk. He cocked his head in what seemed to be genuine puzzlement. "My dear lady, I meet so few young American women. I find them exhausting." He looked down and turned over a paper. "And charming, of course," he added, without looking up.

* * *

When they returned to the Embassy to report, Benjamin Moran was standing in the doorway holding a small white envelope and looking with obvious distaste down Great Portland Street.

"A man left this for you, Captain Oakes." He gave one of his expressive sniffs and held out the envelope. "That man. You just missed him."

Oakes turned to stare, but in the fading afternoon light he could see only the usual pell-mell of pedestrians, bulky and brown as bears in their thick coats. Then at the far corner he saw a heavy-set man with a salt-and-pepper beard turn and stare at him. Oakes slapped the envelope gently against his palm, Moran pulled open the door, and all three of them stepped inside.

"I'll find the General," Maggie said. She nodded at Henry Adams, who had just materialized through a doorway on the left and passed through toward the staircase.

"Hello, Moran," Adams said. "Quintus, what do you have there, a pretty billet-doux?"

Moran murmured something chilly and correct to the ambassador's son and followed Maggie toward the staircase.

"Does the Embassy have any kind of library, Henry?"

"Scraps, law books, what do you need?"

"Smyrnaeus. The General made one of his polymath allusions last night. I didn't know what he was talking about. I think it's Greek."

Adams laughed his unpleasant laugh. "Author of the 'Posthomerica,' a fourth-century continuation of the *Iliad*. Greek indeed, but oddly enough, his first name was Roman— 'Quintus,' like yours. I see our alma mater left a few gaps in your education, Cousin."

"Go to hell, Henry."

"The best part concerns Achilles. I assume that's what our warrior scholar was referring to." Oakes said nothing, which Adams took as an invitation to continue. "In the Trojan War, Achilles hunts down Penthesilea, the queen of the Amazons. When he finds her, he kills her, but then as she lies dying on the battlefield poor dumb Achilles falls desperately in love with her."

Oakes looked down at the envelope in his hand.

"I could probably find a copy somewhere, but I don't think your Greek would be up to it."

Oakes opened the envelope and read the small, precise, unsigned note on the card inside. *Cherchez-moi à l'entrée nord de l'Exposition.*

"The idea," Adams said, "the irony, is that he kills what he loves. Or else"—another laugh—"loves what he kills."

16

OAKES HAD JOINED SHARPE'S BUREAU of Military Information in May 1863, some six weeks before Gettysburg. Before that he had served with George Meade's grandly titled "Military Engineering Cartographers"—in plain English, he drew maps. This strange assignment was apparently due to the fact that, at enlistment, he had rashly admitted to studying two months in 1858 at the Ecole des Beaux Arts in Paris.

Drawing maps, he found out, was terrifying work.

That connoisseur of irony Henry Adams would surely have pointed out the joke that, although the first American President had been a celebrated land surveyor and although the Mason-Dixon line had been laid out by 1767, in the middle of the nineteenth century vast tracts of Washington's native Virginia still remained unmapped.

The first problem facing the Army of the Potomac, then, was usually just to know where it was. Those maps of Virginia that did exist were often wildly inaccurate—in the earliest campaigns, battalions were known to march miles past their rendezvous points, passing each other blindly in the night. Roads and bridges seemed to melt away or slide off the edge of the paper. Whole counties could jump fifty miles. Lee's men were on home ground. But the Union troops were literally marching into uncharted territory.

To remedy this, to give eyes to the army, Meade's military cartographers advanced well ahead of the regular formations, alongside the scouts and skirmishers, and tried to map out the terrain on the fly. They took directions from different surveying points and landmarks and calculated distances by the pacing of their horses. Crouching in the saddle, head down drawing on a tablet, paused on a ridge to do mental geometry, they made perfect targets for the rebel sharpshooters lying in wait just ahead. In the evening, those topographers who had made it unscathed through the day would assemble in camp and compose little maps by firelight. If the next day was sunny, they had photographs taken of the sketches and sent them on to the battalion commanders.

Photography, Oakes thought. Photography. Ingersol and O'Sullivan. What were they doing now, three thousand miles away in New York City? Poring over their equipment lists maybe, readying themselves for their own long-planned, much-dreamed-about march west into the uncharted virgin Wind River range in the territory of Wyoming—"Pursuing the One Great Object of My Desire," as O'Sullivan sometimes crooned while he shuffled about in his darkroom, a phrase he had picked up from an old dance hall song.

It was well past ten o'clock in London, whatever time it was in New York. A chilly mist, not yet thick enough to be called fog, had settled into the city. In two straight rows down Regent Street, delicate gas flares hung in the lamps overhead, yellow stars with the shivers. Up and down the street, late-hour carriages and omnibuses shouldered each other aside like shadowy boats on the river Styx. The sidewalks were thick with pedestrians, cowled, capped, top-hatted, black-bonneted. Oakes's pulse beat in his ears like a drum, his face burned.

He was pursuing the One Great Object of his Desire, and his thoughts were scattering like ants.

No one had noticed him leave the Embassy, but he stopped fitfully anyway, every block or so, and turned around to see who was behind him. The pavement smelled of horse dung and wet straw. The street lamps created velvety pockets of darkness where the damp, trash-littered alleys began. He crossed over to Warwick Street. There was only one "Exposition" that he knew of in London, the only place she could have meant—the "Exposition de Paris," a disreputable gallery of supposedly French erotic paintings and etchings a few blocks from the Haymarket, a place of Hogarthian dissolution that was popularly known, when he lived in London, as "Hell Corner." Presumably there were north and south entrances.

Oakes stopped and looked at his watch. He would go and wait for an hour, that was all. He was only a few blocks from it now, and the rigid gray respectability of Great Portland Street had started to give way to the bargain stalls and public houses and raucous street life he remembered very well from one or two wide-eyed expeditions in the company of his indulgent London cousin. On the corner two women with brandy-sparkling eyes stood arm in arm against a doorway.

"Feel my cunt for a shilling," one of them said matter-of-factly.

Oakes smiled and passed by. Ahead he could hear music, some kind of band. In the army camps there were always boys selling newspapers and magazines and, if you asked for them, flimsy little paperbound books called "Barracks Favourites," which were bawdy novels, usually said to be "translated faithfully from the French." You could also buy photographs of nude women, twelve by fifteen-inch pictures that sold for $1.20 a dozen. The interesting thing, he remembered—the Argyll Rooms came into sight, blazing red and white under some kind of torchlight illumination—the interesting thing was that the plain nude pictures were always of white women standing or lying down alone, posed. If you wanted sexual action in your photographs, those featured only black or Indian women.

He was on Windmill Street now. Next to the Argyll Rooms there was a glass-fronted gin shop and on the sidewalk a five-man brass band was blaring away. Flickering in and out of the yellow streetlamps he could see flashing satins, painted cheeks, two or three drunken couples, more lounging women along the sidewalks and storefronts—the Haymarket was a place of "profound indecency," his London cousin had said, not without a touch of pride.

Oakes pushed aside a mumbling derelict reeking of whiskey and tobacco and took up a position just to the left of the gas-lit doorway whose faded placards announced a "Special Admission Tonight Only—Two Shillings" to the "World Famous Exposition de Paris." The north side.

He would stay one hour, he told himself. Without a doubt the salt-and-pepper beard man was somewhere nearby, as a sentry. In a minute or two she would appear. His hands tingled from the memory of her touch, the curve of her hip in his palm, the lift of her pale white face toward him.

Then he took a deep breath. In Sharpe's war you developed a sixth sense for when you were being watched, when eyes were turned toward you. Oakes stepped back from the lamppost and looked across the street and saw Maggie Lawton and Isaac Pollacky staring back at him.

17

POLLACKY CROSSED THE BUSY STREET with all the aplomb of a native Londoner and ex-policeman. He stared down an impatient hackney driver, guided Maggie Lawton around an impressive mound of what young Mr. Adams liked to call "horse evidence," and hopped up, not quite scowling, onto the sidewalk next to Oakes.

"Captain, sir." He touched one finger to his inevitable shapeless green hat. "Not a good place for a gentleman like yourself, sir."

"What is the gentleman *doing* here?" Maggie Lawton said between her teeth. She turned and inspected the nearest poster on the wall. "Is 'callipygian' the gentleman's preferred female type?"

The same mumbling derelict pushed forward again, out of the lowering gray fog, then stopped when he saw Pollacky's glare. Two bright red cheeks leaned out of the Paris Exposition *guichet* to watch.

"Better to go back to the Embassy, sir."

Oakes realized that he had his fists clenched. His face was burning. "I can take care of myself perfectly well, Pollacky. I came through a war perfectly well."

The brass band in front of the gin shop had caught sight of them and now perversely began to push along the sidewalk toward them.

"Not safe for the lady, though, sir, and *she* says she's not going back unless you do." Pollacky tilted his head in Maggie's direction.

"You *cannot,*" Maggie said, "go off on your own like this. Is it that woman? I should tell Sharpe."

The band was playing something called "Billy Barlow," which Oakes recognized from misspent nights in New York.

"Mister Henry Adams told us where you were going, sir. Read your note over your shoulder, I should think. I couldn't let the lady come off by herself."

Oakes said nothing.

"He can read the print off the page, that Mister Adams," Pollacky said.

Oakes squinted at his watch. If she were nearby, she wouldn't be coming now. With those two in front of him, she wouldn't be coming at all. He was furious at being followed, furious at being caught out. He looked hard at Maggie Lawton. "Do not tell Sharpe," he said with such ferocity that she actually blinked and took a step back.

"I wish I knew what you want," she said in a whisper, and the band marched out of the fog, and all three of them turned to go.

Two-thirty the next afternoon found them back on The Strand in the labyrinthine offices of Coutts & Company, following Sir Frederick Cridland's handpicked emissary, the Second Assistant Director of Foreign Transactions.

"Legare O'Beare," he said with a bow.

"You must be Irish," Maggie said. It was the first thing Oakes had heard her say all day.

"A good guess, yes indeed, but let me assure you, it's not an Irish name." Legare O'Beare chuckled softly at the thought, although given his considerable height and girth it came out more as rumble than laugh. He turned and led them with quick, shambling steps down a grimy, poorly lit corridor, painted once upon a time, Oakes guessed, a pleasant light green, now as faded and cheerless as everything else backstage in the bank.

"It's French, in fact," O'Beare explained. "Some of the ancestors paddled across the Channel with William in 1066"—he glanced in a friendly way over his shoulder. "They still teach you all about that, don't they, Miss Lawton? Back in what my old father always calls 'the Colonies.'"

"The Colonies are very up-to-date."

"D'Aubert is what it was. Mangled by the alien tongue to O'Beare. People do say I look like a bear. Here we are."

O'Beare's office had a floor-to-ceiling window that looked down on a mews. One story below Quint could see a pair of grooms brushing a carriage horse, somebody else going into the stables. O'Beare cracked open a tiny side window and let in a stream of frigid late March air. "Spring," he said happily.

Oakes looked about for chair and a desk and saw only a "highboy" accountant's table with a slanted top, one cracked leather batwing chair, a great jumble of cardboard letterboxes, and two walls completely lined with black and brown account books.

"I write standing up, you see." O'Beare made a vague gesture of apology at the highboy table. "No desk. Easier on the back. The lady can take the chair, of course. Mister Oakes, you and I will have to be like the rugged pioneers and stand. You can push some of those ledgers aside and lean on the wall if you like. I often lean on the wall to think."

The faint pockmarks on Maggie Lawton's cheek were bright with anger, and her mouth had contracted into a steady scowl. "He likes to stand beside walls," she said. "Inside or outside."

"Now, Sir Frederick said you drank tea, Miss, so I've rung for a dish of the same."

Oakes looked around to see how he had rung for anything. At the same moment there was a rap on the door and then the usual five minutes of baroque English afternoon tea arrangements, complicated by the need to bring in a small table for the lady's cup and another for the teapot itself and its entourage of sugar bowl, spare cups, cow creamer, biscuit plate, and red quilted cozy. When the office boy/cup-bearer had backed solemnly out of the room, O'Beare took a great gulp from his own cup and announced with great satisfaction, "Tea."

"Ass," Maggie said under her breath.

"Sir Frederick was rather bothered by your being a woman, Miss Lawton." He took another ursine-like swallow. "I'm not, of course. My wife is rather outspoken on the Woman Question, so I'm accustomed to all that."

"The 'Woman Question?'" Maggie asked in what Oakes heard as a menacing tone.

"The Vote. Female Suffrage. Equality and such. No, I'm more intrigued by the whole idea of your job, you two. Here you are following up—What is it? Two years later?—still following the trail of those wretched assassins. You hanged four people, but I saw Mister Seward's letter—there *had* to be others, I quite agree. And now you've traced some of them to London and you think we may have done—*inadvertently* done—business with them."

"In Canada." Oakes had a duplicate set of notes and reached in his coat pocket for them. "In Montreal, Booth deposited cash and a check in the Ontario Bank on October twenty-seventh, 1864. The cash was in Canadian bank notes. The check was for two hundred and fifty-five dollars. It was endorsed by a Confederate broker here in London named Simon Davis. The check was drawn on Coutts & Company. But we don't know where he got *his* money."

O'Beare nodded and rapped his knuckles on his cluttered writing table.

"I've read the details. I stayed on last night to look into our books. It doesn't appear this Simon Davis had an account with us. Evidently, he bought a banker's check from us, in dollars, and paid for it, as our French friends would say, *en person*, either in sterling or in gold. That's not specified in the slip. It wouldn't be for such a small sum."

"One month later Booth deposited three hundred dollars in gold, either gold coins or a bar," Oakes said. "We don't know the origin of that either."

"Wouldn't tell you anything in Canada, would they?" O'Beare was amused. "This Booth was a fascinating *personage*, you know, at least to us over here. My old father was quite the traveler and actually saw him act once in New York. *Richard III*, I think. Got so carried away in a sword fight that he drove the other fellow off the stage and into the wings. Had a weakness for the bottle, though. I read somewhere that once in Hamlet he was so drunk that he suddenly pushed Ophelia over on her bottom and climbed up a ladder to the crossbars and started crowing like a rooster. Probably because the ghost leaves at the 'crowing of the cock,' don't you think?"

"Spare us your English charm, Mister O'Beare," Maggie Lawton said. "That money was used to finance Confederate covert operations, including the assassination of the President. We want to know where Simon Davis got it."

Oakes put out an arm to calm her, but she pushed it away.

O'Beare looked quizzically at one, then the other. "Well, I can't say, Miss Lawton. We don't have any records for it."

"You're supposed to keep records of all foreign transactions with gold, in whatever form. That's what your office does, yes? You should know where Booth got his gold."

O'Beare shook his head. "Not quite exactly, Miss."

"*Men.*" Maggie stood up abruptly, brushing the tea things aside with her skirt and knocking over her cup. "*Bankers.* These people are useless, Mister Oakes. I'm leaving." When she reached the door, she turned back, face blazing, eyes damp. "Stay and ask him about Sarah Slater, why don't you?" She looked hard at Oakes. "That's his 'Woman Question.'"

She stepped into the corridor and closed the door with force enough to rattle the account books on the shelves.

For a long moment neither man spoke. Then O'Beare gave a little dying sigh that was almost a smile. "She must be the one who's Irish," he said. "Redheaded ladies—my old father always warned me about them. I keep a small bottle of brandy in this drawer, Mister Oakes. A dram or two?"

He fished out a decanter and two fairly clean snifters from the highboy drawer, then said in an offhand way, "I did in fact see an American woman named Sarah Slater, you know. I was going to get around to her."

Oakes stopped the glass halfway to his mouth.

"Just two days ago. No idea she was of interest to you, of course."

Oakes found his voice. "What did she want?"

"Beautiful woman," O'Beare said. "Something about her, you know. She had an unusual conversion request, so the tellers sent her upstairs here to me. Sat in that very chair."

Automatically Oakes looked over at the chair vacated by Maggie Lawton. Her spilled teacup was on its side, brown tea was still running over the saucer and onto the table. "Conversion request?"

"She had American gold to exchange, a great deal of it."

Oakes turned slowly back to him.

"She's quite a rich person now, you see."

PART THREE

Rome

April 1867

1

JOHN SURRATT HAD LEFT LONDON in mid–September, 1865. According to Stanton's earlier investigators he took a train from London to Southampton, a boat from there to Calais, and after that...

After that, no one could be sure.

A hotel in Paris reported his passport on September 17, but in a city of so many tourists and travelers, no one took notice. Twelve days later, a hotel in Marseilles also reported his presence, a matter of indifference to the local gendarmerie, who had yet to receive word that the United States government had declared Surratt a dangerous fugitive. Not long after that the Sixth Conspirator entered Civitavecchia, the ancient port on the Tyrrhenian Sea that served central Italy as its principal commercial entrance. Here he lingered for some days, hidden and housed by sympathetic priests. Then as if drawn by a magnet, he turned north toward Rome.

Sharpe intended to follow the same route. On Friday morning, April 3, he led Maggie Lawton and Oakes down the southernmost platform of the Ludgate Hill Station and they climbed aboard a first-class carriage on the 7:25 a.m. train for Dover. There they transferred to the Great Southeast Steamship Company and bounced and wallowed their way across a gray, windy, and dyspeptic Channel to Calais.

A French express train was scheduled to bring them into Paris at about seven o'clock that evening. Oakes had assumed that they would stop for several days in Paris, and he was eager to leave the gloomy pretensions of London and find himself again in the one city in the world he truly loved. Sharpe had already made a list of French Confederate sympathizers to interview, including—a prospect that fascinated Oakes—Judah Benjamin's estranged wife Natalie. Here too they would wait for the ailing Keach to stagger out of his London sickbed and join them for a frontal assault on certain unsavory French banks. But at the last moment Seward had instructed Sharpe to proceed directly to Rome, bypassing Paris for the moment. So from the newly constructed Gare du Nord the party grabbed two taxi carriages, one for the passengers, one for their baggage, and hurried over the Seine to the Gare de Lyon, where at 9:50 p.m. they boarded yet another train and set off at eighteen miles an hour along a standard gauge mainland route that would, some twenty hours later, terminate in what Oakes recalled as the truly squalid Mediterranean port city of Marseilles.

At least he could sleep. A soldier can sleep anywhere, a soldier is a professional sleeper. He laid his cheek against the cold glass of the train window and dreamed of swaying wagons over Wyoming trails, mountain snowbursts like cotton smoke, range after range of white wind and gray stone.

"Look alive, Captain!"

Oakes blinked and rubbed his cheek and half slipped his watch from his pocket. Sharpe, of course. Sharpe was a notoriously early riser—from the corner of his eye, Oakes could see a pinkish blue dawn rolling past the train window—and like all such people Sharpe thought the world should wake up when he did.

"This is General Parke," Sharpe said. On the opposite bench Maggie Lawton was already bright-eyed and awake. Dimly, Oakes remembered that she had slept in a separate passenger compartment reserved for "Dames."

"John Parke." Sharpe nodded to the portly bald man about his own age, whose wolfish yellow teeth were grinning around a black, foul-smelling cigar and whose eyes were wide with good humor. "You remember him."

"Gettysburg." Oakes sat up and ran one hand through his hair. "The Gettysburg conference."

"Maggie and I ran into him at breakfast. I'm going to sit in his compartment for a while and fight the war all over again."

"Let me know how it turns out this time."

Sharpe snorted, Parke laughed, and the two of them disappeared down the tilting corridor.

"Pair of old coyotes," Oakes muttered and covered a yawn with one hand.

Maggie reached into her snap-bag and extracted a paper sack stuffed with pieces of buttered baguette. "You were having bad dreams." From somewhere else in her traveling equipment she produced a pasteboard tray that contained two waxed paper cups. "Very ingenious," she said. "The dining carriage has these cups to hold coffee. It gets cold very fast, though."

Oakes murmured his thanks and sipped the lukewarm coffee. In the Gare de Lyon, he had found time to have coffee at the station restaurant—strong, black, genuine Parisian nectar, and the bitter taste had sent his taste buds dancing and his mind racing about in search of memories.

"The General says you used to write poetry." Maggie was sipping her own coffee and looking casually out the window at the green and brown fields unscrolling beside the train. Oakes wondered how she managed to look so fresh and *soignée*—he was already thinking in French again—after a day and a night of travel. She frowned at the window. "He said it wasn't very good."

Oakes laughed. You didn't go to George Sharpe for sugar coating. "I did, before the war. I showed some poems to my father once, and he said, 'You don't do much of this, I hope.'"

"Did you write poetry for Sarah Slater?"

He lifted his head in surprise.

"You did," Maggie said, a statement, not a question.

In Marseilles they had their choice of two private French shipping lines that ran weekly packet boats to central Italy, but the next departure was at least four days away and Sharpe was impatient.

The French government, he learned, occasionally dispatched a naval steamer to Messina, Sicily, with a mid-voyage stop at Civitavecchia, and happily one was due to lift anchor the very next morning. At once, armed with his letters from Seward, his excellent French, and his unmistakable military bearing, Sharpe persuaded—or bullied—the local French naval commandant into taking them aboard as "diplomatic personnel." Accordingly, fourteen hours later they climbed aboard a glistening white modern French gunboat and riding the four-a.m. tide, turned their faces eastward, toward the great boot of Italy.

Just before they had boarded the gunboat, the local American consul seeing them off had handed Sharpe a courier pouch from Seward. It was marked "Urgent and Personal," and when Sharpe opened it over his coffee in the gunboat galley, it turned out to contain a copy of the deposition of one Dr. Lewis McMillen, formerly ship's physician aboard the Canadian steamship *RMS Peruvian*. The very ship, Sharpe reminded Oakes, that John Surratt had taken from Quebec to Liverpool in September 1865.

And just as in Montreal, when he was supposedly in hiding, on board the *Peruvian* Surratt had found it impossible to keep from talking about his notoriety. His garrulousness was helped along by alcohol—"three half tumblers of brandy in twenty minutes was normal for him," McMillen wrote with a physician's audible disapproval. Surratt proudly confessed to being part of Booth's original conspiracy and he readily confided to one and all that British Confederate sympathizers would be waiting for him at the docks in Liverpool, with money and papers, to help push him along toward the Continent and ultimate freedom.

McMillen's testimony, however, had somehow been suppressed or misplaced or forgotten in Canada, and it had only reached Seward's desk a few weeks ago—"Priests," Sharpe growled when he read this part aloud to Oakes, "you can bet some god-fearing, slavery-loving meddling priest had his thumb on it." In any case the belated report was of no particular value, since it simply confirmed what Seward and Stanton already knew. Much more important, Seward wrote, would be the testimony of one Henri de Beaumont Sainte Marie, an American turncoat and scoundrel who was waiting to meet with them in the capital of all meddling priests, the walled enclave of the Holy See in Rome.

"The Vatican," Sharpe explained unnecessarily. "The meddling Pope himself."

At half past four on the afternoon of Monday, April 6, some sixty or more hours since they had left London, Oakes stood on the foredeck of the French gunboat and watched a brown, foggy landscape grip the water and begin to lift itself over the horizon like a swimmer coming out of the sea.

"That fog looks like smoke, don't it?" General Parke said. "Cannon smoke, gun smoke. Reminds me of Richmond when I came up the James with Lincoln, the day Richmond fell."

"They're fighting all over Italy," Oakes said, "but that's just fog."

"Garibaldi," Parke said. "They keep beating him down, but the son of a bitch won't quit. He'll take Rome yet. He's like Grant was. You know Lincoln offered him a place in our army, at the start? Major General Garibaldi, he would have been."

"What happened?"

"Garibaldi said he'd only come if Lincoln made him a Lieutenant General and commander of all the Union armies. A little too much to swallow. You were in Richmond, Captain?"

Oakes nodded and squinted at the fog; it was just fog.

"I saw Lincoln walking down the main street with his little boy," Parke said, and Oakes nodded again because he remembered Richmond very well. Sharpe had reminded him of it in Washington City. So had Thomas Chester Morris in Liverpool.

"Memorable scene," Parke said. "All that smoke and ruined buildings and little fires burning in the windows everywhere and that tall, slow Lincoln with a wondering look on his face as he took it all in, what he'd finally done. I saw an old black man bust out of the smoke and walk right up to him, and they both stopped and stared at each other. Then the nigger took off his hat, and Lincoln did the same thing and bowed to him and walked on. Bowed to a nigger. That's why I stuck with him. I wrote my wife I always knew he was abolitionist at heart. You were abolitionist, son?"

Oakes nodded a third time. You couldn't very well be a New Englander and be anything else, though to his secret shame he had never been vocal about it before the war.

"My father," Parke said, "my father—look at that, I see buildings now, a pilot boat coming out—he was *profoundly* abolitionist. He once got in a big debate with some Secesher at a town hall in Elmira. 'Read the Bible!' the Secesher said. 'Slavery is a divine institution!' Quick as that, my father shot back, 'So is Hell!'"

He was still chuckling at his joke when Sharpe and Maggie Lawton came up from below deck. "Talking about Lincoln with your officer here," he told Sharpe. Then he leaned forward and gripped Maggie by the arm. "Listen here, young lady. I'm going on to Rome, just like you. And if you find any of those people that financed Booth, I don't care who they are, and Sharpe won't take 'em down and wring their necks, you call me."

The pilot boat was thumping over the water toward them, not a hundred yards away. The French sailors were suddenly, noisily swarming on deck, hauling in ropes, swiveling wheels and levers, gently slowing the gunboat for the pilot to board. But Parke was not a man to let his point get lost. "He's a fine man, our George Sharpe is, but he's too judicious, too rational sometimes, if you see what I mean. He can be cool and cold, when the way forward is passionate and hot." He dropped her arm and grinned at Sharpe. "Wring their necks," he said.

2

Since Imperial times, Civitavecchia—"ancient city"—had served Rome, some forty miles to the northeast, as its major seaport. The nearby town of Ostia, where the Tiber emptied into the ocean, would have appeared a more logical choice. But the mouth of the Tiber was chronically choked with ship-blocking sediment and silt, while Civitavecchia's deep harbor was kept clear and clean by a long string of protective moles. Roman generals, of course, had understood its advantages perfectly. The first great structure Oakes observed as the gunboat glided into port was a very tall, very square Roman citadel on the topmost hill, towering over their masts, bristling with cannons.

This was the Forte Michelangelo. But despite the quintessentially Italian name, it was the French flag that hung over its main gate and French soldiers who could be seen pacing along its ramparts. Napoleon III had recently stationed them there, Sharpe said in his best professorial voice, to defend his extensive Italian interests, i.e., his money and his real estate. Farther north, other French detachments were fighting for these same noble interests in a crazy quilt of alliances and misalliances, sometimes with Garibaldi's rebels, sometimes with the Papal States or the

Kingdom of Two Sicilies, sometimes all against all. But slowly and inevitably, the professorial voice predicted, the fighting would sort itself out, Italy would all be transformed into one unified country, just as Prussia would be. Meanwhile…

Meanwhile, Oakes looked about curiously at the soldiers swarming the streets and quays of the port. In keeping with the topsy-turvey logic of the situation, these were neither French nor Italian troops. Instead, they wore the beehive insignia of the Pope and therefore served not the emperor Napoleon III, but the independent country of the Papal States, a long, rich swath of territory about the size of Connecticut and Massachusetts together. It stretched from the Tyrrhenian Sea to the Adriatic, and was sometimes called, with pious irony, "the patrimony of Saint Peter." These were, in other words, soldiers of the Catholic Church, and from the very first, their army was the refuge toward which the would-be assassin Surratt had fled.

Oakes's mind took a turn into the past.

As they climbed into a taxi carriage for the railway terminus, he looked back along the streets and for a moment, the red jackets and plumed blue caps wavered and wobbled in the fog and dissolved into the dust-stained blue coats and dark slouch hats of the Army of the Potomac. In the spring of 1864, he and Sharpe had stood by their tent and watched them march off toward what was about to become the Battle of the Wilderness.

In his mind's eye a kaleidoscope of images came tumbling back—knapsacks, tight gray blanket rolls, brown haversacks with the customary three days rations—endless columns of doomed young men winding down out of the open country toward an endless and almost impenetrable Virginia pine forest. Some irreverent private had hung a coffee pot on the end of his musket.

Somebody else had fit a frying pan on his head for a cap. Cavalry trotted by, riders almost obscured by bags of oats and the blankets piled on pommel and crupper. Artillery wagons, teams of sweating horses, bags of forage and oats lashed to the cannons. Later on, they would indicate makeshift graves with names scribbled on pieces of old cracker boxes—the Battle of the Wilderness would be the bloodiest three or four days of the war, until Cold Harbor.

By then, Oakes had seen enough of the war to know what was going to happen next. He remembered thinking how strange it would be if you knew beforehand who was going to survive the battle—if each man who was destined to die over the next few days wore a badge or ribbon on his coat, to mark him out. Maybe, even as you watched them march by, they would already begin to fade and dissolve from view, like ghosts.

Maggie Lawton cocked her head at him. "I fear our leader's going to start quoting Latin at us when we reach Rome," she said, "the way he kept declaiming poetry in London."

But Oakes said nothing and continued to watch the soldiers by the side of the road.

The Hotel de Londres stood at 15 Piazza di Spagna, directly opposite the Spanish Steps. The proprietor was a middle-aged Italian who had once served as an infantryman in the Papal Zouaves and who therefore entertained, Oakes thought, an exaggerated and unwholesome respect for high-ranking military officers, even American officers.

Naturally, he explained, with repeated bows and salutes, General Sharpe's party had the best rooms in the house. Each one boasted a private bath and a balcony overlooking the busy piazza. Each one had fruit and wine as a welcome gift, and for the lady, of course, a little basket of Florentine soaps. When they finished unpacking in their rooms, another military gesture awaited. This time it was an Englishman, former King's Guard Sergeant Matthew Coloris, who snapped to attention in the lobby and led them outside, where a four-seat, two-horse hackney cab and a driver with a bright red hat and scarf waited, ready to take them wherever in Rome the General ordered.

Sharpe consulted his watch and announced in fluent enough Italian—he had once lived six months in Rome—that they still had daylight enough to see a few sights. The driver lifted his hat and the cab bounced and rattled out of the piazza and into a labyrinth of brown and orange buildings.

A new kaleidoscope, this time of alleys to nowhere, pennants from windows, flags, Roman dogs, Roman cats, shoulders and legs and bouncing hats scattering as the hackney sped by. They flashed past fountains, churches, more churches, red and white striped awnings, terrace caffès, churches, yet more churches, and suddenly the cab wheeled neatly around a crowded omnibus and came to a stop beside the grimy church of Santa Maria Liberatrice. A few yards past its columns an assortment of beggars, guides for hire, and idle excavation wagons marked the entrance, twenty steps down into the past, to the rubble-strewn remains of the Roman Forum.

Sharpe had delivered the salutatory address at Rutgers in Latin. At Yale he had supplemented his legal studies with yet more Latin. He was no pedant like Henry Adams, but once down on the confused and overgrown paths, once strolling on the ancient Via Sacra toward the two-thousand-year-old ruins of the Rostra, the Pundit began to percolate ominously, as Quint thought, with Henry Adams-like pomp.

"This is the base of what was the central platform for public speakers."

He stopped and made an expansive gesture that took in a cleared space of pavement about twenty square yards. Weeds and grass grew ankle high between blocks of dusty pockmarked stone.

"*Rostrum*." Sharpe cleared his throat. "*Rostrum* meant a warship's ram, the plural is *rostra,* and at one time the platform had six of them. Cominius Auruncus captured them in the battle of Antium and brought them back as trophies. Now we call any speaker's platform a rostrum, of course. After he had him executed, Octavius had Cicero's hands nailed to one of the rostra and they stayed there for years."

"Why his hands?" Maggie asked.

"Because he wrote out his orations with his hands, the fourteen Phillipics against tyranny."

Off to one side, the guide they had hired was nodding vigorously. "Now that's the Palatine Hill over to your left," Sharpe said. "On the other side, that's the Capitoline Hill. The entire *Magnum Forum* was in this small dip between them. You stood here, and you faced the north side of the *comitium*, towards the Senate House where I'm pointing. This left plenty of room for the plebians to assemble and listen to your demagoging peroration while the Senators lined up on their own steps. Over there."

Somewhere in the overgrown jumble of marble ruins and trash and limestone fragments that was the modern Forum, Sharpe had picked up a long, oddly crooked stick. Now he pointed it toward what looked like a graveyard of chalky fragments and headless statues some fifty yards away, fenced off from the rest of the ruins by excavators' wooden fences. A few wandering tourists looked curiously in their direction.

"Julius Caesar was assassinated somewhere on the Senate floor just behind the fences. But right *here*"—he banged the stick on the stone floor. "*This* is where Marc Antony gave his speech against the traitor Brutus. This is where they burned Caesar's body afterwards. *Here!*" He banged the stick so hard against the pavement that it snapped in half and he tossed the pieces away. "Remind you of anything, Captain Oakes?"

"Caesar," the guide ventured, "very bad man."

Sharpe ignored him. "Caesar made the same mistake Lincoln did. You know what I mean, Captain. He was a fatalist. He dismissed his Praetorian Guard and walked to the Senate House alone. Just like Lincoln. Everybody told him not to go anywhere without a guard. *Bring some Pinkerton men, for God's sake.*"

"He had a guard," Oakes said, "at the theater."

"He had one half-drunk Metropolitan policeman, who came out with him from the Mansion, then wandered off somewhere for the rest of the night. The only guard outside Lincoln's box was his footman, a silly little man named Charles Forbes. Booth just nodded to him cool as could be and opened the door."

It was growing dim in the sunken Forum. The broken stones had begun to fade and dissolve in the late afternoon sun. I'm standing in the wastes of time, Oakes thought. All around lay the ruins of empire. Nearby, scrawny, yellow-eyed feral cats were emerging from crannies and weeds. There was a whispering sound that might have been rats, might have been wind.

"Booth just stuck his wretched face to the peephole in the door and then turned the knob and stepped inside."

Oakes looked away to his left. The huge outer walls of the Coliseum some quarter of a mile away rose crisp and bright in the late afternoon sunlight.

"He leaned in," Sharpe said in a voice so cold and matter-of-fact that Oakes shivered. "He leaned in about two feet behind the President. The Derringer bullet, which is the size of the tip of your little finger, Maggie, went in the left side of Lincoln's skull, kept going through the jelly of his brain, and lodged just behind his right eye." Sharpe stepped off the Rostra and rubbed his hands together as if for warmth. "There were a dozen men in the cabal that killed Caesar. Do you *really* think Booth acted alone?"

He walked briskly off toward an ivy-covered structure that bore a dirty white placard: "Arch of Fabius." Over his shoulder Sharpe said, "That short sword on the statue there was called a *gladius.* Gives us 'gladiator,' of course." He took two more steps and turned around. "Tomorrow we go to the Embassy and find out who helped that bastard Surratt escape."

Maggie Lawton had seen enough of the Forum and, as she muttered to Oakes, she'd heard enough lecturing, too. While there was still light she wanted to see the Coliseum. With a few words to the still preoccupied Sharpe, she and Oakes followed a winding path southward, crossed the crumbling foundation of what signs indicated had been Nero's Golden House, and, with no ceremony or fuss of any kind, passed through an iron-grilled gate into the largest amphitheater in the world.

The Forum was already half-plunged in twilight. But the Coliseum sat on much higher ground than the Forum did, and great dusty lanes of sunlight still filtered down from the west, through the topmost arched doors, and flooded the sandy elliptical arena on the bottom. There were more tourists walking about here than in the Forum, and the competing voices of guides and souvenir sellers set up a muted cacophony that made Oakes shudder.

In its glory days, he seemed to remember, the Coliseum held nearly eighty thousand spectators, as many as Robert E. Lee's whole army at Richmond. An imaginative visitor could hear their echo even now, see the decks and sails of the mock sea battle spectacles that entertained Nero, see the animal hunts, the lions, oxen, elephants, the oiled torsos of the doomed gladiators, the blood puddling thick on the sand. A sign in Italian and English announced that the Pope would begin his annual Good Friday procession from this very spot. But Oakes had shut down his imagination.

He heard his name and looked up.

Most women travelers on the Continent wore heavy dark woolen skirts and thick bodices with mutton-chop sleeves and a stiff white collar. They looked about as attractive as upholstered crows. Today Maggie Lawton wore a tan skirt of some linen-like material, a light green jacket with normal sleeves, and an open white collar. While Oakes had been glancing glumly around, she had climbed a dozen or more ranks of seats to get a better view, and now she was leaping from stone bench to bench like a red-headed gazelle, laughing and calling on Oakes to "shake a leg" and join her.

Suddenly exhilarated, he shouted, "Do you want me to recite some Latin poetry for you?"

"What I really want…" she said, but the rest of her sentence was lost in echoes.

3

THE CONFEDERATE GOVERNMENT of Jefferson Davis never minted any gold coins itself. During the whole life of the Confederacy, the only gold available in the South was either pre-war United States or Mexican coins or United States gold bullion—"ingots." In general, as Oakes well remembered, Union soldiers were paid, not in gold coins, but in Treasury Secretary Salmon P. Chase's "greenbacks," so called because one side of the paper bill was tinted green. Confederate troops were paid in their own version of a greenback, but of course by the end of the war those were utterly worthless. Oakes had a little box of them in his New York rooms as souvenirs.

According to Legare O'Beare in London, the U.S. coins in circulation in Richmond in 1865 would have been twenty dollar "double eagle" gold pieces. These were about an inch and a half in diameter and any large, loose sum of them would have been a very clumsy load for a young woman like the Confederate courier Sarah Slater to carry. More practical were the ingots, which were relatively compact and could be concealed as part of her railroad baggage.

In early April of 1865, as the Confederacy disintegrated behind her, she left Richmond with a trunk of them, intended for

Jacob Thompson's still continuing subversive operation. She left Richmond and headed to Montreal—no mention of a stop and arrest in Washington, O'Beare said—and there she promptly disappeared. Now in England almost two years later, she had come to Coutts & Company with a sample of Confederate gold—a "Kellogg & Humbert" ingot from the U.S. Assay Office in San Francisco. This was California Gold Rush gold, O'Beare pointed out, rather interesting to a European. An ingot of that particular gold weighed not quite fifty ounces and was worth, at inflated 1867 rates, about $4,500.

"She claimed," O'Beare said, "she had twenty such bars in her possession. Not rightfully hers, of course. That was obvious. She wanted to know how much I would pay for them."

"And?"

"Well, the Bank of England is required to offer gold sovereign pieces in exchange for any eleven/twelfths fine bullion offered it, which this was. But you see, they only have to give gold *coins* in return, not what the lady wanted. She wanted bank notes. At the Bank of England that would raise quite a few questions."

"But Coutts is different. You could give bank notes for ingots."

O'Beare shook his head. "Sir Frederick would have had my scalp, as you people say. Doubtful provenance, diplomatic tangles." He poured himself another finger of brandy and sighed. "Hated to turn her down, you know. She was a very damn'd attractive woman."

At half past ten the next morning, Sharpe and Oakes walked along the quay where the River Tiber hooked sharply south, just past St. Peter's, in sight of the grim, gray rotundity of the Castel San Angelo. Past the Ponte Mazzini they turned left onto a crowded street consisting mainly, it seemed, of banks and churches. They were on foot because Rome's carriage traffic had turned out to be even more clogged and chaotic than London's, and Sharpe was in a hurry. Before he went to the Embassy, he had announced at breakfast, he wanted to visit a seminary school called the Venerable English College and interview its Rector, the last of the long chain of godly and dissembling Catholic clerics who had sheltered the fugitive Surratt.

"You notice, in Rome the banks and the churches look exactly alike," he muttered. "Now, I'm not some half-cocked nativist like that idiot Morse. But I swear, the longer we go on like this, Quint, the uglier the Catholic Church gets."

By "that idiot Morse," he meant, as Oakes well knew, Samuel F.B. Morse, the mediocre painter and world-famous inventor of the telegraph. Because in the North, as History would soon conveniently forget, Morse was notorious for his praise of slavery and his poisonous hatred of immigrants, especially Irish Catholics. Even four years after the Emancipation Proclamation, he continued to claim that slavery was divinely ordained—the "beautiful Will of God"—and that slavery had been responsible for two centuries of beautiful domestic happiness in the South.

No matter how much proper society protested, in the gospel according to Morse, "Massa" and slave had lived together in righteous harmony, one cheerful, blessed family, until that blessed family was irretrievably destroyed by the abolitionist puppet Lincoln. Oakes's father used to choke with rage when he heard Morse's name.

But Oakes was scarcely listening to Sharpe. He was looking across the street at the costumed guards and churchly baroque façade of the Banco di Milano.

Twenty ingots. Was it some of the money Judah Benjamin supposedly carried out of Richmond? Did Benjamin give them to her for services rendered? *What* services? Who knew? O'Beare said Sarah had politely but firmly declined to explain their provenance.

He cleared his throat. "Keach told me this is one of the few banks in Rome that will change foreign gold for paper currency."

Sharpe looked at him with a blank expression.

"Does that interest us?" Oakes asked.

After a moment, Sharpe looked away. "I don't see why."

They turned again onto the Via di Monserrato. Oakes had said not one word to Sharpe about gold, gold ingots, Confederate couriers. If the General could have his secrets, so could the Captain. He refused to examine his motives.

At the next corner they stopped to let a meandering convoy of yellow and green Roman omnibuses go past, forty-foot long roofed carriages pulled by teams of eight melancholy, bony-hipped horses, who were encouraged to go faster by the drivers' long whips and constant, ear-splitting shouts from the passengers. Oakes didn't like Rome. Its antiquity depressed him. Its noise and disorder chafed his nerves. Sharpe took his elbow and steered him around a line of fly-ridden vegetable stalls.

Sarah Slater's stolen ingots, he had calculated, would now amount to well over a hundred thousand dollars, an absolute fortune.

Did *Sharpe* know? Had Sharpe known all along?

The Venerable English College was a hundred yards farther down the narrow street—redundant, Oakes told himself; *all* Roman streets were narrow—housed in a non-descript four-story dark brown stone building constructed, according to a plaque by the entrance, in 1807. But the Venerable College itself, Sharpe translated from another plaque, was first established on this spot in 1361.

And did those two Machiavellian chameleons Seward and Stanton know? Had they sent him off to find Sarah Slater because they wanted the money back?

If not...with Booth dead, with the Confederate government a shipwreck, with Jefferson Davis in prison and all his cabinet scattered—even a bad law student might ask—*Whose money was it now?*

The Venerable College had begun as a medieval pilgrim's hospice and over the centuries evolved first into a local religious college, then into an English-speaking pontifical college for foreigners. Most of the students now were Irish seminarians who had come to the Continent to escape the oppressive British hostility toward anything Catholic and worse, hostility toward anything Irish.

Nonetheless, when they were ushered into his dark little closet of an office, the Rector of the College turned out to be an Englishman.

He was a plump, balding, many-chinned Eton and Oxford graduate named Frederick Neve, about sixty years old, and he presented himself with an air of untroubled naiveté and incompetence that suggested a lifetime of academic insulation from the raucous, bustling world about him.

Yes, he cheerfully admitted sending money to Surratt when the boy first landed in Civitavecchia. He couldn't deny it, he was glad he had done it. He had also given Surratt a free room in the College and meals for a week or so, while he went about enlisting in the Papal Zouaves. As a Christian person, not as the official Rector, you understand. He had acted entirely on his own, Neve assured them, smiling vacantly and benignly. His motive was simple charity, nothing else. He was not a political advocate. "Judge not, that ye be not judged" was what he always said. He was sorry that Mr. Lincoln was dead—the cascade of chins rippled in sympathy—but after all, the institution of slavery, as the American gentlemen would remember, was sanctified in the Scriptures. When poor Surratt came to him in Rome, frightened, hunted like an animal, mourning his dead, hanged mother in Washington, what could a Christian do except murmur, "There but for the Grace of God go I?"

"I never quite understood that logic, Rector Neve," Sharpe said drily, rising from his chair and picking up his hat. "It seems to mean that while God may have spared *you*, more or less on a whim, He has come down viciously on somebody else, more or less on a whim. It seems a little ill-tempered and irritable for an omnipotent deity, don't you think?"

The priest blinked and gripped the gold crucifix around his neck, and Sharpe and Oakes set out to re-cross the city and meet the American Ambassador to Rome, who was, as whim or grace would have it, yet another of Sharpe's inexhaustible supply of fellow Union generals.

4

THIS ONE WAS NAMED RUFUS KING. He was tall and heavy set, and he wore a long gray lightning bolt of a moustache, L-shaped side-burns, and a beard that Roman sparrows might have nested in. He looked like a down-on-his-luck gold rush prospector, Oakes thought, not in the least like a brigadier general or a United States ambassador. Rumor claimed that King had been forced to resign his army commission at the end of 1863 because of epilepsy or drink, or maybe both. But he seemed entirely sober and at ease now as he came forward to grip Sharpe's outstretched hands.

"He wants to know," Maggie Lawton said from the ambassa-dorial couch where she had been waiting for them, "if General Sharpe has started quoting poetry yet."

Sharpe gave a snappish bark that would pass for a laugh.

"The General quoted Latin for us at the Forum," Oakes said, "but not poetry."

"They left before I could get around to 'Childe Harold's Pilgrimage,' King. You know, the part about the ghosts in the Forum—"

"Dear God, stop the man!" King said good-naturedly. He looked past Sharpe's shoulder. "You're going to be Captain Oakes,

I think. Saw you once in Washington. This fellow here used to drive Grant crazy with his poems. Sit in the tent in the rain, going over his papers and muttering poems."

"Grant liked it," Sharpe said.

"Grant wasn't afraid of anything," Rufus King said, not quite logically. "Now we're going to lunch right here in the embassy, then I'm going to take you over to the famous Cardinal Antonelli and he'll let you talk to Sainte Marie. But I'm telling you, Sharpe, you won't like him. He's a liar and a braggart and a god-damn'd gasbag, pardon my Latin, Miss Lawton. The Cardinal's all right."

All right as he was, the Cardinal nevertheless did not bother to manifest himself. Instead, his secretary greeted them and, with what Sharpe described as frostbitten courtesy, ushered them into a private conference chamber somewhere in the dark, labyrinthine corridors of the Vatican offices that reminded Oakes of nothing so much as the dusty recesses of Coutts & Company Bank.

The conference chamber, however, was another world entirely. It had a Persian carpet; floor to ceiling windows; two small, exquisite Raphaels on one wall; and cabinet after cabinet of books in luxurious gold and leather bindings, safely locked away behind glass doors.

The secretary muttered something in Italian to Sharpe, who replied in Latin—just for the hell of it, he explained later—and the secretary backed out of the room with an arrogant shrug that Oakes took for a bow. Maggie Lawton sat down beside the conference table, Oakes looked out the window toward the pale green dome of St. Peter's, and Sharpe began slowly pacing along the bookshelves, nose to the glass, as if he were inspecting troops on parade.

After ten minutes the secretary returned with an assistant who carried a tray with a polished silver coffee service, then the two of them left without a word. Maggie Lawton opened the coffee pot and sniffed. "I guess the Pope can't afford tea."

"I asked the major domo for tea," Sharpe said. "Some miracle has turned it to coffee. Quint, your puritan New England soul must be curdled by all this."

Sharpe's gesture took in the beautifully furnished room and the great dome levitating outside the window. Maggie had wanted to go into Saint Peter's for a moment, but Sharpe had made a moue of disgust and led them past the magnificent portico and entrance and down a side street to the Cardinal's private entrance.

"God himself—who is undoubtedly a plain-living busi-ness-like deity—would be nauseated by all this garish piety. As I recall, Quint," he added, "your distinguished father was an Emersonian Unitarian."

Oakes was about to reply that his distinguished father had loathed Emerson—"all those dots of thought"—and never really took Unitarianism seriously. The feather bed of Christianity, he had called it. But at that moment, the door swung open again and in stepped a slightly built man in his early thirties, swarthy, dark-haired, wearing flowing brick-red trousers, a blue jacket and a blue vest trimmed in red with two large gold crosses sewn on the breasts, and a red brimless cap with a gold tassel hanging from the top.

"I'm fluent in three languages," Henri Beaumont de Sainte Marie announced. "But I don't suppose you are. So we will speak English."

Sharpe started to say something—Oakes hoped it was in Latin—but evidently changed his mind and simply smiled.

Introductions done, they all sat down. Maggie Lawton sighed and poured herself coffee. Sainte Marie crossed his legs and tossed his head back and made the little tassel swing.

"This is why we asked to see you, Mister Sainte Marie." Sharpe slid a copy of Seward's letter of instruction across the table. "General King said you came to him in April of last year and told him about John Surratt. We'd like to hear more about that."

"I had hoped you were bringing me my reward." Sainte Marie sniffed. "Your friend Mister Seward"—he tapped the letter with one finger—"offered a reward of ten thousand dollars for information leading to Surratt's arrest. That would be me."

"That would be *I*," Maggie Lawton said, "to those fluent in English."

Sharpe shot her a stern look. "Mister Sainte Marie, perhaps you could just tell us what you told General King."

Sainte Marie smirked and began a long monologue, interrupted only by the occasional question from Sharpe. Maggie Lawton took notes. Oakes listened with only half a mind. Sainte Marie was a Canadian Catholic, but in the early 1850s he had wandered down to Maryland, where he taught school for a year and became acquainted with Surratt. He claimed to have served briefly in the Union army but was vague about units and dates. Early on he was captured by Jeb Stuart's cavalry, he said, but some months later he was released by the Richmond government and returned to Canada.

"There was a little ring of forgers in the prison, you see. Some of the guards, and two or three Union prisoners who used to work in print shops. They were making counterfeit army purchase orders and military passes—quite a lot of money in that—

and I turned them in to the authorities. The honorable Rebs were very grateful and showed me the door."

After the war, he said, more out of boredom than anything else, he had enlisted in the Papal Zouaves. There, to his surprise, he found himself assigned to the same infantry company as his old friend Surratt—now going under the name of Giovanni Watson—who had joined the Zouaves only a few days earlier. As always, Surratt was hopelessly talkative. Yes, he confessed, he had participated in Booth's plot. Yes, Jefferson Davis knew *everything* and completely approved. And yes—best of all—Surratt claimed that certain third parties in New York and London had generously financed the assassination and frequently sent written instructions to him and to Booth.

While he talked, Oakes also made an occasional note. But for the most part he stared over Sainte Marie's head at a row of books. He had no interest in the pompous Canadian's story. He didn't believe most of it. He thought "god-damn'd gasbag" was too kind.

He looked across at Sharpe's hard profile. Seward had chosen the right man to plow this particular furrow across Europe, no question about it. Systematic, tireless—he might casually quote poetry and learned languages by the yard, but if you really knew him, Sharpe was a driven man. Like the rest of the higher army command, he had worshipped Lincoln, and he meant to avenge him. Sharpe's complex character was that simple. What had General Parke called him—*too judicious, overly rational?* He couldn't have been more wrong, Oakes thought. George Sharpe had a profoundly passionate nature. His passions burned cold and distant and forever, like the stars.

"I really do want my money," Sainte Marie complained. "Ten thousand dollars is a very large sum."

"Now as I understand it," Sharpe said, studying his notes, "you went right away to General King at the Embassy—last April it was—and you told him Surratt was here, in the Zouaves. King looked into that and then sent off to Washington for extradition orders. And Cardinal Antonelli authorized Surratt's arrest."

"As soon as that laggard King requested it. He took his time. The Italians behaved very well."

"You have a bit of a history of betraying your friends," Maggie Lawton said. "Those fellow prisoners in Richmond, for example."

"Criminal trash," Sainte Marie told Sharpe. "You would have done the same thing."

"There was some mention of a young woman," Maggie said.

Sainte Marie turned scowling toward her.

"One Sarah Slater," she said. "Evidently"—she pretended to read from a slip of paper—"You were both quite taken with her. Only she preferred Surratt."

"Or Booth or Atzertodt or anybody." He leaned forward and snarled. "A French slut. A skinny blonde tramp."

Maggie kept her eyes fixed on the slip of paper. "Jealousy would be a good reason to betray your friend to the authorities here."

Sainte Marie looked left and right, as if for help.

"An excellent reason," Sharpe said, "for exaggerating what Surratt said. Or for making the story about conspiracies up whole cloth."

Sainte Marie started to rise, then settled back in his chair and crossed his legs the other way. "We heard about you," he said, "in the Confederate prison. The Rebels hated you. 'Torturer Sharpe' was what they called you—strung prisoners up by their thumbs, half drowned them in water buckets. 'Torturer Sharpe.'"

"I have never 'tortured' anyone," Sharpe said mildly.

Oakes watched a raven circle the great holy dome and alight on an eave opposite their windows. It wasn't true that he refused to examine his own motives. He hadn't asked Sharpe about Sarah Slater's gold for two reasons. The first was that Sharpe might lie to him—and he didn't know if he could stand that. The second was that Sharpe might admit he had known all along—and he didn't know if he could stand that either. Used like a blind, dumb tool. Where ignorance is bliss.

"I'll tell you exactly what happened," Sainte Marie said angrily.

Oakes abruptly stood. All three heads turned toward him. "I'm going to let you finish this, General," he said. He hardly recognized his voice. "The two of you can finish it. I'm going to visit some of the banks on Keach's list."

Sharpe said nothing. Maggie Lawton pushed her chair back and looked up at him, expressionless. In his mind's eye, Oakes walked past Sainte Marie and flicked the tassel on his cap in the other direction. In reality, he nodded once to no one in particular and walked out.

He VISITED NO BANKS, of course.

He walked across the endless piazza in front of St. Peter's and continued up the north side of the Tiber in what he thought was the direction of the ancient Pantheon temple, whose famous architecture was something he had told himself he ought to see. But halfway there he decided he had had enough of temples and veered off toward the Palazzo Borghese, where the gardens were coming into bloom and half the city, it seemed, had decided to take an afternoon stroll.

From there he walked the streets aimlessly, clearing his mind of Sharpes and Surratts and Sewards—the conspiracy of 'S's—and beginning to take some pleasure in the constant operatic drama of Rome's streets. He was a New Englander—inescapably so, it appeared—but the warmth of the Roman sun, the unashamed colorfulness of the buildings, the gay bravura of Roman clothes and voices had started to thaw a little of his ancestral granite.

You don't *thaw* granite, he told himself with a laugh. No wonder Sharpe said he wasn't a poet.

He wandered down the via Condotti—perhaps the narrowest, noisiest street he had yet set foot on—and stopped for a coffee at a place called the Caffè Greco, whose sidewalk placard informed him (in four languages) that earlier patrons had included Goethe, Keats, and Lord Byron. Oakes fingered his long hair and decided he fit right in.

His elderly waiter was completely bald, but as compensation had black moustaches so waxed and rigid that they might have served as semaphore blades. The coffee came with a splash of brandy in it. Another waiter handed him a three-week-old London newspaper on a hickory pole. Oakes drank the coffee and pushed aside the newspaper and pictured Sarah Slater here, in Rome, in this very room. Sarah Slater thawing too. Sarah Slater beside him, so close that their shoulders touched and their breaths came in rhythm.

One night, camped in a Virginia pine forest outside Richmond, he had sat alone in front of his tent, watching fireflies. First one yellow dot showed up, then another, then ten, thirty, dozens of them, each one signaling all the others, as if to say, *I am here. Find me if you can.* But on that particular night, they started sparking in unison, synchronized, more and more of them blinking together like one great single climactic pulse of light. It was the most erotic sight he had ever seen.

At eight o'clock that same evening they all found themselves seated around the long, polished dining table in the Ambassador's residence, Mrs. General Rufus King at one end, behind a gigantic blue ceramic soup tureen, General King at the other, behind a gigantic black cigar.

"Don't smoke at the dinner table, General King," his wife said.

General King ignored her, which Oakes took to be their usual style of matrimonial conversation.

"All the elegant polish of the bivouac's rubbed off him." General Parke winked at Mrs. King. Then he turned to Maggie Lawton on his right. "Wring anybody's neck today, young Miss?"

"I wish," she said brusquely. Parke lifted an eyebrow in the direction of Sharpe.

"We interviewed the man who came to King here about Surratt," Sharpe explained. "Miss Lawton was unnaturally polite."

General King snorted and expelled a whitish cloud of cigar smoke that briefly screened Maggie's face.

"He told us," Sharpe said, "that after the Italians arrested Surratt in the Zouave barracks, Surratt pushed his guards to one side and jumped into a hundred-foot deep ravine. He landed on a ledge that was covered with garbage and ran away. They sent fifty soldiers, but nobody could find him."

"Until," King said, "I sent word to Alexandria, Egypt, which is where *we* found him and arrested him ourselves, and he *stayed* arrested."

The men leaned back in their chairs to allow servants to clear the soup course. When King had put down his cigar and begun to carve the lamb, Sharpe added, "The official Italian report on Surratt was translated into rather fine English. 'The escape of Watson,' it said, 'savors of a prodigy.' Miss Lawton here thinks it savors of this two-faced Sainte Marie's helping his friend to decamp while he collected the reward." He accepted a plate from King. "She expressed this thought at some length."

Parke smiled his somewhat mischievous avuncular smile at her. Then he pointed his fork at Sharpe. "But you don't think so."

"I think Sainte Marie isn't capable of that. I think someone else in the Zouaves—"

"Or in the Vatican," King said.

"—or in the Vatican, maybe—somebody else bribed the guards and they simply looked the other way. Which would take a good deal of money, to bribe fifty men. Which is why we poke around in local banks for signs of local Confederate sympathizers. Or Captain Oakes supposedly does." He looked blandly at Oakes and sipped his wine.

In the ambassador's study after dinner, General King passed around a cut-glass decanter of whiskey, hesitating briefly when it was Maggie Lawton's turn—she had declined Mrs. King's invitation to sit in the parlor—but then he shrugged and poured her a ladylike dram.

"I remember you better now, Captain Oakes," General Parke said. He had imbibed fully at the table and now he had a full-size general's ration of whiskey in one hand and a foul black cigar, the twin of King's, in the other. "Whiskey makes me think of it. You were just a lieutenant at the Gettysburg conference. Shy and thin, not longhaired and husky. You see, young Miss," he wagged his glass toward Maggie, who had walked over to the open French window to look at the torch-lit streets. "It was late at night at the end of the second day, and Meade had four of us in his tent for a council of war. Nobody knew if we could go through another day like that, and Meade was thinking about a retreat."

"He wasn't going to retreat," Sharpe said.

"And he had a camp table with a plate of crackers and a half pint of whiskey in the middle of the tent that nobody had touched, and Sharpe comes in to give his report, looking as dry and hungry as a man that's been lost in the desert. Meade looks at Sharpe's numbers—how many troops had Lee already used? How many did he have in reserve? That was the key, you see— how many more people did he have left to throw at us? And

Meade rubs his jaw and looks worried and sends Sharpe off to recheck his numbers. No whiskey offered. No crackers. About an hour later, back comes Sharpe with this young lieutenant here and Sharpe says this is Oakes and I guarantee his numbers. And Oakes gives a little presentation to Meade, Hancock, Slocum and self, and when he was done Hancock, who'd been lying on a cot combing his hair, he swings himself up and says, 'General Meade, we have got them nicked!'"

"What was it you said?" Maggie asked Oakes.

"He said," Parke answered for him, "'Lee's already used every single unit he has except for Pickett's division, and his people are all knocked to pieces, half strength at best. He can send Pickett in tomorrow, but it won't be enough.' And that, by God, was when Meade pushed the plate of crackers and the whiskey toward old Sharpe here"—Parke's round face broke into a huge man-in-the-moon grin—"but he never gave one drop to Oakes! You never saw such a look!"

Parke and King laughed and slapped their legs, and Parke refilled Oakes's glass with a laugh and a shake of his head. Sharpe looked at them both with what Oakes would have called distant affection. Then he stood up and started to examine the books in the room.

Behind him Parke was refilling Maggie's glass. "'Smartest boy I ever met,' that was what Sharpe told me later about Oakes. Once he gets something in his mind, he's like a dog with a bone, determined as hell. Like Sharpe, obviously. 'Love him like a son,' Sharpe told me."

"But he should have given me some whiskey," Oakes said, and the two generals burst into another cackle.

It was nearly midnight when they returned to the Hotel de Londres. Oakes, who had decided early on that alcohol, not epilepsy, was Rufus King's failing, had allowed the general to fill his glass once too often—making amends for Gettysburg, as the older man said.

In his room he found the basket the hotel proprietor had left for him on arrival. It contained some pulpy oranges, a green lemon, and a bottle of blood red wine that came, according to the label, from the far-off region of Puglia. He took it to the bed and sat down heavily. He would not say he was drunk, but he acknowledged that the floor under the carpet was heaving slightly, like a boat at sea. He perched on the edge of the bed, holding the bottle unopened, and listened to the sounds of the Roman streets, which apparently never went entirely quiet. Abruptly, he realized that what he had taken for a carriage rattling was in fact a knocking at his door.

"I seem to be always coming to your hotel room," Maggie Lawton said. She walked in, followed by a hotel servant with a wooden tray containing a teapot, two cups, and assorted ritual items.

"Ganymede," Oakes said, "cupbearer to Zeus."

"Hardly Zeus, don't flatter yourself. And no more wine." She took away the bottle and placed it on a cupboard. "This is cambric tea, good for your head. Also, no more Greek or Roman talk."

"Sharpe told me that every soldier lives the *Iliad* first. Then afterwards, he lives the *Odyssey*." He watched the servant arrange the pot and cup on a little table by the window, then back out of the room, bowing. "Of course, in the *Odyssey* the hero has a home to come back to, and a wife."

"Penelope."

"Penelope."

"It was funny listening to those old men jaw away about the war—Gettysburg and Grant and Meade's terrible temper."

"Funny, no." Oakes took a sip of the tea and made a face.

Maggie sat down on a chair facing the bed. "What happened to you, Captain Oakes? What happened to you in the war?"

Oakes looked up carefully. He tried without success to characterize her tone. She sat very still, hands curled around her teacup, red hair motionless. There were three gas lamps on the wall, hissing softly; compared to American lamps they were dim and ineffective. When they flickered, her not-quite-handsome face receded into indistinctness.

"You saw the war," he said, "yourself."

"But not as a soldier. I saw plenty of horrors after the battles and in the hospitals—ask your foul cousin Henry—but I spent the war traveling around writing reports for Pinkerton and Sharpe, and nobody ever shot at me, or hung me up by my thumbs or threatened my maidenhood, alas. In prison the gallant Rebs even gave me a separate room."

Oakes pushed off the bed and walked to the cupboard where the hotel servant had left the wine bottle. He took a corkscrew from a drawer and pulled the cork. He found two water tumblers, filled them both with wine, and talked to the wall.

"When I went into the war, I had no idea how I would do—the blood, the death, the mutilation—I thought I might be as weak and useless as my 'foul' cousin. I was afraid I'd break apart and fall to pieces. But in fact, nothing bothered me. I saw men shot and dying and I slept next to corpses—once on the supply boat going back to Washington, I slept on top of somebody's coffin—and I felt perfectly indifferent. At Gettysburg, on the third day, when Pickett charged up Cemetery Hill, a sergeant next to me had the top of his skull blown off and he bolted straight up and screamed, 'I'm a dead man' and I had no more feeling about it than if he'd tripped over a rock."

He handed her a glass and drank a long swallow from his own. "Pretend it's tea."

"You made yourself hard."

Oakes shook his head. Nothing special had happened to him, nothing that hadn't happened to thousands of others. She was right, of course. He had made himself hard for the war, that was all. Thousands did it. Sharpe did it. But the war was over and how do you thaw yourself after that?

His mind skipped. Sarah Slater had once told him that a woman makes herself soft for love. A man makes himself hard.

"My mother said I was a happy, chubby little baby," he told Maggie, "always smiling and babbling, a sweet little man." He took another swallow. "I wonder where he went."

Maggie put down her untouched glass and came close to him. In the most extraordinary gesture of Oakes's life, she reached down and pulled his left hand to her lips and kissed it. Then she turned and walked to the door. Halfway into the dim hallway she looked back over her shoulder. Her face was hidden in shadow. "General Parke says when we go to Paris we should be sure to see the Exposition."

PART FOUR

Paris

April and May 1867

1

"WHEN I FIRST CAME TO PARIS—" Natalie Benjamin interrupted herself and peered suspiciously at the pitcher of water that the servant had just deposited on the table beside her. "When I first came to Paris, *ma petite*, all the drinking water was taken from that awful Seine River—what a foul sewer that is—and it was *opaque! Solide!* It looked like a glass of Louisiana mud. If you drank it straight away, God knows what diseases you let yourself in for. They say Mozart's mother died from drinking Paris water. People used to let it sit in a glass for a day until all the *bits* had settled to the bottom."

She shifted in her chair with a formidable crackling of crinoline and silk that made her sound like a fireplace. "You don't mind if we speak French now, do you, dear? English always makes me think of a duck gargling."

Sarah Slater smiled and nodded, and Natalie Benjamin began a rapid cannonade of Louisiana-accented French that Sarah had trouble following exactly. Mostly, it seemed to be a complaint about the enormous excavation pit outside the front doors of her house, where Monsieur Haussmann, the new Prefect of the Seine, was at work on one of his celebrated destructive "improvements." In this case his army of workers, striking through to an unsuspected, paved-over spring, had transformed half the block into a sea of mud. The pit and the haphazard stacks of lumber and broken stone everywhere looked like Mr. Benjamin's descriptions of Richmond after the Yankees had bombed it to ruin.

On the other hand, Natalie Benjamin freely admitted, Haussmann and his new network of masonry *égouts* had done wonders in improving the water. It was odd, of course, for Sarah to hear Mrs. Benjamin talking about water. On the two previous occasions they had met—at John Slidell's house on the chausée d'Antin—she had drunk nothing but wine, and quite a lot of that. But then most things about her hostess were odd.

"You haven't been here before?" Natalie Benjamin hesitated. "I believe Mister Benjamin said I wasn't to ask you too many questions. No, of course, you haven't been here before. Let me show you my paintings."

She stood and gestured expansively toward the far wall of her salon, which was covered with several dozen canvases of various sizes, all of them framed in gold and hung one over the other in columns of four or five after the European tradition.

"These are my old Dutch things. Landscapes." She led Sarah to the column of paintings nearest the big French window and balcony. "A little dreary, but Mister Benjamin buys them for me in London and sends them over and so I keep them to please him. *Husbands*," she added with an ambiguous snort. "I keep hoping he'll send a Rembrandt or something valuable, but Mister Benjamin is much too Hebrew to spend his money frivolously." She laughed and patted Sarah's shoulder with one bejeweled hand. "Whereas my philosophy is that spending money frivolously is the only rational thing to do with it."

The mid-afternoon sun was draining the life and color from the Dutch landscapes. Natalie Benjamin moved several steps to the right. "You might," she said coyly, "recognize one or two of these."

Just for a moment Sarah considered asking, mischievously, whose portrait they were, but good sense prevailed. "These are lovely! Wonderful! They capture you perfectly—your eyes, your skin—" Her eyes were still giving her trouble from time to time, and she stumbled slightly, wondering what to praise next.

But Natalie Benjamin took up the reins quite smoothly. "He made my teeth a little large, but perhaps I was smiling too much. He caught the dress perfectly."

Sarah leaned forward to study the dress. Natalie tugged her sleeve and motioned toward the next portrait to the right. "I was sixteen when this one was painted."

Sarah found herself looking into the eyes of a sixteen-year-old—not *girl*—it was hard to think that the self-possessed, sophisticated woman next to her was ever a girl—a sixteen-year-old woman. Her shoulders were bare, her dark eyes expectant. Her smile was a shade too inviting for propriety. Her hair, exceedingly black, curled and twisted rebelliously down her back, her whole body radiated sensuality. Sensuality and selfishness.

"He gave me perhaps more bosom than I had then." Natalie cocked her head and frowned at the ample *décolleté* of her younger self. "But I was so very proud, you know."

She turned with a grin toward Sarah. "Now I wear a French corset, you see." To Sarah's faint shock she placed one hand under each of her breasts and hefted them like melons. "You probably don't know the French word. It's new—a corset is a *divorce* because it separates them."

"Ah." Sarah found it hard to pull her eyes away from Natalie Benjamin's jiggling breasts.

"Mister Benjamin was twenty-one when that was painted. My father hired him to teach me English because I grew up speaking French in New Orleans, as all little princesses did. And of course"—Natalie made a completely unexpected literary reference—"'that day we read no further.' Dante," she said. "A *divorce*," she added.

Sarah took a breath and stepped toward the next painting, but Natalie stopped her and eyed her bosom critically. "Yours are adorable, you know. But not very large. You have the French figure."

"I like this one," Sarah said, and not to be misunderstood pointed at a pen and ink sketch of Natalie Benjamin, done with a minimum of strokes and a surprising lightness of color.

"My friend Auguste, yes. Young Auguste. I like to encourage young painters. We should go to his studio. He likes a plumper body, but he might want to paint you all the same—lovely skin, lovely blonde hair." Somehow they had arrived at another of the little round tables that seemed scattered like mushrooms everywhere in Natalie Benjamin's crowded sitting room. This one had a cut-glass carafe of red wine and two plates of chocolate-coated biscuits. "You do like paintings? You do follow art?"

Back in Connecticut, Quint Oakes had been interested in paintings and drawing, so Sarah had told herself that she should be too. Together they had gone to a gallery at Yale and he had told her at length what they were seeing, though in fact he was looking at her most of the time. That day they looked no further…"I went to the Left Bank and saw some good things at the Exposition."

"*Bouf*." Natalie dismissed the Paris Universal Exposition of 1867 with an untranslatable Parisian sound. "Tomorrow perhaps we'll go to see Auguste. Meanwhile, tell me how you know that useless old man John Slidell. And tell me how you found Mister Benjamin in London. Is he still too fat? Sit down," she said. "Drink. Talk."

2

SHARPE HAD ORIGINALLY INTENDED to leave Rome immediately after interviewing Henri Saint Marie. The start of John Surratt's trial, he reminded Oakes and Maggie Lawton every morning, was rapidly approaching—the first week in June, some six or seven weeks away—and if they turned up any further evidence against him, it would need to be in Seward's hands before that, written out, cross-filed, double checked, impeccable. The reason for such legal punctiliousness, according to one of Seward's hectoring memoranda, was that the government had now decided to try the Fifth Conspirator, not in a military tribunal like his mother and the others, but in an open civilian court where the rules of evidence would be far stricter.

But Sharpe, despite his fidelity to deadlines and instructions, was not, Oakes thought, a hound easily thrown off the scent.

The day after their meeting with Sainte Marie, when their schedule said they should be packing for Paris, Sharpe announced that he was in fact going to the Vatican again, first to revisit the buffoonish Canadian, then to track down the elusive Cardinal Antonelli, the Pope's Foreign Secretary. Oakes was sent to buy a new set of tickets to Civitavecchia and Marseilles.

"He told me he has to go to the Vatican because the Cardinal still has the British passport that Surratt used to enter Italy and he wants to see it for himself."

"What the General wants…" Maggie said, without bothering to finish the sentence. Sharpe had made it clear at breakfast that the forces of piety in the Vatican would not speak to him again if he were accompanied by a woman. Senora Lawton, Oakes was hardly surprised to see, had taken it with her usual undisguised disdain for manly men's men who were afraid of women. Particularly, she had added, staring at a passing gaggle of priests, men who wore skirts.

Oakes laughed at the memory, at Maggie Lawton's spirit and wit, and pushed away the thimble of warm oily water that passed for mid-morning coffee in the Hotel de Londres. He rubbed sleep from his eyes. He drank, he drank quite a lot sometimes; and usually he paid the price for it with throbbing temples and a mouth so dry it might have been used as a mausoleum for dead insects. Yet this morning, despite General King's whiskey and the several tumblers of wine in his room with Maggie—a visit neither of them had yet alluded to—he felt nothing but restlessness and a certain two-fingered pinching sensation in his nose.

"He told me we should go to the banks on Keach's list today," Maggie said across the table, "and meet him at General King's again for dinner."

Oakes made a different face. "How is Keach?"

"He's a miracle of health. He's coming to meet us in Paris. Are you going to the banks?"

"No."

"Do you want *me* to?"

No answer.

"I don't know enough to ask the right questions. *You're* the one who went to law school." She tapped her index finger on the table in the same slow, impatient rhythm that Sharpe used.

Oakes raised his head and studied the dining room window of the hotel. Rain had just started falling, an event that seemed to have thrown the street outside into a panic and sent the hotel owner rushing from window to window in a loud Italian frenzy of shock and personal insult. When you go to Paris, General Parke had said, be sure to see the Exposition.

"I know where there's a better cup of coffee," Oakes said.

But Maggie was in no mood to go out in the rain. She was going back to her room, she announced, to do something useful and look over Keach's notes. Oakes put on an old slouch hat and set out splashing past the Spanish Steps toward the via Condotti. In the Caffè Greco he found the same elderly waiter and ordered coffee with hot milk, just as before. Then he asked to see a foreign newspaper.

"Inglese?" The old man frowned and stroked the waxy blades of his moustache. "London *Times*?"

"French. Anything from Paris."

The waiter said something in Italian that Oakes mentally translated as "Fucking Napoleon" and went off to fill his order. When he returned, he slid a steaming cup from his tray and a deputy second assistant waiter behind him reached around deferentially to present Oakes with a much-folded copy of *Le Moniteur de Paris*.

"Week old," the assistant apologized. Oakes handed him a coin and turned to the back of the paper, where "Spectacles" were listed and described.

The "Exposition Universelle" was Napoleon III's grand project, intended, along with the invasion and occupation of Italy, to regain for France its rightful place of supreme international importance. It had opened two weeks ago, on April 1, on one of the coldest, wettest April days in recent memory, the paper reminded its readers. Half the exhibits had still remained to be uncrated then and virtually no dignitaries braved the weather to attend. But now the weather had turned brilliant, the exhibitions were all in place, and *Le Moniteur* was devoting the last six pages of every issue to a large-scale map and a long catalogue of displays and events, printed in columns, four to a page, like a railroad timetable.

Oakes spread the plan open on his little café table. The Exposition was taking place on the Champ-de-Mars, the great open field north of the Ecole Militaire where the French cavalry was accustomed to carry out its drills. If you could believe the newspaper's drawing, the Exposition covered the entire space, some one hundred acres, most of them devoted to an astonishingly large oval building about fifteen hundred feet long, twelve hundred feet wide. It was constructed in seven more or less concentric inner galleries that held the booths and stalls for the exhibits. Dozens of separate buildings stood in gardens outside the giant oval, including a Lincolnian log cabin sent over by an American delegation from Kentucky. Oakes bent closer. There was a South Entrance Gate by the École Militaire.

And a North Gate just in front of the river Seine.

Cherchez-moi à l'entrée nord de l'Exposition.

He sat back abruptly and knocked over his coffee. It raced, hot and milky brown, across the table, across the newspaper pages, down onto his trousers and into his shoes. A scrimmage of waiters descended on him with towels flying. He barely saw them. His fingers found another clutch of coins and he dropped them on the bespattered papers and stood.

Outside he tugged on the slouch hat and began to walk. Rain was still coming down in sheets. Behind a windy curtain of water and mist old Rome was gradually disappearing. *Paris*, not *London*? The *Paris* Exposition, not the London one? Did she say she was going to Paris—in Lambeth? Oakes could hardly remember, Oakes could hardly tell.

He turned a corner and Sarah Slater walked toward him out of the rain.

He stopped. Rain spilled from his hat, whipped in his eyes. Pain and desire welled up, ready to burst from him like a jet and the Roman matron in the white dress coming toward him, covering her head with a piece of old cardboard, looked at him warily and hurried past.

I am here. Find me if you can.

John Surratt's—or "Giovanni Watson's"—passport, it turned out, was both forged and, in a sense, stolen. At dinner Sharpe explained that he had enjoyed a long audience with Cardinal Antonelli, who had entered into the spirit of the hunt far enough to bring out all the documents his office had collected relating to the enlistment of Zouave Number 1857, one "John Watson," an American.

"The Italians changed 'John' to 'Giovanni.' Otherwise, they just stamped everything three or four times with the Papal States seal and then tossed the whole batch in a file and forgot about it."

"Until I went to see them," Rufus King muttered.

"I had my London documents," Sharpe said. "It was easy enough to see that the passport was forged—you can't mistake Seward's handwriting. And a little more digging brought out the fact that this 'John Watson' is a real person, but not an American, a Scottish lawyer who lives in Edinburgh. Perfectly innocent. I'm going to guess that Surratt—or somebody—went to the Home Office in London and simply pulled his name and address out of a census book and off he went."

"We don't have to go back to London?" Maggie Lawton was alarmed.

Sharpe hesitated. Oakes knew him well enough to understand that the old Bureau of Military Information chief hated to leave any loose thread, anywhere. Sharpe led an orderly life. He cast a cold eye on anything incomplete, unfinished, ambiguous. Yet he was also too practical and hardheaded to waste time going back to London and revisiting its blank faces and frigid silences.

"If Captain Oakes can arrange the tickets," he said finally. "We might leave for Paris tomorrow."

But thanks to a considerable battle being fought not far to the north of Rome—Garibaldi hammering stubbornly away at the outnumbered Papal States army like an Italian U.S. Grant—Captain Oakes was only able to procure tickets for two days following, back along the railway to Civitavecchia and from there, another frustrating day later, on to Marseilles.

It was in fact, not until the morning of April 18 when they finally climbed aboard the train and set out under a gorgeous Roman spring sky to retrace their steps of two weeks earlier. But long before that Oakes's thoughts had turned toward Paris, swiveling constantly toward one single point, like the needle of a lovesick compass.

3

When she had come over from London ten days ago, Sarah Slater had worried about using the new passport with her "Susanna Foreman" name on it, but as it turned out Paris hotels took no great interest in foreign passports. In the first place she stayed, the Hotel Louvre, they hadn't even asked for it.

But the Hotel Louvre, though recommended by Cassell's Guide, was more like a cattle barn than a hotel. It had endless dark corridors, few facilities for ladies, rather leering and aggressive service, and the constant, unnerving stench of some unidentifiable green mold, the result of a recent flooding by the Seine. It was also intolerably noisy from dawn till dusk, and walls and furniture alike were coated with the dust raised by another of Monsieur Haussmann's massive construction projects just a few blocks to the east.

At the end of three days she switched to the Grand Hotel on the boulevard des Capucines, more expensive but better suited to a woman traveling alone. No passport needed there either, though it too had a Haussmannian drawback—at one end of the boulevard the new Paris Opera House was going up, massive as a pyramid, but the noise and dust were far less in evidence.

Sarah had never been to Paris before—Paris, unlike London, was indefinably *foreign*. The architecture was wrong, the clothes, the food, the voices. Especially the voices. The French was not her father's French, either, though her father had been born on the rue Saint-Antoine, not more than a mile from her hotel. Parisians talked fast, like New Yorkers, and used slang words that sent her puzzling back to her dictionary.

Did she like it? She wasn't sure. The hardest thing in life, her father told her once—the hardest thing in life is to know *how you really feel*.

One thing she *knew*, if not *felt*, was that the city she was seeing was not the Paris her father had known either. Natalie Benjamin was right. Monsieur Haussmann, the omnipotent Prefect of the Seine, "the artist of demolition," as he called himself, was dramatically rebuilding the city; it was obvious even to a newcomer. The morning after she arrived, she had accompanied her precious trunk from the hotel to safe storage at J. Arthur & Co., Foreign Merchants on the rue Castiglione. All along the way she and her driver had encountered smoking chaudières of tar, detours, squadrons of laboring men, great holes and gaps in the sidewalks, deep trenches where the streets were being extended and public squares laid out. Just beyond the rue Castiglione was a scene of such wholesale destruction—shells of buildings, piles of rubble everywhere, stones and beams seemingly fallen at random, free standing staircases to nowhere—that she thought for a moment, just as Natalie Benjamin had said, that she had stumbled backward in time to the day in Richmond when the Yankees marched in and the Old South marched out.

In fact, the date today was April 20, 1867, two years and seventeen days after Richmond had fallen. Two years and six days after Booth had shot Lincoln.

She sipped her coffee and watched from her window as pale Parisian sparrows spun round and round a leafy plane tree like birds in a faded tapestry. If she liked Paris, it was undoubtedly because she wasn't so clearly a fugitive here. In Canada, in London—especially in squalid Lambeth—there were the ubiquitous policemen, there was the vile Thomas Courtenay. Even if you were used to running, even if you were hardened and strong—she dropped her thoughts a register into French—*there,* in London, it had been one long *cauchemar,* a nightmare.

Her coffee was cold. She pushed it away. The money she had borrowed from poor besmitten McRae in London would last just over a week now. By then she would have found a banker willing to change her ingots for cash, and she could plan her permanent disappearance from the world, from a life she had wrecked as completely as anything Monsieur Haussmann could have managed.

As for Quintus Oakes—she jerked her mind angrily away from Quintus Oakes. If a person wanted to find her—if a person wanted not to betray her—wanted to vanish with her—she had left a note. That person could come to Paris, if that person cared.

The sparrows shot into the air like bullets and disappeared.

* * *

Breakfast finished, day's allowance counted out from her little cache, then toilletted, coiffed and bouffed like a true Parisienne, Sarah finally set out on what had become her morning routine.

From the canopied entrance to the Grand Hotel, she walked fifty yards westward to the *station de voitures* and its cabriolets for hire. Thirty minutes and a mile and a half later—fast for Haussmann's Paris—she stepped down from the cab at a busy plaza just by the river, called (she didn't know why) the place de l'Alma.

To the left, along a stone embankment, a long line of sightseers waited with surprising patience for one of the new Seine touring boats, called (also mysteriously) Bateaux Mouches—"fly boats." But Sarah scarcely glanced at them. Across the pont de l'Alma and down a few blocks on the Left Bank of the Seine, was her destination.

There, on a map at least, the venerable grass fields of the Champ-de-Mars stretched southward toward the École Militaire, but no map could possibly render the new and festive reality— the vast complex of military buildings at the other end was lost to view, totally obscured by what was literally a gigantic glass and steel pleasure dome. It was one and a half stories high, surmounted by hundreds of dancing flags. The iron filigree around the glass had already started to oxidize in the damp Paris spring, so that the whole structure had a strange, unearthly reddish hue, as if it had been built on another planet from designs and colors that human beings were not accustomed to. In the gardens around the sides of the great oval ran a long succession of booths, restaurants, and individual exhibitions, all of them swarming with people, so many that the air shook with the uproar. She paid her driver, glanced over her shoulder out of unbreakable habit, and pushed off into the crowd.

A few steps onto the bridge, she paused to look down at the fast-moving river. Little spoons of sunlight flickered on its ripples, a south breeze whisked waves into a froth. She always looked at rivers, water. The best cure in the world, she thought, for low spirits was to stand on a bridge and look at water.

But today, from the moment she stopped, shouting, jostling beggars surrounded her, tramps, beggars, mountebanks with gee-gaws and souvenirs to sell. A boy juggling colored wooden balls hurried toward her while his little sister trailed behind, holding a hat for coins. When she reached the front of the Exposition two different bands were on either side of the Entrance, simultaneously playing different tunes. She thought briefly of the old book's hero Christian in "Vanity Fair," told herself she was no Christian, and joined the pilgrims streaming into the monstrous buzzing hive that was Napoleon III's modestly named "Universal Exposition."

"Madame wishes to leave her coat?"

"Madame wishes to check her messages."

A functionary in frock coat and crimson topper bowed with a brilliantly insincere flourish and led her through the cloakroom, out another door, and back toward the entrance. There was a bookstall here, with a big lid propped open like the ones you saw along the riverbank. Beyond it on one side stood a large open room populated with women of various ages tending to a handful of crying children. In several languages signboards announced *Crèche*—the English notice added, "Refuge for Lost and Straying Enfants."

On the other side of the Crèche, protected by a metal grill from the crowd and, presumably, the Straying Enfants, stood a large corkboard panel and three wooden hotel reception cabinets. These were punctuated with pigeonholes for mail and messages.

Thomas Courtenay had also told her about this in London—because the Exposition was so chaotic and crowded, the management had set up a message center at each main entrance gate.

Visitors who lost sight of each other in the exhibit halls could reunite here, or leave notes for friends, or mail letters and cards. Sarah had paid a *poste restante* fee at the Northern Gate, good for exactly two weeks.

"The beautiful American Mademoiselle again." The smiling young girl behind the counter knew her by sight now. "No reply, *désolée*." She held up the beige-colored envelope and read the inscription in a French accent that made the plain old English words sound almost lyrical: "Q. O. /Guilford, Connecticut."

Then she pinned the envelope back on its place on the corkboard and made the same untranslatable sound that Natalie Benjamin had made. "*Bouf*."

"If someone comes, perhaps you could just send me word here." Sarah had thought of this at breakfast. "To save my coming every morning." She handed the girl a ten-franc note and a card from the Grand Hotel with her name on it.

The girl was twenty perhaps, with the saucy air of a born Parisian *grisette*. She dropped the money between her breasts and put the card in a pocket. "It's a man, isn't it? 'Q.O.' of Connecticut?"

Sarah had practiced deceit and evasion for three full years in the war, and now two years after the war. It was almost an instinct now. "Yes, a man I know."

"American too?"

"He was in the war. Our war."

People were bustling around them, so noisy and frenzied that Sarah had to lean forward herself to hear the girl's question. "Why hasn't he come? Was he hurt in the war?" She touched Sarah's elbow. "A beautiful woman like you." She shook her head and said in slangy French. "He can't be that dumb."

Sarah patted the girl's hand and turned away. Maybe, she thought, because he thinks I helped kill the President.

There was a barker of some kind on the other side of the grill, shouting that a musical demonstration was about to begin in Gallery Three, but Sarah paid no attention. Her mind had slipped into what she called its endless, maddening seesaw. She admitted it—she knew she had left a deliberately ambiguous note for Oakes in London, cryptic even, so terse as if to defeat the whole idea of the message. She hated herself for it. People in Richmond had called her cold. Booth himself, in his cups—and when wasn't he?—had called her cold and hard, harder than a soldier. But Quintus Oakes was clever, he had always been clever. If he wanted her, he would decipher it.

The hardest thing, her father said, was to know how you felt.

She stepped outside into the sunlight, but the noise from the Exposition was still deafening, the crowds unbearable. She had no idea how she felt.

4

"HOW MANY CONFOUNDED UNION GENERALS were there?" Maggie Lawton groaned. They climbed down from their carriage and looked warily up and down the rue de Chaillot. "There must have been an army of them."

Sharpe laughed and told the driver to wait right there. Maggie pulled off her big wide-brimmed traveling hat and smoothed her dress. "And why did they all have to come to Europe after the war?"

Oakes shielded his eyes from the sunlight and squinted down at his folder. John Adams Dix, yet another confounded general—and yet another Adams, though not a cousin—was now the United States Minister Plenipotentiary to France. According to Sharpe's notes Major General Dix had been responsible for arresting the entire Maryland state legislature at the very beginning of the war and thus preventing Maryland from voting to secede. After that, he had commanded the New York district and had quite ruthlessly put down the draft riots in that city in 1863, while the Battle of Gettysburg was going on.

"Well, this is one general I didn't know," Sharpe said. He turned on the sidewalk and satisfied himself that the wagon with their baggage was safely anchored behind the carriage. "Seward said he'd find us a hotel."

"Not *this,* I hope." Maggie hitched up her skirt to avoid trailing it on the filthy sidewalk, crusted like so much else in Paris by Haussmannian detritus. "*This*" was a quite shabby six-story limestone *immeuble*. A broken awning hung sadly over the entrance. Half its windows were boarded up, apparently to keep out the noise of the street. Midway along the rue de Chaillot, dozens of workmen in paper caps were pulling up paving stones with what looked to be a set of horse-drawn plows and a nonstop ringing chorus of pickaxes.

"This is the United States Legation office, my dear fastidious lady. Notice the flag on the balcony. We'll put you up in your accustomed elegance somewhere else." Pleased with his humor, Sharpe nodded to the doorman and led them inside, where the noise and the sunlight abruptly ceased.

Up two dark and winding flights of stairs they found a brass American eagle over a door, and inside a pair of clerks morosely stamping passports. One of them rapped on an inner door for them, and moments later John Adams Dix himself swept them in with a grin.

"Beautifully timed, General Sharpe, beautiful. We close the office to the public at three and it is now"—he inclined his head toward the clock on the fireplace mantel—"three-forty-five." A quick pursing of the lips, the door again. "Jourdan! *Chaises!*" He stood back while the two clerks wrestled chairs through the door and positioned them in a semi-circle in front of the desk, whereupon Ambassador Dix slipped behind his desk and sank into his own chair. Oakes had a moment of déjà vu, thinking his life was one damned office after another—Rufus King's Roman chambers, Charles Francis Adams's handsome rooms in London, Seward's Washington office where the whole grim chase had begun. There would be no offices in Wyoming, no chambers.

But this was not to be mistaken for one of those grand functionary offices. In Paris, the United States Minister Plenipotentiary had been given an ordinary medium-sized room, unimpressive in every way. No carved and handsome walnut desk like Seward's, no paintings on the wall, no shelves of leather-bound books. Dix had a fireplace made of gloomy black marble, and an equally gloomy black marble clock on the mantel. In a fraternal spirit, the dark green rug was worn nearly black.

Introductions made, tea and biscuits brought in by Jourdan, the ambassador leaned back in his chair and stroked his neat little white beard. "Didn't know you in the war, Sharpe. Barely knew Lincoln. Knew Grant, of course." He looked a question at Maggie Lawton, who was performing the mystic rites of tea. "Don't quite understand what a woman is doing in all this, though."

"Miss Lawton was a Pinkerton's agent in the war," Sharpe said.

"Is that so?"

"Some of Booth's sympathizers or financers here in Europe may have been women."

Dix made no effort to keep the skepticism out of his voice. "Well, maybe."

"We certainly want to see Missus Judah Benjamin, for example."

Dix laughed outright. "Now, I'm sure you do! Good luck getting a word in edgeways! I don't think she could stop talking long enough to shoot somebody." He nodded in Oakes's direction. "Very opposite of Grant and Grant's wife. You know Grant in the war, Captain? You're kind of quiet like him."

"I saw a lot of General Grant, from Cold Harbor on," Oakes said, and added diplomatically. "A great man."

Dix nodded and grinned and launched into a whole series of Grant stories—Grant's terrible headaches that he used to treat with chloroformed handkerchiefs, Grant's odd habit of wearing an old private's coat instead of an officer's jacket, the way Grant would sometimes take a nap on a plank in front of a fire, Grant when an artillery shell burst a hundred feet away and everybody ran for cover except him. "He just sat there on his horse smoking his cigar and staring at the Reb lines," Dix said. "The rest of us were flat on our bellies. The horse wasn't any more bothered than he was."

"We're particularly interested in an American woman," Maggie said. "Sarah Slater. Sometimes she uses the name Kate Thompson."

Dix didn't like having his reminiscences interrupted. He looked first at Sharpe, then at Maggie. "I wouldn't know anything about that," he said finally.

"Do the hotels here keep a record of foreign passports?"

Dix thought about it. "Some do."

"The embassy in London found us a retired police detective to help check hotels and track down former Rebels. Could you arrange that, too?"

Dix frowned. "Is that what you want, Sharpe?"

"It would be a help, General."

"There was a whole nest of Secesh here, you know—Bigelow, Slidell, Caleb Huse, plenty of others. Only one still here is Slidell, and I'd be surprised if he'd see you. His daughter married Baron Ehrlanger." He nodded helpfully toward Maggie and explained. "Ehrlanger et Cie is a banking house. They lent the Confederates money to build ships in Liverpool and took cotton bonds in exchange. Then of course they sold the bonds for profit. Made a killing. They won't talk to you either."

"Seward wrote Baron Ehrlanger a personal letter," Sharpe said.

"Did he?" Dix massaged his beard a little more. "Well, I'll do what I can, but it seems to me like too little, too late. Lincoln's been dead two years. You caught the last of Booth's gang. I'd let it go. 'Vengeance is mine, saith the Lord.'"

"You didn't know the President, General." Sharpe came slowly to his feet. "You don't know me."

* * *

The hotel Dix found for them was named the Hotel de Lille et d'Albion and it occupied a pleasant, fairly new building on the north side of the rue Saint-Honoré.

Then it was a question of one more meeting to plan their agenda. As usual, a hotel cat materialized and curled itself around Sharpe's ankles. And as usual, the general had come armed with a list. First, he intended to pick up where he had left off in Rome and pay a visit to the Papal States envoy in Paris, who may well have seen Surratt and sheltered him on his passage through to Rome. Then there was the Ehrlanger Bank matter. And a routine check of hotels for Sarah Slater, since Isaac Pollacky had thought she might have fled London for Paris. And finally, certain French military officers, observers who had spent time with the Army of the Potomac in the last year of the war—they were back at the École Militaire and might have names. And, course, the matter of Agent "B."

"All that in one week." Maggie Lawton was using her London street names notebook for work notes now. She scribbled something in it with a gold pencil she had bought in Rome. "Exhaustion is mine, saith the Lord. I don't think I know syllable one about Agent 'B.'"

Nor did Oakes know syllable one. Obligingly, Sharpe pulled out a set of papers from his manila notecase and then, to their surprise, next pulled a pair of reading glasses from his coat pocket. He gave them a tired smile over the top of the lenses. "What was it Washington said when the soldiers rebelled? 'I've grown old and nearly blind in the service of my country.' Well, not blind. But old."

Sharpe rubbed his forehead and snapped the sheets of paper to order. There are some people, Oakes remembered, you just love.

But did they love you in return? Or just use you?

"'Agent "B,"'" Sharpe read, "'was placed in Paris by Secretary Stanton. He was paid with War Department funds, not State Department monies. Secretary Seward knew nothing about him. Toward the end of March, Agent "B" wrote Stanton that Confederate conspirators in Paris were sending a man to assassinate General Sherman, in retribution for his'—I quote—'*lethal savagery* in Georgia.'"

Sharpe put down his notes and looked at something far away. "Stanton ignored it, of course, being Stanton. But after the President was…After April fifteenth, he wired a warning to Sherman down in North Carolina. Sherman sent me a copy. All we knew was that the assassin's name was Clark, no first name given. 'B' said he was slender, medium height, dark brown hair, moustache and goatee, high cheekbones. He never came close to Sherman."

"They should have sent a woman," Maggie said. "She would have shot him."

Sharpe nodded. "They should have sent you."

There was more. When the war ended, Agent "B" went off the payroll and out of sight. Clark was never identified or found. Stanton's records on that were lost or misfiled, but a former agent in the Lloyd's shipping office in Nantes might recall payment information, meeting places. Nantes was only a day's travel from Paris.

Oakes half listened to them. He found himself marveling at how immensely, how insanely *complicated* the war had been—so many people, so many stories—so many names, battles—so many dead, so many deceits and lies. Scholars would write about it for a thousand years, like the *Iliad,* but no one mind could ever take it in or see it whole, not even Sharpe's.

At their hasty dinner, Maggie and Sharpe were still going over his papers, rearranging the agenda, refining the search for what Sharpe—his French coming back very nicely—described as *banquiers dégueulasses*—"disgusting bankers." Maggie wrote more reminders in her notebook and pondered out loud whether a trip to Nantes was worth the time. Oakes toyed with his food, drank no wine, and thought about ways he might slip free from Sharpe and Maggie and go to the Exposition, which was open every night until midnight. Just before nine he excused himself and left them, heads bent over yet another missive from Seward, murmuring and humming together like a couple of bees.

Outside on the rue Saint-Honoré he began to walk, aimlessly at first. It was still faintly light and the streets were almost as crowded and busy as at mid-day, but reluctantly he decided it was too late to attempt the Exposition. Just as in London, while he walked his mind filled slowly with memories of the first time he had been to Paris, when he had broken away from the elderly London cousins and crossed the Channel to see a place where they didn't speak English—an irresistible thought to an unimaginative boy of eighteen. Not speak English?—For a long time he imagined that all the Parisians were talking in a made-up language just to trick him, so that if he wheeled around quickly enough he would catch them really speaking English.

He looked up to find that he was on the boulevard des Capucines, a street he barely recognized. Ditches, trenches, piles of lumber, and building stone littered the boulevard toward the east, as chaotic as a battlefield. Yet a hotel was open not fifty yards away, and farther down a pair of cafés. The night was chilly, but the French, in his experience, would eat outside in a snowstorm, so the terraces of the cafés were little islands of light and tinkling laughter.

He stopped and studied the faintly illuminated windows of the hotel. Sarah might be in one of those rooms, he thought. Or at any moment she might step out of one of those islands of light and turn toward him. He remembered the weight of her cheek in his hand, the weightlessness of her hair.

He changed direction and started walking south toward the Seine. He concentrated on Paris sensations, Paris sights. In front of him now, for instance, was a "rambuteau," a one-man public urinal shaped like an upright cylinder and named irreverently after the former Prefect who had installed them. No chance of seeing such a thing in Boston. Possibly in New York. The rambuteau was plastered with *affiches* showing a line of female legs kicking high in a dance called "the cancan." In the drawings, men in top hats sat by the stage, watching breathlessly, mesmerized.

What had Maggie Lawton said in London?—He was pursuing a woman he didn't want to catch.

At the Pont Neuf he paused to examine the statue of Henri IV riding his horse boldly forward, as if ready to vault over the fence and onto the street. Behind the statue, upstream on the other side of the bridge, more construction rubble and a black gap where a building was being demolished and another was going up. Beyond the black gap rose the great gray Gothic apparition of Notre Dame. Its two towers barely showed now, light-colored stone shafts propping up the darkening sky. Some unexplained torchlight hung in an open space. Below it, a dot of color where stained glass caught the reflection of God's thought.

Vengeance is mine indeed, saith the Lord. But He didn't mean it. He meant for *Sharpe and Seward* to avenge his slaughtered saint. And *they* meant for Oakes to find Sarah Slater and bring her to them, because if Sarah had known about Booth's plot, Oakes was duty-bound to Lincoln, honor-bound to country to find her. And if he found her, they would hang her. He thought of the postcard Sharpe had bought, Mary Surratt on the gallows.

Pedestrians still hurried in both directions across the bridge. An omnibus and horses rattled close by. A hooded woman approached him, then veered away.

Somehow, without even knowing it, Oakes had come to agree with General Dix. It was over and done. Let the unchangeable past roll away and vanish, like this river, into the empty distance.

A couple walked past. Under the gas lamp at the end of the bridge he could see that the woman was carrying cut flowers in a paper cone. Parisians, he remembered, loved flowers. For a long time now, he thought, all the components of his nature had been at war with each other, the soldier, the son, the rebel who wanted to escape his life in the east and begin again in the west. What if there was no need to avenge the President?

Because, more and more it seemed to him, Lincoln must have willed his own death, as atonement for the unbearable ordeal of freedom he had forced upon the nation.

"YOU HEAR STORIES ABOUT HIS PENIS," Natalie Benjamin said.

Sarah was about to take a step closer to the shop window. Now she stopped herself, straightened, and very slowly turned her head to look at her companion. She willed a smile to her face, though she was quite sure it didn't reach her eyes.

"I beg," she said quietly, "your pardon?"

"Wilkes Booth," Natalie said. "His penis. You hear stories about his penis."

"You do?"

"Well, everyone knows he had—what's the disease that starts with a G?"

"Gonorrhea," Sarah said, and could have kicked herself for knowing. First, that awful Courtenay in London, now this.

"And of course," Natalie said, "that sometimes makes the poor little thing twist about terribly and get misshapen. Over here they treat it by laying it on a table and hitting it with a book to flatten it out again."

Sarah looked about to see if anyone was listening. But though the arcades of the Palais Royal were bustling with people, mostly women come to visit the famous shops, no one appeared to be paying them the slightest attention.

"I believe," Natalie added thoughtfully, "they use a dictionary. In any case, seeing that you traveled so often with Booth, I naturally assumed—"

"What in the world made you think of this?" Sarah worked to keep her voice both friendly and dismissive. How much did this strange woman know about her and Booth? And who else did?

"Why that window, the next one over."

They had been examining the window of Chevet's, a shop that offered exotic foodstuffs to jaded Parisians—birds' nests from China, ortolans from Italy. In the center was a huge, gray mushroom labeled *Tête de Mort*, "Death's Head," which must have weighed ten pounds and looked to Sarah for all the world like a human skull.

But it was not the Tête de Mort that had set off Natalie Benjamin's train of thought. The next window over was consecrated to the latest "mania"—Natalie's word—to seize fashionable Parisians: collecting photographs of notorious criminals. And holding the place of honor—Natalie's word again, not without irony—was a large framed portrait of John Wilkes Booth. It showed him dressed in a beautiful frock coat, standing beside a marble Doric column, his right elbow leaning against a balustrade, his gaze into the camera direct and intense. Next to him was the photograph of someone identified as "Phillipe, the Strangler of the rue de la Ville l'Evèque."

"And it continues over here." Natalie led the way toward the theater that occupied the northwest corner of the arcades. The current play was a musical drama by Offenbach. But coming in a month, a poster said, was a piece in seven *tableaux* entitled *La Vie et la Mort d'Abraham Lincoln*, by one M. Reuben.

"It's already been performed at the Odèon," Natalie said. "Last year. Quite remarkable and quite crazy, I thought. It has Booth appear as a suitor for Lincoln's niece, who rejects him and of course this makes Booth hate the President. The play they go at the end to is *King Lear*, of all things, and Jefferson Davis shows up in act four asking someone, anyone to kill this man and save the South."

"*King Lear*?" It was all Sarah could think of to say.

"Nothing about his gonorrhea, though."

At tea back on the Boulevard des Italiens, Natalie reverted to Lincoln and Booth. "One of the lycées here offered a prize for the best poem on the death of Lincoln, you know. But the French couldn't find a good rhyme for 'Lincoln.'"

"No, I didn't know."

Natalie touched her hand. "You mustn't be out of sorts, my dear Sarah. Mister Benjamin told me a little about your time in the war. I quite admire it."

"How is Mister Benjamin?"

Natalie smiled her catlike smile. "Do you know that in some parts of England, when the couple joins hands at the marriage ceremony, the woman keeps a thumb free, as a sign she won't be dominated?" Then, as was her unsettling habit, she simply changed the subject. "I wonder if Jefferson Davis really did look for an assassin," she said, "the way he does in that play. I asked Mister Benjamin once."

Sarah carefully added sugar to her already well-sweetened tea. "What did he say?"

Natalie Benjamin evidently shared Sarah's belief that it was not necessary to answer a question just because it was asked. She changed the subject again. "People in Louisiana used to say, behind my back, that Mister Benjamin couldn't perform his masculine duties."

Sarah, fascinated and appalled, decided to stare at the pedestrians coming along the boulevard.

"They called him 'the Eunuch,'" Natalie said, with a trace of bitterness in her voice. "When he was a Senator in Washington City the rumor went around that our daughter wasn't his. I heard it all."

"Was that when you moved to Paris?"

"That was the second time I moved to Paris. Look at that wonderful man."

Natalie had chosen the ultra-fashionable Café Tortoni for their tea, and she had chosen a pavement table to see and be seen. The wonderful man in question wore a yellow cut-away coat, a white wig and a parrot on one shoulder. His shoes were red, his trousers green. "I love this boulevard. Everybody comes here. Everybody dresses."

Natalie herself was wearing a deep purple silk dress, cut very low at the bosom, and what she had told Sarah was called a "Chapeau Pomponette," a wide-brimmed blue bonnet adorned with real roses and tied beneath her chin with a large bow. She was certainly in her forties, possibly in her fifties, and she carried a kind of middle-age plumpness that Sarah had once heard described as "pneumatic." But her face was as animated as a schoolgirl's by the Parisian scene.

"We must get you some clothes," she said, as if Sarah were sitting naked on the boulevard des Italiens. "And you have to tell me about 'the man.'"

Sarah looked quizzically toward the bewigged dandy, but instinctively she knew what Natalie was about to say and she felt her throat constrict.

"You are far too pretty, my dear, and too passionate"—she held up a hand—"I know women very well. I know men better, of course, but that's because they're simpler. A *passionate* woman like you comes to Paris alone. She has a letter of introduction to John Slidell. She has a certain furtive side to her history. There's a man, obviously. Are you fleeing him or looking for him?"

Sarah shook her head.

"Have you seen him here? Have you made love to him?"

Natalie had an irresistible force in her personality. Or perhaps, Sarah thought, I've been by myself for far too long, and it's not force but sympathy she has. "I saw him once in London before I came here." She corrected herself. "Twice. I saw him before that in Washington. We knew each other before the war."

"A Northerner." Natalie nodded as if to confirm some suspicion. "When you saw him again, was he what you expected?"

"Worse."

"Worse?"

"He was what I remembered," Sarah said.

6

ALMOST AS SOON AS THE FIRST CANNONBALL splintered the walls at Fort Sumter, the Confederate States of America began putting together missions to London and Paris. In both cities, their aims were the same—secure diplomatic recognition for the new country, and find, beg, or borrow money to finance the war.

In London, though the aristocratic upper classes tilted their monocles and looked down with disdain on the plebian North, the Confederate envoys were unable to bring the cautious and gun-shy Foreign Office to the point of diplomatic recognition. The Southern States, no matter how sympathetic and romantic they seemed at a distance, were still a slave-holding power, and the British public had a long-standing revulsion against chattel slavery. *Money*, however, was different, and this the Confederate mission found in abundance, so that armored warships purchased with cotton bonds sailed for a time from Liverpool entirely undisturbed by the Queen's government.

In Paris the chief of mission was John A. Slidell, a former Senator from Louisiana and a notoriously hotheaded Secessionist. By his own account, he was greeted with great warmth by the Emperor Napoleon III, who repeatedly (but not publicly) declared his support for the South in its noble, not to say French-like attempt to throw off Tyranny.

The Emperor also met with the glamorous one-time Confederate spy Rosa Greenhow, who had come to Paris after her release from a Washington prison. Such was her allure that the Emperor allowed her photograph to be taken with him—an unusual favor, but she was indeed beautiful, and he was indeed French. He assured her, as well, that his heart sided with the South. But nothing could be done by France alone, he sadly told both Slidell and Rosa Greenhow. The very moment that Great Britain recognized the Confederacy, France would recognize her too, he promised. After Gettysburg it became plain to everyone that that moment would never come.

In the second aim of his mission, Slidell had more success. Certain French shipyards quietly admitted, repaired, and even constructed ships for the Confederate Navy. But the Emperor, possibly mindful that French financial support for the Americans in their Revolution had bankrupted his country and brought on its own Revolution, never quite managed to pull open the strings of the royal purse.

Slidell, however, had a very beautiful and charming daughter, Mathilde, who so entranced the great Parisian financier, Baron Frédéric d'Erlanger, that a stupendous loan of some fifteen million dollars was privately arranged for the Confederacy, backed by the sale of still more cotton bonds. After Gettysburg, again, most of them sank to zero and fell out of the market. But if d'Erlanger lost on his bonds, he won the hand of Mathilde.

"And that," Sharpe said as they mounted the steps of an extremely elegant *hôtel particulier* on the rue de la Chausée d'Antin, "is why he's still in Paris, living like a king. I wonder if he misses his slaves." He paused at the door and looked up and down the street, blessedly free of Haussmannian chaos. "I think Thomas Jefferson had a house on this street, when he was ambassador, or the next one down."

"Another slave owner," Maggie said.

Oakes had a soft spot for Jefferson, although his pious father always called him "Atheist Tom," so he remained silent while Sharpe rapped twice on the door. Sharpe had decided not to send a letter ahead to Slidell, reasoning that "to come cold," in his words, would be more likely to surprise the Louisianan into receiving them. But when a servant pulled open the door, he had a letter from Seward in his hand, ready just in case, which he sent in with his card.

They were bowed into a foyer richly furnished in French antiques, but with engravings and watercolors of Louisiana land-scapes covering two walls entirely. After no more than three min-utes wait, the inner door opened and a pale, clean-shaven man in his mid-seventies shuffled forward. He was tall, but growing stooped. He had a nimbus of white hair around his ears. He wore a formal black frock coat, a black silk ribbon at his collar and, Oakes was startled to see, shabby brown house slippers and thick cotton stockings. His own grandfather, he remembered, had dressed the same way.

"Mister Benjamin wrote that you would probably call on me," John Slidell said softly. He handed back both the letter and the card. "I would have sent you away at once, but I didn't want to pass up the chance to see for myself the celebrated General Sharpe."

"Then undoubtedly he also told you why we're here," Sharpe said.

John Slidell looked slowly from Oakes to Maggie Lawton. "Three of you," he said. "You always did outnumber us."

"May we come in?"

"You may not."

Sharpe tried a diplomatic smile. "You have the reputation of an honorable man, Senator Slidell. I would like to think you could help us establish innocence—or guilt—in the murder of the President."

"You refer to Mister Lincoln." He looked curiously at Maggie. "A woman. On such a business." Then to Sharpe: "I have no information that would possibly help you. If you come again, the door will be closed." He turned away, stopped and looked over his shoulder back at Sharpe. "You have the reputation of being an exceedingly hard man, General Sharpe. Now that I see your face, I believe it."

* * *

The rest of the day passed no more successfully. Sharpe disappeared to interview someone at the Papal States Legation. Maggie went to Dix's office to meet the French detective he had turned up. Oakes, even without Keach to lead the way, was assigned to interview an officer of the Crédit Lyonnais bank, which had handled Slidell's Confederate mission accounts. He got as far as the second receptionist before he was politely but definitively turned away.

From the bank's offices near the Bourse he walked under a hot blue sky to the Exposition. At the north entrance he ignored the hawkers, the hundreds of printed advertisements for exhibits, the competing bands of musicians stationed by the ticket booths.

He stood, stupidly, for twenty minutes beside the main gates, staring at the crowds that flowed in and out in a wild, noisy, unending cacophonic bustle.

Then he bought a ticket and stepped inside and found himself brought up short by a sudden nerve-shredding wail of horns. This came from the exhibit of Modern Musical Instruments just to his right, where seven kinds of "saxophones" were being enthusiastically demonstrated, one after the other. The saxophone, he remembered, hurrying past the blare, was hardly "modern." It had been invented at least two decades earlier by Napoleon III's "Imperial Instrument Maker," Adolphe Sax. Next to it the Steinway Company of New York had set up a series of pianos progressing in size from small upright to large to larger to "Grand." A woman in formal evening dress played waltzes on the Grand.

He found himself pulled by the crowd toward a *"Crèche* for Lost Enfants." Next to it was a wooden bookstall and a pretty French girl. Idly, curiously, he took a step forward, then explosions broke out fifty yards away in the Swedish gallery, and with the perverse instincts of a U.S. Grant he ran toward them, not away.

"Dynamite," it turned out to be, not the gunfire he had imagined—dynamite was a newly invented alternative to black powder, just patented by a Swede named Nobel. The explosions were to demonstrate how small sticks of the material could be set off in a controlled manner, one going off after another in a big metal barrel like Chinese firecrackers. Oakes held his ears and backed away. The idiotic Swede must have thought the world badly needed one more way to blow itself apart. He wheeled about, passed the *Crèche* again, and regained the outer plaza.

Stupid, he told himself again, meaning first Nobel, then seamlessly, in the manner of obsessive thought, Sarah Slater.

Stupid. Foolish. Frustrating. What could she have meant, "meet me at the northern entrance?" *When? How?* Stand there every morning, hat in hand?

On the train from Marseilles he had thought hard about her note. For a time, he considered the possibility that it was all a code, an encryption he was supposed to break. People on both sides of the war had been bedazzled by secret codes—the Confederates had even resurrected a sixteenth-century cipher called the "Vigenère," based in turn on the ancient "Julius Caesar" code in which each letter was replaced by the letter three steps beyond it in the alphabet. The old classical scholar Sharpe had simply laughed the first time he saw it. Toward the end of the war, some agents in Canada were sending extremely small photographic negatives, folded and hidden inside buttons.

But those weren't codes and her note was no button. He stood by the pont de l'Alma and watched the barges thump their prows upriver. Stolen gold ingots. Maddening vagueness. Women, he thought.

Back at Dix's office he found Maggie and a retired French detective who was just on his way out and was introduced to him in passing only as Daudré. Dix was busy hanging up a print in his grubby office. While he hammered and frowned and readjusted, the ambassaddor explained to Maggie that, like many Americans, since coming to Paris he had discovered a whole new artistic side to his nature, and he was slowly, happily spending down his pension on paintings and engravings.

Maggie nodded and turned away, uninterested, to the desk where Daudré had left his preliminary passport lists from the six or seven hotels he had visited that morning. She stood next to Oakes and passed him slips of paper on which she had already crossed out almost every name. No Sarah Slater. No Kate Thomson. Nobody.

Satisfied with his print, Dix came around to them and watched with an avuncular smile. "You two seem well suited," he said. "Work together like a team."

"No."

"Yes."

Dix looked puzzled, then decided to be amused. "Well now, which is it, Miss Lawton?"

"Mister Oakes and I," she said, "are like the wrong ends of two magnets."

"I don't follow you."

"Every time I come close." She raised her head and stared at the black marble clock on the mantel. "Every time I come close, he pushes away, repelled."

Dix stood with his mouth agape. Oakes found himself wincing in pain. Before either of them could speak, the door swung open and Sharpe marched in, muttering curses against the Papal States and the unholy Catholic Church, and it was back to business again.

7

One of the oddest features of the war, Oakes always thought, had been the constant presence of spectators.

On the very first day of the First Battle of Manassas, Virginia, when the war was barely under way, carriage loads of men and women, most of them furnished with champagne and picnic hampers, had rolled gaily out from Washington City to witness the fighting, as if the whole thing were a sporting event like a baseball game. And even though a few hours later they fled back to the city in terrified disarray—along with the terrified and retreating Union soldiers—from that point on, there were few days when somebody's wife or sister or maidenly cousins didn't come to tour a camp and flirt with the officers and go up as close as they dared to hear the distant "pop-pop" of rifle fire along the skirmish lines.

He and Sharpe were just then crossing a bridge over to the Left Bank, and despite the rattle of horses' hooves, Oakes could hear similar warlike percussive noises off to the left, coming from construction of a new boulevard to run past the Saint-Germain church. In the army they had used a peculiar and infuriating word for skirmish fire—the enemy was "annoying" the forward lines—"annoying" when sometimes half a company of men went down, a minié ball in their guts, bleeding to death, annoyed.

He pulled his mind back. Sharpe called out directions in French to the driver, who ignored them. More understandable than the visiting ladies were the foreign observers. The Austrian army, he remembered, had sent someone to study American telegraph and signal techniques, a reasonable idea, except that the Austrian colonel in question spoke no English and appeared to be stone deaf. There were Mexican officers, too, who strutted about in brilliantly colorful uniforms and exceedingly tall leather hats, lovely targets for Confederate sharpshooters. Russians came as well, a Roumanian once. Members of Congress often showed up when the fighting was calm, pulling importance into their faces. The ordinary soldiers called them "chickenhawks." Sharpe and Grant regarded the congressmen as alien creatures but treated them with brusque courtesy. Englishmen (and some quite young English boys) arrived by the trainload. And of course, there were the French.

The French not only came to observe. In the case of the man they were about to visit, they came to serve. Early in 1862, in the Peninsula campaign, the Prince de Joinville attached himself to McClellan's headquarters, as, he remarked in flawless English, "amateur and friend." But his two nephews actually went to work as aides-de-camp for Allan Pinkerton, who was at that point responsible for estimating Confederate troop strength (Pinkerton was hopeless; no reliable estimates were ever presented until Sharpe took over).

Both Frenchmen had been living in exile in London—the older, Louis Phillipe, being the deposed comte de Paris, official "Pretender" to the French throne—and their English was likewise perfect, so much so that the "Orleans Brothers," as everybody called them, were given the ranks of captain and assigned the task of writing daily summaries of the field reports. Oakes had heard they refused a salary and claimed they were only following in the footsteps of the great Lafayette.

"Rue de Varenne," Sharpe announced, and a moment or two later their carriage rolled through open gates and into the cobblestoned courtyard of a handsome *hôtel* not unlike John Slidell's on the other side of the river. For political reasons, neither the Prince de Joinville nor Louis Phillipe lived in Paris—the Emperor's hostility to their family was notorious—but the younger brother Robert, the duc de Chartres, being "Pretender" to nothing in particular, had boldly returned to the old family residence.

And almost before their wheels had stopped, the duc himself was unlatching the carriage door and bestowing warm Gallic kisses and embraces, assisted in these courtesies by a huge gray Russian wolfhound who placed both front paws on Sharpe's shoulders and began to howl.

Then followed yet another session of wine and food and wartime reminiscences, a kind of talk that more and more Oakes considered to be like shackles holding you prisoner to the past. He wanted to remember nothing from the war. What he wanted was to find Sarah Slater and vanish with her, vanish and reappear a continent away, in Ingersol's Wyoming wilderness.

But Sharpe was not like him, Sharpe of the prodigious memory, the student of Latin, the erudite lecturer in the Roman Forum. Sharpe reminisced, recalled, and recounted the past with deep, self-evident pleasure, every day of the war, every name, every bullet. Sharpe's life was one continuum, Oakes thought, a single long path of consciousness. It was not broken up, like his own, into discontinuous fragments, with innumerable gaps and holes, like one of Haussmann's violently fractured boulevards.

The duc de Chartres (generally known to the soldiers as the "Duke of Chatters") had been an early enthusiast of military observation balloons—and he was in fact now the proprietor of such a balloon for peacetime sightseers, a gorgeously painted blue-trimmed golden hot-air ship that was anchored in the Tuileries Gardens and took paying customers up for half an hour at a time. Oakes had seen it the first morning of their stay and thought for a moment that the sun had come untethered from the sky and flown over, like everyone else, to see Paris.

Single-minded as always, Sharpe carefully led the conversation from balloons and signal flags around to Lincoln, whom the duc had once met and, surprisingly for an aristocratic Parisian, admired. His murder, the hunt for Booth, the theatrical pageant of Lincoln's week-long funeral cortege—all this had greatly appealed to the French mind, as did the idea that some still darker conspiracy lay behind Booth's plot. The duc knew plenty of Parisians who had spoken out for the Rebels and sent money and jewels to the Confederate treasury. In the salons of Saint Germain many of them still raged wittily against the Northern "aggressors." But no one he knew would have ever done more than talk ("our national pastime") and ridicule the ugly and unfashionable President. And no, Mrs. Natalie Benjamin was above suspicion, entirely indifferent to politics, and no, John Slidell had never shown enough energy or enterprise to engage in assassination.

"Though the woman you mention—"

"Sarah Slater."

"A spy like Miss Greenhow? Booth's lover?"

"She was a courier," Oakes took it on himself to answer. "She carried messages between Montreal and Richmond. Nobody," he also took it on himself to add, "actually knows if she was Booth's lover."

"Captain Oakes knew her before the war," Sharpe said.

"Ah, our old friend 'the green-eyed monster.'" The duc was a lean, graying man in his mid-forties. He had the big aquiline nose of his race and a small, greedy mouth. In McClellan's camp he had enjoyed the reputation of a man who enjoyed his pleasures. The room in his hôtel he had chosen for their talk was lined with paintings of stallions and women, neither clothed. He smiled at Oakes. "Good hunting," he said in French.

Their carriage back to the Embassy arrived promptly at two, leaving them time, Oakes suggested, for a visit to the Exposition. But Sharpe had early on announced that he had no interest in seeing that colossal monument to godless commerce and imperial self-love. Instead he dismissed the carriage and proposed, for the exercise, that they walk along the Seine, eastward toward the Ile de la Cité and Notre Dame.

"Not a useful meeting," he allowed as they started out.

"Friendly at least," Oakes said. Sharpe had returned to Dix's office in such a foul temper because the Papal States representative in Paris had just treated him, he reported, with complete disdain. If John Surratt had come to the Papal representative on his passage through the city, it was certainly no concern, he was told, of a minor, non-ambassadorial military person. Seward's letter of introduction had struck him as irregular, possibly forged. Until and unless he received instructions from Rome, he chose to believe that the un-credentialed Mr. Sharpe had certainly not met with the Papal Foreign Secretary, Cardinal Antonelli.

"He called you a liar?" Oakes stopped cold on the sidewalk.

"I've been called worse," Sharpe said mildly. They moved on again, parallel to the Palais des Tuileries on the opposite bank. "After law school, you know, I traveled a certain amount in Europe—Austria, Switzerland, Rome. I loved Rome. But my best memories are of Paris."

"You liked the art? Like John Dix?" Oakes was looking at the distant immensity of the Louvre.

"The pleasures," Sharpe said. His tone left no doubt as to the pleasures he meant. "I haven't pried, Quintus. I *won't* pry into your private history. But you need to understand that I will find this woman. And for my sake, and the President's sake, *you* will act honestly, honorably."

Oakes stiffened. He opened his mouth to reply, then closed it.

They walked silently for what seemed like many minutes, though when Sharpe spoke again they had barely reached the Pont des Arts. "You know I'm fond of that old Roman backstabber, Cicero," Sharpe said.

Oakes's face was still red and hard. His mind was still back on Sharpe's declaration. Or command. Or warning.

"Cicero would have enjoyed analyzing our friend Chatters," Sharpe continued in a casual, conversational way. "Did you see those decadent paintings?" Oakes glanced over and reminded himself that for all his worldliness, the rugged general had a prudish streak. "Horses and naked women. Cicero once said that men's greatest pleasures are only narrowly separated from disgust."

Oakes concentrated on Paris thoughts, Paris sights. The Pont des Arts was relatively new, the first completely iron bridge thrown over the Seine, closed to carriages and horses, beautifully decorated with flowerbeds and potted trees. He had read some-where that people used it for picnics.

Sharpe put his arm on Oakes's shoulder and dug in his grip. "Cicero also said that the most difficult battles are not between good and evil, but between *good* and *good*. We have five more days here, Quintus. Do the right thing."

* * *

When they returned to Dix's office, there were two surprises waiting for them.

First, Daniel Keach himself, considerably paler and thinner, rose to give the general and Oakes a mock salute. Then he sat back down with a sharp, rib-cracking cough.

And second, a somewhat hesitant Dix handed Sharpe an ele-gant and—if Oakes's nose didn't deceive him—perfumed enve-lope. "Came this morning," Dix said rather gruffly. "From Missus Natalie Benjamin, you-know-who's wife."

Sharpe, his mind evidently on something else, simply handed the note to Maggie.

"It's an invitation to a 'gala' dinner on Saturday," Maggie Lawton told the others. She cocked her head at Dix. "But it's addressed to the 'Honorable Ambassador Dix and Family,' not us. You don't mean for us to go?"

"Rude to leave you here on your own," Dix said. "That's what my wife said, anyway. Can't leave you here to sleuth and starve alone. She loves Natalie Benjamin's dinners. So does my daughter. So I sent back a message to ask if I could bring three diplomatic guests. Didn't say Seward sent you over, of course—no sense stirring up that particular bed of coals. She's a friendly old duck, Natalie Benjamin, but in view of who her husband is, still pretty Secesh."

"I'll cough and give her germs," Keach said.

"I'll go buy a dress," Maggie said.

8

PROPER WOMEN, PROPER SINGLE WOMEN, didn't ride on buses in Paris.

This was the inflexible rule of the day, according to Natalie Benjamin. On the same afternoon that Daniel Keach arrived at the Embassy, a mile and a half to the east, Sarah Slater looked longingly at an *omnibus à l'imperiale* jingling past, pulled by four great Percherons. The busses were everywhere, they cost thirty centimes to ride inside, and only fifteen centimes to ride on the upper deck, though Natalie had warned her that the railings on the upper deck were so flimsy that people often fell off.

So Sarah took a hired carriage everywhere. She was normally a defiant person, unconventional, obviously. But there was nothing to be gained by calling attention to herself, a lady alone on a common omnibus. Nothing to be gained, but something to be saved. She sighed and felt, discreetly, the dwindling bulk of coins in her purse. Paris was far more expensive than London, and the money she had brought over was rapidly evaporating.

At her hotel she debated for a moment whether to walk a block down and take tea in the fashionable Café de Paris. Single women could walk unaccompanied on the boulevards and in the center of the city. Otherwise, said another inflexible rule, she needed to be accompanied by *une amie* as she had been the other day with Natalie. Tea and cake would cost four or five francs. On the other hand, she would be gone in a week. Tea, no cake.

Or maybe she wouldn't be gone in a week. The Banque de France was as impossibly hidebound as the Bank of England. In London, neither of the two bankers Colin McRae recommended had worked out. Then, not really understanding why she asked, he had written down the names of two more private bankers in Paris with, he said, "flexible scruples."

But Paris was no better than London. The first banker on McRae's list had turned out to be no more than a Jewish money-changer working from a squalid little room off the rue de Balzac. He offered twenty percent of the official Bank of England price—forty thousand dollars—a great deal of money, but nothing like what her gold was worth.

The second man, just seen that very afternoon, after a long back and forth correspondence about terms, had finally refused to help at all without better documentation for the gold's provenance.

If she had known how complicated bank exchanges were—a thought that came much too late—she would have found someone in London to forge papers for her. Surely the besotted McRae or Courtenay would have known how to reach such a person, or even Huggins in a pinch.

Today's banker had been her best hope, she thought. He had a lecherous eye, and she had leaned forward as often as she dared, grazed her fingers across his, held him in a spotlight of admiring feminine attention. No luck. Not even a nibble, as the people in North Carolina used to say. So much for amorous Frenchmen.

She studied herself in the glass of the café window. She was certainly not too old.

But Sarah Slater rarely gave up. There were still two people in Paris to ask before she went back and threw herself on the mercy of the moneychanger.

Natalie Benjamin, she guessed, had no business sense whatsoever. But Natalie Benjamin knew everybody in Paris, beginning with the Emperor himself (there was a thought!), even though she'd described him to Sarah as dull and looking like a melancholy parrot. Natalie, married to a rich man, would know where money was to be made and found.

And if not, there was the former Confederate agent John Slidell, whose son-in-law was fabulously wealthy. Slidell was a shuffling old man now, but like many old men he was a passionate hater. On the one occasion they had met, he had quickly turned small talk into a poisonous denunciation of the North and the "ape-tyrant" Lincoln.

She would ask Slidell about banks. She would ask Natalie Benjamin about the Emperor—why not? As she rose from the table, Sarah stole another glance at herself in the window. She would ask Natalie about clothes. Because, she thought, laying three francs on a saucer, she was going to have to spend still more money for a gown to wear to Natalie's ridiculous Saturday evening "supper." A waste, foolish, but she couldn't offend Natalie by refusing to come, though she wouldn't know a soul. Unless, perhaps, Slidell came. In the window reflection she minutely adjusted a strap on her dress and smiled sweetly. Certainly not too old. And Slidell was a Southerner, not a Frenchman.

That evening Oakes and the others dined with General Dix in his house on the rue de Presbourg, a cobblestone's throw from the Champs-Élysées. The dinner was presided over by the general's wife, a very strange woman who sat through the meal with a fixed, vacant, tight-lipped smile, the very picture of implacable serenity. She may have spoken—surely, she spoke—but Oakes couldn't remember a word she may or may not have said.

The married daughter, however, Mrs. Charles Blake—Dix had brought his whole family from New York—more than made up for her mother with an unending fund of stories about Parisian eccentrics. There was, for example, the disreputable actress at the Comédie Française known only as "Madeleine," who famously wrote in the autograph album of an admirer: "I prefer Dishonor, of course, to Death." And the elderly baron who used to go to Tortoni's every afternoon and order a bowl of strawberry and a bowl of vanilla ice cream, then pour one into each of his shoes and walk away barefoot."

"Well, our hostess-to-be on Saturday," General Dix said, "Missus Natalie Judah Confederate Benjamin, is supposed to have her newspaper specially printed on rubber, so she can read it in the bath."

Amid the general laughter, Mrs. Blake, not to be outdone by her father, clutched Sharpe's wrist and added breathlessly, "And just yesterday, General, I found a pamphlet at Galignani's—you'll never guess—'The Last Will and Testament of *Nero*.'"

"The Roman Emperor?"

"No! Nero was *our* Emperor's Newfoundland dog. He died in January. It was in all the newspapers. The dog stipulates in his Will that there should be thirty-five statues of himself sculpted after his death and erected in the various *quartiers*, none of them to show him on horseback. It was evidently penned by Napoleon III himself, who fancies himself a humorist."

"Which reminds me," Maggie Lawton said. She asked one of the servants for her traveling bag. When it arrived, she plunged one arm in it and pulled out a rectangular package wrapped in white tissue and a red ribbon. This she presented with a ceremonious bow to Sharpe, who bowed back in great good humor, and unwrapped it quickly. With a little cry of pleasure, he held up a folio-sized book for all to see.

"*Les Chats*," he read. "Cats."

"I bought it this afternoon," Maggie said, "at the bookstall at the Exposition. It claims that by census there are 700,824 cats in Paris—"

"More," Dix muttered.

"—and it tells the history of cats from the Egyptians till now. You have the names of famous cats in literature—here's Doctor Johnson's cat 'Hodge'—and all these illustrations."

Dix had taken the book from Sharpe. "Japanese woodcuts," he said with the approving tone of a connoisseur. "Very handsome."

While the book passed from hand to hand, Keach leaned close to Oakes. "Doing well, are we, Captain Oakes? Prospering?"

Oakes pulled away from Keach's raw breath.

"Went to the banks in Rome, I hear? Made a proper fuck of it, I suppose."

Oakes touched his empty wine glass and made a motion to the hovering butler. "Welcome back, Daniel." From his seat at the other end of the table, Sharpe turned and looked at them.

"We should go to the banks here together," Keach said. "Tomorrow. I'll show you how to ask for what you want." He took the bottle from the butler's hand and filled his own glass first.

Then he gave his own unpleasant version of a tight-lipped smile. "You'll be good as gold."

"I don't like Natalie Benjamin!" Mrs. Dix suddenly, loudly announced. From the slur of her words it was instantly clear that she was drunk.

"Mother!'

Her head tilted to one side, like a puppet with a broken string. "Her Jew husband killed Lincoln. All her friends too—God will beat them with His fists!"

She slumped forward, elbows sprawled. Through her serene, unearthly smile, she murmured, "Kill—Kill—Kill."

9

ON THURSDAY MORNING, MAY 11, two days before Natalie Benjamin's supper, Sarah spent another four francs for a table at the Café de Paris and a cup of tea she didn't want. But anything was better than staying cooped up in her hotel room staring at the gray sky.

She had taken an inside table because the weather had turned suddenly wet and windy—normal in what passed for spring weather in Connecticut, but surprising here. Or not. What did she know about geography? A waiter slammed open an outside door and the wind slung in a fistful of rain. Her papers flapped on the table like startled birds, her inkbottle slid.

Inventory. One letter to John Slidell. Ripped in half. One letter to Baron Frederic d'Erlanger, ripped in quarters. One sheet of paper covered with slanting, crossed-out numbers meant to calculate how much forty percent of her ingots value would come to, if she could talk the Jew moneychanger down.

The rain was coming down in ropes now, and she wondered what that did to the paving machines and the gooey macadam tar that workers had laid down yesterday on the boulevard. Some of Haussmann's work sites now included towers with spotlights—gas lamps behind a giant magnifying lens—so that the work of tearing Paris asunder could go on day and night.

Under her scraps of letters were two timetables, one from Lloyd's Shipping, the other from The Great Steam Navigation Company on the rue Vivienne. She had spent another fifty centimes to send a boy from the hotel to buy them.

In the war, she remembered, she never wondered which step she was to take next. In the war, she went upstairs to Secretary Benjamin's office on East Clay Street in Richmond and he gave her instructions in his soft, sad-eyed way. Then she collected her train tickets from Mr. Benjamin's clerk and set off, sometimes with an escort, and went just where he had told her—this hotel in Montreal, that hotel in Ottawa. Stop at Washington City. See Mrs. Surratt's son, who should have a waiting carriage at the terminus. A discreet exchange of papers out of sight.

Now she had no instructions, no escort. If she could get her money changed into what the French inexplicably called *liquid*—she pictured greenbacks bubbling up out of a spring—she could go anywhere in the world that Lloyds or the Great Steam Navigation Company would take her. Not Connecticut, of course, or North Carolina or New York or Richmond—going back to America would be like throwing herself to the hounds. But Malta was cheap. She had heard Malta was very cheap and welcoming for foreigners.

She sighed and stood up. The rain was slackening, growing thin. Fickle rain, French rain. At the café door she peered at the street. What had she read about icebergs? What showed on the surface was the least part of an iceberg, the smallest part. Its real bulk and nature were below the surface, underneath the water, hidden. What people saw on *her* surface was her coolness, her competence. Below the surface, she thought, all the usual female weaknesses—indecision, timidity, greed. She shook her head and snapped the wings of her bonnet. Where was Quintus Oakes? She didn't care. She stepped boldly into the rain.

Quintus Oakes was in fact not quite half a mile away, in one of the side streets surrounding the Paris stock market called the Bourse. Keach poked him in the side and said, "You ain't sugar, my man, you won't melt in a little rain. Come on, turn up your coat, remember the Wilderness."

Oakes had never forgotten the Wilderness, surely the most savage battle of the whole obscene war, when it had rained so hard and long that after that battle—something you would never believe if you hadn't seen it—their horses actually sank down in the mud to their shoulders. The artillery limbers were bogged so deep that whole teams of oxen, lunging and bellowing at every whip crack, still couldn't budge them. Keach was right. He wouldn't melt in a little Paris rain.

"I had no luck at the Crédit Lyonnais the other day," Oakes said. "They wouldn't even talk to me."

"Of course, they wouldn't. They didn't deal with Richmond during the war, and they were pretty wary of the Canadians. Same reason why there's no point at all going to the Banque de France," Keach said. "Those big banks didn't touch Secessia money. It was the private ones."

"Erlanger," Oakes said as they crossed the rue Vivienne. Everybody knew about the Erlanger loan to the Confederates.

"Erlanger and some of the others. Lloyds over there doesn't do just shipping, they do insurance and commercial loans, too. My old bank in New York saw plenty of Lloyds."

"You go, then."

Keach coughed and half turned his back to avoid the splashing wheels of an omnibus. "You go to Lloyds. I wrote down for you all the accounts we care about, and the right questions. I'm going *there*." He pointed to a red and black painted model steamship suspended over the sidewalk and beneath it the sign, "Great Steamship Navigation Co."

Oakes must have looked puzzled, because Keach added, "Sharpe wants me to look for his fantasy assassin, the famous Agent 'B' that was supposed to kill Sherman. Sharpe thinks he might have bought ship passage in Paris, then left from Nantes. Waste of time, too. That redhead Lawton likes you, Oakes, you do know that, don't you? You ought to pay attention to her."

"That's another fantasy, Keach."

Keach laughed and coughed and waved a kind of dismissal and joined the pedestrians hurrying through the rain. As his coat flapped in the wind, the butt of his Navy revolver glinted a moment in the rain.

The Great Steam Navigation offices reminded Sarah of the Hotel Louvre—a big dark barn of a space, noisy as a cattle yard, dotted with unexplained doors, corridors. Desks and counters made a long concave semi-circle in the central lobby.

The difference was, there were men everywhere you looked, not cattle, men in tall hats, men in wet coats and wet slickers, men smoking and laughing. As she swept in from the street many of them turned to stare.

Some of them laughed, a few made catcalls in a garbled French she didn't quite catch, but she understood the tone perfectly well. There was no other woman in sight. It would doubtless have been better to send a boy from the hotel to buy her ticket, but it would have cost her more money and of course the boy would bungle something. She made herself look amused, perfectly comfortable. She smiled and the men slowly parted, with more catcalls and mutterings, to give her a path toward the counters. She swept her skirt along the dirty floor, over the cigar butts and ashes, and as the buzzing voices resumed their normal volume she made her way toward the desk under the sign "*Passages Individuels*—English Spoken."

Somebody found a chair for her, and she sat down in front of a harassed French clerk who glanced up at her in mild surprise and continued writing. Sarah looked around, more curious than nervous now. In the war she had moved among far larger masses of men than this, many more men.

"*Madame. Je peux vous server comment?*"

"*Passage à Napoli, une personne, moi seule.*"

The clerk studied her with obvious disapproval. "*Vous seule. Pas de mari?*"

No husband, she agreed.

The clerk snorted. Of course not. "*Aller, retour?*"

Sarah declined, as her father would have said, from French into English. "Not a round trip. To Naples. First class cabin, your next sailing from Le Havre."

To her left, standing at the desk two places over, a short, unpleasant looking American was speaking English too. As far as she could tell over the noise of the office, he wanted to talk to a manager, someone in charge, but he kept interrupting himself with a cough.

The French clerk examined him with distaste and shook his head, a Gallic match for Anglo-Saxon disagreeableness. He looked past the American to the next person in line, ready to call him forward, and as the American swung around to wave the person back in anger his coat caught and lifted. In the war Sarah had also seen many men with pistols in their belts.

10

"A 'PINCER' MOVEMENT," GENERAL DIX SAID, "is when the two flanks of an army close around the enemy from each side, like tongs squeezing around a fire log. Sheridan was a master of it."

"Is that what you did at Appomattox, Papa? 'Pincered' Robert E. Lee?"

Mrs. Charles Blake had taken a great interest in the company of a celebrated general like Sharpe. She was also fascinated by the presence of Maggie Lawton, a woman traveling with men, a spy and a female detective. Hence her own presence that afternoon at her father's office, where normally she never showed her face. A paper sack of home baked scones and a canister of black tea from her mother's kitchen served as her excuse.

"I was already ordered back to New York by then," Dix said, a little grumpily. "Replaced by Ben Butler. So I missed Appomattox."

Mrs. Blake made a face to show what she thought of Ben Butler.

"But Miss Lawton here was in Richmond when it fell," Dix said. "She saw the Rebel armies move out."

"She told me last night—it must have been thrilling!"

Maggie twisted her mouth and looked sideways at Oakes. "I think Captain Oakes here was with General Sheridan when they closed in on Appomattox, Miss Blake," she said, "pincing away like crazy."

Mrs. Blake cocked her head in puzzlement like her mother, and Oakes recognized that he ought to say something. Dix was busy arranging various items on his desk to demonstrate a pincer movement—a penknife for Sheridan, the teapot for Lee's army, a brass paperweight shaped like a bear for Grant. He had set out cups and saucers and a set of ivory napkin rings in reserve. George Pickett's infantry was three white sugar cubes.

Oakes reached over and moved the penknife around the sugar cubes and toward the teapot. "Sheridan was cavalry, Missus Blake, coming down from the Shenandoah Valley, on Lee's left flank. He was supposed to drive the Confederates southwest toward the Appomattox River."

"And Grant was coming up the river, turning Lee's right side, folding him back like a piece of wet rope toward Pickett," Dix said. "That was the other point of the pincer."

"More like a blade," Keach said from the corner of the office and coughed.

Dix had yielded to numbers and ordered his clerk to bring in three more chairs. There was also an incongruous love seat that nobody could account for, discovered in one of the outside closets. Keach, with the perfect instinct of the bad-mannered, had claimed it at once.

"Like a bloody blade is more like it," he said. "Grant was the Grim Reaper that last month. He swung that army across Lee's people like a big blue scythe, just cut them down like corn."

"In fact, Missus Blake." The Pundit had left the corner where he was conferring with Keach and come to the desktop battle-field, ready to lecture. "Technically, Grant ordered an 'enveloping attack' against Pickett, not a pincer movement. In a pincer the tension is much greater. The two points of the tong are coming together, blindly but inevitably toward each other, like fateful lov-ers in an opera. They don't *see* each other coming, but they can feel it. At the end they almost dash into one another."

"And that *was* the end," Mrs. Blake said. "The end of that traitor *Lee*. You should have put *him* in prison with the others."

Oakes, who knew that Sharpe had personally handed Robert E. Lee his safe passage home in exchange for Lee's simple *parole*, stirred uneasily. But Sharpe was thinking of something else, Sharpe was looking through Dix's window at the clouds, toward the ocean, home.

"He helped kill Lincoln, with all those others," Mrs. Blake said emphatically. "You'd have to be out of your mind to think a no-account, washed-up drunken actor could kill the President by himself." She turned toward Maggie. "We all met Mister Lincoln at the President's Mansion, our whole family did. He was the *ugliest* man I ever saw, but sweet natured, so kind to his little boy." She hesitated, evidently remembering something, "and to his wife, too. He called her 'Mother.'" Another pause. "She *was* out of her mind."

Sharpe was at the window studying the gray sky. "*Le temps se leve*, as the French say. Strictly translated, it means the weather is 'picking itself up,' very odd expression. But the streets will start drying off now. Of course, the rain can always start again later. I remember that it can rain and turn cold in Paris any time it wants, winter, spring. The second May I was here, before the war, it actually snowed."

He rubbed his eyes with a tired gesture and spoke to the room over his shoulder. "We won't get anything else done today. Quintus, I concede that the very humble Exposition of the Entire Universe might finally be worth a visit."

It took the two Union Army generals more than an hour to mobilize their party, so that it was almost six o'clock in the evening before they arrived at the North Entrance. But that, as Mrs. Blake explained, made no matter. You could eat and drink at any number of pavilions, and at any time, in the informal, mingling fashion that the Exposition seemed instantly to have introduced.

Instantly introduced as well was the new fashion in women's dresses, something Mrs. Blake enthusiastically pointed out to Maggie—the Empress's English couturier Frederick Worth, she rhapsodized, with more seriousness than humour, was the "Great Liberator" of Womankind, the "Lincoln of the Ladies." He had freed them all from the tyranny of that awful billowing crinoline that, swelling mountainously under the skirt, made walking and sitting such an adventure in volume management. Now—she stopped near the *Crèche* and made them all observe the new, svelte lines of the crowds of women passing around them—comfort, ease, naturalness of silhouette.

"Shorter hemlines, too," observed Sharpe, who never ceased to surprise Oakes with what he knew.

"Yes indeed! The Empress likes to take long walks. They make it *much* more comfortable."

Pointlessly, Oakes looked about for Sarah Slater, imagining that they might suddenly be caught between pincers, like faithful lovers in an opera.

"They all look like ladies of the trade," Keach said in his ear, bringing a sour smell of mucous and medicine. "Street girls here. I read they call them *cocodettes*."

That surprised Oakes, too. "Cocodette" was one of innumerable slang words Parisians used for the *demi-monde*; there were *cocodès, lorettes, petit crevés*, and—best of all—*grandes horizontals*. How in the world did Keach know that? But he was right. Off to one side a scowling man dressed all in black was offering Bibles to the passing women.

"I want to buy you a beer," Keach said in his ear again. "In a minute."

"I want you to show me the American exhibits, Quintus," Sharpe said. "These old eyes have had about enough of Europe."

The first of the concentric ovals in the great hall was devoted to French exhibits. The second one was given over to British displays. The remaining galleries were a hodgepodge of nations and included, if Oakes translated the placards correctly, a genuine Turkish bath (two francs), a Russian izba, and a Kyrgyz yurt. The only American sight so far had been the Steinway pianos at the entrance—to the indignation of the French, they had just won the Grand Prize for Musical Instruments, beating out all their European competitors.

To track down other exhibits soon became a matter of bumps and elbows, false starts through the crowds and the corridors, retracing steps again to the central garden. But soon enough Mrs. Blake was in the fifth concentric gallery, admiring a newly improved safety elevator by the American Otis Brothers & Co. General Dix and his daughter wandered off to see a fifty-five-ton cannon on exhibit from Prussia. Sharpe and Maggie Lawton decided to linger in the American painting salon.

"The Captain and I are hungry," Keach said. "We'll be outside in the food pavilions."

Sharpe scarcely nodded. Keach gripped Oakes's elbow and pulled him toward an exit.

Ordinarily, Oakes would have pushed Keach's hand away and gone on with his business. But Keach's whole manner since he had rejoined them was disturbing. Keach's pistol was disturbing. Oakes allowed himself to be led back past the Steinways and out into the night air.

Hardly night sky, however. The outside gardens were festooned with hundreds of brilliantly colored Chinese lanterns. Gas lamps marked winding pathways through the grass of the Parc du Champ-de-Mars, and a breeze off the Seine made the lights pitch and dance across the passing faces and the otherworldly red of the great hall's façade. Top hats sailed in and out of shadows like stately galleons. Ladies' white faces swayed on their new silhouettes like blossoms on stalks. Mrs. Blake, with her mastery of cliché, would undoubtedly have said it was like a fairyland. Oakes looked again at the North Entrance—nothing, no golden fairy. He followed Keach's back down the nearest path.

As it happened, just as he had read in the newspaper in Rome, the American pavilion in the gardens did in fact include a replica of a log cabin, proudly labeled as the actual and authentic cabin where Abraham Lincoln was born. Next to it stood a full-sized (and working) replica of a frontier saloon. Here Keach shoved his way through until he found space at one of the upright barrels that served as tables. The waiter wore a coonskin cap and went off in search of beer.

"Nice to hear our Sharpe correct old Dix about the pincer movement."

"He was kind enough about it."

"That was a butchery, though, that time with Sheridan at the end. I won't forget that soon." For a few weeks just before the end, both Keach and Oakes had been seconded over to Sheridan's cavalry, because Grant's lines at Petersburg had not yet started to move, and Sheridan—nobody, Oakes thought, had ever seen Sheridan not in motion—Sheridan needed information gathered at top speed. Sheridan needed *everything* at top speed or faster. Sheridan's ruthlessness made Grant look tenderhearted.

"You remember how Shridan treated Warren?"

Oakes did remember and took no pleasure in it. Gouverneur K. Warren of Rhode Island was a decent, not incompetent general—during Gettysburg he had organized a famous defense at Little Round Top. But like most Union generals he showed little inclination to hurry his troops or rush into combat. On the last day of March 1865, when Sheridan's cavalry were slaughtering trapped Rebels in a scene of almost biblical carnage, he committed the unpardonable sin of being slow to bring his brigades up to join the fight.

So for Sheridan—Oakes had thought afterward that the old Greeks had it right with their gods—there really was such goddess as Lyssa, the daemon of madness and fury in war—and for one whole day she seemed to have come to earth and inhabited the mortal form of little brick-shouldered, black-haired Phil Sheridan, who galloped from line to line, trampling corpses, whipping his saber about his head like a man truly possessed. His dark face thundered with blood, his eyes flashed—when a soldier at his side was struck in the throat and the blood started spurting in a fountain, Sheridan violently yanked him to his feet and sent him staggering forward—"You ain't hurt a bit! *Move!*"—till the soldier dropped his musket and fell down dead.

"Fired Warren on the spot," Keach said with obscure satisfaction. "Sheridan did." He took the first swallow of his beer. "Demoted him from general then and there, wrecked his career. I think even Lincoln was afraid of little Phil Sheridan. Not Grant, though." Keach swallowed more beer and nodded his approval to the hovering waiter. "Lincoln was too soft."

Oakes had heard Abraham Lincoln called almost everything, but not until now had someone spoken of him as "soft"—on the contrary, like Grant, Lincoln in his quiet way had been implacable Will incarnate.

Will incarnate, and also Mercy incarnate. At the end of the long unforgettable day when Richmond fell, Lincoln had gone into the Executive Mansion of the Confederacy, now ghostly empty, deserted hours earlier by Jefferson Davis and all his people. He had sat down in Davis's chair at the head of the cabinet table. Oakes was standing by the door with another guard, watching the stairway. He heard the President politely ask an elderly black servant to bring him a glass of water. Then somebody—probably Admiral Porter—had asked what the President wanted done with the still bitter and hostile white population of the city. And Lincoln had run his hand across the smooth wood of the desktop, as if to erase a deep cut or gouge, and said, "I'd let 'em up easy, I think. Let them up easy."

"What do you want with me, Keach?"

"You already have the tickets home—Wednesday next, May fifth, Paris to Havre, Havre to New York, right?"

"That's what the general asked for."

"You're going too?"

Oakes had pushed aside his beer as undrinkable. Now he straightened and stared at Keach. "Am I going, too? Is *that* what you said?"

Keach pulled the untouched glass next to his own. "You see, Captain Oakes, sir, I've had a couple of deep thoughts all along, ever since we started this trip. Deep thought number one—why all this trouble about Sarah Slater, or whatever name she uses now? Small fry, don't you think, a little female courier? If she knew about Booth's plot, well, so did some other people, but Sharpe and Stanton don't care about them. She wasn't in the Ford's Theater, she didn't have anything to do with pulling the trigger. Why bother with her? And why bring *you* along just to identify her? Because—deep thought number two—you're useless, Captain Quintus Oakes, sir. True, you went to college. True, you had an officer's commission. But face it, my friend, you don't know anything about banks or commerce. You never worked for a living your whole life. Sharpe could have gotten along fine with just me."

Oakes stretched his neck and looked through the inauthentic glass window of the cabin. A nice French irony, putting a saloon next to the teetotaler Lincoln's actual and authentic log cabin.

Keach, of course, was correct. And Keach's bitterness—put yourself in his place, Maggie had said. Keach was poor and Irish and had no future—clerk in a bank—you had to make allowances, Maggie said. On the other hand, Keach had let the violence in his nature take over too many times and warp him. Maybe his Ruling Passion wasn't money, but mayhem.

Oakes brought his gaze back around.

Keach was looking intensely at him. "While you and Sharpe were off in Rome wasting more time, Captain Quintus, I climbed out of my bed of sickness and sorrow and on a hunch went over to see one Mister Legare O'Beare at the Coutts and Company bank."

Oakes felt his whole face turn to ice. He made himself stand up straighter, but slowly, in no hurry at all.

Some people you just love.

"A very nice man," he said, "Legare O'Beare." At the other end of the frontier bar, under a big tilted mirror, a trio of French musicians was now thumping out an unrecognizable tune on two horns and a bass.

"A very nice man," Keach said. "Drank sherry and talked his plummy old English head off." He paused significantly. "About gold ingots mostly."

Oakes was remembering a phrase in a novel he'd read years ago, something about "the incredible velocity of thought." But his own thoughts were moving as sluggishly as an ox in Virginia mud. Sheridan would have fired him on the spot.

"Here's a geometry lesson," Keach said, "from the Irish streets of New York. For your information, parallels actually meet."

The pedant in Oakes stirred. "No, they don't."

"In real life they do. You and Sarah Slater, same little town in Connecticut, at the same prison on the same day in Washington City. Somehow, you're on duty and she gets away—don't act so surprised, I know a lot more than you think. The point is, *your* two parallels come together in the end. I think you found her when we were in London and you helped her get away to Paris. I think when the rest of us trot up the gangplank to New York, you're going to be back here in old Paree, you and her and all the Confederate gold money she stole. And before that happens, my fine Harvard friend, you're going to take me to her."

"Did you tell any of this to Sharpe?"

"O'Beare said she has at least two hundred thousand in Kellogg and Humbert ingots—you wouldn't know what they are, but there's not a bank in Europe will touch them without another bank's credentials, so she'll have to go to some private money-lender and change her ingots into notes. But a moneylender isn't going to give her two hundred thousand. *Maybe* she can get sixty or seventy thousand. *I* could probably find a way to get more. But either way, it's a nice little pot. I want that money, Quintus. And you have to take me to her."

"Why should I do such a thing?"

Keach laughed his unhealthy laugh. Laughed and coughed leaned over the table. His breath was sour, his grin tight.

"Why you should do it is so that Sharpe doesn't find your girl first and hang her."

11

THE NEXT MORNING DAWNED gray and damp.

Sarah Slater wrote the day's date at the top of a blank sheet of paper. *May 6, 1867. Saturday.*

Then she began writing down numbers in the neat hand she had learned in the tiny brick schoolhouse out on Sachem's Head, back in Guilford, Connecticut, a lifetime ago. For some reason, she always found it harder to add and subtract in French than in English. She squirmed on the uncomfortable chair provided with the impractical table in her hotel room and moved her papers randomly around, with the vague idea that they would spontaneously arrange and total themselves up on their own.

On the single occasion she had met Quintus Oakes's formidable father, that granite-jawed old New England lawyer had been remarkably gracious, a surprise considering her lowly station as dancing master's daughter—how had Quintus escaped the snobbery of his father and all the other gentry? Mr. Oakes senior had even made a kind of playful joke about himself. Other people, he said, knew mathematics and astronomy and Euclidian geometry—his only intellectual tool, alas, he allowed, was "The List."

"Whenever you're confronted with a problem, Miss Gilbert, I advise you always to 'Make a List.'"

Under the date, as a stalling tactic, she added the place: *Paris, France*. Then, *List*.

Next came *Liabilities*. A long column of numbers, indeed. One-way ticket, First Class cabin, from Le Havre to Naples, by way of train from Paris to Le Havre. One stop in Marseilles, two days sail to Malta—940 francs. One new dress, quite beautiful and expensive, bought from Natalie Benjamin's favorite dress-maker—320 (!) francs; to be worn tomorrow at Natalie's "souper." Grand Hotel through Sunday morning, 142 francs.

There was more, but they were small sums and tedious to add up—carriage fares, perfume from Natalie's perfumer. Guidebooks, newspapers, something for the porters at the train and docks. Female supplies at a pharmacy. Natalie had wanted her to go to Nadar the Society Photographer and have her portrait taken in her new dress, but Sarah didn't have her photograph taken, ever.

Impossible to explain to Natalie, who didn't listen in any case and went off on an amusing speech about the popularity of photographs of naked women that were being sold behind tobacco counters all over the city. And of course, the *scandale du jour*, somebody's painting of a prostitute named "Olympia" that was so much talked about. She would miss Natalie.

Assets.

Sarah pushed back the uncomfortable granite-bottomed chair—what did her own disloyal father say? "I hate French furniture!"

She walked across the room and opened the wardrobe with a key. Behind her dresses and shoes, behind a lady's traveling box, sat a black leather bag with two locks and two folding handles. The Jewish moneylender had given it to her as a present after she had come back to his squalid little coffin of an office, and they had, with far less trouble than she expected, settled their terms. Under *Assets* she could put the assorted francs and leftover English pounds in her purse, amounting to something like $400. She could also put the leather bag, which contained the equivalent in francs and Italian lira of $88,500.

Eighty-eight thousand, five hundred dollars. Compulsively she unlocked the bag, verified that the banknotes were still there, and locked it again. As soon as she locked it, she felt the urge to unlock it and check the money all over again. There was a line Booth particularly liked, from some forgotten play—"Play the man, Polycartes! Play the man!" *Play the man, Sarah!* She shook her head firmly to impress an unseen audience, pushed the bag back, and clicked the wardrobe shut.

At the window she pulled back the curtain and watched the gray air give up the fight and turn to thin, glassy rain. Her mind jumped from compartment to compartment like the ball on a spinning roulette wheel.

If it kept on raining, what would happen to Natalie's party tomorrow night? If she left the hotel at six on Sunday morning, she would reach Le Havre with three hours to spare before the ship sailed. John Wilkes Booth—her mind skipped back to Booth and Polycartes. Thomas Courtenay was right, of course, about Booth's penis. According to an actress she knew, he did have a seemingly permanent case of Senor Gonorrhea, but she had never seen it for herself. Despite the gossip about her, Sarah had felt a visceral dislike for Booth, she had always kept her distance from him. Whatever people said, whatever Quintus Oakes had heard, she never...

Through a gap in the buildings across the street she could see the flickering silvery line of the Seine. If her room were a few floors higher, she could surely see the Exposition building as well, a mile or so downriver. In the war the Confederate army used four basic flag motions to signal messages over distances like that—you could make all twenty-six letters and ten digits with combinations of the basic four moves. You could write a book with your flags. If he was in Paris, if he was at the Exposition, why didn't Quintus Horatius Flaccus Oakes pick up a flag and signal her? *I am here. Come find me.*

The hotel had sent up tea for her at ten o'clock, and even though it was cold now, Sarah sat down on her bed and poured a new cup. Years ago she had read a story about a woman at her birthday party—the woman had been happy to have a party, but *un*happy that a former lover was going to be there. She was happy that people would see she was pregnant, but *un*happy that her husband was displeased—and so on. In real life just as in the story, for every emotion there was an equal and opposite reaction. Newton's Law, Sarah's Law. She wanted to go to Malta and start over, she wanted to go home to America. She wanted to go home to 1859. She wanted to see Quintus Oakes. She never wanted to see him again.

For every cup of cold tea in Paris, there was an equal and opposite cup of hot coffee. She put on her bonnet, her new impermeable, picked up her umbrella, and prepared to walk out into the slow, sad Parisian rain.

12

"I WROTE AN EPITAPH A LONG TIME AGO for sentimentality," Maggie Lawton said. "For 'Mother Europe,' for travel. I never want to travel again. But I guess I'm glad I saw London and Paris—"

"And Montreal," Oakes said.

"Less glad to see Montreal. Glad to see Sharpe again. If I were his valet, he'd still be my hero. But I need to be in New York, I need to be back in America. You're at home here, Sharpe's at home anywhere, but I'm American to my bones."

"Like Lincoln." Oakes's mind was on too many other things. He was scarcely listening.

"Lincoln was a troubled man," Maggie Lawton said.

It took a moment for Oakes to register what she had said. He turned slowly back from the lobby window.

"I told you once," she said. "I wake up every morning mad at Lincoln. He could have let the South go out, they had every right to go. But he took it on himself to save the glorious Union, as if a dusty old eighteenth-century political contract is a holy sacrament. Thousands of men died to satisfy his ambition. I hate the way he always called the war 'this big trouble.' Not 'this big bloodbath that I started.'"

Oakes sat down opposite her. He wanted to object, but didn't.

"Of course, he didn't do it alone," Maggie said. "You can't start a modern war without a lot of help. Newspapers, for instance. Wars sell newspapers. And the bankers, too, the bankers rubbed their palms and grinned like monkeys at the thought of all those contracts and graft. Hypocrites every one of them—blessing the sword with a cross and a dollar sign. When that half-blind old fraud Chase put 'In God We Trust' on his greenbacks, I think every banker in New York had to snicker."

Oakes watched a woman with a very wet white dog under her arm bang the bell at the hotel reception desk. He exhaled, a long sighing sound that seemed to have begun a hundred years ago. "I hope you don't say these things to Sharpe."

Maggie leaned forward and said quietly, "I only say things to you."

Oakes didn't know where to look. He twisted toward the woman with the dog. He frowned at the rain. There was a drum-roll of thunder, like the distant gathering of troops. "What time is our gala dinner tomorrow?" he finally said.

"I don't know. There's something else I've been meaning to tell you about Sharpe. In Rome, while you were out moping or trawling for Rebels or whatever you did, our dapper general dragged me off to the Spanish Steps to see the house where Keats died."

"Keats the poet?"

"Keats the poet. One of his many best favorites. Apparently Keats died at an early age."

"He was twenty-six. He had consumption."

"Well, somebody has made a museum of the house where he died in Rome, and Sharpe wanted to see it. We went up to the second or third floor—I never remember how they count floors in Europe—and there wasn't much to see, just old bookcases and furniture and a guestbook to sign. And a guide holding out his hand, of course. You know you can't cross the street in Rome without hiring a guide. As it happened this was an Englishman named Clarke, not a Roman at all. He showed us Keats's books and a bad painting of him and then he took us into the bedroom where Keats actually died."

She stopped abruptly. Oakes waited a long minute by his own count. "And then?"

"And then our general fell apart. He started to recite a poem, naturally. I remember the first line—'When I have fears that I may cease to be.' He got that far and then he began to cry."

Oakes had no idea what to think or say. He had never seen George H. Sharpe cry. His mind erased the image, and substituted the trim, hard figure of the general cutting through the Willard Hotel lobby like the prow of a ship, people silently standing aside to let him pass. He was the much-feared spymaster of Grant's invincible army. There was no place in Sharpe's makeup for tears.

"He cried and told me to look at that room—it was hardly a room, it was not much bigger than a closet. It had one narrow bed and a pair of windows that looked down on the Spanish Steps and the fountain, and a little bedstand with a water pitcher and a glass. He told me Keats was the greatest young poet in English history and he couldn't bear the thought of this genius lying on that awful little bed and coughing his lungs up instead of going on to write glorious poetry. Then he recited what I guess was the end of the poem—'on the shore/Of the wide world I stand alone and think,/Till Love and Fame to nothingness do sink.'"

"The most surprising man," Oakes said stupidly.

"He told me he was crying at the thought of that wasted young life, all that beautiful lost literature."

Oakes raised his head to meet her eyes. "But you think he was really talking about the war. He was thinking about all the wasted lives in the war, thrown away for no good reason."

"No, I don't think that," Maggie said impatiently. "He quotes poetry, he cries about somebody he's never seen. But he's not bothered about all those soldiers he sent off to be killed. That was just his job, like Grant's job, and in some awful way you have to admire him for it. *You* think he's complicated, deep, full of contradictions. You think he loves you like a son and if it came down to it, he'd look the other way for you. But he's just *hard*, Quintus. He's not sentimental. If he finds your Veiled Lady, he's going to put her in a cell twice as narrow as John Keats's room and then he's going to walk her out to the gallows and watch her hanged and he won't shed one solitary tear. But you would cry. And I would cry because you cried."

Maggie shoved back her chair and stood.

"If l were your lady friend from Guilford," she said, "I would run as far away from you as I could."

13

THE GALA DINNER was to begin at nine.

As preparation for a life together with Natalie that would probably never happen, Judah Benjamin had built for her a three-story mansion at 41, avenue d'Iena, just half a mile from the Arc de Triomphe—the imposing presence could easily be seen from the upper floors. This was the house where Sarah had first seen her paintings.

To Natalie's disgust, however, the avenue d'Iena was still being widened by Haussmann's crews, while other workers were also digging trenches for new sewers, so that the usual chaotic construction process was going on below ground as well as above. The muddy excavation pit for the sewers stood directly across from Natalie's front door; the digging and stockpiling of stones and tools and machines extended half a mile north, as far as number 163.

When the crews finally finished their work, the great Prefect had assured the the world in a somewhat Olympian pronouncement, the sewers would perform to perfection and the avenue would be wide enough for six carriages at a time—like the "broad back of the sea on which the Greek fleet sailed to Troy." His erudition amused no one who had to pick his way through the present ruins of fallen trees, half-demolished walls, paving stones and mud. Certainly not Natalie Benjamin, who expressed her displeasure in a constant stream of outraged messages and notes. To her most recent letter of complaint, Haussmann had himself personally and philosophically replied, "Nine-tenths of Progress is Destruction."

As it happened, on Saturday evening the excavation caused very few problems for Natalie's dinner. Helpful workmen had cleared a path for carriages, right to her door. But the rain, which had held off most of the day, came creeping back late in the afternoon. By six o'clock regrets and excuses because of the weather had been delivered by the dozens, though more than a hundred guests were still expected.

For the occasion, Natalie had transformed her extensive rear gardens into a miniature replica of the Exposition gardens, complete with white and orange Chinese lanterns in a shrubbery maze. From six to eight she spent a good deal of time throwing open the back doors and cursing Jupiter Pluvius in both English and a thoroughly unladylike French.

At Parisian dinners of the best society one usually didn't dance—that was for the music halls and theaters—but music was always provided. With a nod to convention, Natalie had hired three flutists from the Opera to wander the grand salon and the gardens—but the gardens would be too wet now, of course. And for a completely original touch she had also engaged, as a surprise, the "Theatre Pupazzi" of Lemercier de Neuville to perform before the food was served.

"He has a touching story," she told Sarah, "Monsieur de Neuville."

"Is he Italian?" Sarah stood in Natalie's second floor dressing room, adjusting ribbons, patting stray hairs, and generally putting the mirrors, as Natalie said, through their paces.

"Of course not. He was born in Laval. He's as French as can be. Until five years ago he was astonishingly poor"—she paused as if to consider what that was like—"and one day his little boy went deathly sick. There was no money for toys, so to amuse him Monsieur de Neuville made some funny puppets out of colored paper and strings. Then his friends told him he should put on a show like that for the public, *et voilà*!"

"Is John Slidell coming tonight?"

"And bringing the weight of the world on his shoulders, or at least the weight of the Confederacy, yes."

"How do I look?"

Natalie's emotions were never hard to read. "Damn your lovely eyes," she said, only partly joking. "Also damn your lovely blonde hair—mine always looks like little black wires sticking out of my head—also damn your dress. Emerald green silk, perfect with blonde hair. You appear," she sighed, "very presentable."

Sarah tucked in a rebellious strand of hair and asked a question that had been in her mind almost from the first moment she saw Natalie. "You talk all the time about Mister Benjamin," she said. "You write him every week. Why don't you live together?"

Natalie glanced at the maid who sat in a corner assembling a corsage. Something resembling telepathy passed between them, and the maid rose, curtsied, and left. Natalie spread the folds of her gown, which was ample and voluptuous and not at all in what she called the "pinched thorax" style of M. Worth.

"Once when we were living in Bellechasse," she said, "outside New Orleans, Mister Benjamin worked so hard he damaged his eyesight and had to stay in a dark room for three months. He didn't come out at all. I never even saw him. He sent me notes. Now, being blind and living like that would have driven me mad. But Mister Benjamin is made of different stuff. He just hired a man to read to him and kept on with his law practice as if nothing were wrong. He said he had an obligation to his clients." She paused and frowned. "Do you see what I'm saying?"

"You're talking," Sarah said slowly, "about a sense of duty."

"I'm talking," Natalie said, "about the 'woe that is in marriage.'"

At a quarter past nine the first carriages splashed up to the portico of number 41. Inside, the flutists wet their lips, a servant came down the front steps holding an umbrella, and with a burst of laughter and a shaking of wet hats and sleeves, the dinner began.

Like a good general, Natalie had stationed herself close to the front lines. In Paris she was indulged as an American—and therefore somewhat exotic—hostess, less formal and rigid than most French women. Once, she had hired dancers from the Jardin Mabille to teach the cancan to her guests, including (people said) the Emperor himself in disguise. And though the spectacle of Paris's social elite kicking their legs in chorus had been considered "delirious" and "magic," in the aftermath polite shock set in, and Natalie was cautioned never to be quite so exotic again.

Tonight, she simply stood decorously at the entrance to her grand salon and welcomed her guests with becoming commiseration— *"Such a rain!"*—and an elegant, sympathetic gesture toward the display of champagne and lobster by the window. As the crush of people grew and the room became nearly impassable, she quite forgot about Sarah Slater.

Which suited Sarah. She was not a shy person. She held her own now in the rapid Parisian French that had at first tripped her up. She felt easy enough among strangers. But her mind was busy elsewhere, picturing the next morning, the ship's pitch and roll, the long Mediterranean horizon that would mark the end...She hardly knew what it marked the end of—being a fugitive? John A. Slidell, expatriate Confederate, shuffled up to her.

"Hiding among the flowers, my dear Miss Slater—'herself a fairer flower.'"

Sarah smiled at the compliment, but then Slidell spoiled it by adding like a schoolmaster, "*Paradise Lost*, Book IV. John Milton talking about Proserpine."

"Is your beautiful daughter here, Mister Slidell?"

Slidell was wearing a silk crimson cravate, which he now twisted violently to one side of his neck. "Damned French clothes," he muttered. "Just as soon bloody strangle you. Language, beg pardon. No, my son-in-law wanted to come, but she wouldn't budge."

"Because of the rain?"

Slidell had turned away, scanning the crowded salon. Two of the flutists had come together beside Natalie Benjamin for an impromptu duet. Champagne sailed by on trays held high above a sea of powdered and pomaded hair, and the old man raised his finger toward a waiter.

"Not the rain," he said. "She heard General Dix was coming, and that horse-faced daughter of his, and then some other people from the Embassy, too. She can't stand Dix. I speak to him, but I don't shake his hand." He snagged two glasses from a passing tray and handed one to Sarah. "Tell me more about when you were living in Richmond."

But Sarah knew General Dix by sight, from the war, and she saw him at that moment stepping inside the room, extending his hat and gloves to a servant. She had no more desire than Slidell's daughter to meet him. With a murmur of apology and a touch on the old man's sleeve, she turned and slipped away.

Daniel Keach saw her leave but had no idea who she was. The whirl of her blonde hair made him think for a moment of gold.

Then he said, "Don't just stand there, Oakes. Give the man your hat."

Oakes, who was looking in the other direction, turned and gave his hat to a servant. General Dix frowned back at them, seemed to count, and over the rising and falling noise of the room asked loudly for Sharpe.

"Finishing a letter," Maggie Lawton told him. She planted herself next to Dix, hooked his right arm over her elbow and smiled across his middle-aged rotundity to Mrs. Blake on the other elbow. "General Sharpe never stops writing reports. He'll come, but he'll be late."

"My father's the same way. He says the best things are written in anger."

"And I'm always angry." Dix beamed complacently at the room and acknowledged with a nod his hostess on the other side of the room. "I like what the Duke of Gloucester said to Gibbon—'Another damn'd thick square book, eh, Mister Gibbon? Scribble, scribble, scribble!' Sharpe'll have trouble getting through that excavation mess outside."

"Don't you like Miss Lawton's gown, Captain Oakes?" Mrs. Blake said. "Emerald green, with her red hair, so *daring*!"

Oakes scarcely heard her. His mind was still back in the hotel lobby, where Maggie had said she would cry because he cried. But he made a little bowing motion that he ruined by frowning.

Then he stepped away toward the center of the room, followed closely by Keach. If it hadn't rained, half the guests would have been outside, strolling among the flowers and lanterns. Now they were all inside, packed shoulder to shoulder. The men pulled their elbows in and the ladies' skirts swayed like bells.

Natalie's house, thoroughly modern, had gas lamp fixtures. But either because of the storm or because of the forthcoming puppet show, these had gradually been dimmed and given way to candles in sconces along the walls, so that against a background of turning shadows the faces of the partygoers looked like white petals floating in a vase.

Keach planted himself on Oakes's left. "Go away, Keach."

"You're not skipping out, Captain. Think of me as glue."

The flutists brought their duet to an end, and servants began to arrange three rows of oval-backed chairs. While they clattered about and herded guests out of its path, to a gasp of pleasure, two footmen rolled out a portable stage.

This was no more than a wagon about six feet long, such as might be seen at any open market in Paris, resting on four differently colored wooden wheels. Its panels were cleverly decorated with bright, busy paintings of puppets and dolls. Above the wagon box, blue curtains extended up another three feet, supported by brass uprights. An open square in the center revealed a black velvet interior. Suddenly a pretty girl wearing a jester's cap ducked behind the wagon. An instant later two thin poles snapped up high above the topmost curtain, stretching between them a scroll with the flaming red words—"*Les Pupazzi de Neuville!*"

Quickly, excitedly, chattering like sparrows, the ladies besieged the chairs. The men pushed forward behind them. Out of somewhere—to the evident disdain of the flutists—an accordion player appeared and began to caper and play. What the tune was, Oakes had no idea. But most of the audience recognized it, and some started to applaud, while others waved champagne glasses and shouted *Bravo!* A smiling Natalie emerged from the foyer.

Oakes circled the room restlessly, going in a clockwise direction. Keach kept a steady, unfriendly stare on him. Meanwhile, the accordionist swung his instrument over his head and with a burst of chords and a wild whoop, M. de Neuville himself bounced out of the shadows like a jack-in-the box and into the circle of candlelight around his stage.

Oakes stopped far off to one side of the wagon. Natalie's grand salon had the usual tall French windows, but twice the normal height, it seemed. The curtains had been roped back to the window jambs and the glass panels propped slightly open. The damp night air was creeping in, making him shiver. Distant thunder rattled the glass.

At almost the same moment the little curtains in the center of the stage closed and snapped open again, and three big, silly puppet heads popped up. As they started to slap and punch each other, the audience broke into loud, knowing laughter.

Oakes had read that de Neuville's satirical puppets were all supposed to be contemporary French politicians and notable *boulevardiers*. He wouldn't understand the jokes and, in any case, he disliked puppets. He had always disliked—even as a boy—manipulation, strings, hair-trigger violence; puppets were far more lifelike than any actor.

A plump, not unhandsome woman came to the side of the stage, poised and self-delighted, clearly their hostess. Her smiling face drifted through shadows.

Another face appeared beside her and stopped, frozen in a point of light.

14

Two THOUGHTS FLASHED like pistols.

Sarah Slater hadn't seen him.

Keach had.

And not only Keach. Anyone watching Oakes would have caught the sudden stiffening, the arch backward as if he had been stung or shot. From the other side of the room, Keach started forward. Behind Keach, Maggie Lawton stared.

Oakes had been standing on the left side of the grand salon, near the half-open window. Sarah had appeared exactly opposite him next to the wagon-stage, where the puppets, to everyone's delight, were now pummeling each other with brooms.

Impossible to cross to her in front of the puppets. Oakes took two steps slowly to his left, and as soon as he dared, bent his head and circled fast behind the stage. In a blur he saw a man's crouched back, hands working the puppets. The girl with the red jester's cap knelt beside him. A burst of laughter drew every eye to the stage and Oakes stepped out from the shadows on the other side, beside a startled Natalie Benjamin, who turned and spoke to him in surprise. Whatever she said was drowned out by another burst of laughter, but next to her Sarah Slater caught a sound, a movement and she too turned, wide-eyed, toward Oakes.

If he thought he had found her, if he thought she would rush into his arms in a burst of light—nothing happened—nothing had ever happened as he imagined, except the war. Without a word she spun about and pushed through the laughing crowd. Annoyed or puzzled faces looked back as she passed, then closed ranks again and pressed closer to the puppets.

Oakes dodged around Natalie Benjamin. Not quite running, not quite walking, he shoved past the stocky figure of John Dix and elbowed his way into a hallway. He saw carpeted stairs and and an open window where rain hissed on an awning. At the second floor landing he saw a door begin to close. He pushed it open again, and when he entered the room he saw Sarah Slater by a gas lamp, a shadow come to life.

By the time he reached her, six years had passed. In a gesture so natural, so perfect and unexpected he would never forget it, she lifted her right hand to his cheek and rested it there a moment.

"I never gave up hoping," she whispered, "I left messages," and if it was a lie, he never had time to ask. He bent toward her and the door behind them slammed shut.

"Captain Oakes," Keach said. "And Miss Thompson Slater Gilbert, Etcetera, I presume."

From below came a cascade of laughter. From the window, thunder and a whiplash of rain across the glass. Keach advanced into the room. Somehow Oakes had time to see that the walls were covered with paintings of women, little feminine tables with cups and vases were everywhere. A side door cracked open and a maid's face peeked in.

"Time to choose, Oakes. Your country or your girl. You always knew you'd have to."

"Get out."

"The Captain and I have an understanding," Keach told Sarah. "You're going to take me to that nice yellow gold you stole from Jeff Davis."

And suddenly it had never been a choice at all.

"No," Oakes said.

"Yes." Keach pulled back his coat to reveal the butt of the Navy revolver he had brought all the way from the war to Paris. "You stole a lot of money, Miss Gilbert. You can take me to it, or I can take you to General Sharpe."

"Quint—"

"General Sharpe is the man who would hang you for treason. He's right downstairs."

Oakes took a step toward him. Sarah moved backward toward the wall. Keach drew the revolver from his belt. Thunder clapped just overhead and a zigzag of lightning outside the window made the air in the room jump and the gas lamp go black.

In the darkness Oakes could hear the maid screaming. To his right came the noise of Sarah scrambling over something. Blindly he dove toward her and his shoulder hit Keach and he swung hard and cursed. Phantom hands, fingers struggling, then next to his ear a single loud snap.

The *crack* of a pistol sounds nothing at all like thunder. In a room, in a house it can sound tiny and angry and human. And yet, the instant after Keach fired the whole house seemed to have heard it and gone silent, even the rain and the wind. It must have been like that for Lincoln, Oakes madly thought, the whole great theater voiceless, mute while the pain shot like a fist through his skull. The maid screamed. Oakes swung again and felt blood on his knuckles. A second terrible *crack*, then the door to the hallway opened and in another tongue's flicker of lightening he saw Sarah Slater, running away from him once again.

The gas lamp on the landing still worked. Oakes stumbled out, grabbed the banister, and felt a jolt of pain run down his wrist. There was just time enough for the thought to form—chasing a woman you don't want to catch—then he was bouncing down the stairs three at a time. The double doors swung open from the grand salon on the right and shouting guests flooded into the entrance hallway. He glimpsed Maggie Lawton's red hair before Keach's fist hit the back of his neck like a a brick and sent him tumbling and rolling onto the wet tile of the entrance.

The front door of the house banged open; Sarah Slater disappeared into the black rain. Oakes felt himself buffeted sideways and backwards by the people still streaming out of the salon—so many by now that he had no chance at all of getting to the front door and out.

With a lurch he came to his feet and pushed the other way against the crowd, back into the salon. Here the gaslights were coming on. He could see the half-open window by the puppet stage. He threaded his way through overturned chairs—somebody shouted that he was bleeding—the puppet master jumped out of his way. At the window he braced one arm on the sill, registered in some part of his brain that now his whole arm was burning with pain, and vaulted over and into the shrubs that Haussmann had providentially left intact on Natalie's side of the street.

"Quint!—"

Great-hearted Maggie Lawton, Maggie Lawton who would have shot Sherman dead if they'd sent *her*, who leapt through the Roman Coliseum like a deer—in the cold rain and colder

wind Maggie Lawton had somehow gotten ahead of the hysterical crowd. Another flash of lightning showed her tottering at the
edge of the excavation pit. On the other side of it, halfway up a
slick muddy incline, Sarah had fallen in the mud. She was standing now, gripping a plank with both hands like a club.

Oakes could hardly see through the rain. He ran toward
Keach with his arms windmilling to keep his balance. Something
snagged his trousers and ripped them, a shoe sucked and filled
with mud. Maggie Lawton jumped into the pit and started
toward Keach.

"Get back, Maggie!"

Rain scoured his face. Sarah swung her plank and struck Keach
a slicing blow on the head, but the revolver stayed in his hand. In
the next lightning flash Maggie had caught up. The two women
were no more than a yard apart, swaying patches of wet green silk,
brown mud. Oakes saw his left hand grab Keach by the shoulder
and fall away. As the wind lifted the next curtain of rain aside,
he saw Sarah scrambling up a wobbling pyramid of construction
stones. In another moment she would be at the top of the pit, on
the open street, next to the river that ran to the faraway sea.

Then Keach clutched her trailing skirt, and Maggie came
between them and pushed him away. Thunder broke open the
sky. The streetlamps went out. In the staccato motion of a dream,
their shadows flowed together and fell apart. The pistol barrel
glinted, but thunder rolled over them again, jealous, obliterating
every other sound, so that Oakes never heard it fire, he saw only
an orange spurt of light, a green dress turn to red.

When he reached her Maggie was sprawled on her back and
blood was pumping from her chest. Above them Sarah Slater

paused and looked down. Her face hung in the darkness, far out of reach, and vanished.

"You stupid, stupid man," Maggie whispered.

Oakes knelt and cradled her head. Someone knelt on the other side pressing a cloth against Maggie's breast, but the dark blood pumped on, relentless, reddening the water on the ground.

She opened her eyes for a moment and Oakes bent so close he could feel her breath as it slipped away. "Sweet man," she said, "you should have chosen me," and her head flopped to one side in the mud.

Some people you just—but the thought never finished itself.

Keach was off to one side, yelling. Rough hands lifted Oakes to his feet and dragged him aside. Not speaking, not even glancing at Keach, Sharpe lunged to his knees beside Maggie.

Oakes staggered up. More hands guided him toward the sidewalk and automatically, mindlessly, like a wind-up automaton he walked a few stiff steps down it, toward the river. His arm felt on fire, his sleeve was bloody and sticky. He looked back once to see someone wrenching Keach's arms behind his back as if to arrest him. There was no point in that, he thought. Keach would get away. Keach would say it was an accident. Nobody in France would care.

Three steps farther and the North Entrance of the Universal Exposition came into view at the bottom of the avenue. Its orange and white lanterns winked like fireflies through the leaves of the plaza. *I was here. I am gone.* Sarah would have melted into the crowd by now or got away into the carriages and cabs that swarmed along the avenue. In a matter of hours she would be far from Paris. He could go after her, but there was no point in that either. She was gone. She was as unreachable as Maggie.

The rain was still falling, but the storm had exhausted itself. The weary clouds were curling away to the east now, bruised and gray from their battle. He slowly turned in a circle. The ruins of Paris lay all about him. He looked like someone who had lost his way in a distant country.

15

THREE DAYS LATER, OAKES STOOD at a window looking out at the clear, clean, thoroughly scrubbed Parisian sky. Ambassador Dix had found temporary office space for them in the building that housed his own offices, but the room was on a lower floor and on a different side from the rue de Chaillot, so that the gray alley below them was undisturbed by pickaxes or shovels or the shouts of mud-smeared workmen. Silent as the grave, he thought.

"Are you interested in making yourself useful, Captain Oakes?"

Sharpe was seated on some kind of folding wooden chair, at an incongruously elegant Louis VI desk, studying his inevitable folders. His eyes were red-rimmed. His voice was flat and dull. His voice had been flat and dull since the night of Maggie Lawton's… Oakes let his mind turn over various possible nouns—"accident," "demise," "murder"—but finally settled on the exquisitely uncommunicative word the French police and Sharpe had been using in their official report exculpating Keach, "*décès*"—decease.

"How so?"

"Dix has found us another ship to New York, so somebody has to go exchange our tickets."

"Keach too?"

"Keach too."

"I won't go with him."

Sharpe sighed, "Quint, Quint," just as he had when they had first sat down together in Seward's office. But he didn't argue or drum his fingers in anger. "Seward will probably pay for a separate ticket. Find yourself another passage."

Oakes's right arm hurt where the bandage had peeled away from his not very consequential wound. A single bullet across the top of the bicep. A little lower, the French doctor had cheerfully said, no more elbow. Probably no more arm either. He could have sat on the sidewalks in New York and begged, a real veteran at last.

"There's a ship out of Liverpool three days from now," he said. "I'd have to go to London tomorrow to catch it."

This time Sharpe looked up and spoke harshly. "She won't be there, Quint." He squared his folders and rapped them hard on the desk. "She didn't go back to London. She left Paris for Naples the day after…the day after. From Naples, God knows where she went."

"We only saw the ticket register. We don't know that she really sailed. Nobody said she actually sailed. You taught me to be skeptical."

Sharpe stood up stiffly, like an old man, and Oakes noticed that he was wearing the same dirty shirt and trousers he had been wearing since Natalie Benjamin's gala dinner. Where was our dapper general, as Maggie Lawton used to call him? Where was Maggie, for that matter? But he knew the answer to that, because he had already made himself useful yesterday and arranged the transport of the big lead-lined coffin that Sharpe had paid for himself. In the geometry of desire, the perfect figure was a triangle.

"Quintus." Sharpe looked around at the featureless little room and appeared for a moment to lose interest in what he was about to say. "Quintus. I've been watching you for four months. Half the time you hung back and dragged your feet because you didn't really want to find this girl."

"Because you would hang her."

"And half the time you were so much on fire to find her I thought you were going to push us all out of the way and break into a run, just run straight for her. She's gone. Leave it. Go to Wyoming, go back to school. Just…go."

He flapped the steamship tickets impatiently in his hand. Oakes took them and walked to the door. When he looked back, Sharpe was already seated at the incongruous desk again, staring at the bare wall.

"Do you think she did it?" he asked from the door.

Sharpe twisted on his chair. "Did what?"

"Helped Booth."

Sharpe's face was as blank and unreadable as the wall. "I think she stole our money," he said finally, "and spent it." The ghost of a smile came and went. "That's all I ever thought."

* * *

Outside, Paris was green and preening, holding its beautiful white face up to the unaccustomed sun.

She wouldn't have gone north, Oakes thought, to England. She didn't like to be cold. If she had gone anywhere, she had gone south, toward warmth. If she had gone anywhere.

The steamship ticket agencies were located near the Bourse, on the other side of Paris. He could walk there, or he could hail a cab or swing aboard an omnibus. Or he could go and sit on a bench and watch the river and think about how little he had understood Maggie Lawton. Or how well she had understood him. What had she said once, in London? There was nothing to be done about the desire of the moth for the flame. Who was the moth? Maggie or himself?

Hope and fear, he had read somewhere, were the only two real motions of the human mind. Toward what we want, away from what we fear. Tell that, he thought, to the moth.

As he started to walk toward the nearest hackney stand, he saw Keach coming up the rue de Chaillot, and he turned abruptly away. Keach had been investigated, castigated, disciplined, but at the end of it all the Paris police had shrugged and marked her death down as an accident, a diplomatic episode with no French citizens involved, only a question of paperwork and regrets. Sharpe wouldn't press any charges. Keach would be going home, free and alive.

To avoid meeting him, Oakes moved downhill at a rapid pace. He stumbled three or four times on roots and deformed pavement blocks but didn't slow down until he had curved around the new *immeubles*, six-story residential buildings that now enclosed the place de l'Alma on three sides. The fourth side, of course, opened onto the bridge and the great carnival-like scene of the Exposition.

I left messages for you, she had said, just before Keach burst in on them. But there had been no messages at his hotel, not ever, not here, not in Paris, nothing ever at the Embassy.

There was always a crowd streaming over the bridge toward the Exposition. Today, thanks to the brilliant weather, it was bigger and noisier than ever. Indifferent, directionless, Oakes let himself be carried along, flotsam or jetsam—he could never remember—over the arched, dolphin-like back of the bridge and toward the North Gate. For some reason admission was free today. He bumped and floated along straight up to the entrance turnstiles and then a moment later found himself inside, shaded suddenly from the sun, blinking.

On his left was the bookstall he had noticed the first time he came—Maggie Lawton, he remembered, had bought her present for Sharpe here, the book about cats through history.

Next to the bookstall he saw the *Crèche* sign and he heard the squall of crying children—not a usual Parisian sound—which mixed oddly well with the bawling of a saxophone from the music exhibits down the corridor. And a grilled cloakroom gate and a big panel behind it where hundreds of fluttering envelopes hung pinned to a giant corkboard. *Poste Restante. La Ville Lumière.*

I left you messages. Heart suddenly racing, he pushed rudely past a doorman and hurried forward, bumping people left and right, until he was towering over the desk. A pretty young girl seated behind it, twenty perhaps, raised her eyebrow.

"Monsieur cherche quelque chose?" Was he looking for something?

He didn't know. He gripped the edge of the desk with his good arm and squinted hard at the corkboard, and then at the three letter reception cabinets with their alphabetically arranged pigeon holes. *There are some people you just love.*

"Vous cherchez, Monsieur—?"

An Englishman behind him poked him hard in the back and told him to mind the queue. Oakes flung his arm sideways to move him back. The girl gave a disapproving scowl.

"I'm probably mistaken," Oakes said in French, "but perhaps a young woman, blonde…"

"Americain? I speak English."

Oakes felt his face stiffen in puzzlement.

"*Votre accent, Monsieur.* Your accent is *américain.* You are look-ing for a message from a young American woman?"

Oakes nodded. The Englishman behind him was muttering indignantly, an ocean of voices and music drowned him out. The girl, grinning now, stood up. "Under the letter O?" she asked.

He nodded silently again.

"*De l'état de Connecticut?*" she said, but Oakes was no longer listening, Oakes could hear nothing but the drumbeat in his ears. The French girl had suddenly turned away, toward the open grille, where the long corridor was swarming with sightseers. There was a little rise here in the muddy turf of the Champ de Mars, and so the Exposition pathway rose too, and at the top of it and under an open skylight, Sarah Gilbert stepped out.

As the sunlight reached her face he broke into a run.

EPILOGUE

Washington City

December 1867

1

MESSAGE FROM THE PRESIDENT
OF THE UNITED STATES
Transmitting
To the Speaker of the House of Representatives
United States Congress Assembled

A Report Of George H. Sharpe Relative to
the Assassination of President Lincoln

SIR: I have the honor to lay before you, with a view to its communication to the House of Representatives, a transcript of the report made to this department by General George H. Sharpe, ret., who, under its instructions, visited Europe in the first part of the present year to ascertain, if possible, whether any citizens of the United States in that quarter, other than those who have heretofore been suspected and charged with the offence, were instigators of, or concerned in, the assassination of the late President Lincoln, and the attempted assassination of the Secretary of State.

Respectfully submitted: WILLIAM H. SEWARD
December 17, 1867

Summary Conclusion of the Report:

Conscious that earnestness was brought to the attempt at identifying the loathsome instigators of the great crime, and that every possible assistance was received, I have to report that, in my opinion, no such legal or reasonable proof exists in Europe of the participation of any persons there, formerly citizens of the United States, as to call for the action of the government.

Acccordingly, I traveled to British North America (Canada), Liverpool and London in the United Kingdom, Rome and the Papal States, and Paris. This mission was conducted during a space of a little over four months.

I did not conduct my investigation unaided. I was accompanied throughout Canada and Europe by Sergeant Daniel Keach, formerly under my command in the Army of the Potomac, now an employee at Ward & Company Bankers of Manhattan; by Captain Quintus Oakes, formerly under my command in the Army of the Potomac, now thought to be a resident of the Territory of Wyoming; and by Miss Margaret Lawton, spinster, formerly of the Alan Pinkerton Agency. Miss Lawton died in an unfortunate accident in Paris while serving on this mission and should be remembered by this government with great respect.

I will add that I met everywhere in Europe great courtesy from the foreign officials I interviewed, with the exception of the Consulate of the Papal States in Paris, where my reception was discourteous in the extreme.

Very respectfully, your obedient servant,
GEORGE H. SHARPE

2

From the *New-York Times*, July 31, 1867:

"Today following two months of testimony before Judge David Carter in the Federal Court in the District of Columbia, John H. Surratt, Jr. was released from custody. This is the John Surratt, Jr., of course, the so-called 'Fifth Conspirator,' accused of conspiring with Booth and his accomplices to murder our late and irreplaceable President. Eight jurors voted 'not guilty'; four voted 'guilty.' The proceedings were officially declared a mistrial. The statute of limitations on charges other than murder has run out. Surratt was released immediately on $25,000 bail. No person this reporter spoke with thinks an appeal to another court will succeed. For all intents and purposes, the Fifth Conspirator is as free as a bird.

"When he had finished his formal remarks, Judge Carter delivered an angry, stinging rebuke to the federal prosecution for the 'totally inept' fashion in which it had carried out its work. He then struck his gavel three times and announced that, as far as the government was concerned, the investigations were closed.

"'There are now,' he declared as he rose from the bench, 'no more Lincoln assassination conspirators anywhere in the world to be sought or tried.'"

ACKNOWLEDGMENTS

How much of this story is true?

Well, most of it. General George H. Sharpe was a real person. And in the conspiratorial atmosphere following Lincoln's death—anyone who remembers the assassination of John F. Kennedy will understand that atmosphere—Secretary of State Seward did indeed send General Sharpe to Canada and Europe, searching for more conspirators. Probably the fictional characters, Oakes, Keach, and Maggie Lawton didn't accompany him. But all the other historical actions and details are as accurate as I could make them, and all of the obvious historical personages here—Judah Benjamin, John Surratt, Charles Francis Adams, even Thomas Chester Morris—did and said pretty much what I have them doing and saying here. That includes, mostly, the very real Sarah Slater.

Readers wishing to know more will find a good account of George Sharpe's years in the service in Edwin C. Fishel, *The Secret War for the Union*. Sharpe's report and correspondence with Seward is in the National Archives, best accessed through microfiche and microfilm. The best source of information about

Sarah Slater is an article by James O. Hall, "Veiled Lady: The Saga of Sarah Slater," *North & South*, August, 2000.

The definitive study of John Surratt's escape is Andrew C. A. Jampoler, *The Last Lincoln Conspirator*. Mr. Jampoler is a distinguished historian and a generous correspondent. I have also drawn on information passed on to me by the very learned Peter G. Tsouras of Alexandria, Virginia. Professor George Selgin of the University of Georgia kindly answered my queries about Confederate gold. I am indebted to all of them; any errors are surely the work of the Muse of Fiction.

Those who suspect me of personal hostility to Henry Adams are right, but in my defense I should add that most of what he says here is taken directly from his letters and books and from the extremely detailed diary of Benjamin Moran (long out of print), another real person who came to know him very well in London, and to regret it.

Finally, I've taken every opportunity to get the historical setting right: the American Embassy in London was really on Great Portland Street and the Langham Hotel was around the corner. It really did cost thirty centimes to ride inside on a Paris omnibus in 1867. The repellent Mr. Sainte Marie in Rome (another real person) dressed as badly as I say, and so on. The confusion of railroad times and timetables described in the trip from New York to Canada was real. It was not until 1883 that William Allen, one of Sharpe's former Bureau agents, proposed a series of standard national time zones. All the information about the Universal Exposition comes from contemporary newpapers and guidebooks.

First and always, I thank my wife Brookes, who is sugar and spice and Patience herself. And my warmest thanks, also, to Diane Johnson, John Lescroart, and William P. Wood for their interest and support, and thanks especially to literary agent supreme, B.J. Robbins.

ABOUT THE AUTHOR

MAX BYRD is the author of bestselling historical novels about Ulysses Grant, Thomas Jefferson, and Andrew Jackson. Winner of the Shamus Award for his mystery novel *California Thriller*. Other widely reviewed novels include *Shooting the Sun* and *The Paris Deadline*. Byrd's earlier novels, *The Wall Street Journal* says, "vaulted him into the first rank of American historical novelists." *The Sixth Conspirator* is his finest book yet.

DON 91-02971

Donofrio, Beverly
16.95
Riding in cars with boys.

WITHDRAWN

RIDING IN CARS
WITH BOYS

RIDING IN CARS WITH BOYS

CONFESSIONS OF A BAD GIRL WHO MAKES GOOD

BEVERLY DONOFRIO

WILLIAM MORROW AND COMPANY, INC.
NEW YORK

Library of Congress Cataloging-in-Publication Data

Donofrio, Beverly.
    Riding in cars with boys: confessions of a bad girl who makes
    good / Beverly Donofrio.
        p.   cm.
      ISBN 0-688-08337-4
      I. Title.
    PS3554.O536R5   1990
    813'.54—dc20   89-78126
                                                                          CIP

Printed in the United States of America

First Edition

1 2 3 4 5 6 7 8 9 10

BOOK DESIGN BY JAYE ZIMET

91-02971

To my mother, my father, and my son

This book would not exist without the help, encouragement, and affection of my teachers Richard Price and Tony Connor; Dr. Joseph Finkle; my agent Gail Hochman; my editors Jim Landis and Jane Meara; and my good friends Robin Tewes, Terry Reed, Sheryl Lukomski, Kirsten Dehner, Trudy Dittmar, Janet Donofrio Rieth, Peter Alson, Alex Kotlowitz, and Thomas deMaar.

P r o l o g u e

I'M driving my son to college. It's dark and pouring rain out. I always imagined it would be sunny, like after a storm, magnificent puffs of clouds moving a hundred miles a minute across an electric blue sky. And there I'd be, hanging out a window, waving my arms and shouting hallelujah as my son disappeared around a corner. I thought it would feel like Bastille Day did for the starving French masses. But instead of a freedom frenzy, I'm having a nervous breakdown.

A few days ago I saw this kid on the uptown bus. He was dangling a GI Joe from his mouth as he dug in his backpack, then pulled out some drawings to show to his mother. He watched her face as she placed the pictures on her knees, smoothed them with her hands and smiled. The scene made me blubber. I know everybody cries when their kid goes to college. But this was not supposed to happen to me. I was not supposed to be driving in a downpour, mumbling, "Oh God," and using every molecule of will in my body to keep from crying.

I was not supposed to have a kid to begin with.

I try to pass a bully truck. A gust of air pushes me to the edge of a lane and sprays water on our little Honda, so the windshield floods and I can't see through it for a second. Jason grabs the handle on the dashboard and closes his eyes—not hysterical, but indulgent. He thinks I'm a terrible driver, a notion he picked up when he was seven and eight and nine and I'd fly over bumps to make him scream or slam on the brakes for no reason except I loved to scare him. When he was four, I soaped up my face, then scrinched it into a horrifying grimace and chased him screaming through the house. Lately, I've been thinking of the things I did and feeling like a maniac mother. Lately, I've been looking at my life like there's something to learn.

I look at my son as he pushes buttons on the radio. How could I have raised such a kid? He's tall and handsome and calm. Mostly calm. That's what you think when you see him. You think, That kid's got self-possession. Like Jimmy Stewart or maybe Gary Cooper. People say I'm lucky, but I always thought different.

I hear Frank Sinatra singing "My Way." I tell Jase to stop there and I think, That's it. I wasn't a terrible person. I just did like Frank Sinatra. Then a picture of Sid Vicious singing the same song comes to mind and makes me feel awful all over again.

PART
ONE

CHAPTER 1

TROUBLE began in 1963. I'm not blaming it on President Kennedy's assassination or its being the beginning of the sixties or the Vietnam War or the Beatles or the make-out parties in the fallout shelters all over my hometown of Wallingford, Connecticut, or my standing in line with the entire population of Dag Hammarskjcld Junior High School and screaming when a plane flew overhead because we thought it was the Russians. These were not easy times, it's true. But it's too convenient to pin the trouble that would set me on the path of most resistance on the times.

The trouble I'm talking about was my first real trouble, the age-old trouble. The getting in trouble as in "Is she in Trouble?" trouble. As in pregnant. As in the girl who got pregnant in high school. In the end that sentence for promiscuous behavior, that penance (to get Catholic here for a minute, which I had the fortune or misfortune of being, depending on the way you look at it)—that kid of mine, to be exact—would turn out to be a blessing instead of a curse. But I had no way of knowing it at the time and, besides, I'm getting ahead of myself.

By 1963, the fall of the eighth grade, I was ready. I was hot to trot. My hair was teased to basketball dimensions, my 16 oz. can of Miss Clairol hairspray was tucked into my shoulder bag. Dominic Mezzi whistled between his teeth every time I passed him in the hallway, and the girls from the project—the ones with boys' initials scraped into their forearms, then colored with black ink—smiled and said hi when they saw me. I wore a padded bra that lifted my tits to inches below my chin, and my father communicated to me only through my mother. "Mom," I said. "Can I go to the dance at the Y on Friday?"

"It's all right with me, but you know your father."

Yes, I knew my father. Mr. Veto, the Italian cop, who never talked and said every birthday, "So, how old're you anyway? What grade you in this year?" It was supposed to be a joke, but who could tell if he really knew or was just covering? I mean, the guy stopped looking at me at the first appearance of my breasts, way back in the fifth grade.

In the seventh grade, I began to suspect he was spying on me, when I had my run-in with Danny Dempsey at Wilkinson's Theater. Danny Dempsey was a high school dropout and a hood notorious in town for fighting. I was waiting in the back of the seats after the lights dimmed for my best friend, Donna Wilhousky, to come back with some candy when this Danny Dempsey sidled up to me and leaned his shoulder into mine. Then he reached in his pocket and pulled out a knife, which he laid in the palm of his hand, giving it a little tilt so it glinted in the screen light. I pressed my back against the wall as far away from the knife as I could, and got goosebumps. Then Donna showed up with a pack of Banana Splits and Mint Juleps, and Danny Dempsey backed away. For weeks, every time the phone rang I prayed it was Danny Dempsey. That was about the time my father started acting suspicious whenever I set foot out of his house. He was probably just smelling the perfume of budding sexuality on me and was acting territorial, like a dog. Either that or maybe his buddy Skip Plotkin, the official cop of Wilkinson's Theater, had filed a report on me.

Which wasn't a bad idea when I think of it, because I was what you call boy crazy. It probably started with Pat Boone when I was four years old. I went to see him in the movie where he sang "Bernadine" with his white bucks thumping and his fingers snapping, and I was in love. From that day on whenever "Bernadine" came on the radio, I swooned, spun around a couple of times, then dropped in a faked-dead faint. I guess my mother thought this was cute because she went out and bought me the forty-five. Then every day after kindergarten, I ran straight to the record player for my dose, rocked my head back and forth, snapped my fingers like Pat Boone, then when I couldn't stand it another second, I swooned, spun around, and dropped in a faked-dead faint.

I was never the type of little girl who hated boys. Never. Well, except for my brother. I was just the oldest of three girls, while he was the Oldest, plus the only boy in an Italian family, and you know what that means: golden penis. My father sat at one end of the table and my brother sat at the other, while my mother sat on the sidelines with us girls. You could say I resented him a little. I had one advantage though—the ironclad rule. My brother, because he was a boy, was not allowed to lay one finger on us girls. So when his favorite show came on the TV, I stood in front of it. And when he said, "Move," I said, "Make me," which he couldn't.

But other boys could chase me around the yard for hours dangling earthworms from their fingers, or call me Blackie at the bus stop when my skin was tanned dirt-brown after the summer, or forbid me to set foot in their tent or play in their soft-, kick-, or dodgeball games. They could chase me away when I tried to follow them into the woods, their bows slung over their shoulders and their hatchets tucked into their belts. And I still liked them, which is not to say I didn't get back at them. The summer they all decided to ban girls, meaning me and Donna, from their nightly softball games in the field behind our houses, Donna and I posted signs on telephone poles announcing the time of the inoculations they must receive to qualify for teams. On the appointed day they stood in line at Donna's cellar door. Short ones, tall ones, skinny and fat, they waited their turn, then never even winced when we pricked their skin with a needle fashioned from a pen and a pin.

By the summer of 1963, my boy craziness had reached such a pitch that I was prepared to sacrifice the entire summer to catch a glimpse of Denny Winters, the love of my and Donna's life. Donna and I walked two miles to his house every day, then sat under a big oak tree across the street, our transistor radio between us, and stared at his house, waiting for some movement, a sign of life, a blind pulled up or down, a curtain shunted aside, a door opening, a dog barking. Anything. Denny's sister, who was older and drove a car, sometimes drove off and sometimes returned. But that was it. In an entire summer of vigilance, we never saw Denny Winters arrive or depart. Maybe he had mononucleosis; maybe he was away at camp. We never saw him mow the lawn or throw a ball against the house for practice.

What we did see was a lot of teenage boys sitting low in cars, cruising by. Once in a while, a carload would whistle, flick a cigarette into the gutter at our feet, and sing, "Hello, girls." Whenever they did that, Donna and I stuck our chins in the air and turned our heads away. "Stuck up," they hollered.

But we knew the cars to watch for: the blue-and-white Chevy with the blond boy driving, the forest-green Pontiac with the dark boy, the white Rambler, the powder-blue Camaro, the yellow Falcon. I decided that when I finally rode in a car with a boy, I wouldn't sit right next to him like I was stuck with glue to his armpit. I'd sit halfway there—just to the right of the radio, maybe.

My father, however, had other ideas. My father forbade me to ride in cars with boys until I turned sixteen. That was the beginning.

"I hate him," I cried to my mother when my father was out of the house.

"Well, he thinks he's doing what's best for you," she said.

"What? Keeping me prisoner?"

"You know your father. He's suspicious. He's afraid you'll get in trouble."

"What kind of trouble?"

"You'll ruin your reputation. You're too young. Boys think they can take advantage. Remember what I told you. If a boy gets fresh, just cross your legs."

It was too embarrassing. I changed the subject. "I hate him," I repeated.

By the time I turned fourteen, the next year, I was speeding around Wallingford in crowded cars with guys who took corners on two wheels, flew over bumps, and skidded down the road to get me screaming. Whenever I saw a cop car, I lay down on the seat, out of sight.

While I was still at Dag Hammarskjold Junior High

17

School, I got felt up in the backseat of a car, not because I wanted to exactly, but because I was only fourteen and thought that when everybody else was talking about making out, it meant they got felt up. That was the fault of two girls from the project, Penny Calhoun and Donna DiBase, who were always talking about their periods in front of boys by saying their *friend* was staying over for a week and how their *friend* was a *bloody mess*. They told me that making out had three steps: kissing, getting felt up, and then Doing It. Next thing I knew, I was at the Church of the Resurrection bazaar and this cute little guy with a Beatles haircut sauntered up and said, "I've got a sore throat. Want to go for a ride to get some cough drops?" I hesitated. I didn't even know his name, but then the two girls I was with, both sophomores in high school, said, "Go! Are you crazy? That's Skylar Barrister, the president of the sophomore class." We ended up with two other couples parked by the dump. My face was drooly with saliva (step one) when "A Hard Day's Night" came on the radio and Sky placed a hand on one of my breasts (step two). Someone must've switched the station, because "A Hard Day's Night" was on again when his hand started moving up the inside of my thigh. I crossed my legs like my mother said, but he uncrossed them. Lucky for me, there was another couple in the backseat and Sky Barrister was either too afraid or had good enough manners not to involve them in the loss of my virginity or I really would've been labeled a slut. Not that my reputation wasn't ruined anyway, because sweetheart Sky broadcast the news that Beverly Donofrio's easy—first to his friends at the country club and then, exponentially, to the entire town. Hordes of boys called me up after that. My father was beside himself. I was grounded. I couldn't talk on the phone for more than a minute. My mother tried to intervene. "Sonny," she said. "You have to trust her."

"I know what goes on with these kids. I see it every day, and you're going to tell me?"

"What's talking on the phone going to hurt?" my mother asked.

"You heard what I said. I don't want to hear another word about it. You finish your phone call in a minute, miss, or I hang it up on you. You hear me?"

I heard him loud and clear, and it was okay with me—for a while, anyway, because my love of boys had turned sour. Sophomore year in high school, my English class was across the hall from Sky Barrister's and every time I walked by, there was a disturbance— a chitter, a laugh—coming from the guys he stood with. My brother was the captain of the football team and I wished he was the type who'd slam Sky Barrister against a locker, maybe knock a couple of his teeth out, but not my brother. My brother was the type who got a good-citizenship medal for never missing a single day of high school.

Meanwhile, his sister began to manifest definite signs of being a bad girl. My friends and I prided ourselves on our foul mouths and our stunts, like sitting across from the jocks' table in the cafeteria and giving the guys crotch shots, then when they started elbowing each other and gawking, we shot them the finger and slammed our knees together. Or we collected gingerbread from lunch trays and molded them into shapes like turds and distributed them in water fountains.

The thing was, we were sick to death of boys having all the fun, so we started acting like them: We got drunk in the parking lot before school dances and rode real low in cars, elbows stuck out windows, tossing

1 9

beer cans, flicking butts, and occasionally pulling down our pants and shaking our fannies at passing vehicles.

But even though we were very busy showing the world that girls could have fun if only they'd stop acting nice, eventually it troubled us all that the type of boys we liked—collegiate, popular, seniors—wouldn't touch us with a ten-foot pole.

One time I asked a guy in the Key Club why no guys liked me. "Am I ugly or stupid or something?"

"No." He scratched under his chin. "It's probably the things you say."

"What things?"

"I don't know."

"You think it's because I don't put out?"

"See? You shouldn't say things like that to a guy."

"Why?"

"It's not right."

"But why?"

"I don't know."

"Come on, is it because it's not polite or because it's about sex or because it embarrasses you? Tell me."

"You ask too many questions. You analyze too much, that's your problem."

To say that I analyzed too much is not to say I did well in school. Good grades, done homework—any effort abruptly ended in the tenth grade, when my mother laid the bad news on me that I would not be going to college. It was a Thursday night. I was doing the dishes, my father was sitting at the table doing a paint-by-numbers, and we were humming "Theme from Exodus" together. My mother was wiping the stove before she left for work at Bradlees, and for some reason she was stinked—maybe she had her period, or maybe it was because my father and I always hummed while I did the dishes and she was jealous. Neither of us acknowledged that we were basically harmonizing. It was more like it was just an accident that we were humming the same song. Our favorites were "'Bye 'Bye Blackbird," "Sentimental Journey," "Tonight," and "Exodus." After "Exodus," I said, "Hey, Ma. I was thinking I want to go to U Conn instead of Southern or Central. It's harder to get into, but it's a better school."

"And who's going to pay for it?"

It's odd that I never thought about the money, especially since my parents were borderline paupers and being poor was my mother's favorite topic. I just figured, naively, that anybody who was smart enough could go to college.

"I don't know. Aren't there loans or something?"

"Your father and I have enough bills. You better stop dreaming. Take typing. Get a *good* job when you graduate."

"I'm not going to be a secretary."

She lifted a burner and swiped under it. "We'll see," she said.

"I'm moving to New York."

"Keep dreaming." She dropped the burner back down.

So I gritted my teeth and figured I'd have to skip college and go straight to Broadway, but it pissed me off. Because I wasn't simply a great actress, I was smart too. I'd known this since the seventh grade, when I decided my family was made up of a bunch of morons with lousy taste in television. I exiled myself into the basement recreation room every night to get away from them. There were these hairy spiders down there, and I discovered if I dropped a Book of Knowledge on them they'd fist up into dots, dead as doornails. Then one night after a spider massacre, I opened a book up and discovered William Shakespeare—his quality-of-mercy soliloquy, to be exact. Soon I'd read everything in the books by him, and then by Whitman and Tennyson and Shelley. I memorized Hamlet's soliloquy and said it to the mirror behind the bar. To do this in the seventh grade made me think I was a genius. And now, to be told by my mother, who'd never read a book in her life, that I couldn't go to college was worse than infuriating, it was unjust. Somebody would have to pay.

That weekend my friends and I went around throwing eggs at passing cars. We drove through Choate, the ritzy prep school in the middle of town, and I had an inspiration. "Stop the car," I said. "Excuse me," I said to a little sports-jacketed Choatie crossing Christian Street. "Do you know where Christian Street is?"

"I'm not sure," he said, "but I think it's that street over there." He pointed to the next road over.

"You're standing on it, asshole!" I yelled, flinging an egg at the name tag on his jacket. I got a glimpse of his face as he watched the egg drool down his chest and I'll remember the look of disbelief as it changed to sadness till the day I die. We peeled out, my friends hooting and hollering and slapping me on the back.

I thought I saw a detective car round the bend and follow us down the street, but it was just my imagination. Now that my father'd been promoted from a regular cop to a detective, it was worse. Believe me, being a bad girl and having my father cruising around in an unmarked vehicle was no picnic. One time, I'd dressed up as a pregnant woman, sprayed gray in my hair, and bought a quart of gin, then went in a motorcade to the bonfire before the big Thanksgiving football game. We had the windows down even though it was freezing out and were singing "Eleanor Rigby" when we slammed into the car in front of us and the car in back slammed into us—a domino car crash. We all got out; there was no damage except a small dent in Ronald Kovacs's car in front. He waved us off, and we went to the bonfire.

Back home, I went directly to the bathroom to brush my teeth when the phone rang. In a minute my mother called, "Bev, your father's down the station. He wants to see you."

My heart stalled. "What about?"

"You know him. He never tells me anything."

I looked at myself in the mirror and said, "You are not drunk. You have not been drinking. You have done nothing wrong, and if that man accuses you, you have every reason in the world to be really mad." This was the Stanislavsky method of lying, and it worked wonders. I considered all my lying invaluable practice for the stage. There were countless times that I maintained not only a straight but a sincere face as my mother made me put one hand on the Bible, the other on my heart, and swear that I hadn't done something it was evident to the entire world only I could have done.

My father sat me in a small green room, where he took a seat behind a desk. "You were drinking," he said.

"No I wasn't," I said.

"You ever hear of Ronald Kovacs?"

"Yes. We were in a three-car collision. He slammed on his brakes in the middle of the motorcade, and we hit him."

"It's always the driver in the back's fault, no matter what the car in front does. That's the law. Maybe your friend wasn't paying too much attention. Maybe you were all loaded."

"You always think the worst. Somebody hit us from behind too, you know."

"Who was driving your car?"

"I'm not a rat like that jerk Kovacs."

"That's right. Be a smart ass. See where it gets you. I already know who was operating the vehicle. You better be straight with me or your friend, the driver, might end up pinched. It was Beatrice?"

"Yes."

"She wasn't drinking but you were?"

"*No!* Did you ever think that maybe Ronald Kovacs was drinking? Did you ever think that maybe he's trying to cover his own ass?"

"Watch your language."

I put on my best injured look and pretended to be choking back tears. It was easy because I was scared to death. Cops kept passing in the hall outside the door to the office. I was going out on a limb. If they found concrete evidence that I'd been drinking, my father would really be embarrassed. He might hit me when we got home, and I'd definitely be grounded, probably for the rest of my life.

"They're setting up the lie detector in the other room. We got it down from Hartford for a case we been working on," he said. "Will you swear on the lie detector that you're telling the truth?"

A bead of sweat dripped down my armpit. "Good. And bring in Ronald Kovacs and make him take it, too. Then you'll see who's a liar."

Turns out there was no lie detector; it was a bluff and I'd won the gamble.

When I got home, I played it for all it was worth with my mother. "He never trusts me. He always believes the worst. I can't stand it. How could you have married him?"

2 4

"You know your father. It's his nature to be suspicious."

"I wish he worked at the steel mill."

"You and me and the man in the moon. Then maybe I could pay the doctor bills. But that's not your father. He wanted to be a cop and make a difference. He didn't want to punch a time clock and have a boss looking over his shoulder."

When I was four, before my father became a cop, he pumped gas at the garage on the corner, and every day I brought him sandwiches in a paper bag. He'd smile like I'd just brightened his day when he saw me, then I sat on his lap while he ate. Sometimes I fell asleep, leaning my head against his chest, lulled by the warmth of his body and the rumble of trucks whooshing past. Sometimes I traced the red-and-green American Beauty rose on his forearm. I thought that flower was the most beautiful thing in the world back then. Now it was gray as newsprint, and whenever I caught a glimpse of it, I turned my eyes.

"You should've told him not to be a cop," I said. "It's ruining my life."

"It's not up to the wife to tell the husband what to do," my mother said.

"He tells you what to do all the time."

"The man wears the pants in the family."

"I'm never getting married."

"You'll change your tune."

"And end up like you? Never in a million years."

"You better not let your father catch you talking to me like that."

CHAPTER 2

MAYBE it was poetic justice for being so contemptuous of my mother and her position in life—as my father's servant—that landed me, before I graduated high school, at the altar.

I met Sonny Raymond Bouchard on New Year's Eve in the eleventh grade. As usual, I didn't have a date and neither did my best friend, Fay Johnston. Her parents were away for the weekend, so I was sleeping over. We were drinking gin and Fresca in martini glasses and pretending we were rich and famous and living in New York City when her brother Cal showed up with two of his hoody friends, Lizard and Raymond. I'd heard about a friend of Cal's named Raymond and how his brother was in jail for holding up Cumberland Farms with a gun. Raymond's hair was black and greased high back. He wore tight black pants and pointy black shoes.

Cal crammed a case of Colt 45 in the refrigerator, then stood in the doorway of the living room and said, "Happy New Year!" as he slammed his heels together and pointed a can of beer in the air like a Nazi salute. Then the three of them came into the living room and started talking about Lizard's giving a guy at the Farm Shop a bloody nose.

"Why'd you hit him? What did he do?" I asked.

"Nothing," Lizard said.

"He ranked on Lizard's sister," Raymond said, opening a beer.

"Called her a douche bag." Cal giggled.

I liked that. Hoods had their drawbacks—like using *dems* and *dose* when they spoke and wearing their hair like Elvis's—but usually they weren't afraid to fight for a girl's honor.

Ray took a long drink of beer, and when he put the can down, his eyes landed on me. Then Cal put "Sunny" on the record player. It skipped: "Sunny, thank you for the . . . Sunny, thank you for the . . . Sunny, thank you for the . . ." Cal said, "First one to change the record's a pussy."

This went on for ten minutes. I kept an eye on Ray to see how he was taking the torture. That's when I noticed he smoked Lucky Strikes, like my father. I wondered what he was thinking. He sat still in the chair like the Lincoln Memorial, except every once in a while when he lifted a heel off the floor then put it back down. I wondered if he carried a gun like his brother. I figured he could probably fix cars because that's why hoods were called greasers.

Cal flung his shoe at the record.

"Eh-heh," Fay said. "Cal's a pussy."

"Shut up, chicken legs." He swigged his beer.

"Drop dead, raisin nuts." She threw a pillow at him, knocking his beer in a gush across the carpet.

Fay stood up and dropped into Lizard's lap. He was called Lizard because he'd eat any kind of insect. Only thing was, it had to be living. Fay didn't care who she flirted with.

"Do my bones dig into you when I sit on your lap, Liz?" Fay said.

"You're light as a bird."

"Do you think I'm too skinny?"

"Nah, you're just right."

I knew she was thinking, Well, you're fat as an ox and ugly as sin or something like that. Fay was always flirting with guys who didn't have a chance in hell. Usually, I thought it was mean, but this night I thought maybe she had the right idea, so the next time I returned from the kitchen with a gin and Fresca, I coasted into Raymond's lap and said, "Hi, I'm Beverly."

"Raymond." He nodded and shifted his weight. I suggested we move to the sofa.

"I never saw you around school," I said.

"Quit."

"Why?"

"Buy a car."

"Your parents didn't care?"

"Nope." He stretched and laid an arm across my shoulder. I thought of Danny Dempsey and wondered if Raymond carried a knife. I put my head on his shoulder and interrogated him.

"So, you have a job?"

"Yep."

"What do you do?"

"Work down Cyanamid. Is your old man the cop?"

"Yes. I hate him. Is your brother really in jail?"

"Yep."

"For what?"

"Armed robbery."

"That's terrible. Did your mother cry when she found out?"

"Yeah." He kept flicking his thumb with his index finger. I took his hand in my lap to hold it still.

"What about your father?" I asked.

"He don't know. He ain't been around for a couple of years."

"Where is he?"

"Bowery."

"In New York?"

"He's a drunk."

Raymond was a high school dropout, his brother was a thief in jail, and his father was a Bowery bum. He needed me. More than anything else in the world I wanted Raymond to cry on my shoulder. I kissed his forehead. He pulled his face away and kissed my mouth.

It would be like *On the Waterfront*. He'd be Marlon Brando and I'd be Eva Marie Saint. I'd tutor Raymond for his high school equivalency; he'd listen to me recite Shakespearean soliloquys in my cellar. Pretty soon he'd wear crewneck sweaters and loafers. He was lying on top of me. It was probably too late to turn back now: I had a hood for a boyfriend.

By the time Raymond and I came up for air, the room was deserted. I told Ray I had to go to the bathroom, and as soon as I sat on the toilet, Fay barged in. "What are you doing? You like Sonny?" she said.

"I think so."

"I don't believe it."

"Tell me about him."

"What's to tell? He was the neighborhood simp. We never let him play baseball and shit because he was such a slug. Used to call him spider after a hairy mole he had growing under his earlobe. Teased him so much he had it removed, surgically."

"Poor Raymond." I flushed the toilet.

"Sonny Bouchard is retarded, Beverly." She sat on the toilet. "I can't believe you like him. Are you sleeping with him on the couch?"

"I guess so."

"Have fun." She flushed the toilet and walked out. When I went back to Raymond, I looked for the mole scar. It was a silvery patch the size of a quarter beneath his earlobe. I kissed it and we lay down. I told him I hated the name Sonny and would always call him Raymond. Soon he was breathing regularly and I slid off the couch, tiptoed outside, and stood on the carport. There was no moon, but the sky was heavy with stars. My breath puffed white clouds and there was no sound except for I-91 in the distance. I walked to Fay's window and tapped it. She got up and opened it. "What're you, crazy? It's freezing out."

"Nice though." I spread my arms to demonstrate.

In a minute she stood beside me, a blanket around her shoulders. She wrapped me in. "Let's walk," I suggested.

The grass cracked under my bare feet. When we stepped onto the main road, a car whizzed by beeping. Soon it would be light out. I spotted a red flag sticking up on a mailbox. I pushed it down, then back up, and without thinking about it, I bent it back and forth until it snapped off in my hand. "Wow," Fay said. She went across the street and did the same. We hurried around the block breaking off every flag in sight, until we'd circled back to her house. We had about thirty of them wrapped in the pouch of our blanket. "What'll we do with them?" I said.

"I don't know." Fay hugged herself. "I bet we could get arrested."

"Willful destruction of federal property or some shit."

"I know," she said. I followed her into a vacant lot. She knelt down on the ground and banged a flag in with a rock. I hammered in the next one. We made a circle of red flags in the middle of the field, then stood for a long time looking.

"Maybe no one will touch them," she said.

"Maybe they'll be here forever." I shivered.

One year later, almost to the day, I was shivering again, this time from nerves. I was in Fay's bedroom and at one o'clock on the dot, I dialed the phone to find out if I was pregnant. I dropped the phone and fell face first on the bed.

"Well, what did they say?" Fay asked.

"Positive."

"Postitive? What does positive mean?"

"Pregnant."

"But it could mean you're positively not pregnant, couldn't it?"

"Could it?"

"Call them back and ask."

"You call."

I slid onto the floor and rested my forehead on her knees as she dialed. She hung up and said, "You're fucked."

I broke the news to Raymond that night as we sat at the drive-in, the little portable heater between us on the seat, a motorcycle movie called *The Wild Angels* (Raymond's all-time favorite) on the screen.

"Raymond," I said. "Our lives are ruined."

"Don't you love me?"

"Yes. But still. I mean, why'd this happen to us? Why me? Do you think I have bad luck?"

"You probably got it from me. I told you you shouldn't love me. I'm trouble."

Raymond always said things like that. In the beginning, it made me hug him and kiss him. The first time I'd said "I love you" was when he was drunk and crying. It was in response to his saying, "You shouldn't love me." Now his self-pity just made me mad. Possibly because I was thinking he was right, I shouldn't love him, because if I hadn't, I wouldn't be sitting at a stupid motorcycle movie, pregnant.

But what I said was, "Don't say that," then changed the subject to other depressing topics. "You're going to have to work so hard," I said. "You wanted to quit. Now you can't."

"I'll get another job maybe."

He didn't seem nearly upset enough. "We can't spend any money," I said. "We have to save everything."

He nodded his head, then at intermission he bought hot dogs, sodas, and fries, and I got furious at him for spending the money. But I ate my hot dog, my fries, and half his fries anyway. I was starving.

For the next month, behind Raymond's back, I bumped my ass down stairs, punched myself in the stomach, and threw myself from couch to floor ten times every night before bed. Anything. Anything was better than telling my parents, especially my father, that I'd been screwing Raymond in the basement recreation room while he sat above me watching television in his reclining chair every night. How could I mention the word *sex* to him when I couldn't stay in the same room through a Playtex living bra commercial?

It was 1968 and abortion wasn't legal. If I'd known you could get one in Puerto Rico, I'd have sold my onyx ring, opal necklace, and Raymond's canary-yellow Bonneville to get there. Fact was, I never really thought about the baby, pictured it or imagined being a mother. I was too worried about telling my parents. And I was depressed, despondent, deeply disappointed. I always thought it was my destiny to become a star. But now I'd be married to Raymond for the rest of my life. I'd be a housewife with no money, a station wagon, and a husband whose intellectual curiosity could be summed up in his favorite expression: How come dat?

It seemed to me that God or the will of the world or fate or whatever it is that determines a person's life had turned against me. It's true I'd been the first of my friends to lose my virginity, but within a week of my breaking the news, three of them had followed suit. Now we were trading how-to-have-orgasm tips and none of *them* was pregnant. Fay had even been given a third-of-a-carat diamond and was due to marry a twenty-six-year-old sailor stationed on a nuclear submarine a week after graduation. Why was it my lot in life to be singled out for public humiliation?

Every night for that long month I lay on my stomach on the sofa saying, Next commercial, I'll tell my parents next commercial, but I never could make the words come out of my mouth. So finally, on my way to school one Monday morning, I left a note in the mailbox saying, "Dear Mom and Dad, I'm really sorry. I know I've disappointed you I'm pregnant. Love, your daughter Beverly.

School that day was a nightmare. As if I didn't have enough on my mind, Mr. O'Rourke, the history teacher, decided to notice I was alive and pick on me. "Miss Donofrio," he said.

I didn't hear him.

"Miss Donofrio, I hate to interrupt whatever you're doing [I was cleaning out my pocketbook]. We were talking about Andrew Jackson, a president I'm sure in your vast wisdom you have a good deal of respect for." The class snickered. "I was wondering if you would do us the favor of shedding some light on the subject. Tell us anything, anything at all, about Mr. Jackson."

"I don't know anything."

"What a pity. Then I must assume you didn't read the assignment. I think you'd better write me two pages on the topic."

"You want me to tell you anything?"

"That's what I said."

"He was a president. He wore a white wig."

"Not good enough."

"You said anything."

"Three pages."

"That's not fair."

"Another word and you've got detention."

I wrote *cocksucker* in my notebook.

I had the car that day, and after school I drove my friend Virginia and her boyfriend, Bobby, to Virginia's house. We ate Mystic Mint cookies and drank Cokes in her kitchen. I kept sighing, and V kept saying, "Poor Bev. I'm glad I'm not you." When I got up to leave, Bobby dove onto the floor, hugged his stomach, and rolled around laughing until tears fell down his cheeks. When he caught his breath, he said, "Your father's going to kill you." Bobby should know. His father was as much of a maniac as mine, only a Baptist. I walked out the door as though to an execution.

It was a half hour before dinnertime, and my parents were waiting for me at the table. I dropped my books and slumped into a chair. My mother stood up, leaned against the stove, and crossed her arms against her chest. "Well, I hope you're proud of yourself now," she said.

"No," I said.

"What are you going to do?"

"Marry Raymond."

"It's that easy. You're so smart. You know everything." She always said that. Probably because, since the seventh grade, I'd been rolling my eyes at everything she said and constantly correcting her grammar.

"No I don't."

My father was leafing through the pages of my notebook.

"And what about your boyfriend? What does he think about all this?"

"He's very happy. We're getting married."

My father tore a handful of pages from my notebook and threw them in front of my mother. On the table lay the pictures I drew in English class that day of balls and cocks erect and coming, with the words *suck, fuck, cocksucker, motherfucker* written in block letters and shaded like titles on a book. "Look, look what your daughter thinks about in school."

I ran out of the kitchen, past my sisters in the living room watching the *Mike Douglas Show*, and thought, Thank God my brother's not around to hear this—he was in the middle of the ocean somewhere, in the navy. I sat on the top step of the stairs to my room, pinched my face between my knees, and listened to my parents yell at each other in the kitchen.

"I knew it. I knew it. Trust her, you say. Leave the kid alone? So help me God, Grace, don't you ever tell me to trust those other two daughters of yours."

"Oh no, Sonny, you're not blaming me for this. She's your daughter too."

"What did I tell you she was doing in the cellar with her boyfriend? What did I tell you?"

All I could think about was Mindy Harmon. Mindy wasn't bad like me. Mindy was a cheerleader, never wore makeup, got drunk only rarely, didn't smoke cigarettes, and still she got pregnant. Her mother dragged her to all the basketball games where she was supposed to be cheerleading, just to shame her. Mindy was pathetic. She had to sit sideways at her desk, and she wore her skirts with the zipper open and the waist fastened with the three-inch safety pin she got from her cheerleading kilt. But whenever anybody asked her if she was pregnant, she'd blink her eyes twice and say no. I'd already told half the town about my condition. I might be pregnant, but I'd rather die than act ashamed like Mindy Harmon.

"Rose," my mother called. "Go tell your sister to get back here."

My nine-year-old sister stood at the bottom of the stairs and looked up at me. "Bev?" she whispered.

I was embarrassed to meet her eyes. She looked like she might start bawling. What was I doing, banished to the stairs like a scarlet woman? What kind of an example was I setting for my sisters? You'd think I'd murdered somebody the way my parents were acting, when all I did was have sexual intercourse—and not even that often.

My father was sobbing into his hands and my mother was picking crud from the crack down the middle of the table with a bobby pin when I sat back down and dug my heels in.

"You're killing your father," my mother said.

I shrugged my shoulders.

"Your father and I think you should give the baby up for adoption."

"No." I'd already made up my mind about that.

"Then keep it and live at home."

"No!" She had to be out of her mind. The one and only good thing about having a baby was that it would get me out of my parents' house.

My father blew his nose.

"Your father and I have discussed this. If you want, we'll adopt it. You're too young to get married. You'll regret it the rest of your life."

"Adopt it?" I stood up shouting. "You just want to steal my baby. I'm keeping it. I'm getting married. It's *my* baby."

"All right. All right." My father wasn't crying anymore. "You just calm down. You're underage, smart ass. You need our permission."

"I'll elope."

"You think it's fun? You think it's easy? You think that boyfriend of yours will be a good provider? You think he can keep a job and support you and a baby?"

"Mom was pregnant when you got married." This was my ace in the hole. I'd figured it out by subtraction, years ago. This was the first time I'd mentioned it.

"That was different," my mother said. "We were older. We knew what we were doing."

"Daddy was unemployed. You didn't have any money. You told me yourself. You lived in a shack."

"That's enough." My father stood up.

At the risk of getting slapped, I said one more thing after my father told me enough. "All I'm saying is it worked for you."

"All right. I give up. She knows everything." My father smacked the back of his chair. "I'm telling you, Beverly. You better be good and goddamn sure, because once you leave this house, you mark my words, you can't come back. You made your bed, you sleep in it."

I stared at the floor.

"Go to your room," he said.

I ran to my room, threw myself on the bed, and sobbed my heart out in spite of myself.

CHAPTER 3

THE weeping segued to the eve of my wedding. Ray was off at his bachelor party and I was sitting in Fay's kitchen with her mother and her mother's friend Joyce the manhater. They were drinking gin and Fay and I were drinking coffee. Joyce, who was a staple at Fay's house, was a vociferous opponent of marriage and a devout deballer of men. She liked nothing better than to drink her second martini and hold me and Fay captive with her invectives and warnings: "They're all big babies. You're better off alone, doing for yourself. Who needs them sniveling and complaining and pawing at you." Mr. Johnston walked in and poured himself a scotch, and Joyce went on like he wasn't there: "There's not a woman in the world that doesn't regret getting married. But they'd rather choke than admit it. I bet your mother just loves being married to a guinea. [Joyce and Fay's mother were Italian, too.] Does he slap her around if his meatballs are overdone?"

I liked that Fay's mother had a friend like Joyce. Fay's mother came from the Bronx and wore gaudy plastic jewelry and bright red lipstick and smoked cigarettes in an ivory cigarette holder. She let us smoke and swear in her house. One time she came home from work with a migraine in the middle of the day and found five of us playing hookey and dressed up in her clothes. She didn't say one word except, "I'm sick. I'm going to bed." This night she hardly said a word to me either. I thought she didn't like me anymore because I'd deserted to the enemy's camp. This made me very sad, and after my second piece of pie, I left Fay and her mother and Joyce to lie on the sofa in the living room, where Mr. Johnston sat doing the crossword puzzle under a lamp and sipping his scotch.

"So, Beverly," he said. "Big day tomorrow."

"Yeah."

"I thought you were going to be a great actress."

"I was."

"Well, you never know what might happen. I know what you need. What you need's a stage name, that'll perk you up."

I sat up. "Yeah?"

"I know, Viela, Viela Scaloppini, how's that? That's a good stage name for you."

Viela Scaloppini, I repeated the name to myself. It sounded familiar. It would stick in people's minds. "Hey, Fay," I called to the kitchen. "Your father made up a stage name for me, Viela Scaloppini."

"That's an Italian dish, Beverly," she said. "Veal and peppers or something."

Her father was laughing so hard the newspaper shook. I felt like bawling right there in front of him, but then I'd really seem a fool, so I waited until I went home shortly after, passed my sisters and parents watching TV in the living room, said good night to the floor and heard my mother say, "Got a big day tomorrow, don't stay up late," as I walked up the stairs to my room. I laid on top of my bed and thought, That's the last time my mother will say those words to me. This is the last time I'll sleep in my bed, the last time this will be my room. I looked around at the knotty-pine panels my father had hammered up one by one to make my brother, Mike, a bedroom. I'd moved in as soon as Mike left for the navy. I'd rearranged the furniture, but it had never really been my room anyway. I turned off the little lamp hanging by my bed. My mother had bought it on sale at Bradlees, where she worked in the candy and stationery department. It was bulbous and made of milk glass, with little lumps all over. Fay had said it was diseased and that the lumps looked like warts. I should have told her to shut up. I jammed a pillow over my face and cried myself to sleep.

It worked out for the best that Fay's father was a cruel man, because by the wedding ceremony the next morning I was all cried out, or maybe I was just so much of a contrary person that I was smiling because 90 percent of everybody else was crying. When I saw Fay and Beatrice, we broke into a giggling fit.

I avoided looking at Ray until he was five feet away. When I finally tried to meet his eyes, he was looking down at his hands. I remembered about his father. I looked in the front seat of Ray's side of the aisle. His mother and sister were leaning heads together weeping, and there was no sign of Ray's father, who had shown up in town fresh from the Bowery a couple of weeks before. We'd sent him an invitation, and then this morning Raymond was supposed to drop by his room with a red carnation in a see-through plastic box and bring him to the wedding.

At the altar, my father's eyes looked greener somehow. When he kissed me his cheek felt smooth as silk from shaving and slippery with tears. My mother looked beautiful in her new pink dress but she was practically convulsing with my two little sisters in the seat behind me, and then when Raymond came and took my hand, his mouth started trembling. I got annoyed because I wanted him to act like a man. But then when I took his hand and it was cold and shaking, I felt the way I did whenever I saw a midget or dwarf or a hunchbacked person—like I wanted to take them home and adopt them or something. So I covered his shaking hand with my hand, looked him in his eyes, and said, "I love you," even though a minute ago, at the top of the aisle, I wished he'd die before I turned thirty-five. The kid would be eighteen then, a legal adult, and I could start another life while I was still reasonably attractive.

By the time we'd reached Ray's sister's apartment in New York City for our honeymoon weekend, I was tired and grouchy and mad at Raymond for drinking shots of Seagram's 7 in the bar next to the hall, then for being found puking in the bathroom when it was time to cut the cake. I'd had my first drinks and cigarettes in front of my parents. I'd danced nearly every dance. I'd led the Bunny Hop and laughed and joked and passed out cookies. Now that it was over, I felt like a discarded flower. Ray's sister had left us a bottle of champagne in the refrigerator and two champagne glasses with our names engraved like frost across them. Ray and I linked arms and took a sip, then slunk into bed. After we fumbled around in the dark for a while, I remembered about Ray's father. "What happened to your dad?" I said.

"He didn't answer the door."

"You brought the flower and knocked and he didn't answer?"

Ray nodded his head.

"How do you know he was there?"

"I could hear cartoons on."

"Do you feel bad?"

"It would've been weird if he came."

"I wish I could meet him."

"No you don't."

I pulled Raymond's head to my chest. He put his hand on my belly. Dionne Warwick's "Do You Know the Way to San Jose?" came on the radio. It made me think of dancing with my father at the wedding. I'd looked forward to it for weeks. I pictured us doing the cha cha, the lindy, the fox-trot, a waltz, just like he'd danced with my mother for us kids in the kitchen Saturday nights when they were all dressed up and about to go out. I pictured the whole group of people down in the basement hall of the Italian Club stopping just to watch me gliding across the floor with my handsome father. But my father never asked me to dance again after the first one, when he gave me away. In bed with Raymond, I thought I should've been brave enough to ask him.

After the reception, everyone had gone to my house. Ray and I changed in my bedroom and counted our money. We had eight hundred dollars, which would pay for the hospital. Then we played the Four Tops in the basement with my cousins and friends for an hour or so before Bobby and Virginia drove us to the train. When Bobby peeled out of the driveway, I saw my father look out the window.

"There must be a dozen cops in that house," Virginia said.

"They ain't going to do nothing to me," said Bobby. "I'm going to Nam in a couple of months."

"A real hero." Virginia flipped her fall off her shoulder and looked out the window.

At the stop sign, when Bobby slammed on the brakes and peeled out again, Raymond said, "Hey, we got a pregnant girl here, man." I don't know why, but I'd felt like Raymond and Virginia were on one team and Bobby and I were on another.

"Put a dollar down and buy a car," Dionne's song brought me back to my honeymoon and future life— "In a week maybe two they'll make you a star"—and I felt the tears coming. Raymond put his head on my belly. "I think it's moving," he said.

CHAPTER 4

FOR most of my life my family and I lived in a little mint-green house that was officially part of the public-housing project but was perched on the very edge of it. Across our back lawn and down a field of weeds sat the rest of the publicly owned homes, tiny Cape Cods on minuscule plots of scorched grass or long brick apartment buildings set at strange angles to the street. Teenagers peeled out from stop sign to stop sign down there and kids ran around in huge stick-wielding packs. But across the road from our front lawn were big privately owned houses, fire-engine-red, snow-white, and forest green, with long lawns, generous trees, and kids who said please and thank you. At the very top of our hill was the country club.

Whenever I told anyone I lived on Long Hill, they assumed it was in one of the big houses and I didn't correct them. There'd been a time when I hung out at the project by a chain-link fence, French-inhaling cigarettes and flirting with boys who said *pussy* and *twat*. My best friend Donna broke up with me over my attraction to the project. But that was a long time ago, back during the fall when everyone at Dag Hammarskjold Junior High School mistook that plane for the Russians. Since then I'd come to think that most of the people from the project were two things: poor and weird. Like Susan Gerace and her father, Anthony, whose backyard I could see from my bedroom window. Anthony dressed up in his World War II uniform to play his bugle every chance he got—like on Memorial Day, at high school graduations, assemblies after assassinations, and every other evening after dinner. He stood with Susan in their backyard and made her play "Taps," too. If she got even one note wrong he slapped her on the ear and made her do it over until she got it right. Only then would Anthony answer her with his sad, clear high-pitched horn, putting her playing to shame no matter how perfect her notes. It seems that every night of my life I'd digested dinner to "Taps." For this I blamed my parents. I looked down on them for landing us in the project, for not owning their own home, for not graduating high school—so they could get good jobs and afford their own home—and for never having enough money for anything, like dancing lessons or enough expensive clothes.

So I took it as yet another kind of poetic justice, or should I say just punishment, that I ended up leaving school before I graduated and being grateful to my father for pulling some strings and jumping Raymond and me to the top of the public-housing-authority waiting list. We got an apartment in a peeling mint-green duplex house on a dead-end street called Backes Court, which, luckily, was separated from the rest of the project by about a mile. On the first floor we had a kitchen with an emerald-green floor, blue brick contact paper behind the stove, and a living room with a picture window. On the second floor were two small bedrooms, ours and Baby's, and a bathroom at the top of the stairs, with a Chiquita banana sticker on the doorknob. In our yard we had one dead bush and no trees. **4 5**

On our new road, kids rumbled on Big Wheels all day, dug holes in yards, which they filled with water to make mud balls to throw at each other. The mothers shook blankets from upstairs windows and sat in the sun on front stoops, their hair rolled up and drying. The few remaining fathers drove off in cars and returned once a day, which was what Raymond did, while I plopped around the house like a fat tomato. Most of my time was spent at the window, watching and wishing I'd have the nerve to ask one of those women over for tea and cinnamon sticks or something—when I wasn't stuck doing schoolwork, that is.

It had been arranged for me to be tutored so I could graduate high school. That meant I had to invite every teacher I'd formerly sassed into my impoverished teenage home decorated in cast-off furniture that had made a detour to my house on its way to the dump. In other words, I ate crow as my teachers wiped their feet on my welcome mat and sat in my Flintstone furniture— old stuff that belonged to an aunt and had been reupholstered hard as rock. When I handed them my meticulously done homework assignments, not one of them, not even O'Rourke, who chain-smoked and smelled vaguely of booze, ever made a crack, which made me feel pitied instead of relieved. I never had to hear I told you so, but I did have to put up with my home economics teacher's conversation—like when Bobby Kennedy got shot and she objected to there being no day off from work like there'd been for Martin Luther King. She said it was "just because Martin Luther King's black." I figured that was a good enough reason, when you considered how many black leaders we had in the country, but I kept my mouth shut because she was the teacher and I was the pregnant teenager making a pink dress with five seams so I could let one out every time my stomach grew another inch.

Then came graduation, which I couldn't attend because of my big belly, not to mention that I wasn't invited. My friends called me the next day to give me the details. They told me the principal had stood at the podium after handing out the diplomas and said, "And congratulations to Beverly Donofrio, who couldn't join us today." My friends swore to me that nobody, not one person, snickered or yelled out a joke, and I was so grateful, I felt love for every single classmate I had formerly called a jerk or moron or imbecile.

I wasn't so in love with my friends, though, because they'd deserted me to go have the best time of their lives at a cottage they'd rented by a lake an hour away. So all summer long my main companions besides Raymond were Bam Bam, a retarded three-year-old, and my mother, who stopped by every morning and every afternoon too, since my house was on her way to everywhere and since she figured I was lonely and needed her.

One morning she came in the back door and called, "Yooo hooo."

I was still in bed. It was ten-thirty.

"You up?"

"Yeah."

I heard her banging around in the kitchen, and pulled on my jeans with the stretchy stomach pouch, which my mother had bought me on one of our afternoon jaunts to Barkers, Stars, or Caldor. I padded down the stairs and into the kitchen.

"It's gonna be a scorcher," she said, placing two coffee cups on the table.

"I don't want any."

"What do you want, juice?"

I nodded.

"I brought you some leftover stew." She pointed to a plastic container in the refrigerator. "And there's some of those stuffed peppers, too."

"They give me heartburn."

"That's one thing I never got. But I held my water, especially with you. My legs swelled up like balloons. And the poison ivy that year? I thought I'd die. Ray likes peppers. Warm them up for him."

She sat down, lit another cigarette, and took a sip of coffee. "When'd you do the wash last?"

The last time I did the wash was when she'd done it. "I don't know," I said.

"You got to keep on top of it. Do you want to do a load now?"

"No, Ma, it's too hot." She was beginning to piss me off.

"You can do it tonight, you know. I used to do that. Once it cools down, throw a load in, then hang them out, they'll be dry before noon."

"I'm so bored I can't stand it."

"It's not like you don't have plenty to do—you just don't do it. When did you mop the floor last?"

"I don't want to talk about housework."

"I'm just telling you for your own good. You get into a routine, then it's easy."

"Ma!" I yelled. "I don't want to talk about housework, okay?" She got up and started sponging off the counters. I looked at the clock. I still had an hour before my first soap opera.

"Tell me how you and Daddy met." I said it to change the subject and keep her around, even though I'd heard the story a hundred times, like I'd heard all her stories a hundred times—because I'd been her main

confidante since the day I was born, only back then she

was fun. She used to sing in the kitchen, tap-dance down the hallway, and sometimes do back bends on the lawn.

She sat down and lit another cigarette. "We were at a dance at Rockaway Park. All the big bands came there. Your father was with his buddies and they were teasing him in front of me, saying, 'Why don't you jitterbug with Grace?' He wasn't asking me because he had the piles and they knew it."

"He couldn't dance because he had piles?"

"Well, you know, they were uncomfortable. He was shy. The next Saturday I asked him to dance. You know your father, he's a good dancer. And then we started dating, and six months later we married." I figured my mother must've been a hot number because she didn't hold sex off very long. "My family disowned me. They never liked Daddy, said he was a bum. I don't think your father ever forgot that."

"Do you wish you never got married?"

"Oh, you know. When I was single, I had a job, I had money, I bought nice clothes, went on vacations. I did what I pleased. Then when you marry, you go where the man wants. I moved to Wallingford. I hated it. I didn't know nobody. Then you kids came. I don't know. If you want to be happy, you stay single."

"But you love Daddy?"

"Oh yeah. But I cried in the beginning. I was so homesick. I missed my friends. I missed my job. And your father never wanted me to work. A man has his pride. But once I got my license—you were, what were you, fifteen?—I said, the hell with this. We needed money. That's when I started down Bradlees. Now, my legs, standing on those concrete floors. And taking care of two houses. I'm not getting any younger, you know." My mother could only talk for so long before she started complaining.

"Ma, you don't have to clean my house." I tried to nip it in the bud.

"Yeah, well, once you have the baby, I won't, believe me." Just then Bam Bam knocked on the door with his head. Bam Bam never said a word except "Bam Bam" and he only said that when he knocked on your door with his head.

"Are you going to let him in?" my mother said.

"Yes." I got up and opened the door.

"What you let him in for?"

"I like him."

Bam Bam sat at the table between us.

"Honest to God, Beverly, I can't believe you're having a baby in a couple of months. You better grow up." This was her favorite and most irritating thing to say. "Have you met any neighbors yet?"

"No."

She raised her eyebrows.

I should want to talk to Bam Bam's aunt—the woman he and his sisters lived with? She ignored her children, looked like a walrus, and lived with a guy who had no teeth. Or the lady across the street, who polished her red GTO as often as she changed her clothes? It was true sometimes I wished I could invite one or two of the prettier ones over, but the one time I did talk to neighbors it had been a big mistake. They were Stu and Marsha Heckle, who lived on the other side of my house. I called them the Uglies because he had big angry pimples and a pin head while she was shaped like a mushroom and you could see her pink scalp through her hair. As if being so ugly weren't enough, they were also Jehovah's Witnesses. I was sitting on the front steps, while Raymond watched a

baseball game inside, and Mr. Ugly came out and offered me a brownie "the Mrs." had made for a meeting
they were having that night of the Parents Against Sex
Education in Schools Committee. "You really think
sex education's wrong?" I ventured.

"Darned right," said Mr. Ugly. "Some stranger
telling our kids about the birds and the bees? What
gives them the right to take prayers out of the classroom and replace them with sex?"

This made me want to barf, since I figured if somebody had given me the scoop on birth control, I might
not be stuck, a pregnant teenager on a front stoop in
the public-housing project listening to a perverted
Christian confuse prayers and sex.

"Like the Uglies?" I said to my mother. "I'm supposed to talk to people who don't believe in sex education?"

"Everybody's entitled to their opinions."

"And so am I. I *like* Bam Bam. And I wish you'd
butt out. It's my business who I talk to."

"I better go."

I immediately felt bad for yelling. "What're you
cooking tonight?"

"I don't know. It's so hot, I thought I'd just have
kielbasa and potato salad. And you?"

"Sloppy joes."

"Why don't you have the stew? I don't know how
you kids can eat that stuff."

"Ma."

"All right, all right. I got to go pick up a few
things at Jeannie's. You want to come, you need anything?" Jeannie's was my father's cousin Jeannie's
store, and every time I went there, she threw a box of
goodies in my bag, like Ring Dings or Drake's Coffee
Cakes or a gallon of ice cream.

"No," I said.

She opened the refrigerator and lifted the quart of milk. "You need more milk." She opened the freezer. "That was the last can of juice? I'll pick some up."

She washed the cups and left.

I turned on the TV and watched my soaps with Bam Bam; then at around five I told the Bammer to go home for dinner. I opened up a can of sloppy-joe mix, put two hamburger buns on each of our plates, and warmed some Green Giant corn. Sometimes Ray and I sat in front of the TV and ate off snack trays, but tonight I thought we'd sit on the back stoop, where it was cooler.

When Ray hadn't shown up by five-thirty, I sat on the stoop with my plate balanced on my knees and tried not to get too worried. The first few times Ray was late I let my imagination run away, picturing him in his car wrapped around a tree or swallowed by a machine at work or simply driving and driving away from me and out of sight. But this time I figured he was probably just getting shitfaced as usual in a bar with some guy from work I'd never met.

After I finished dinner, I switched to the front stoop to watch for Ray's car. I hoped Bam Bam and Berta and Betty, his two beautiful five- and six-year-old sisters, would show. Berta and Betty had bright red hair and startling blue eyes, but they were always filthy dirty and ragged just like their little brother. I almost felt as sorry for Berta and Betty as I did for Bam Bam, because sometimes I'd look out at night and there the two of them would be—their curly heads in the dark—walking in the gutter, Berta in front, Betty in back, just walking up and down the street looking at their feet.

They came running from their yard when they saw

me. Bam Bam sat up close as I directed Berta and Betty in acrobatics. They did cartwheels around the rim of my yard, then crisscrossed each other in a big X, doing back flips. They did the routine over and over until they got the timing right and wound up in front of me at exactly the same moment. Then I taught them to curtsy, their arms curved like the necks of swans. I swear, the two of them would've made it to the Olympics if their aunt would only push them.

It was just getting dark when Berta and Betty's aunt stood on her back stoop and called, "Beeertaaa, Beeetteeey." If she looked my way, she would've seen them, but she didn't. Just stood on her stoop, round like an apple, with her hands cupped to her mouth, then went back in the house. Berta and Betty stopped dead in their tracks. The screen door slammed like a gunshot. They took off and didn't look back. They never said goodbye.

I heard Bam Bam rustling under the bush and making that whiny noise he did. I'd lost track of him, and now his knees were caked with dirt and there was snot dried on his face. "Crying out loud, Bam Bam," I said. "Doesn't your aunt ever wash you?" He smiled a slit smile and wagged his head back and forth real fast. "Want me to wash your face for you, Bammerang?" He kept shaking his head back and forth. I took a rag and loaded it with suds then washed his face like I was polishing a car. He squirmed around and squealed. It's not that I was a nut for cleanliness. That was my mother. I think it was more that Bam Bam was the type of kid people naturally liked to torture—like the neighborhood psychopath, Andrew, who could chase Bam Bam with a willow whip for hours.

Bam Bam pointed at the refrigerator, turned his palms up next to his shoulders, then shrugged them to his ears. He had some cute ways about him. You know how they say retarded people are closer to God? I believed that about Bam Bam. He didn't have a mean bone in his body, and his life was pretty grim. I think his aunt wished he'd just disappear, get kidnapped or run over by a truck or something. You never heard her calling, "Berta, Betty, Bam Bam."

It was late, near nine o'clock, and I was trying hard to keep my mind off of Raymond so I wouldn't get furious. I got Bam Bam a Ring Ding Jr. and poured him a glass of strawberry Kool-Aid, then I sat at the table across from him with my Ring Ding and glass of Kool-Aid and he did like Simon Says. He peeled the wrapper exactly like me, then held the round chocolate thing with his pointer finger and thumb the same as me. Then I licked under it to be sure it wasn't my imagination, and he licked it too. Bam Bam cracked me up.

It was pitch-black out; a breeze was kicking up and whipping the shades against the windows. I was spooked and glad Bam Bam was there. "Hey, Bam," I said. "You want to dance?" He nodded his head up and down fast. I put *Sgt. Pepper* on the stereo. I was careful not to lift my arms up high because my mother was always warning me that I'd strangle the baby with the umbilical cord. So I twirled and swayed my gigantic hips and Bam Bam did little hops and wiggled his head.

I collapsed exhausted and sweaty in the rocker.

Bam Bam tried to climb on my lap.

I didn't want him to touch me. "Get off," I said. He made like he'd start crying.

"Don't you cry, Bammer, or I won't let you in anymore. Hear me? You better go now." I opened the front door. He just stood there. "Bam Bam," I said with forced patience.

He bent his chin to his chest and crouched down like an ape. When he finally passed through, I locked the door and headed upstairs. He banged his head on the screen, "Bam . . . bam, bam . . . bam," he said.

I screamed, "Bam Bam, get lost. I mean it!"

I ran up the stairs and sat on the edge of our bed and stared out the window in the dark. I spotted Bam Bam sitting in the gutter a few feet down the road, swishing sand with a stick and rubbing his eye with the back of his hand. I felt bad kicking him out, but I didn't want to call him back, either.

Just then a car approached in a whoosh of light and I thought maybe it was my mother. It was Raymond. He slammed the door a little too hard.

His feet made a lot of noise on the floor. He called, "Beverly."

I didn't answer.

"Fuck," he said.

He opened the refrigerator door and closed it. I heard the water go on. He walked up the stairs, took a piss in the bathroom. I held my breath. He looked in the room and said, "What're you doing?"

"You should have called."

He leaned against the door frame. He smelled of cigarettes and booze. "That guy, Sal? Got laid off. He didn't expect it, either. Some of us guys went down the Aviation for some drinks to make him feel better."

I laid down on my stomach and started to cry.

"What's the matter?" he said.

"I don't know," I lied. The matter was I wanted my mother.

I had big plans for my marriage. They went something like this: My friends come over every night. We have pajama parties and play music as loud as we want. Instead, like I said, they deserted me to Spring Lake, where they had new and changing boyfriends, went skinny-dipping and floating on inner tubes, and never thought of inviting me, because I was pregnant. The only girlfriends who called me up were Virginia, who would be going to college in the fall and had to stay in Wallingford to work for the summer, and Fay, because she was married now too. She'd married the guy from the nuclear submarine the day after graduation, as planned.

Finally, my friends invited us to a huge party. Ray and I drove Virginia and Bobby, who would be leaving for boot camp in a couple of weeks. Everybody would be there except for Fay, because she was visiting her in-laws in Virginia. By the time of the party, it had been positively confirmed that Fay had conceived on her honeymoon. I was ecstatic that now I wouldn't be the only mother.

I could think of nothing but the party for weeks. I was sure everybody would be shocked to see how fat I'd grown and that they'd make a big fuss over me. But my girlfriends seemed different. For one thing, their skin was tanned, and for another, they were surrounded by guys I'd never laid eyes on. There were empty beer cans and scotch bottles overflowing from garbage bags in corners. Beatrice, who used to think she was ugly, was wearing tight hiphuggers and a low-cut jersey. She was with a guy named Donnie, who'd just come back from Vietnam, where he'd been a paramedic. But his last three months all he did was load bodies in plastic bags onto planes. Beatrice told me this in the bathroom while she plucked her eyebrows. "I'm such a mess, Beverly. I've been drunk for a month."

"Really?"

"We have beer for breakfast. Beer and toast."

"You're lucky."

"I'm broke. I spent all my graduation money. We all are. In two weeks I start at the Knights of Columbus with my mother. I don't want to go back to Wallingford. You're lucky you don't have to work."

"I know."

No one made a fuss about my hugeness, so after my third rum and Coke, I lifted my shirt up in the kitchen to show off my belly. People gathered around to touch it. "What does it feel like?" they wanted to know.

"Heavy. I get backaches and heartburn."

"Ugh."

"But it moves. Sometimes you can see it under my skin."

"How weird."

Then I got drunk, noticed this beautiful guy walk in the door, and forgot myself. I asked him to dance. We did the Jerk and I forgot all about the umbilical cord and fetus strangulation and that I was even pregnant. I closed my eyes and really got into it. I imagined he was watching me and wishing I wasn't married. I imagined that if I weren't married, I would dance with this guy for the rest of the night. Then we'd go outside and talk by the lake. He'd be from a different town. We'd go there and I'd meet new people. I felt his hand on my arm and opened my eyes. "Won't you hurt the baby?" he said.

I turned and walked through the kitchen and out the back door, stunned. I sat on the ground between two parked cars until I was sure I wouldn't cry, then I looked for Raymond. He was leaning against a car. He took the last swig of a beer, then squashed the can in his fist and burped. He was with Armond White, who was home on leave from the army.

"You're drunk," I said when I stood next to Raymond.

"Tell me one thing," Ray said. "We were just talking. How do you lose my socks in the wash? What the hell happens to them?"

"You've had too much to drink," I said.

"Ah, come on."

"I want to go home."

"We just got here."

"Why don't you leave the guy alone?" Armond said. I had a longstanding gripe with Armond. He was the moron who told Raymond that if you had sex more than once in twenty-four hours then you were safe after the first time. I knew Armond was stupid, like most of Raymond's friends, but I believed him because I thought they taught guys all about birth control in the army.

"Mind your own business, Armond," I said.

"You let your wife talk like that, man?"

"*Let* your wife? I talk however the fuck I please."

"Nice language."

"Raymond." I thought I'd murder him if he didn't walk away with me that instant.

"You think you're pretty tough, huh?" said Armond. "Remember, tough cookies crumble."

"All over your face."

"Beverly, come on." Raymond hugged me from behind and pinned my arms to my sides as he walked me away backward.

"You have such assholes for friends," I said.

"So? I'm an asshole," Ray said.

"Let's go home."

"I'm having fun. We never have fun anymore. Don't let's leave yet. Please? Besides, what about Bobby and Virginia?"

"How can you even talk to somebody so stupid? I'm so tired."

"You're always tired. You hate my friends. We never have any fun." He tried to kiss me on the neck. "Come on, Bevy. All your friends are here. You been looking forward to this for weeks. Why aren't you having fun?"

"If we stay longer you'll get drunker."

"I promise. If we stay another two hours, I won't drink anymore. Maybe one beer."

"One hour."

"All right."

One hour later I couldn't find him. An hour after that, I found him lying on his back on top of a picnic table by the lake. Drunk. I told him I wanted to go home.

"I want to go home. I want to go home. You know who you sound like? What's her name in *The Wizard of Oz*." He thought that was a riot.

"You said only one beer."

He sat up and swayed so far to the right he almost fell off the table. I felt like hitting him. "Give me the keys," I said.

He dug in his pockets, then shook his head up from his chest. "What am I doing? No way. You're really something." He pointed his thumb at me. "The big boss. Everybody thinks I'm pussy-whipped. That's why I got drunk."

"I'm going," I said, and started walking toward home, which was fifty miles away. The road was dark and deserted. I passed the little stand, closed now, where the year before I'd sat on a picnic table and flirted with some college guys who'd asked me if I was a nonconformist, a word I'd never heard. I'd walked nearly a mile and was not only getting cold but scared, because the trees made an arch over my head and blocked off the moonlight, when Raymond finally pulled up with Virginia and Bobby in the backseat. "You walked far," he said.

"I'm freezing," I said.

"Get in, baby," he said.

"Let me drive."

"Please, Bev?"

I felt sorry for him. I could be a bitch. Plus, I didn't want to make a scene in front of Virginia and Bobby, who'd seen too many already, so I got in and ignored his weaving all over the road. About ten minutes later, Raymond nodded out and our VW flipped like a pancake. Sand chimed around me and time slowed down as I thought, Now, at last, I'll lose the baby.

Then everything was still and silent. Virginia said, "Bobby?"

"I'm all right," he said.

"Beverly?" she said.

"I'm okay," I said as I squeezed myself out of the upside-down car. Bobby and Virginia looked dazed standing a foot apart staring. The only sound was the whir of wheels spinning. "Where's Ray?" Bobby said after a minute. It was strange we'd forgotten him.

We walked like zombies to the other side of the car. Raymond was lying on the ground, unconscious, with the car door resting on his shoulder and a big blob of blood gelling on the asphalt under his nose.

"Do you think it's his brain?" I said.

Bobby put his ear to Ray's chest. "He's alive," he said.

We walked across the street and banged on a door. A woman's voice yelled, "Get out of here before I call the cops."

Bobby said, "Fuck you, lady."

At the next house, the woman called an ambulance and we went back to the car to wait.

"Goddamn!" Bobby kicked a fender.

"Bobby, don't," Virginia said, because Bobby could get crazy.

"That's my buddy," Bobby said. "Look at him, man."

I couldn't. Neither could Virginia.

At the hospital they wheeled Ray away, then a doctor examined me. He listened to my stomach with a stethoscope and said the baby seemed fine. Then he bandaged my knee and my forehead where it had hit the windshield and told me I could go home. Bobby and Virginia got picked up by Virginia's father, and I hung around to wait for Ray to get out of X rays. His eyes were black-and-blue and opened. When he saw me, he started crying.

"His collarbone and his nose are broken," a nurse told me.

"I should've let you drive," Raymond cried.

"It's all right," I said.

"I could've killed you. I love you so much."

"I love you too. Don't cry."

The nurse rolled him away sobbing.

"You all right?" my father said when I called home for a ride. I'd been praying I'd get my mother.

"Yes."

"Him?"

"Broken collarbone and nose."

"Was he drinking?"

"A little."

"Did they book him?"

"No."

"The car?"

"Totaled."

"Jesus Christ. What's the matter with you kids? I ought to have his license taken away. Now, what're you gonna do for a car?"

My mother came to pick me up, then it was her turn. "He's gonna miss work," she said. "What're you going to do for money? I do what I can, but you know your father and me don't have a pot to piss in. I don't know, you kids think you can go around acting like teenagers."

"We are teenagers."

"You're having a baby. You have responsibilities. What's it going to be like when the baby's born? How would you've felt if you lost it? You better smarten up."

I leaned my head back on the seat and watched the streetlights disappear into the car roof and hummed not a song but a drone, like a bumble bee.

"What's that?" my mother said.

I kept humming, and she never knew it was me.

Once I got home, I was afraid murderers and escapees from mental institutions were lurking by the windows, so I went directly to the bathroom, locked the door, and sat on the floor next to the toilet. I felt so lonely, I even confessed to myself that I wished I could've gone home with my mother. I hugged the bowl and yowled great sobs like opera.

Then the baby moved. It was the first time since the accident. My crying trembled to neutral.

Maybe I'd been lonely for the baby. I realized I'd been talking to her for months without thinking. Maybe I would've been sad if she died.

I went to a fortune-teller by the railroad tracks. Her trailer smelled of cat piss, and she was as wide as a Volkswagen. She sat me down and dealt some cards.

She said I was having a girl, which I already knew, and that within five years I'd have two more children and move into a split-level house. My daughter's name would begin with *J*.

I began making plans. My daughter would look just like me, and when she was born she'd have a round little baseball head covered with black hair. Her eyes would be big and brown. She was going to be my best friend and there'd be nothing in the world we wouldn't talk about. I'd tell her every last detail about my life up to her birth and after. She'd definitely go to college, and I'd call her Nicole, after a schizophrenic on my favorite soap opera. Ray said if it was a boy, he wanted it named after him. I said, no way. I wasn't naming our girl after me. We settled on Jason, after Jason McCord in *The Lawman,* and his middle name would be Michael, after my father.

CHAPTER 5

LABOR started on a Sunday night in the middle of September. It was so hot that week that the neighborhood dogs had taken to roaming in packs in a flurry of heat madness. Cats dived under cars and into open cellar windows to escape them. One day I saw the dogs toss a doll in the air and rip it limb from limb, a cloud of white foam clinging to their coats. I was almost two weeks late, and if I didn't deliver soon, I was planning to throw myself in the middle of that pack of mangy dogs and be done for.

We went for macaroni at my mother's on Sunday, a ritual I'd missed maybe a half dozen times in my entire life, only this time I felt a pain after dinner while we were watching *The FBI* and eating lemon meringue pie, but I didn't say anything. Raymond wanted to stay for the Sunday night movie, but I told him I didn't feel too well and wanted to go home. As soon as we walked into our house, a slimy liquid drooled down the inside of my thigh. "Oooh, gross! Raymond!" I yelled. "I think I'm in labor."

"You're kidding," he said.

We tossed my overnight bag into the backseat of our Chevelle (my father had found it for five hundred dollars and co-signed for the loan), and I suggested we take a ride once around the duck pond before we went to the hospital. The new Beatles song "Hey Jude" came on the radio.

"That's it!" I said. "That's what we'll name her—June." I'd misheard the lyrics.

Ray drummed his thumbs on the dashboard, jerked his chin in and out, and said, "Cool."

I was scared to death in the labor room. First they shaved me, then they gave me an enema, then after I waddled out of the bathroom and back into the room, they laid me in a crib like a beached whale. Immediately, the nurse poked some fingers in. I was three fingers, the middle circle. Five fingers was the biggest. When you stretched that wide it was bingo, birth. The Puerto Rican women came in and left within half an hour, screaming, *Mama! Mama! Mama!*

There was a pretty woman lying in the crib across from me. "Hi," she said after the nurse left.

"Hi."

"I'm Louise Baker. This is my first baby. You too?"

"Yeah. My name's Beverly Bouchard."

"If I scream like those ladies, shoot me, okay?"

"You think it's gonna really hurt?"

"I'm sure it does, but it can't hurt that much."

"How long you been here?"

"About an hour. I haven't seen a doctor yet. I go to the clinic."

"So do I. I never saw you."

"That place is the pits." She pulled back her long blond hair and began making a braid. "I go to Central Connecticut College. I mean, I did. After I was six months, I quit. My boyfriend still goes there. I'll probably go back after the baby."

"What were you going to school for?"

"My major? Anthropology."

I wasn't sure I knew what that was, but I'd rather die than ask her. I noticed her legs weren't shaved. I wished I'd seen her at the clinic. Everybody else spoke Spanish, and there never were enough folding chairs to go around. I'd had to wait a minimum of four hours every time, and if I'd met Louise there, we could've talked for whole mornings. By now we'd be good friends. But, probably, a person who went to college would think I was too stupid.

"Do you have medical insurance?" she asked.

"No. You?"

"Do you realize if you don't marry, your boy-friend's insurance won't cover you? We refused to marry. We put our politics in action. Art and I believe it's an archaic formality binding you together by law. My parents don't even . . . oh boy. Here comes one."

My pains had stopped altogether. I told the nurse. A doctor came in. He was young and handsome. His hands were slender and long. I'd never laid eyes on him before. "Hello," he said. He looked at my chart. "Mrs. Bouchard, I hear your pains have stopped."

"Yes."

"We're going to give you a little something to get them started again, speed things up."

The nurse handed him a needle and he stuck it in my ass. Within ten minutes, I was in agony and there was no breather between contractions. The doctor came back and said, "Okay, Mrs. Bouchard, we're moving right along. Now, I'm going to give you some Demerol to ease it up a bit." He gave me another shot in the ass. Before I passed out, I had a hallucination. I saw the kitten I'd had when I was a kid. It was jumping up over and over again, trying to get in the crib with me.

I don't know how long I was out before I awoke to Louise screaming, "Oh God, oh God, oh God. Ah ah ah ah *aaaahhhhhh!*"

Sweat started raining from every pore of my body. When she stopped screaming, she saw me looking at her through the bars and said, "I'm sorry, but it hurts so much," then she started crying.

I wished I could die.

Louise was long gone when the nurse rolled me onto my back, put my ankles in my hands, and told me to push. It was too humiliating. I kept thinking how even Jacqueline Kennedy must've held her ankles in the air and grunted like she was taking a shit. The next time the nurse appeared, she looked between my legs and started breathing heavily. "Okay, Mrs. Bouchard, I'd like you to stop pushing now. We're paging your doctor. Don't worry, everything's fine."

"I can't help it," I cried. "I have to."

"Please, Mrs. Bouchard, try not to push," she said as she wheeled my cot into the delivery room. I felt betrayed by every living mother. Why hadn't they warned me?

"This is horrible." I started crying. "Where's the gas? Give me the gas," I yelled. "Don't I get gas?" The nurse strapped my knees into stirrups, then positioned a round mirror above to distract me. "Look, Mrs. Bouchard, look. You can see the head." It was slimy green and protruding. I covered my eyes and yelled, "Take it away, I can't stand it, I don't want to!" Finally, an Oriental intern walked in. They clamped a gas mask on my face and it was over.

When I awoke, the nurse held a wrinkled, ugly red baby in a white cloth out to me. "Congratulations, Mrs. Bouchard, you have a healthy eight-and-a-half-pound baby boy."

"Boy!" I screamed. His head was huge and shaped like a football. "What's the matter with his head? He has blond hair!" The nurse blanched. I covered my face with my hands and sobbed. It was as though my daughter had died. The baby girl with the pretty round head who'd been hiccupping, rolling over, and kicking inside me—the daughter who'd been my best friend for months—had been a boy all along. What would I do with him? I didn't even like boys anymore. He'd have army men and squirt guns and baseball cards and a *penis*. What would we talk about?

My mother brought me a strawberry milkshake and kissed me on the cheek, then sat down and settled her pocketbook on her lap. "So, how does it feel to be a mother?" she asked.

I shrugged.

"Hurt, huh?"

I bit my lips to keep from crying.

Later, I took a walk to the nursery and saw him, a little lump under a white blanket. I thought if it weren't for his name on the bassinet, I wouldn't even know he was mine.

My mother came back at the next visiting hour and brought my father and my sisters, Rose and Phyllis, with her. Ray's mother came too, and so did three of my girlfriends. Everybody sat on my bed or the windowsills. Rose sat on my father's lap. When Ray came by after work, there was no place for him. He seemed like an outsider, and I felt sorry. He handed me a bunny with an ivy plant in its back, and the first opening he got, he rocked forward and back and said, "Hey, Bev, you know something? The song's 'Hey Jude,' not 'June.'"

Since the Beatles had been singing about a boy all along, maybe having a boy wouldn't be too bad. Besides, if the fortune-teller had been wrong about the sex of my baby, then she was probably wrong about the other two kids and the split-level house, too. "Do you think we should name him Jude instead of Jason?" I asked Ray.

"I guess."

"Jude?" my mother said. "What kind of a name's that?"

I'd never heard of St. Jude or *Jude the Obscure,* and the name reminded me of Judas, Jesus' traitor. I changed my mind. "Let's call him Jason," I said.

"Cool." Ray dragged on his cigarette.

The next day, when Jason came to my room, he was soft and warm and smelled sweet like baby, but he moved his head like a dinosaur in a Japanese movie. I was scared of him. Then he got the hiccups after half an ounce of milk and started crying.

He was still crying when I gave him back to the nurse. "Only half an ounce?" she said.

"He got the hiccups," I explained.

She shook her head as if to say, Stupid teenage mother.

The next time he came to my room, I made myself be braver. I shut the door, then took off his undershirt and memorized exactly how his diaper was pinned so I could duplicate it, then took it off too. I'd never seen an uncircumsised penis before. It looked like an elephant's trunk. I kissed it. I nuzzled his stomach, his armpit, his neck. I put his whole foot in my mouth.

The day we left the hospital, I dressed Jason in a blue suit with a plastic Tweety Bird glued on the chest. Ray carried him to the car like he was a tank of nitroglycerin. At a traffic light, when I noticed his head being led around by his mouth, I stuck my finger in. He sucked on it.

My mother was at our house when we got there and it looked like she'd been there for weeks. For one thing, it was spic-and-span, and for another, she'd moved the kitchen table from kitty-corner to flush against the wall. She was sitting at it with a tray of pastries and a pot of coffee in front of her. "You have more room this way," she said. I sat down and said, "Ma, look." I stuck my finger in.

"Take that finger out of his mouth! Are you crazy?" she said.

"Why? He likes it."

"You got germs on your hands. Everything that passes that baby's lips has to be sterilized. Come on, Jason." She held out her arms. I handed him over. "How you doin', little fella? What a big boy you are." She pinched his cheeks. "How you doing? How you doing? How you doing?" she shouted at him, nodding her head every time, poking his chin with her finger. "Look at those fat cheeks. I could eat him up. Your mother's tired, so your Mimi's taking over, let her get her strength back. Isn't that right?"

"Your *Mimi*?"

"It's cute, don't you think?"

"I like it," Ray said, taking off his jacket and sitting on the couch.

"Raymond, hang it up," my mother said. "Your wife just had a baby, she can't be picking up after you."

"I think Mimi's stupid."

"What's the matter with it?"

"It sounds like a dog."

"I like it. It'll be easier to pronounce."

I figured either she wanted to be called Mimi because she was only forty-five and embarrassed to be a grandmother or because Mimi sounded more like Mommy than Grandma did.

My mother came over for hours every single day. I hardly had to do anything, and when I did do something, she watched me like a hawk. "Watch out for his head, Beverly, don't forget the soft spot. His neck isn't strong yet, he could snap it. . . . Better put him on his stomach, he might spit up and suffocate if you lie him on his back."

By the time she started bringing my fat aunt Alma with her, I'd had it. They perked a pot of coffee, broke open an Entenmann's coffee cake and gave detailed infant histories of every one of their children. "Jerry was colicky, kept me up six months straight, but Willie, God bless'm, slept eight hours the first night."

"That's like Beverly. You were the best baby. Never a peep. Loved to sleep. You're lucky Jason's like that. You don't know. Your brother—up every night. I didn't mind, though. You get attached. Wait. You'll see."

One day, around the same time I first smelled winter in the air, I sat at the table with my mother and aunt and Jason, who was in his little seat on top of the table. I watched my aunt's fat fingers roll a cake crumb on her plate and couldn't take them another minute. I stood up and said, "I'm bringing Jason to the library."

"You can't," my mother said. "You can't take a baby in public until he's had all his shots."

"You said I could after six weeks. I'm going crazy."

"Then you go. I'll watch him."

"No."

"You can't take him, and that's the end of it."

"He's *my baby*."

"It's awfully breezy," my aunt said. "Might be hard to catch his breath." She shrugged and bit her lips.

I ignored her, put a jacket and bonnet on Jason,

then made a triangle out of a blanket and wrapped him up.

At the library, I checked out *David Copperfield,* and when I returned, my mother had lost her stand as big chief the baby expert. I invited my girlfriends over every night. Virginia was commuting to college. The rest had jobs, except for Fay, who was pregnant and still living down in New London. I felt sorry for Fay, but I figured it was my duty not to deceive her and to tell her the truth about the horrors of childbirth when she visited. "It hurts like hell," I said to Fay and Beatrice and Virginia as we drank coffee one night in the kitchen. "That miracle shit is a bunch of propaganda. I'll never, no matter what, have another one as long as I live. And Jason? He's all right. I love him, but it's not what you imagine. It's more like you'd love an abandoned puppy you found on the street."

With my friends around, I liked to make fun of Jason. I took off his clothes, strapped him to his changing table, then imitated Diana Ross in my "Love Child" routine. "Started his life in old cold run-down tenement slum . . . love child, always second best, love child, different from the rest." I swung my hips, spun around, and pointed at him to the beat.

If we laughed too loud, Raymond called from the living room for us to keep it down.

By winter, Ray was working four to twelve and leaving me alone every night. And just about every night, Virginia came by to keep me company after she'd finished her homework. She gave me all her books to read as soon as she'd finished them, like *The Ego and the Id,* from Psychology 101, and some Hemingway, Fitzgerald, and Ford Madox Ford books from a course called "The Jazz Age." I joined the Literary

Guild and got four more books by Hemingway, four by Steinbeck, and four by Faulkner, which I read whenever Jase went down for a nap or I could get him to shut up in his playpen for a while. I was trying to make myself smart to make up for not going to college.

The thing V and I liked to do best, besides talk about her classes, was to play with the Ouija board. Usually, we asked it questions like if I'd ever get divorced; when Raymond would die; if Jason would go to college; when Bobby and Virginia would marry; how many children they'd have; and if Bobby would make it home from Vietnam in one piece. Then one night we contacted a spirit. Her name was Nancy and she told us her history: she'd died at the age of eighteen, had three brothers still alive and one sister dead, lived somewhere in Michigan, and was a B student in high school. We carried on a dialogue with Nancy for a couple of nights before she turned nasty.

It was early spring and one of those moonless nights when little puffs of wind pushed the shades away from the window, leaving a black gap where someone could peek in. We were a little scared to begin with, but then when the magic indicator started jerking around the board spelling out profanities, I thought my heart would beat a hole through my chest. "Nancy, is that you?" I said.

Fuck, bitch, bastard, asshole.

"Why are you swearing?" Virginia asked.

Dirty twat, scum, cunt.

Then we heard a crash behind us. We jerked our hands off the magic indicator. The utensil rack was swinging from one screw in the wall and the utensils were strewn all over the floor.

We walked over to the wall to get a good look.

Here's the thing. The rack was made in such a way that you had to squeeze it together to pull the round holes over the screws. The only way it could be swinging there would be if the other screw had fallen out of the wall or if someone had squeezed the rack together, then pulled it off. Both screws were still in the wall.

V and I looked at each other, screamed, ran up the stairs, and locked ourselves in the bathroom. We sat on the floor with our backs pressed against the door. "What about Jason?" V said.

"Oh God," I said. "We have to get him." We ran across the hall on our toes, went into his room, locked the door, and peeked in his crib. He was lying on his back. His eyes were wide open with only the whites showing.

We ran back into the bathroom. "He's possessed," I said.

"Oh, Mary, Mother of God." V was my only religious friend. She went to mass every morning—she said it was for the peace and quiet, but I knew she probably prayed for Bobby. Just then we heard banging at the front door. We stopped breathing. Then we heard banging at the back door, next the cellar hatchway being pulled open, then footfalls on the stairs. By the time the door opened from the cellar to the living room, we were weeping. "Bev," I heard. It was Raymond. He'd lost his keys.

We ran down the stairs and told him everything. He looked at the baby and said his eyes were normal. Then I looked, too, and they were.

Virginia was too spooked to drive home, so she slept on the sofa. The next night, she was back in our kitchen. "Nancy went nuts because of Bobby," she said. "He's dead."

"What?"

"Shrapnel. They said he didn't feel a thing. His mother called. It'll take a couple of days for his body to come home."

"You're kidding," I said.

"Right. I made it up. It's a big joke."

"I'm sorry. I didn't mean . . ." I said.

Virginia started crying. I couldn't think of a single thing to say. I wished I could cry too. I hugged her and we rocked, stretched between our seats. When Ray came home, he sat in the rocker to take off his work boots, and we told him the news. He threw a boot across the floor, then flung himself back, pressed the heels of his hands into his eyes, and said, "My buddy. My buddy."

The night before the funeral, Ray and I didn't put Jase to bed at six o'clock as usual. We sat on our steps, and Jason, eight months old now, pushed a dump truck around our feet. We put the "White Album" on and, one by one, as if they'd been invited, people began to pull into our driveway and park on the road. There were about a dozen of us sitting on our steps and lying on our lawn that night, listening to the Beatles, reminiscing about Bobby. He'd gone to Dag Hammarskjold with me and had been responsible for the rash of bomb scares one freezing fall. The whole school had to stand outside while the cops searched every locker and desk in the building. A guy named Lenny flicked a cigarette into the night and told us how he'd been waiting for his turn outside the vice-principal's office when Bobby called the vice-principal an ape, then decked him. Bobby was expelled for that one. Rather than face his father, he ran away to Maine and got a severe case of frostbite. But then in high school, he'd joined the football team, and made more touchdowns than anyone. His father was proud of him. Which was Virginia's theory of why he joined the marines: to keep his father that way.

On leave after boot camp, Bobby'd come over for Sunday dinner. He hardly ate any macaroni, then he drank so much he puked in the living room. After he'd come downstairs from washing his face, I'd asked him if he was scared to go to war.

"Bev," Ray said.

"What?"

"You don't ask a guy those questions."

"Oh," I'd said, and Bobby turned his face away.

Sitting on the steps, I pictured Bobby the way he'd looked at my wedding, wearing a shirt with huge polka dots and maroon bell-bottoms. Then I pictured him in the photo he'd sent me from Nam. He had a rifle slung over his shoulder and his hair cut like a Mohican. He was standing on a hill and looked like a statue. I wondered if I'd still remember Bobby when I was thirty or forty. I'd be an adult, but in my memory he'd still be a kid. I wondered if Bobby would've always been wild or if he'd have calmed down, settled in a job somewhere, had a couple of kids, a bald head, a beer belly. I wondered if Bobby was the lucky one. I looked at the back of my son's neck—he was passed out on the grass. It looked so delicate, so tender. Finally, I wept.

"Blackbird" was playing in the background, and I thought how Bobby would never get the chance to spread his wings and learn to fly. I wondered if any of us would.

CHAPTER 6

A year after that—in June 1970, to be exact—at the tail end of the most glorious spring of my youth, if you can still consider the age of nineteen youth, my heart broke.

The thing that got me, the real kick in the ass, was I was happy. Really happy. Marriage was working, because marijuana had changed our lives. Not only did Ray and I dress differently—we both wore sunglasses (we called them shades) day and night, and bell-bottom jeans that were so long they dragged on the ground and frayed on the bottoms—but we had a dream: to live *Easy Rider*. Raymond had even borrowed a thousand dollars from the credit union to buy a chopped Harley-Davidson, then managed to get laid off so we could hang out together and collect unemployment. He'd also become tight with a bunch of guys from the Animal Pack, the local motorcycle gang. I could take or leave the Animals—obviously, they were nothing like Peter Fonda and Dennis Hopper—but the important thing was I was dreaming again. There was California, there were communes, there was free love for married people. Not to mention how beautiful the world looked, in the spring, under the influence of drugs. I began to write poems.

My mother thought I'd gone off the deep end. I'd

regained my independence. I was different from her. So what if I was disorganized and a slob, I was imaginative and a thinker. "Jason," she said when he stuck his finger in his nose at a year and a half. "Get your finger out of your nose."

"Leave him alone, Ma."

"What, you're not going to teach him manners?"

"If everybody picked their nose when they felt like it, everybody would be a lot happier. You pick your nose, I pick my nose, everybody picks their nose, so why hide it? We got ruined from socialization."

"You're saying I should've let you pick your nose?"

"Yes."

"Honest to God, Beverly, I don't know who you take after."

And my father, never a slouch when it came to detective work, took one look at the cars that ended up in our driveway at all hours and knew exactly what was going on in our house. He refused to set foot in it. Which was fine with us, since he was a cop and we were doing illegal drugs.

Raymond finally had friends, so instead of sitting alone in the living room and not playing Scrabble with my friends in the kitchen because he felt too stupid, he had guys to go out with. Plus, he had long hair and a beard and was handsome. Sometimes when there was company, I'd sit across from him in a miniskirt and I'd catch the way he looked at me and want to leap across the room and land on top of him.

It was almost as though Ray and I were single. Life was blissful. One night I'd go out with my friends, and Raymond would baby-sit. The next night Ray'd go out with his, and I'd baby-sit. My friends and I rode around town smoking superb red marijuana sent from Vietnam. The air through our windows smelled of damp earth. We were awed by each leaf flapping separately on the trees. We peed in cornfields and ran through sprinklers on golf courses.

I even had a crush that spring. His name was Peter Dodd. Raymond had met him at the Crystal Spa and told me about this guy who'd shot off his toe in Vietnam to get discharged, which made him a hero to us because we thought the war was bullshit. Peter wasn't only missing a toe, he'd been born with only one testicle. I fell in love before I even laid eyes on him, then fixed him up with Beatrice. He was tall and skinny and drove a school bus. He wrote songs. Some mornings he'd pull his yellow bus across my front lawn and we'd sit in the kitchen eating toast and drinking coffee, Jason on Peter's lap. We talked about people. I read him my poems, which were very short: "Lemon days alone and lost. What will happen in the dark?" That was one. "Swing high. Swing low. Never know. Where to go." That was another. Sometimes at night with Raymond, Peter sang us his songs and I read them my poems. I felt a little sorry for Raymond because all he did most of the time was listen, but he didn't seem to mind. He nodded out in the rocker, and I watched Peter fold his long legs this way and that as we passed a joint back and forth and Peter laughed at things I said. We talked until dawn many nights. I looked at Raymond, asleep by then in the rocker, and I felt tender.

That sleeping in the rocker was the beginning of the problem. Or the beginning of my noticing there was a problem at all. Raymond had taken to half sleeping in the rocker for hours and hours, kind of scratching his nose, which was peeling from all the rubbing, and sitting there with his head on his chest nodding out. Since it often happened when we were smoking marijuana, I thought maybe it was giving Raymond

7 9

brain damage. But since I was so happy, I didn't pay much attention until one night.

Beatrice and I had gone to the Coleman Brothers' carnival and I'd left Ray at home baby-sitting and expecting some friends to come over. Ever since I was a little kid, I'd loved the carnival. I had this friend, when I was very little, named Joannie Devon, who lived on top of some rickety ill-lighted stairs in a shabby apartment alone with her mother. Rumor had it that her mother had had an affair with a carnie who left town and her pregnant with Joannie. Joannie was very poor but extremely beautiful. And even as a little child, though I couldn't put a word to it, I knew Joannie had grace. There was something in the way she looked at you and moved and smiled that I thought saintly. In other words, if the Virgin Mary were going to appear to anybody, it would be Joannie. We moved away from our first house and I lost track of her. But I remembered her every time the Coleman Brothers came to town. Then I'd look at all those carnies in their booths with tattoos on their arms and voices daring you on and I'd wonder which one had fathered Joannie Devon, the angel.

Beatrice and I smoked some pot, then rode the Ferris wheel. Then we saw a trailer advertising Siamese twins. Inside there were two boys around my age, attached at the hips. They sat back to back watching the same shows on separate TVs. The pink printed sheet we were handed at the door said they were born that way and that their parents had put them in the carnival to help pay for college. The twins just sat there, their eyes riveted on their TVs, as though they were completely unaware that hundreds of people were walking behind a rope in their living room, gawking. I felt so sad after I saw those twins, I wanted to cry. The twins,

I knew, would never go to college. I got the idea that maybe the next day I could drop by, real early, before the carnival opened, and make friends with them. Have a real talk, maybe about books. I didn't tell Beatrice any of this. I just said I felt depressed. She said, "Me too."

We drove back to my house, where Peter Dodd had said he might stop later.

Ocho Perez's truck was in the driveway, which meant some of the guys from the Animal Pack were probably with Raymond.

When we walked in, Raymond was in the rocker and three guys dressed in black and blue sat shoulder to shoulder on the couch. I only knew Ocho Perez, who was in the middle, his thumbs in his belt, his head on his chest, snoozing with everyone else. Raymond heard the screen door slam, pulled his head up, opened his eyes, which took a while to focus, then he blinked at the TV. It was flashing silver specks. "Hey, man," he said. "Why don't one a you change the fucking channel?"

"Why don't you change the channel, man?" Ocho said when he pulled his head up too.

"It's my house, man. My TV. You want to watch it, you change it."

"For Christ's sake," I said, embarrassed at Raymond's rudeness. "What channel do you want? I'll change it."

"Shit, Bev," Ray said. "You home?"

I whispered to Beatrice in the kitchen that I thought the pot was making Raymond retarded.

"Do you think it can?" Beatrice asked.

"I don't know. Maybe. But they're all like that. Look at them."

"Maybe they're just tired," she said.

"I don't know what from. None of them work."

"What's dat show?" one of the guys said.

"I don't know," Raymond said.

"Ain't that Clint Eastwood?"

"Shit, man," Ocho said. "If that's Clint Eastwood, I'm John Wayne."

"John Wayne?" Raymond guffawed. "Try Sal Mineo." Ocho was small and dark and Puerto Rican, just about the only one in town.

"That ain't Clint Eastwood, man. That's what's his face," the other guy said. "You know, man. *The Rifleman*."

"That was a good show," Raymond said.

"It sucked," Ocho said.

I rolled my eyes at Beatrice.

Peter Dodd came in the front door, and Raymond said, "Pete, my man." The guys on the couch just looked at him.

"Hey, Ray, how's it going," Pete said. "Bev, Beatrice." He smiled, walking toward the kitchen. The guys on the sofa obviously didn't know or didn't like Peter, and vice versa. This made me uneasy.

I decided it was time Raymond found some work and stopped hanging out with the Animal Pack.

The next day I suggested he look for some kind of part-time job, maybe under the table so he could still collect unemployment, and mentioned that the motorcycle we'd been hotly awaiting seemed stalled indefinitely. Ray's reports on the state of the bike went like this: First the guy wasn't sure he wanted to sell it after all; then Raymond decided the guy should fix the exhaust before we handed over any money; then the guy cracked up the front fender and didn't have the bucks to fix it; and on and on. I told Ray we should take this opportunity to stockpile some money for our trip across country.

To my surprise, Raymond agreed with me and went out nearly every day looking for work. It was a drag not to have a car and boring to be stuck home alone with Jason again. There was only so much you could do with such a little kid. We danced to *Sgt. Pepper,* the "White Album," *Abbey Road.* I lay on the floor and he sat on my belly. I pushed his features around like his skin was made of Play-Doh. He touched his finger to my eye and said, "Nose." I said, "Eye." We played patty cake, this little piggy, itsy bitsy spider. He tried to sing along. I bent my knees and stood him on my feet and lifted him high in the air like an acrobat, which made him laugh and fall forward so I'd catch him. Jason spent as many waking hours on my lap as off it. When he napped, I read and then reread *Rebecca* and dreamed about living in a mansion and having no children, just a maid who ran my bath while I sat at my desk every morning and answered letters with a gold pen.

Then one day Ray left home around noon as usual and didn't return till nine in the evening. I was a little worried, but mostly I was bored to death and had such a craving for a Dairy Queen ice cream cone I thought I'd go out of my mind. Of course there was no way to get a Dairy Queen without a car or a baby-sitter, and watching that clock creep forward little by little, later and later, while I envisioned that vanilla cone with chocolate sprinkles, made me furious. I was beside myself. It wasn't like this was the only time he'd been too late for dinner lately, and always with some lame excuse like a flat tire. I was so pissed I couldn't sit still. I thumbed through an old *Life* magazine that had pictures of all the dead soldiers who got it that week, but I couldn't concentrate. I sat on the front stoop, but the Uglies were planting things on their side of the yard, so I went back in and shuffled through our records. I pulled out the Jefferson Airplane album Raymond had bought. We'd had an agreement that we couldn't buy anything because money was too tight. I said, "Raymond, I thought we agreed."

"I didn't buy it. Ocho gave it to me."

"He just gave you a brand new record?" It was still sealed in cellophane.

"It was a present," he said. Later I found a receipt from Spinner Records in his pocket. There were other records too—Jimi Hendrix, The Who, Led Zeppelin, but they were used. Did Ocho Perez really just lay them on Raymond out of the goodness of his Animal Pack heart?

Thinking like this just added fuel to the fire, so when Ray finally rolled in, I was fuming. I ran to the door and locked it.

Ray broke the window with his fist to unlock it.

I thought about the Uglies watching outside and would've giggled if I wasn't so crazy with fury. I stomped into the kitchen, then handed Raymond a whisk broom and dustpan. He took it and began sweeping glass when he realized what he was doing and dropped the broom like a hot potato. "I don't believe it. You fucking lock me out of my own house. My fucking hand's bleeding. Then you give me a broom to sweep it up? You are a bitch, you know that?"

"Where were you, Raymond?" I said, determined not to believe a word he said.

"What is this, the Inquisition?"

"Let me guess. You ran over a dog and had to bring it to a vet."

"I don't have to take this." He turned around and left.

Why did he always get the car? Wasn't it both of

ours? I kicked myself for not taking off first. I could've gotten a Dairy Queen, then gone to visit Beatrice.

From the moment Ray left until the moment he walked through the door at midnight, hunger, boredom, and frustration worked together to clear my head. I knew like a clairvoyant that Ray hadn't been looking for work the past weeks and had probably been getting screwed up every day. I decided when Raymond returned I would talk to him calmly and maybe he'd tell me the truth.

When Raymond returned he bumped into the hassock, then slumped into the rocker. "You'll never guess who I talked to tonight," he said.

"Look, Raymond," I said. "I don't care if you don't get a job. I've been thinking I like it better when you're home anyway. But you've been lying, haven't you?"

"Your old boyfriend Robby Costa . . ." I stopped short. Robby Costa was the first boy I'd ever kissed. I was in the eighth grade and we kissed on a hammock, then the next day when we went for a walk, he held my hand and rubbed his middle finger up and down my palm. It made me nauseous and I never went out with him again. "Robby Costa was not my boyfriend," I said.

"That's not what he says. He says, 'That old lady of yours is a nice piece of ass.'"

I just looked at him.

"How am I supposed to feel when some guy tells me my old lady's a nice piece of ass? That's why I got fucked up."

"You're making this up."

"Were you really a virgin or were you lying?"

I threw the first thing that came to hand, which happened to be Jason's workbench with different-colored pegs. I threw it as hard as I could at his head. He deflected it with a forearm.

"Are you saying I wasn't a virgin?" I was screaming now.

"All I want to know's how am I supposed to feel?"

"How *you* feel?" I threw the contents of Jason's toy box one by one. Raymond tried his best to dodge them. "I was a goddamn virgin when I fucked you and got fucking pregnant and ruined my life. You lousy son of a bitch. How dare you come in here and tell me some ass-wipe moron imbecile told you I'm a pig. Why didn't you punch him out? You're a wimp and a retard. I should've killed myself before I ever married you." I was crying uncontrollably now. I was pummeling him with my fists now. He was backed up against the wall, blocking my blows. "Jesus, Beverly," he said. "I'm sorry. I'm sorry. I didn't know you'd get so upset." I believed I could beat him up, tear him limb from limb, kill him with my bare hands, but he really looked sorry, and scared. I ran out the door and peeled out. I had to stop every mile or so because I was crying so hard I couldn't see. I decided to kill myself and drove around looking for the right spot.

I found it by the old reservoir. A huge oak. But then I thought, What if I ram the car into it and I just total it then we won't have any wheels, and I might get arrested and my father would kill me. Then I thought, And what about Jason? Do I want him to be raised by Raymond? To use double negatives when he speaks? Raymond probably wouldn't even raise him. He'd give him to my parents or, worse, his mother. I got out of the car, leaned against the tree, then slid down the oak and sat with my back against it. Raymond obviously had brought up Robby Costa to deflect any blame from himself for not looking for work and for lying, and I'd fallen for it. But that Raymond could stoop so low as to accuse me of not being a virgin, when it was sex with him that had ruined my life, was unforgivable.

It was dawn when I got into bed.

"Hon?" he said.

I didn't answer.

"I'm sorry."

I ignored him.

"I know you were a virgin."

Silence.

"I don't know why I said that. I'm a loser. I'm no good. I wouldn't blame you if you divorced me."

"You are a loser."

"You hate me."

Silence.

"Bev?"

"All right. All right. All right. I don't hate you, now can I go to sleep? And you get up with Jason." Raymond fell right back to sleep. I inspected his arm for needle tracks, but there weren't any.

When I got up at noon, Raymond looked like a ghost and so did Jason. Jason's forehead was hot, so I took his temperature. It was one hundred degrees. I gave Raymond our last money—which was five dollars, until he got his unemployment check in a couple of days—to pick up some baby aspirin and orange juice. This was noon. By four o'clock he still hadn't shown, which I was figuring was grounds for murder, but Raymond wasn't that much of a creep. Something bad must've happened. I was worried. Finally, the phone rang. It was my mother. "Bev, your father called from the station. He has Raymond with him," she said.

I pictured him handcuffed in a cell.

She said my father was coming home with Raymond and that he wanted to talk to me. She would pick me up.

I put on Jason's sweater. His cheeks were flushed. Jason might grow up and say, My father is an ex-con. In a way, it was Jason's fault. He should've never been born. I hugged him to me and felt his hot face against my neck and his hands holding on to my shoulders while I waited for my mother. When I walked out of the house, she moved to the passenger's side so I could drive and she could hold Jason. "Poor honey," she said, taking off his hat and pushing his hair away from his face. "You coming to your Mimi's? I made you some chicken soup. We can put pastina in just like you like it. Poor baby. It's awful when your throat hurts."

"Ma, what do you think this is about?"

"I don't know a thing."

Why was she so worried about Jason and not worried about me?

I left Jase with my mother and went down into the basement recreation room, where Ray and my father were sitting in chairs, not talking. I sat on the couch and my father nodded to Raymond. "He has something he wants to tell you," he said.

Raymond stared at my knees as he said, "I spent the money for Jase's aspirin on dope. My son's sick, and I spent the money on dope."

"What dope?"

"Heroin."

"You're a junkie?"

He nodded his head. "I went to your father for help. I'm no good, Beverly."

"You went to the police station?"

"He wanted to talk to me. He's sick, Bev," my father said.

"Where are the tracks?" He turned his arm palm upward and exhibited a purple scar on the cleft of his left arm. I'd looked at his right.

"We're going to help him straighten out," my father said.

I could only breathe in short spurts. All I could think was, This is a coward's maneuver. He was scared to face me alone, so he'd gone to my father for protection. How could I be mad at him with the representative of the law, and my own father, on his side? And why was my father sticking up for him, anyway? What about the time he called me to the station and believed some stupid jerk instead of me? Tried to bully me into admitting I was drinking? Threatened me with a lie detector? What was this anyway? Guys against girls?

"How?" I asked.

"They got a program at the hospital in Meriden. Maybe we could get him in. He's got to stop smoking that marijuana, too. No drinking. He needs to get a job. Keep busy."

What about me, Dad? What will you do to help me? I wanted to say, but never would. I'd never in my life had the courage to say what was in my heart to my father.

On the ride home, Ray opened the glove compartment, pulled out his harmonica case, and said, "Open it." It contained a hypodermic needle. "That's where I keep my works. You know the belt hanging on the hook in the bathroom? That's what I used to tie off." I pictured the times his friends went off to the bathroom, one by one, and took too long for pissing. I pictured myself driving around on winding roads with my girlfriends while Raymond tucked Jason in, then stuck a needle in his vein.

"The thousand dollars for the Harley?" he said. "Spent it all." Then he started crying.

"You spent the thousand dollars!" There went the dream.

"I bought some of that Panama red. I was partners with Cal and the son of a bitch ripped me off. He claims somebody stole it. I'm a loser, Bev."

No shit.

He told me that at first a nickel was enough. But then he needed more. He broke into houses. He stole money and TV sets, a couple of stereos. I pictured me and my friends eating jelly muffins in the kitchen and Raymond with a stocking over his face climbing in a window. "Did you steal albums?"

He nodded.

"All them days I was looking for jobs? Dope," he said.

I pictured Raymond going to the beach with the Animal Pack, sitting shoulder to shoulder in the water nodding out.

"I'm sorry, Bev," he said. "I fucked up." Then he started crying again.

"I will try to help you, Raymond," I said, feeling betrayed to the bone, thinking, I will never believe another word out of your mouth. "I will really try. But one more time, one more lie, and it's over." I was half wishing he'd screw up that one more time.

"I won't lie, Bev. I promise."

"Promise on Jason's life."

"That's stupid."

"No it's not. Promise on Jason's life that you will never lie again."

"Okay, I promise."

"Say it."

"I promise on Jason's life I won't lie."

Raymond hadn't been a junkie long enough to need a padded cell like in the movies. But the next day he had the chills and a runny nose. I made Lipton soup· and dropped an egg in it. Ray shivered under a blanket and took tiny sips from a cup. When Beatrice called to come over, I told her we were sick. Ray put his feet in my lap and I rubbed them.

I figured the first couple of weeks would be the hardest, so I stayed with him twenty-four hours a day. I played martyr, which isn't hard when you've been raised by an Italian mother. I stopped smoking pot and drinking, too. I even let Raymond watch his TV shows without arguing. We sat Jase in the car seat between us and rode around town picking out our favorite houses, pointing out moo cows and horses to Jason. Then Ray found a job landscaping for two brothers. I dropped him off every morning, then at noon I drove back to where he was clipping hedges or mowing a lawn or digging a hole in the sun. We sat under a tree on the grass and ate the sandwiches I'd made. We didn't say much, just watched the cars go past and Jason pick dandelions.

After a couple of weeks, Ray said, "Bev, no offense, but the guys are calling me pussy-whipped. Maybe you shouldn't bring me lunch anymore." Two weeks later, Ray didn't bring money home on pay day. He said the brothers hadn't been paid so they couldn't pay him.

The next week it was the same story.

The following week, I was lying on the grass while Jase filled up cups and emptied them in his plastic pool when the phone rang. It was Virginia. She said, "Bev, I know it's none of my business, but I don't think Ray has that job anymore."

"What do you mean?"

"His car's at the Crystal Spa. It was there yesterday too. Did he tell you he was working?"

There wasn't enough time to answer between breaths.

"I got to go, V," I said.

I collapsed onto the couch and sobbed. Then I remembered Jase in the pool and stopped crying as suddenly as I'd begun. After all, I'd be better off without Raymond. Who wanted to marry him to begin with? Really, it was a godsend. I could divorce him and be exonerated. No one would blame me. If I were still a Catholic, I could probably get an annulment.

I went outside and turned the hose on. I ran cold water over my face, then walked back to Jason. Jase splashed his hands on top of the water in his pool. "I'm going to kick your father out," I said.

Jase stood up and splashed back down, laughing.

"You won't have a father. You'll have divorced parents."

Jason picked up a red cup and threw it out of the pool, then looked at me. I squirted water at a cat, which fluffed out its tail and darted under the dead bush.

"We won't have any money," I said, and moved my face closer to Jason's. "We won't have any food." I moved my face closer and crinkled my nose like a witch's. "We'll starve to death."

"No," Jason said, turning his back and trying to climb out. He slipped back in and started crying. I started crying. I sat in the pool with my clothes on. Jason sat on my lap.

"It'll be just you and me," I said.

CHAPTER 7

"THIS is unfortunate." The young social worker with thick glasses and chubby cheeks bounced his pencil on my application and smiled. "But you won't be on welfare long. When your son's old enough, you'll get a job. I'm sure of it. Unfortunately, some people come to view welfare as a, well, a crutch." Then for some reason—he was bored, he liked me, he liked to hear himself talk—he took an hour to describe his caseload and the problems he faced: the utter impossibility of getting these people's feet off the ground. The majority, he said, were either former citizens of Agua, Puerto Rico, who settled near their families in Meriden and spoke no English, had no skills and no interest in working, or the wives of formerly unemployed men, who'd traveled south from Maine to find work in factories. Once they got their jobs, they had more money than they knew what to do with, so they spent it drinking in bars, eventually becoming hopeless alcoholics who were known to beat their wives. Then, for one reason or another, the men deserted and their wives stayed and, I guess, had to come listen to this guy too. I wondered what he talked about to them. When he finished his talk, he said, "But obviously, you're different." He smiled again and winked at me. Then I signed some papers and was told

I could expect enough money for rent, utilities, food stamps, plus what averaged out to be about five dollars' spending money each week.

I appreciated the guy's vote of confidence, but when I was a kid and pictured myself being interviewed, it was by Johnny Carson or Merv Griffin, not a social worker. I was disappointed in myself, but I wasn't complaining. One week before, I'd thought I might be forced to ask my parents if Jase and I could live with them, when number one, there wasn't enough room, and number two, my father had said, "Once you leave this house, you're not coming back," and number three, I'd rather die than be reduced to living by my parents' rules again.

Ray, however, had no qualms about moving in with his mother. After I told him to get out, he stuffed his clothes into two pillowcases, said, "It's better this way. I'm glad it's over," then let the door slam behind him on his way to his mother's. Soon the credit union repossessed his car, which was formerly our car, and Ray landed on the town green nodding out and crying to anyone who'd listen, "I lost my car. I lost my son. I lost my wife," in exactly that order.

The guy was falling apart. It hurt my eyes to look at him. Whenever he managed to keep a date and pick up Jason for an outing, he'd stand on the other side of the screen door, his pants falling from his hips and his neck like a skinned chicken's. He hid his eyes behind mirrored sunglasses. His voice was thick with drugs. He nodded his head and said one word—"Bev."

Meanwhile Jason, who was twenty months old now, would be running from the door to me as soon as he saw him, saying, "Daddy's here. Daddy's here." Then I watched from the window as Ray tilted Jason into the car and next to whatever Animal he'd recruited to drive him and Jason to the community pool or Dairy Queen or Hubbard Park to feed the ducks.

The first time we said more than two words to each other was in public, a month after we'd split up. It was at Big Top Hamburgers, a hood hangout, where my girlfriends and I used to cruise Friday nights after we got bored with the collegiates at the Farm Shop.

I practically had to fall down on my knees to get my mother to baby-sit for me. "Men see a divorced woman and they're out for one thing," she said.

"For Christ's sake, Ma. I'm going to the *movies* with *Beatrice*."

"They figure once a woman's had it," she kept going.

"Had *what*?" I wanted her to come out and say it.

"You know what I'm talking about."

"No. Tell me."

"Once a woman knows what it's like, she wants it. Men can sense it."

"Like dogs in heat?"

"Don't be disgusting."

Look who's talking about being disgusting. "Ma," I said, as calmly as I could, then waited a beat between each word. "Just say yes."

After she said she'd have to think about it, which meant ask my father, she agreed to take Jason overnight on Wednesday. A weekend night was out of the question.

Beatrice and I went to see *M.A.S.H.* at the new movie theater forty minutes away, then smoked pot as we drove and listened to all of *Tommy*, which a radio station was playing uninterrupted. The air hit my face from the open window. I got a whiff of spring, damp and potent, and thought, I'm free. Right now, Beatrice and I could go to Big Top Hamburgers and hang out all night. I have no husband, and my parents would never know it. I could have a rare charcoal-broiled burger. I could actually flirt with some guys in the parking lot. Which was exactly what we did: order a charcoal-broiled burger, rare. But I never got the chance to flirt, because Raymond, the newborn derelict, showed up, weaved into the building, and said without stopping for air, "Where's my son?"

I saw red. What nerve. Raymond probably went to Big Top Hamburgers every night of the week, and now he was insinuating I wasn't taking good care of *his* son? "In the trunk of the car. Where do you think?" I felt people turn on their stools to look at me.

"I'm serious," he demanded.

"It's none of your business," I said.

"I'm his old man."

"Father. Say father." I knew I should shut up, but I couldn't stop. "If you're such a good father, tell me what your son's new word is? You don't even know. Where the fuck were you Sunday? What makes you think you're entitled to know anything about him?"

"He better have a baby-sitter."

"Bev," Beatrice said, and opened her eyes wide as if to say, Let's get the hell out of here.

I brushed past Raymond, got into Beatrice's car, and she drove out of the parking lot so fast my grape soda tipped in my lap.

So much for hanging out at Raymond's spots.

Eventually, though, we cooled down enough to make small talk whenever he dropped by, mostly about Jason and people we both knew. Then one night late in August, almost three months after Ray and I'd split up, I heard a light knocking at my front door. I'd fallen asleep reading *A Tree Grows in Brooklyn* and got up to look out the window. I could see Raymond from above. He was standing on the front stoop looking at his feet. When I answered the door, I realized I should've put something over my nightgown, because I saw Raymond's eyes drift over my breasts from the other side of the screen.

"I have to talk to you," he said.

I opened the door, and crossed my arms on my chest as I sat on the sofa and he sat on the chair across from me, his knees wide open. He took a pack of Luckies from his shirt pocket, shook out a cigarette, and lit it. The way his wrist and fingers moved, where he put the cigarette between his lips, and the way he pulled the cigarette away so his lips kind of stuck to the filter were so familiar, I hugged my heart to protect myself from getting reinvolved.

"Bev," he repeated. "I got something I have to talk to you about."

I nodded.

"I volunteered for Nam. The 101st Airborne Division. I'll be a paratrooper."

"What! Why?"

"I don't know." He shrugged and looked away. "I don't know. Bobby died over there, and I don't know. I got nothing going for me here. I figured I should defend my country."

"But you don't believe in the war."

"I figure, my country's in it, I should fight. And besides, I don't have you no more, or Jason."

"You have Jason. He's your son."

He stared at his hands and shook his head.

I resisted the urge to pull his head to my chest and rock him.

That night I stared at the ceiling in the dark. When I first knew Raymond, he drove a yellow Bonneville with a black roof and had plenty of money for beer and pizza, the outdoor movies, or Riverside Amusement Park. He was living with his mother then, too. He was planning to maybe join the navy to get his high school equivalency and a skill like electronics. Then I got pregnant and his life was ruined. I wept imagining Raymond thousands of miles from home, scrunched down in some rice paddy to avoid the bombs raining shrapnel over his head. I wept harder when I thought of Bobby's wake. The coffin was closed because Bobby's body had been too old. His family had placed his graduation picture on a little shelf above, so we could all remember what he looked like. Raymond wouldn't have a graduation picture to put above his coffin.

In the morning I woke up as usual to Jason calling, "Mommy." I lifted him out and changed his diaper. I hugged him and smelled the Johnson No More Tears baby shampoo in his hair as I carried him down the stairs. I put him down in the kitchen and he walked straight to the cupboard, put his hand on the knob, and looked at me to check if I would say no or not. Then he began emptying the pans out for the first time of the day. I made us some cinnamon toast, then cut his into strips and put him in his high chair. He said, "Mmmm good," as he daintily picked up the first strip and took a bite. "Good?" he said, prompting me to say my line.

"Mmmm, good," I said, biting my toast and realizing I had no appetite. I had a picture in my mind of Raymond standing in the hospital room looking afraid, holding the ceramic rabbit. The ivy plant had died almost immediately. I had no idea what I'd done with the bunny vase. Then I had another picture of Jason the week before, standing on the rocker in front of the window looking down the street for his father, who never showed. Jason's father was a liar and a junkie.

I handed Jason his plastic cup of juice. He took a sip, his eyes watering, and handed the cup back. It became crystal clear. Raymond was going to Vietnam for the heroin, the abundant, pure, and cheap heroin. He wasn't going to Vietnam to defend his country and avenge Bobby's death. He was going there because it was easier than staying here. Besides, who knew with Raymond. It could've all been a ploy to get me feeling sorry for him, to get me to open my arms and say, Don't go. Come back. I called Raymond up.

"Raymond," I said. "I've been thinking. If you go to Vietnam, Jason'll be almost three when you return. He won't remember you."

"That's true."

"What if I said to you I decided to go live in California for a year and a half, and just assumed you'd take care of Jason?"

"That's different."

"No it's not. You can't just leave him for me to take care of."

"I'm going to defend my country."

"Bullshit. You're going so you can afford to be a junkie."

There was silence on the line.

Jason crammed the last strip of toast in his mouth and said, "More." I gave him mine. "Raymond, you have a son. I've been thinking. Either you stay and make up your mind that you're taking responsibility for Jason, or you give him up. Don't come back after Vietnam."

"He'd probably be better off."

I didn't disagree.

"You know me. I'm a fuck-up. I'm as bad as my old man."

"So you're giving him up."

"He'll be better off."

"I got to go."

I wiped Jason's face and his sticky fingers with a washcloth, then released him from the high chair. He went to the cardboard box filled with toys in the living room. I watched him as he dug through the box and came up with a golf ball, which he rolled to me.

I'd read up on kids of divorced parents and how they tended to think they drove the deserting parent away. I would be sure to tell Jason it wasn't his fault. I'd tell him his father and I had fights and didn't get along. I would not make Raymond into a bad person. I'd tell Jason his father wanted to go fight for his country. I'd tell him his father was brave. I could even tell him his father died and that's why he never came back. But that would definitely be a mistake. Jason may have inherited his father's lying genes, and I'd better set a good example. Raymond's mother had told me that Raymond's father was the same as Raymond, lying for the pleasure of it. I'd rather have Jason turn into a drooling idiot. I'd tell Jason the truth about all things. I'd tell Jason his father was a drug addict who couldn't help himself. I'd tell Jason the way things really are, so life wouldn't slap him in the face when he grew up. At that moment, I wasn't sure if I'd even let him believe in Santa Claus.

Jason was quiet by the toy box for a minute, then I got a whiff and knew it was time to change his diaper. That made me picture a scene. It was from when Jason was an infant. Every evening when Raymond came home, the three of us would eat dinner, then Raymond would take off Jason's clothes and dip him in the kitchen sink for a bath. Sometimes I'd sit at the table, smoke a cigarette, and watch. I was mesmerized by the gentleness of Raymond's hands as they cupped water and released it over Jason's shining wet body. Sometimes I'd wonder what it must be like for Jason to feel the largeness of his father's hands and the sureness as they supported his back.

My mother walked in then. I hadn't even heard her car pull up. "P.U.," she said. "Somebody stinks."

Jason laughed and made a game of running away.

"Oh no you don't," she said, dropping her pocketbook onto the couch and grabbing him. She rinsed out the washcloth, with Jason on her hip, soaped it up, then laid Jason down on the floor for a diaper change.

"So, what were you doing?" my mother said.

"Nothing," I said. "Just thinking."

"Better not think too much," she said. "Your hair'll turn gray."

C H A P T E R 8

RAYMOND wrote me letters that I threw away without reading, until the one that made an even dozen. In it he'd enclosed a snapshot of himself passed out on a bed, with a hundred beer cans and empty liquor bottles jumbled on the shelves above him. His shirt was bunched up at his armpits, and his arm, displaying a tattoo of a devil holding a pitchfork, was draped across his bare belly. I guess this was his idea of sexy. He wrote, "I just saw *Love Story*. I am Oliver and you are my Jenny. I've lost you." Did he think we had this great love fit for books and movies, a tragedy to make millions weep, when I, the heroine, hadn't shed a tear since the night I pictured him floundering in a rice paddy? I ended his illusion by writing to him a few hateful words: "I don't now, never did, and never could love you, so do me a favor and forget I ever existed." Then I marched to the middle of the driveway and in a gouge in the asphalt made a pyre of his picture and letter.

The only thing I thought about marriage after that was, Never in a million years, not for a billion dollars, and never again if it kills me.

Then it was a year since Raymond deserted us, the close of the summer of 1971. Jason was about to be three, and a few days later I'd be twenty-one, drinking age, voting age, and a legal adult. I was at a picnic in Beatrice's backyard with Jason and Fay, her two-and-a-half-year-old daughter, Amelia, and a bunch of Beatrice's friends from work. Fay and I'd had a plan. We'd split a hit of acid, then once we got to Beatrice's all-girls picnic, all the girls would take care of our two kids. Problem was, we didn't let Beatrice and her friends in on the plan and they were too dense to pick up on it. First of all, they had no idea we were tripping, because they'd never tripped themselves and wouldn't know a tripping person from a lunatic, which is probably what they thought we were. And second of all, they just didn't understand. This was our logic: Fay and I had gotten knocked up, which made us the scapegoats or fall guys. In other words, if it hadn't been us it would've been them, so the least they could do was take up some slack by easing our kids off our backs during one measly picnic. No such luck.

So I'm lying on my back in Beatrice's parents' aluminum pool and I'm tripping peacefully, listening to the trees talk to me in a language I'm sure I'd understand if only I could concentrate harder. But then here comes somebody handing me my son. By the blinding orange of her bikini, I know it's Beatrice. She says, "Somebody wants to swim with his mommy."

Couldn't she tell somebody didn't want to swim with her son? But she's dangling him over the water, so I reach out to get him and he slips through my fingers and underwater. I catch him just after his face goes under, but he starts crying hysterically anyway, spitting and coughing and making me feel awful. Now I understand every word from the trees. They're saying: You're a terrible mother. You almost drowned your son. He'll remember this moment forever.

I hugged Jason and bounced him around the pool to distract him. When we climbed out, I lay on my back and Jason sat on my stomach. His head was ringed by the sun, and for a minute I thought it was a halo, but then a cloud obscured the vision and I concentrated on his face. He had three freckles on his nose and blue-gray eyes that were shaped like almonds. Did Raymond have eyes shaped like almonds too? I closed my eyes to change the subject, and what I saw was the Blessed Virgin standing on a world with the infant Jesus perched in the crook of her arm, like on a plastic card, and that's when I remembered about my mother. She said she almost drowned when she was little, even went down for the third time, but then she saw the Virgin Mary holding out her arms, and the next thing she knew she was lying in the sand, saved.

Jason had had a vision too, of an old lady floating outside his window, trying to get in. He was afraid of her. I told him she was probably a fairy.

"She's too old," he said.

"Not for a guardian angel. It's probably my great-grandmother Irene dropping by to give you good luck."

"You think so?"

"Sure."

My great-grandmother Irene was on my mind a lot these days, because every time I turned around, my mother was saying, "I don't know who you take after. Not *my* family. It must be your father's grandmother Irene." Personally, I took this as a compliment, but although my mother liked Irene, she meant it as an insult, because Irene had committed the cardinal sin of Neglecting Her Children. Irene, too, escaped from her house every chance she got. She liked to walk around the neighborhood stopping here for a cup of coffee or there to check out some other Italian immigrant who'd just landed on her block. Her favorite thing in the world was the movies, and she went every chance she got. This made her husband—who traveled around the country shooting off fireworks—furious, especially since she left her house a mess and her kids running wild. So, the story goes, one day he loaded the dirty dishes into his wheelbarrow, then pushed it straight down the center aisle of Wilkinson's Theater, to shame her. My story goes that when she saw him, she burst out laughing.

Irene's story does not have a happy ending, though. By the time I met her, her husband was dead and she'd squandered all her money, had no house, no teeth, and was a pauper. She lived with various nieces and nephews but refused to live with her own kids— maybe because she didn't like them, maybe because they tried to boss her around and trap her behind four walls. Meanwhile, my father had just become a cop, driving in his cruiser, and never did a week go by without his seeing his grandmother, dressed in black, her white hair darting from her head like dandelion spores, looking like a witch wandering on the edge of town near some cornfield or cow pasture. He'd stop to ask her if she wanted a ride, but she always refused it. Now, this was his grandmother, so he couldn't order, "Get in," like he could with me. So what he did instead—the day after he spied her at Woolworth's trying on glasses and squinting at a popcorn sign—was order a powwow with his mother and his aunts and uncles, who decided the only thing was a nursing home. When they checked her in, she refused to give up her shoes. When she died three months later, they found them hidden beneath her pillow.

I sometimes wondered, given the authority, if my

father would stick me in an institution too. Especially since he'd reverted to his old trick of stalking me. Like I said, this was 1971. I was a hippie. I wore no bra, walked barefoot, had sex indiscriminately, plus I hitch-hiked and went shoplifting with Jason. My son was the prefect lure for rides (who could refuse a white-haired three-year-old standing in a gutter next to his mother and sticking out his thumb?) and the best decoy for shoplifting (all I had to do was let him run wild in a store and the ladies were so riveted on his grubby little hands they never even noticed me, except to shoot dirty looks that meant, Will you please control your child, you stupid hippie). Probably, there were times my father and his buddies saw me sitting on the lawn of Robert Early Junior High staring at a fluorescent light thinking it was a television. Certainly, they kept track of the multitude of cars that spent the night in my driveway, not to mention the various men who drove them. I wonder if they could distinguish which guy was for Fay and which for me.

Fay and I had no problem keeping track, because we had a list stuck behind a picture of an onion skin Fay had painted and hung on the wall. Fay and Amelia had moved in with me and Jase in the springtime, after Fay had found a pair of bikini underpants in the backseat of her car and surmised, correctly, that her husband was an adulterer. So she drove up from Pennsylvania in her yellow Dodge, dragging half her furniture behind her, and moved in. We'd thrown my old Flintstone furniture out and moved her beautiful furniture in before she'd painted the picture of the onion skin. We didn't know yet that we'd have a list to hang behind it. That started about a month after she'd moved in.

We'd been driving around town with our kids,

really happy. True, we both had failed marriages. True, we were both on welfare. True, we had little kids keeping us from hitchhiking to California or through Europe, joining a commune, and about a million other things we could be doing in the world, but here we were, best girlfriends living together with our kids. It was like a dream come true. One of my fantasies as a kid was that my best friend Donna and I and our Betsy Wetsies were living together because it was wartime and our husands were off fighting. Then we'd get a telegram saying our husbands had been blown to smithereens, which meant the two of us could live together forever if we wanted. Well, that's what it felt like now. We cruised around town, Jase and Amelia singing the ABC song over and over till we finally yelled, "Shut up, you little rodents!" then they bounced around the car laughing and bumping their heads on the ceiling, until they settled into their customary positions: heads out windows like dogs. Meanwhile, Fay and I hunted for wildflowers, which we picked by the bucketful, and cute guys, mostly in sports cars. When we saw one of them approaching, we'd say, "Wave, kids!" which they did like windup dolls.

Then it was dusk of a paralyzingly hot day. We'd just gotten ice cream cones for the kids and were driving around a part of town that was strange to us, the part of town where great aluminum sheds loomed near factories with smokestacks, at ends of streets with old shingled houses and forlorn-looking bushes. And there, in the distance, we saw a cluster of those same sports cars parked by a ballpark.

We recognized a couple of guys. They were on the Italian Club team, which was playing the Elks team. The Italian Club guys wore jeans. Bandanna headbands dammed the sweat on their foreheads and kept their long hair out of their faces. They smoked cigarettes in the outfield and clenched them between their teeth to make catches. They pranced around the bases instead of running when they hit homers. Some of these guys were the same boys who drove by me and Donna when we had sat under the tree, sticking our chins in the air, waiting for Denny Winters. I knew their names from my brother's yearbooks. They were older than us by three or four years. They were the type of gone-by hoods who stole hubcaps and had fights with chains and bricks in high school. Only now they were hippies. "Far out," I said to Fay. "Groovy," Fay said to me.

After that, the Italian Club bar was our hangout. It was the same room where Raymond had gotten drunk on Seagram's 7s at our wedding. The room was big and dark like the belly of a whale. The bar was mahogany, and lined with guys called Rat and Indian, Chip and Skip, Buzzard and Deacon. Half of them were married and thought nothing of the fact that they were drinking at a bar every night. If their wives called looking for them, automatically the bartender said, "Haven't seen him." If they talked about their wives at all, it was as though they were aliens, who flushed their pot down toilets and had fits when they showed up drunk at dawn, then wouldn't talk or have sex for days after.

"What," I asked, "do you think gives you the right to drink at bars and have all the fun you want while your wife is stuck home with kids?"

"Hey, Hank, hit me."

"Aren't you going to answer?"

"Maybe, maybe not. Why don't you put a bra on? You ever think your tits are going to end up at your waist by the time you're thirty?"

"Like your balls'll end up at your knees?"

"Hey, you're all right. I like you."

I'd read Betty Friedan, Germaine Greer, and Simone de Beauvoir, and I was ready, I was willing, I was chomping at the bit to personally fight for the rights of all women, with the help of my best friend and fellow victim, Fay. Since they wouldn't listen when we talked, we took action.

On our list, we made columns headed: name, age, astrological sign, penis size, and performance, rated one to ten. Then we dressed up in our hiphugger jeans and skimpy jerseys that left our belly buttons exposed and strutted into the club to lure men home (never the married ones) to lay, fuck, hump, ball, screw—that's the way we talked to amuse each other—and dispense with any nuance of love or romance. We got right to the point, which was to say, "Do you want to fuck?" If ever some guy had the audacity to try to light our cigarettes, say, we jumped all over him. "What do we look like, damsels in distress?"

Which in a way we were, because soon after we'd found the club, Fay's creep of an ex-husband sneaked up in the night and stole back the yellow Dodge, leaving us carless and furious—because it had been men who'd knocked us up, men who'd left us with kids, and men who got the cars.

The night of Beatrice's picnic, Fay and I were hoping we could get our mothers or Trudy our neighbor to take the kids so we could hitch to the club and pick up some guys, or at the very least have some drinks to take the edge off the acid. Which at the moment was making my ears fill with static. Jason had taken to burying me with grass and was almost finished. He was talking to himself in a murmur, "All I have left are

109

her feet," he said. "The toes are the hardest. . . ."
Amelia ran up. "What're you doing?" she said.

"Burying my mother."

"Can I?"

"All right. When we're done, we have to find a flower. We can stick it in her mouth so it'll stand up."

"That's enough," I said, sitting up.

"*Maaaa!*" Jason yelled.

"What do you want? You were making me dead."

"Let's do it to my mother," Amelia suggested.

"Okay," Jase said, then he and Amelia ran off.

I felt abandoned, adrift, without Jason's anchoring me down. I watched him and Amelia run across the lawn to Fay. They bumped shoulders and ran at exactly the same speed. Jason was six months older, but they were constantly mistaken for twins. Jason was the type who liked to go first and win, and Amelia let him. They got along as well as their mothers did. They slept in Jason's room and got up together every morning before me and Fay, poured each other cereal, and ate it in front of the TV while watching cartoons. Fay and I slept in my room across the hall, but whenever one of us invited a man to sleep over, the other one slept on the couch and told the kids they couldn't watch television. Then they sat in the kitchen and chatted like chipmunks or went out earlier than usual.

When I had a guy over and at some point of the morning we appeared in the kitchen, Amelia flirted with him, while Jason suddenly forgot how to do everything, like put on his own sweater or pour his own milk or talk if asked a direct question by anyone but me. As I'd always figured, Fay lucked out having a girl, because girls didn't have a male territorial thing about boyfriends.

Jase had laid a bombshell on me the last time I had a

guy stay over. The guy had left and I was talking to Jase in a pretend foreign language to get him mad. I don't know why—maybe because he was the wrong sex. Finally, he stood up, red in the face, and yelled, "Stop!" I was shocked. Jason hardly ever lost his temper. I burst out laughing, then he looked like he might cry, so I said, "What's the matter? I was just asking you what you want to be when you grow up, and you wouldn't answer."

"You were talking stupid."

"I know. Sorry. But answer me. What do you want to be?"

"A cop."

"A pig! What do you want to be a pig for?"

"So I can shoot people."

This coming from a kid who never had a toy gun in his life? This coming from a kid who'd been taught, make peace not war? Then the obvious dawned on me. "You want to be one because Pop is."

"No sir."

"Jason, if you become a cop, I'll disown you."

"What's disown mean?"

"It means I'll never talk to you and you can't come in my house anymore."

"Don't say that." Now he looked like he was going to cry again.

Then I remembered reverse psychology. "Go ahead. I don't care. If you want to be a cop, be a cop."

As I watched him and Amelia at the far end of the lawn reaching into a bag of marshmallows Beatrice was holding, I began to dream, one of my favorites: What would my life be without Jason? I'd be living in New York City, appearing in a play. Probably *Hair*. One night John Lennon would show up without Yoko and we'd go out for drinks. Then I axed the fantasy. I

111

tried to Be Here Now and think of the good things about being a mother. I couldn't think of one good thing. Not one. What I thought of was Lenny LaRoyce and his bus. Fay and I'd gone to high school with Lenny, and when he got out of the service, he converted a school bus and drove it across country. When he returned recently, he parked his bus on his friend's lawn for a couple of months and began dropping by the club. Fay seduced him. Then one night he invited Fay and Amelia and Jase and me to sleep on the bus. Wouldn't you know the couple in the bunk above Jase and me would have to get hyperactive in the middle of the night and start humping and bumping and moaning and groaning to beat the band? Jason woke up and said, "Ma, what're they doing?"

"Having sex," I said.

"What's sex?" he said.

I'd told Jason the facts of life since the day he was born practically, because I believed sex was a natural part of life and nothing to be ashamed of. But he never remembered. It wasn't the time to repeat the whole thing again, so I said, "Sh, go to sleep."

When Lenny invited me and Fay to go on his next trip and to bring our kids, I seriously considered it. But then I thought, Oh right, and then I'd have that feeling of guilt, like I was doing the wron thing, whenever Jase woke up in the night hearing people screwing.

I watched him sticking up his face and hands with marshmallow and thought I should tell him he's had enough, but who wanted to listen to him whine? Fay walked over then, sat next to me on the grass, and watched the party from a distance with me: Beatrice and her nine-to-five friends eating hot dogs in bikinis. Finally, she said, "Let's blow this stupid picnic," which was exactly my sentiment.

Of course, Amelia and Jase had a fit because of the marshmallows, but our timing was right, because a minute after we stepped onto the road, we got a ride home.

We found no one to baby-sit that night, so after the kids fell asleep, we sat on the front stoop and tried to will some guys to our house. I was thinking specifically about Hal, the bartender, who hurt my feelings because he gave me drinks on the house and let himself be seduced but had never once called or even spent the day with me after a night together. The last time he'd dropped me off in the morning, he'd said, "You're hostile, you know that? You think you're Janis Joplin. You'd better get it while you can. What do you think's going to happen when your good looks fade?" Then he'd reached over and opened the door for me to get out. He said, "Better make hay while the sun shines," as he backed out of the driveway. This struck me as mean, which was probably why I liked the guy to begin with.

Now Fay said, "The only time they come by is when they know we have drugs."

"All we ever do is talk about guys, think about guys, and go to the club to look for guys," I said. "How can we call ourselves liberated?"

"We do what we want and we don't take shit."

"We need money," I said.

"I'll be rich one day," Fay said. "Then I'm coming back in a red Ferrari."

"We could go to the club. They'd all want to drive it, but we wouldn't let them."

"I would."

"I wouldn't. I think I hate men more than you do. Maybe it's because you had two brothers."

"You had a brother."

"Come on. He was the only son in an Italian family, plus, we never talked."

"That's my problem with this women's lib shit. I'd rather hang out with men than women. Face it. Women are boring. All girls talk about are their babies, their husbands, or their boyfriends, or the fucking sale at some stupid store. Look at Beatrice. Pastel *pantsuits*. Her makeup in a goddamn tackle box. Fucking push-up bras. And she thinks we're crazy? Most women are dumb."

"That's only in Wallingford. And they're not stupid, just unliberated."

"That's what you think. They're worse in Pennsylvania."

"I disagree."

She took my cigarette and dragged from it. "Well, I think we're alike anyhow. We're both tactless. I couldn't believe when you said to Beatrice, 'Nice bathing suit. It matches your skin.' Her bathing suit was fucking *orange*."

"I didn't even think it was rude. I guess it was."

"That's what I mean."

The next morning, we didn't talk. We took our last two hits of speed and set to cleaning the house. Fay took the kitchen and the bathroom. I took the living room and the bedrooms. After a couple of hours I heard the kettle whistling in the kitchen and sat down at the table for a break. Fay had finished the kitchen. The counters were bare and shiny and the emerald-green floor looked like it was covered with ice. She'd picked bright yellow flowers for the table, and by the end of the day there'd be flowers in every room, including on the tank of the toilet. As I sipped my tea— from a cup Fay always made sure had a saucer beneath it—I thought how much better life was now that Fay was my roommate. I watched her take the cellophane off my Kools and crinkle it in her fingers, which moved like spiders' legs. I felt like I was studying a person who was alone. She bit the inside of her lip and began forming the cellophane into a sculpture of a discus thrower. Fay was a great artist. Back in high school, when the art teacher asked her to paint a Santa on the glass ramp between two buildings, she painted him giving the finger. When the teacher told her to go erase it, she erased everything but the hand with the finger, and got two weeks' detention.

Fay was only five feet tall, and everything about her was miniature, except her hair, which was like a lion's mane. It was in two thick and long pigtails that stuck out from the sides of her head and draped over the tops of her arms to her elbows. I thought she was beautiful. She thought I was too. She said I had a classic Roman nose and an interestingly angular face. She'd done several sketches of me during our evenings alone. She said she would make a painting one day when she could afford oils. She said she'd call it Beverly. I wondered how long living together would last. I supposed it would end as soon as one of us fell in love. Maybe that's why we always made fun of each other's men, because each of us was afraid the other would get too attached. Fay got up and put Carole King on the stereo. I wondered if she thought about me whenever she heard "You've Got a Friend," the way I thought about her. I sat back, closed my eyes, and realized I was actually happy.

We'd made a deal with Lenny for that night. He'd use our house to sell eleven pounds of marijuana, because his bus was being watched by the police, and we'd get an ounce of pot for our trouble. Since Fay and

Lenny had to stay home to sell the pot anyway, Fay would baby-sit for Jason while I went on a date with this guy named Brad I saw sometimes, even though Amelia was spending the night at her grandmother's.

I was probably shooting at cans in the moonlight with Brad's .38 when Fay and Lenny and the buyer, who Fay said had a long ponytail and smoked incense-smelling cigarettes, were weighing pounds of pot in my kitchen, and Fay noticed the Uglies on the front stoop. Without thinking twice, she did what we always did: positioned the stereo speakers in front of the screen door to drive them off. This was in retaliation for their forbidding Jase and Amelia to play on their side of the yard, because we sometimes let them run nude in the neighborhood.

This time the Uglies called the police, who appeared at the front door. When Fay answered it, she slammed the door in their faces and said, "We're fucked. It's the pigs."

When I returned home in Brad's pickup truck, three cop cars were crisscrossed on the lawn, their red lights spinning and bouncing off houses. "Turn around," I said, feeling a lump like an apple in the middle of my chest.

We went directly to a bar. "Let's book," Brad said. "I got this buddy on a commune in Colorado."

"With what money?"

"I got five hundred in the bank."

"No strings? If we were just friends, that would be cool?"

"Cool." He nodded.

I looked at him then and knew for certain the only reason I was with him was because when I squinted, he looked like John Lennon. "If I left, after seven years I could get clemency and come back?"

"I don't know. Sure. I think so."

Jason would be ten. The fifth grade. Maybe my parents would've destroyed my pictures and never mentioned my name. Then, when I surprised him in the playground, he'd look at me as if to say, And who the hell are you? When I said, "I'm your mother," he'd say, "She's dead."

I went home to get arrested.

CHAPTER 9

WHEN I walked into my house, Lieutenant O'Reilly, my father's best friend, said, "Have a nice ride with your boyfriend? We figured you'd be back." He was showing off. This was supposed to make me think he was Svengali.

I sat down at the kitchen table where O'Reilly indicated as though it were his house. Cops were ripping the purple, blue, and magenta slipcovers off the furniture in the living room; they were flipping through books and throwing them on the floor; they were opening jars in my refrigerator. Then his sidekick, another plainclothesman, Detective Beaumont, started shaking every pill bottle in the house in front of my face. "Sunshine? Windowpane? Speed? THC?" I knew he was trying to impress me with his knowledge of names, which made me think he was a jerk, which made me less afraid. "Vitamins, aspirin, Midol," I said. It was a good thing I took that last hit of speed for housecleaning.

"You may as well come clean," O'Reilly said. "We're sending them to the lab in the morning anyway."

"Waste your money," I shrugged.

"You don't seem to understand the trouble you're in. We found eleven pounds of marijuana in your house, miss. That's intent to sell, a felony. Your father was here. He was very upset. We told him to go home. He took your son with him."

I looked at my hands on my lap. They were so tanned from hitchhiking in the sun all summer, my nails looked white.

"You got anything to say for yourself?"

I sat on my hands and said nothing.

"All right." O'Reilly stood up. "Bring her downtown. We're gonna book her."

I saw neighbors in the windows across the street watching as I rode off in the backseat of a police car.

At the station, Beaumont dragged my arms beneath spotlights and said, "No tracks. Must be skin popping, huh?" I took pride in never touching heroin or sticking a needle in my body, and his accusation made me furious. But I figured that's what he wanted, so I acted nonchalant. He fingerprinted and mug-shot me, then deposited me across a desk from O'Reilly. I examined the ink on my fingertips while O'Reilly laid into me. "We gave you leeway," he said. "We gave you a chance, for your father. We've had ten loud-music complaints, but we ignored them, hoping you'd straighten your act. You just didn't know when to give up. Your father says, Throw the book at her. He's fed up."

I kept thinking of the time O'Reilly and his wife had come to pick up my parents to go out dancing. His wife had huge breasts that were barely concealed by her low-cut dress. I was having a pajama party with six of my friends and we all walked into the kitchen one by one to get a glass of water and a gander at Mrs. O'Reilly. The next morning, my mother said, "We knew what you were doing. It wasn't very nice."

"Well, miss," O'Reilly said. "Your ass is fried now.

Next time we see a car parked in your driveway overnight, the door's coming off and you're busted for prostitution."

I should've known. It wasn't the drugs, it was sex.

They locked me in a cell. Fay was in the one next door. "Do you believe this?" she said.

"No," I said.

She started giggling.

"I can't laugh," I said.

"One day you'll think it's a riot. I picked my nose and stuck the booger on the wall."

I wished I had her spirit.

My parents didn't bail me out. Some of Lenny's friends did. When Fay got out she went with her mother, who'd bailed her out.

All of the houses were dark on the court, except mine, which was lit like a birthday cake. The doors were flung open, and the inside looked like a hurricane hit it. The cops had left the cushion covers lying on the floor. Every can and pan and vitamin pill was spilled from my cupboards onto my counters and floors. My bedroom was the most upsetting. The contents of the drawers were dumped into a heap on my bed, with my bikini underwear and my diaphragm on top. Our "Love the One You're With" poster had been torn from the wall and ripped to shreds.

Fay had told me back in jail that my father had gone nuts and torn up the poster. After he did that, his buddies advised him to go home. Which he did, but not before he confiscated Jason.

The next morning, when I walked into my parents' house to reclaim my son, my father was weeping at the table again. I didn't sit down. My mother, the lioness when her husband was hurt, stood up. "Well, you've had your fun. Now you're going to pay the price.

What'd you think, you could just do whatever you want and get away with it? I thought you were the one who's supposed to be so smart. You're killing your father. You put every gray hair on that poor man's head."

"Where's Jason?" I said.

"Never mind where Jason is," my father said. He blew his nose and looked out the window. "*Now* you think about him." He wiped his eyes and stuffed his hankie in his back pocket. Then he looked at me. "You mark my words. You get in trouble again, the first complaint, I'm filing for custody. You'll lose him. I'll have you declared an unfit mother. You think I'm kidding? Just try me."

An unfit mother? I wanted to scream. *And you call yourself a fit father?* You never even knew how old I was on my birthdays. But I knew from a lifetime of experience that if I uttered one word in response to an accusation leveled by the big man, the boss and the king, I was "answering back," which was just cause for a slap across the face.

So I stood there and looked contrite. I guess my look made him sick, because he walked out of the room.

Next, I expected my mother to go get the Bible and make me swear on it never to do another bad thing. But she said, "What did you think when you were in jail?"

"Nothing," I said.

"You got a beautiful son. I don't know why you can't be happy with that."

"There are other things in the world, Ma, besides being a mother."

"Like what? Getting drunk? Having boyfriends?"

"Like fun," I said. I could've said, Like an education, a career, travel, experience, but I would've started crying.

My sister Rose, now twelve, walked into the kitchen and smiled at me like she felt sorry. She sat down at the table. Next my other sister, Phyllis, now seventeen, walked in and made her mouth clench and go crooked as if to say, This is so stupid. She sat next to Rose and across from me. Phyllis was running for secretary of the senior class. I wondered if she'd lose if my arrest made the paper.

"Where's Jason?" I said.

"Watching *Mighty Heroes*," Phyllis said.

"I wanted to watch *Lucy,* but I lost the flip," Rose said.

"Oh, you," my mother said. "You're the older. You should tell him. You're such a softy."

"Hi, Ma," Jase said as he turned the corner into the hall from the living room.

"Hi, son," I said.

He sat on my lap. "Could I get a GI Joe?" he said.

In this way, I knew that he'd interpreted getting plucked from his bed and carried through a house of marauding cops as my having done something I should feel sorry for. Because he was trying to get a payment, a reward. And not just any reward. He was asking for something he knew I'd never buy him in a million years. Maybe he thought GI Joe was like his father.

"What do you want one of those stupid things for?" Phyllis said.

"He wants it because everybody else does," Rose said.

"No sir," he said.

"Leave the kid alone," my mother said. "I don't know why he can't have a GI Joe."

"Because toys like that encourage violence," I said.

"It's just a doll," she said, not listening.

"It's just drugs. It's just sex," I said into the table.

"What?" she said.

My sisters giggled.

"Ma!" Jase said, and slapped my hand.

C H A P T E R   10

THIS is what I wondered as I waited for my trial date: Why did my parents decide to name their first daughter Beverly Ann Donofrio and forever brand me with the initials B.A.D.? What did they think? I mean, as a kid those initials were a heavy burden. That word carries a lot of weight when you've just come off being a baby. "No, no. *Bad* girl."

In the second grade, my teacher made us put our initials in bold letters on the face of a folder we'd store our artwork in all year. Every time I pulled that huge manila thing from my cubby, somebody pointed and jeered, "Beverly's bad." Then the rest of them chimed in, "Bad Beverly, bad Beverly." To a normal second grader, it could be rough. To a hypersensitive little girl such as I was, it was devastating. I mean, I was the type of kid who cried every time I saw a kitten without its mother. And I was dainty. I freaked out if I got dirt on my hands or water on my feet. Until I was four, I refused to set foot off the porch without a babushka because I was convinced that birds would dive-bomb me and yank out all my hair. Come to think of it, maybe my parents should've named me Catherine Rose Ann Zelda Yolanda.

Now, at the age of twenty-one, with my name spelled out in the newspaper, which called me a member of an alleged drug ring caught with ten thousand dollars' worth of marijuana (the asking price was actually a thousand dollars), you not only could've called me *bad* and *crazy* but notorious.

First thing, the public-housing authority threatened to evict me if I didn't kick Fay out. So one windy Saturday, I helped her load her stuff into a van and we hugged goodbye in the driveway. She was only going to her mother's, but it felt like the other end of the world. When we pulled out of the embrace, her hair was flying all over her face and whipping against mine. Tears came to my eyes, but I don't think she noticed. She and Amelia climbed into the van. Jason held my hand. Fay rolled down the window and said, "Do you believe this shit?" then started to laugh. As she backed down the drive, she said, "Hey, Bev," shot the finger to Backes Court, and said, "Fuck'm." For my part, I have to admit, I didn't think it was all that funny.

I walked into the house with Jason. It was empty now, except for Jason's old crib mattress shoved into a corner of the living room and a white-topped table in the kitchen that Fay's mother had given me out of the goodness of her heart.

I sat on the mattress. Jason sat next to me. "Why do they have to go?" he said.

"Because I got arrested for something I didn't do."

"Why?"

"Because life's not fair." He was only three and a half but I wanted to give it to him straight, so he wouldn't be the type of kid I was. We're talking warped. I used to fling myself on the ground, bury my face in the grass, and kiss dirt because I loved America that much. If some kid told me to get out of his yard, I jammed my hands on my hips and wouldn't budge an inch. "It's a free country," I said. What an idiot.

I still hadn't changed as much as I thought though, because come the spring of 1972, I expected my trial to be like TV: my lawyer as clever as Perry Mason, as nice as Fred MacMurray. He'd foil the police with a technicality like illegal entry or coercion or inadmissible evidence, and I'd be off scot-free.

But I didn't get to meet the guy until five minutes before court. He was short, ugly, and a man of few words. Nineteen to be exact: "We can make a deal. I'll ask for a suspended sentence plus probation."

"It wasn't my pot," I said.

"It's the best I can do."

Then the prosecutor said to the judge, "We recommend a six months' suspended sentence and two years' probation."

The judge scowled, ran a hand through his hair, shook his head, and said, "Humph. A mother on welfare, using public funds to buy drugs. I'm not inclined to go easy on you, but there is the child to consider," and gave me exactly what the lawyers asked for.

Which translated into a visit every Wednesday with Mr. Stanley Stupski, Wallingford's crack probation officer. I sat on a bench in the town hall while Jason slid around the shiny floor playing with his Matchbox cars. Sometimes my father walked by. Then Jason stood up on his knees and said, "Hi, Pop." My father mussed his hair and winked at me. Which I appreciated. After all, he was probably embarrassed. I was his daughter and I was sitting on the same bench with every other derelict in town, some of whom he'd no doubt busted.

Sooner or later, Stan the man appeared in his doorway, pointed at me, said, "Bouchard," then stabbed his thumb at his office. I squeezed past his beer belly, pulling Jason in behind me, then lifted him to my lap like a shield.

"So, been to any pot parties lately? Orgies maybe?" Stan began the session.

"That's disgusting," I replied.

"What? I thought that's what all you hippies are into. You'd tell me if you knew about any, wouldn't you?"

I rolled my eyes and looked out the window.

"You got anything to say to me?"

"No."

"You got a bad attitude. That's your problem. Now, if you came in here and acted civilized, said, 'Hello, Mr. Stupski, how are you?' I might treat you better. Maybe you'd come in every other week. Once a month. I'd say, Now, here's a nice girl. I think I'll give her a break. But you act like a snot. Didn't anybody ever teach you you win more friends with sugar than vinegar?"

"No," I said truthfully.

By the summer, Fay had deserted me to move to Minneapolis with her new boyfriend, who was a graduate student in psychology. After a couple of months, she wrote me that Amelia was in a Head Start program and by the New Year of 1973, she would be enrolled in college, which her older brother was going to pay for. I was jealous. Wallingford had no Head Start, and obviously, college was out of the question for me. My older brother wasn't going to pay for anything. In fact, my older brother had just made a return appearance in town from four years in the navy, where he'd been in a top-security position, and now would tell no one where he'd been, what he'd done, or where he got what looked like a bullet wound in the muscle behind his left shin. As soon as he got home, the chair at the dinner table, the one at the other head of the table from my father—the chair I'd been sitting in every time I ate over for four years—reverted to him and I retreated to the sidelines with my mother, sisters, and Jason. Come to think of it, I'm surprised Jason, being of the master sex, hadn't gotten the seat across from my father all those years. And guess what profession my brother chose after the service: *cop*. He hadn't been on the force more than a few months before he was written up in the paper as a hero. He'd been on the beat when he spotted a car careening crazily around a corner, then screeching away as fast as the wind. My brother heard a siren in the distance and figured the car was being pursued, so acting on instinct, he dropped onto one knee, aimed his pistol, and shot at the runaway car's tires, which went flat. It was rumored he would probably get the cop-of-the-year award for his action, while I thought he should've been suspended for reckless endangerment of the citizens who'd been all over the sidewalks, going to the post office or the bank. What if one of those bullets richocheted off the asphalt and into one of them?

In any case, there was my older brother, the prince to my father's king, being Mr. Good Citizen again while I was being a nothing, trapped with a kid. I decided that even if I couldn't go to college, I would educate myself. I'd pick authors then read every book he or she had written and then I'd read their biographies. I figured maybe I could be a writer too. I still wrote an occasional poem, but now I would switch to prose to make money. That was the real beauty. I wouldn't need a car or a baby-sitter. I could make money and do it from home. Exactly one year after I got busted, I wrote a story and applied to the Famous Writers School. I tried for irony. It was about a girl in the fifth grade who got the hiccups when she went to confession and they wouldn't stop. For days, weeks, months, whenever she opened her mouth, she had a hiccup attack. Since they started in confession, of course she thought it was the wrath of God, so she bent over backward acting like a saint. But then one day, out of habit she lies to her mother and the hiccups miraculously stop. They gave me a B and said I had talent but needed instruction—for a price. What a dope. I never considered the cost, or maybe I just thought I'd get an A and they'd beg me to be their student, or maybe I'd get discovered by a famous writer. After the disappointment had time to sink in, I got real and went to an employment agency.

The counselor, Mr. Kelly, told me not to expect much. I had no skills or experience, but he'd see what he could do. He called at the end of the week. He had a job as a clerk for a little over minimum wage at Cyanamid, the plastics plant that fumigated Wallingford with noxious chemical stink. He told me to get a pen and jot down the time, the date, and the office number. Then he said, "There's just one more thing. I'd like you to wear a bra. It makes a better impression."

I hung up the phone and heard my ears drumming. I was shocked that I was so shocked. I'd never give that guy the time of day after he'd said that. How could he possibly think it was any of his business whether I wore a bra or not? And if that's the way jobs were, if you had to wear a bra to get one, I'd rather stay poor, unemployed, and true to my principles, thank you. With no car and no one to care for Jason (my mother worked every night at a factory now and I couldn't ask her), the job had been a pipe dream anyway. It all boiled down to the same old thing: the trouble I'd gotten myself into having sex with a hood in high school. And the name of the trouble was Jason. My jailer.

I read him stories every night, to encourage a love of reading early on. That way he might go to college and not end up like his mother or, worse, his father. He played mostly with three foul-mouthed sisters from across the road, who bit their mother, Trudy, to get her attention, but luckily they didn't seem to be rubbing off. His favorite thing in the world was to go to the brook, catch a couple of frogs, then keep them in a coffee can in his room. When he'd do this, I'd hear the thump thump thump of frogs hitting their heads against the plastic lid. This went on all night, until I woke up in the morning screaming, "Let the goddamn frogs out!" He begged me to take him fishing, because he dreamed of catching a good one-footer and keeping it in the bathtub. What was it with boys and the way they liked to imprison other creatures?

Jase was beautiful to look at, knew his please-and-thank yous, liked to kiss and hug and cuddle, but still he was like an alien creature. I still wished he was a girl. Even so—boy, jailer, bane of my life—he was my main companion.

We went to my mother's nearly every day for dinner. I watched soaps with my sisters when they came home from school while Jase hung out with my mother in the kitchen. He colored and played with Lincoln Logs or his remote-control car, then when dinner was served, if he didn't like what my mother made for everyone else, she made him something special, treatment that previously only my father had received. Occasionally, I borrowed my mother's car to ride with Jase around the countryside, which usually ended with a visit to the Friendly Cows. As soon as we pulled up, they came sauntering from their shed to the barbed wire. They slobbered our hands with wet noses. We gave them names and fed them fistfuls of grass. I felt an affinity with the Friendly Cows, and so did Jason. When we left, he always said, "Poor cows." It killed me they were earmarked for slaughter. Neither Jason nor I liked to eat beef during this period. At night, sometimes I told Jason stories about the Friendly Cows, in which the Cows went through all sorts of hardships and misadventures but ended up happy in India, where they were sacred.

But the monotony of my life was about to end, I thought. It was the fall of 1973 and Jason's first day of kindergarten. I'd have half of every day free, kidless, by myself, alone—a state I'd been looking forward to since the day he was born. The next year, when he was gone all day, maybe, just maybe, I could get a job and join the world. I dressed him in gray boy pants, the type with a belt instead of a stretchy waistband. Then I pulled a light blue jersey over his head, to bring out the blue in his eyes. He was a beauty. I knew the teacher would love him. Most women did.

I'd borrowed my mother's car for the occasion. The kindergarten room was plastered with the ABCs, pictures of animals, domestic and wild, and chaotic with mothers and kids. I thought the other mothers were staring at me because I was too young to have a kid in kindergarten, but then I thought people stared at me everywhere I went since the day my name appeared in the paper.

We stood in line for our turn with the teacher, who wore a bright red skirt, a white blouse with a Peter Pan collar, and had translucent skin like a nun's. One second, I wished I hadn't worn my jeans, and the next, I was glad I'd been true to myself and dressed natural.

Jason squeezed my hand tighter and leaned his head into my waist. "You scared?" I asked.

He nodded.

"What of?" I said.

"I don't know."

Half the time, Jason was afflicted with the Donofrio male habit of noncommunication. So I helped him out. "I was afraid when I went to kindergarten," I said.

"You were?"

"Everybody is."

"Why?"

"I don't know. I guess you're afraid to leave your mother. Afraid of all the strange kids. Just afraid because you don't know what's going to happen next. Right?"

He nodded his head and relaxed his grip on my hand. "Well, I'm not going anywhere; some of the kids you'll like and some you won't; and school will get to be such a routine so fast you'll wish you didn't know what's happening next."

"Mm-hm." Jason believed everything I said, because I always told him the truth. Then he added, "You'll pick me up, right?" He had to check.

"Right."

Mrs. Deerie, the teacher, stuck a name tag on Jason—"So I can learn your name, young man"—then pointed him to a chair at a large square table. Jason sat down and stared straight ahead. "Well, Jase," I said. "I guess I'll be going."

He nodded and kept staring.

"Don't I get a kiss?"

He stood up and kissed me quickly, then sat back down and took the same position.

Back home, I drank a cup of coffee. The birds outside the window seemed louder, seemed to make a hysterical racket, because the neighborhood was so silent. I envied Jason and all the kids. First days of school were exciting. My mind crowded with pictures of Jason's beginning: playing ring-around-the-rosy, eating a graham cracker and drinking milk through a straw at snack time. The teacher telling some kid, who definitely would not be Jason, to stop blowing bubbles. While I imagined him learning to raise his hand to ask permission to go to the bathroom, I knocked my coffee off the table. It broke, and I cried. And do you know what I thought? Not, What will I do without Jason. Not, I wish I could go to school too. But, I must be getting my period; I can't wait till menopause.

I was depressed that autumn, and it didn't help that Jason's teacher thought I was a faulty mother. First, at Halloween, I poured green food dye into white baby shoe polish and painted Jason's skin to make him a green Martian. I thought it showed imagination. But when he came home, his face was washed clean. He said, "Mrs. Deerie said it was poison."

Then, at my first parent-teacher conference, she said, "I'm concerned about your son. Whenever there's a little roughhousing, you know the way boys do, Jason retreats to a puzzle or off with the girls. Is there a man in his life?"

"No," I said.

"Nobody to throw around a football or play catch?"

"Well, my father, but . . ."

I could tell she thought me pathetic and Jason's life impoverished because I couldn't provide him with the essentials. I figured her assessment of me was on target.

A month later, after Jason had been bugging me

and bugging me, "I want a butch, I want a butch" (I guess to look like every other little redneck in town), I took out my electric razor, purchased with S&H green stamps, and buzzed off his beautiful hair. Problem was, it came off in patches that made his skull look like a map of the United States, so I had to shave him bald. The kids called him Bald Eagle at the bus stop. They said, "Snatch a pebble from my hand, Grasshopper," from a kung fu TV show that featured a bald guy. This never failed to make Jason shoot me a dirty look.

I was standing at the bus stop with him, because I'd volunteered to work in the school library to have something to do. I rode the bus with him two days a week and Jase didn't seem the least bit embarrassed to sit next to his mother—I guess, because he didn't think of me so much as a mother as another kid growing up. On the ride, I indicated other kids and asked if he liked them, to which he usually answered yes. At his school, I pretended I was a real librarian as I put books back on the shelves in alphabetical order and recommended *Horton the Elephant* or *The Phantom Tollbooth* to kids who came in with a pass.

Then one freezing November day, Jason's teacher was on duty when we disembarked the bus. She took me aside and said in a whisper, "I was wondering. Did Jason have lice?"

"No," I said. "He wanted a butch and I went too far."

"I see," she said, not seeing.

Then she wrapped her arm around Jason's shoulder, bent to his height, and said, "So, how are you today, my little helper? Do me a favor, dear. Put my pocketbook in my desk, will you? Well, back to work," she said, dismissing me.

She thought I was a miserable mother and that she

cared more for my son than I did. Maybe it was true. I'd been dating a schoolteacher who wouldn't park his car in my driveway because he said he might end up fired. He pretended I didn't have a kid. And so did I. So whenever we went out, I never invited Jason. One time, it was a Sunday, we were driving down Main Street and I saw my parents in their car with Jason, coming from the opposite direction. When we passed, I looked out the rear window and saw Jason looking out the rear window too. He kept looking, and then he was too far away for me to tell. I'd felt sad then, and in the library that day, thinking about it, I felt sad again. I couldn't concentrate. I stamped *received* when I should've stamped *date due*. I rested my elbow on the stamp pad and ruined forever my favorite shirt. Then there was the kicker.

The teacher across the hall was a screamer, and today was no exception. She said, "All right, class, attention, pay attention. . . . What's a factory?"

No response.

Louder: "What . . . is . . . a . . . factory?"

No response.

Screaming: *"Where do your parents work?"*

That did it. I ran into the bathroom to start crying. Factory work was all I could hope for, and maybe it would be all my son would hope for too. I was a white-trash person who shaved my son's hair. I might as well be living in West Virginia. Who was I kidding, pretending to be a librarian? People like Jason's teacher thought I was an idiot. I cried so hard the janitor knocked on the door to ask what was the matter. Finally, I controlled myself. When we got home, I called my mother and said I was sick. She volunteered to take Jason overnight and bring him to school the next morning.

As soon as he left, I called the hospital and asked for the emergency room. I said to the man who answered, "If someone took a hundred aspirins, would they die?" He said one hundred aspirins could eat out the wall of his stomach, which would make him hemorrhage and die. He said I should most certainly bring him in. Then he asked who was calling, and I hung up. Next, I carried my bottle of one hundred aspirins along with two glasses of water to my room, emptied the pills onto my bed, and took two and two and two. Probably, it would be my mother and Jase who'd find me. Probably, when she dropped him off after school the next day, they'd call for me, and when I didn't answer, she'd send Jase up to see if I was sleeping. Maybe I'd leave a note on the table so Jason wouldn't have to see me dead. But what could I say? Dear Mom and Jason and Rose and Phyllis and Dad and Mike, forgive me for offing myself, Love, Bev?

I took two more, and lines like "It's always darkest before the dawn" and "When winter comes, can spring be far behind?" came to mind. I didn't believe them. I took two more.

Pregnant at seventeen Divorced at nineteen. Arrested at twenty-one. Killed myself at twenty-three. There was a beautiful symmetry. I took two more.

I didn't like my destiny. God had it in for me. I didn't believe in him anyway, but still I said, "Oh God," or "Please, dear God," or "God help me." I promised myself to never again ever mention his name. But what was I thinking? I'd be dead. I took two more. That made fourteen.

The first time it occurred to me there might not be a God, I was twelve and had just discovered Hamlet's soliloquy. I couldn't sleep that night. A mulberry branch beat on my window while Mr. Gerace played

"Taps" over and over in his backyard. He must've been drunk, because it was late. I had closed my eyes and tried to imagine myself dead—what it would be like, to be dust, no memory, nothing. I'd decided even then it could be bliss. Now, I took two more.

Jason would be better off, no question. Even if he did have to live with my smothering mother and mean father. At least my father wasn't mean to him. Not yet. But wait till the kid reached high school and got caught sneaking a beer. Don't think about it. I took two more.

My formerly beautiful son looked like a concentration-camp victim. I took two more. And two more. That made twenty-two.

Then I remembered my first suicide attempt. I'd been thirteen and in love with Trevis Glasker, who was sixteen and lived around the block. He wore sunglasses, said his name was Ray and that he was blind. I made a fool of myself mooning over him and yelling at his friends when they made fun of his condition. Then one day Ray walked up, took off his sunglasses, said, "I can see you," and started laughing. His blindness had been a big joke that everyone was in on. I ran home wailing so loud birds flew off treetops. I took a razor from the medicine chest, then dove into my closet. I hugged my clothes and started singing "The End of the World." By the end of the song, I wanted to sing it over. I did and got so carried away with the drama, the razor slipped from my fingers and fell between two floorboards. I decided I didn't want to kill myself anymore. For years after that, whenever I thought about Trevis Glasker, my face got hot and I wished I could forget the incident forever.

But then, one day, it seemed funny.

If I didn't kill myself now, one day I'd probably

laugh: being a convicted criminal while my father *and* my brother were cops, riding a bus with a bunch of kindergarteners to get to a fake job, making Jason look like a victim of lice. Maybe one day we'd discover some pictures of him, looking like a little Gandhi, in a shoe-box and we'd roll around laughing. What song should I sing now? "It's My Party and I'll Die if I Want To?"

I decided not to do it.

CHAPTER 11

THERE'S definitely something to that darkest-before-the-dawn line because the next morning I called the psychiatric clinic at the hospital and my life started to look up. My social worker, Mrs. Goldfarb, took out a pad and a pencil and made a list of all the drugs I'd taken in my lifetime: LSD, mescaline, Percodan, horse tranquilizers, Seconal, cocaine, opium, amphetamines, hashish, and marijuana. She nodded her head and said, "That's quite an arsenal." When I told her about what a creep my probation officer had been, she was outraged. When I told her I felt guilty that Raymond became a junkie because I got pregnant and ruined his life, she told me that was ridiculous. When I told her I was afraid I didn't love Jason, she said she was sure I did. I appreciated her rage at Stanley Stupski, but I didn't believe her on the other two points. Still, it was great to have somebody on my side. Then after two months of once a week, she pronounced me an aesthete and said, "You're too intelligent to be wasting away. You should go to college."

I started crying.

She set up an interview for me at DVR, the division of vocational rehabilitation, where they'd give me a battery of tests: psychological, personality, aptitude, and achievement. If I scored crazy and smart enough, they'd send me to college; if I scored crazy and wasn't smart, I'd get vocational training.

DVR had been established after the Second World War to give veterans with physical disabilities some physical therapy and job training so they could join the work force. Then it was expanded to include everybody who was disabled, including psychologically or emotionally disturbed people, of which, obviously, I was one.

The day of the tests, I arrived at seven and was told to sit at a long metal table in a green room. Soon, a psychiatrist arrived. He wore wire-rim glasses and must've been seven feet tall and four feet wide. My strategy was to answer the questions like a crazy person so I'd be considered disabled and a candidate for college or training.

But it turned out I couldn't distinguish between crazy and sane, which made me think I really was a nut. First, there were the college board-type tests. Then the shrink asked me questions like, "What does the statement 'Shallow brooks make the most noise' mean?" I gave him figurative and literal. He looked impressed. He gave me inkblots. He gave me cartoon pictures to put in sequence. He gave me weird tests with questions like, "If you found a letter, addressed and stamped, lying on the ground, what would you do?" I figured to touch it would be a federal offense. Plus, towns don't have lost-and-founds. I knew that "Open it" was the wrong answer, although it sounded like something I'd do. "Mail it" never occurred to me. I said simply, "I don't know." Then he gave me pictures to make up stories about, and each time the psychiatrist held up a new one, it seemed there was only one story in the world that went with it.

In one picture there was a woman lying at the bottom of the stairs. Her eyes were closed, and an older woman was holding the young woman in her arms. I said, "The mistress of the house just fell down the stairs and broke her neck. She's dead. Now the maid's holding her and wondering if it was her fault because she put too much wax on the stairs. She's worried she'll get fired."

I probably should've said it was her mother and that the young woman just fainted or something, because a couple of weeks later, when I sat in the DVR counselor's cubicle to hear the results, the geriatric Mr. Randall lifted his feet onto a milk crate and said, "Our testing shows you're having a difficult time adjusting to adult life. You hate your mother." He blinked his eyes real fast and said, "Not unusual. Nothing you can't overcome. You have problems with your father, too. You buck against authority. Somebody tells you what to do, you do the opposite. If somebody told you to wear a bra, for example, you couldn't do it."

How did he know? And why do they all notice I'm not wearing one?

"You make it hard on yourself. It seems you also hate men. I understand. I can imagine it's not easy being a divorcee in this day and age. Men think they can take advantage."

They never stopped thinking about sex—even if they're about to croak in a minute like this one.

"You are very intelligent, I'm pleased to report." He leafed through the papers. "You scored in the ninety-seventh percentile of all freshmen entering college this year. That's quite high. The doctor was very excited. He recommends we send you to college."

I felt like Hester Prynne must've felt in the next chapter, the one that never got written, the one where she's in the woods on her way to the rest of her life and finally rips off that ridiculous *A* and throws it in the camp fire.

"No sense sending you to vocational training; you'd never be happy in a subordinate position. I can't see you going further than a master's degree, however. You couldn't play the politics.

"One thing bothers me, though. You're like Esau, in the Bible. You'd sell your birthright for a bowl of porridge. You live in the moment. This is what worries me. Say we were to give you money for college, then you get your degree and decide working's for the birds. You're going to live on a commune or be an artist or something. Never pay taxes. Then DVR wasted its money. The whole idea is to make you a *contributing* member of society. We're investing in you. We're saying, This young woman is going to be productive. She's going to have a place in society, not drop out of it. So I'm in a bind. We send you to college, we're taking a gamble."

Sell my birthright for a bowl of porridge? What did that mean? That I'd go for the easy thing? That I'd go for instant gratification, like an infant? And what did "live in the moment" mean? Was that like Be Here Now? I thought that was good. Maybe that was too Buddhist. Maybe Christians—and if I'd ever seen one, it was this guy—didn't think like that.

The creep wasn't going to send me to college.

"Here's my problem. I want to help you, but you only value what you work for. I want you to prove to me that you want this education. We'll pay for your tuition and books at community college; you couldn't get into a better school, with your high school record."

Why did relief always make me feel like crying?

"You'll still get your welfare. But you're going to

have to find your own transportation and day care for your child. I want you to feel you had to work for this opportunity."

Not the goddamn car and not the goddamn kid. Let the problem be anything but the car and the kid. If I had a car and a baby-sitter to begin with, I wouldn't be sitting in this old coot's office listening to how I'm an emotional and social basket case, based on ten hours of testing administered by a friggin' giant. Why didn't they just do the tarot cards? I was beginning to hyperventilate. How could he give me college in one breath and take it away in another? I couldn't talk. But I had to. I could feel my mouth contort, "Middlesex must be fifty miles away." The words came out in a shout, and I couldn't help it. "How am I supposed to get there?"

"I don't know. Maybe you can car pool it. Call the school. Find out who goes there from your area. Show some initiative. You have a lot of potential. Use it. You'll just have to figure it out. You're not going to get a free ride here."

CHAPTER 12

I'D been told by Mrs. Goldfarb I could get a college loan to buy a car. Now my mother split the blinds to take a first look at my new car in her driveway.

"Nice, huh?" I said.

"So clean," she said. "Better keep it that way."

That was the thing about my mother. I'd bought this beautiful fourteen-year-old with-a-rebuilt-engine emerald-green Volkswagen after four years without a car—which, incidentally, was not only going to take me to college but eventually off welfare—and all my mother had to say was, Better keep it clean? It's true, I'd been rude to my mother—probably, since puberty—but she had her faults too, and this took the cake. It was nearing last-straw time, and I don't mean just with her but my whole family.

I hadn't even bothered telling my father about college, since we hardly spoke and I knew my mother'd tell him anyway. Now tonight, after I'd arrived proudly with Jason in my new car, my father came home late for dinner, placed his walkie-talkie staticking next to his plate, and said, "So how many miles she got on her?"

"Ninety-seven thousand, but her engine's rebuilt."

"How much you say you paid for her?"

"Five hundred dollars."

He shook his head like there was a bee in it.

"Cupcake," Jason said.

"What?" my father said.

"That's what my mother named her."

My mother clicked her tongue.

"What?" I said. "She looks like she has white frosting." Her snout was painted white, which also made her look like a pit bull, but I preferred to see her as pastry.

"I don't know, Beverly," my mother said.

"You don't know what?"

"Never mind."

"You think it's childish to name a car. You think I'm crazy."

My father kind of snorted, but nobody answered.

"I think she looks like a cupcake," Jason said after a minute, which surprised me. Usually, even if we were having fun, even if it seemed like he was my best friend for one minute, as soon as we got in front of my mother, he turned traitor. He was forever threatening to tell my parents I smoked marijuana. Right now, he must've felt sorry for me.

"Me too," said Rose, who was now fifteen and smoking pot every morning, noon, and night of her life. At least there was one other person in my family I could halfway relate to.

I suppose the point wasn't so much the car but that everybody always had to make a big deal about what a weirdo I was, while they hardly noticed I'd be going to college, which to me felt like all those corny songs— "Climb Every Mountain," "The Impossible Dream." I mean, it felt like I'd moved heaven and earth, and then when I told my mother the good news, she'd said, "I thought you wanted a job. Now you got to go, what, four years?" Any normal parent would be proud that her kid was going to college, but not mine, mine was worried.

Then, when my brother walked in for the meatloaf dinner, it was the last straw. First of all, he was in uniform. And second of all, he stood next to me waiting for me to get up. My brother didn't live at home either, but he ate over as often as I did. When we showed up on the same night, I deferred the chair to him. But not this night.

"Bev, you're sitting in your brother's chair," my mother said.

"Who said it's his chair?"

"Move," my brother the blue bulk said.

I wanted to say, What're you going to do, asshole, clobber me with your billy club? but then who knew what would happen. He might pull me off the chair by my elbow. My father might yell. Whatever. I was too much of a coward to find out. I left the table, and as I seethed in the living room waiting for Jason to finish, I thought, How the hell did I get stuck with this family? A mother who seems afraid of her own flesh-and-blood daughter's being successful (because then I'd be different from her), growing up in a house where the men were served first and the women had to give their chairs to them. I swore my son would go to college and that never in his life would he think he deserved anything by virtue of his being born with a penis. Then I comforted myself with the thought that at least now I had my car and would be going to college. As soon as I heard the chairs scrape away from the table, I said, "Come on, Jase, we're going."

That was the spring of 1974, and I had to wait until the fall for my first day—when I woke up with the jitters. I stepped into the shower and combed my already pixie length hair with a straight-edged razor. As I watched the strands go down the drain, I thought how when I was little I'd made my mother set my hair with bobby pins for first days so I could look like my idol, Betty Boop, and make a good impression. I thought about how far I'd come. Now I walked by mirrors without looking, never wore makeup, shaved my legs, or plucked my eyebrows, and had even developed a vise-grip handshake. This was thanks to the women's consciousness-raising group I'd joined in New Haven soon after I got Cupcake.

By the time I stepped out of the shower, you could say I'd talked myself into feeling macho. I dried off, then put on my farmer's jeans and dropped a pen and a pencil in the pouch at my chest, which naturally made me think about writing something, which made me think about learning—which was the whole point of college, after all—and I got the jitters again. I figured now I'd have to prove I was as smart as I'd always thought. This would not be easy. I'd taken pride in being a borderline moron in high school and maybe now I'd pay for it. For all I knew, I might get thrown into remedial classes, in which case my pride would force me to jump out a window.

Down in the living room, I paused to look at Cupcake before making coffee. She shimmered like an emerald in the driveway. Behind her, a piece of paper skimmed along the gutter propelled by spurts of wind. I figured that paper was some kid's spelling homework. My chest filled, and I had to stop myself from crying. I could hardly believe my good fortune. I was joining the human race.

Then Jason came slouching through the room. He was capable of black Donofrio male moods, the silent broods. He could be the slug that came to breakfast, lunch, or dinner. And the last thing I needed right now was him acting like a dark cloud and reminding me of what had held me back from everything in life so far.

I knew he felt needy now because his mother was going off to college, but when he sat at the table and stared dazedly at nothing, I figured it was for attention and it pissed me off. It put me on the alert for kids-making-mothers-turn-cartwheels behavior. I said, "So what're you having for breakfast?"

"What is there?"

"What do I look like, the waitress? You want a menu?"

"Maybe I'll have Rice Krispies," he said.

"They're going to come floating to the table and pouring into your bowl, like a commercial?"

"No," he said, pushing his chair back hard and going to get the Rice Krispies.

"Today's my first day of college, remember?" I asked rhetorically, wanting to put the issue on the table.

"I know," he said, pouring milk on his cereal, then spooning two spoons of sugar in.

"Sugar's bad for you," I said.

"Can I come?" he said.

"No, you can't."

"Will you be home when I get home?" He was six years old and already knew how to act like an Italian husband.

"Aren't I always?"

"No."

"When have I ever left you home alone?"

"Once. I went over to Cassie's. Remember?"

"Oh, right. Excuse me. I was ten minutes late. You could've died."

"I could."

Being liberated did not just mean from men but from attitudes and kids, and Jason was not going to make me feel guilty about doing anything I wanted.

When he came back downstairs from brushing his teeth, I noticed his ears sticking out of his hair and that he was holding his Mighty Heroes lunch pail. For some reason the sight of him made me giddy. Then, when I hugged him goodbye and felt how small his bones were, how small he really was, I probably hugged him too long, because he squirmed and said, "Ma, the bus."

As I drove to school up winding roads, by cow pastures and cornfields, I slowed down for a blind curve and thought of Raymond's car accident. Where was Raymond, anyway? What did he do every day? Did he have new kids? Did he ever wonder about me? Then I wondered what the hell I was doing on my first day of college thinking about a junkie husband. Maybe good fortune made me think of bad. Maybe when things start to change, you want to hold on to something familiar.

Middlesex Community College was a bunch of flat, new, economically constructed buildings bunched up on a hill, with as much parking lot as class space. It was a school for commuters that was not long on beauty or aesthetics or little extras like protection from glaring sun in windows, but it was paradise to me. It was an inspiration of the sixties, a college of last resort. If you were a jerk-off in high school, this is where you could start over. If you were formerly too poor for college, you could go now, because Middlesex was cheap. Plus, they had counselors there to get you loans.

The education? Maybe because the students mostly had no money, we were often assigned one textbook per course that digested material for you instead of going to the sources, which was a little too much like high school for me.

Teachers? Well. There was Kirk Donnelly, my English Composition 101 professor, who had us bring in advertisements from magazines to show how pictures can do the job better than words; assigned us papers ("Describe a Room" . . . "Use a Paradox" . . . "Write a One-page Conversation"), which he collected and never handed back; and liked to talk for whole periods about his two-year career as a technical writer, producing manuals for the home repair of a brand of car I can't remember. On the other extreme was Phillip Henry, a Rhodes scholar who taught us philosophy by posing formerly unthought of questions, about the immateriality of the material world, the subjectivity of truth, and the circuity of time, which got me thinking so hard I felt brain cells growing.

Then there were my fellow students. There was one about my age, who, when asked to please read the essay assigned in English, picked up a blank piece of paper and pretended to be reading something she never wrote. I was sitting next to her when she did it, and seeing her actually pretend to read a blank page, for a good three minutes, threw me into a fit of laughing I couldn't stop. Mr. Donnelly smiled good-humoredly when she finished and said, "Maybe you'll share the joke, Bev?"

The woman shot me a dirty look.

I couldn't share the joke, because I didn't know myself what I found so paralyzingly funny. Except maybe it had brought to mind the ridiculous book reports I used to make up in high school. But making up book reports was nothing compared to this woman's performance, which was pure virtuosity. This was what you'd call unfulfilled potential. I admired her at the same time I thought she was a fool for not doing her assignments. Why come if you didn't want to work?

Maybe I was expecting everybody to have my experience, which was the same as gorging myself at a feast every day after living on nuts and raisins. I felt extremely lucky. I pitied the eighteen-year-olds in the back of the class, the gum-snapping, chair-slouching, class-skipping, bad-habits-from-high-school students. They were probably being forced into attendance by their parents. But they were in the minority. In the front of the class, at the other end of the spectrum, were the highly polite grandmothers, some sharp-tongued middle-aged women, a nun, and a retired insurance salesman. The majority of the students, though, were about my age, which was twenty-four, and fellow victims of a previously rocky life. There were some GI-bill Vietnam vets, other mothers of small children, though they were mostly married, and then there were my two new friends—Arlene and Lizzy. Arlene was a native of Middletown and used to run with a girl's gang in high school. She had a scar on her shoulder from a knife fight and a tattoo on her knuckle. Now she wrote the most beautiful poems, using nature for metaphors, and worked as a book-keeper. Lizzy had actually hitchhiked to California and back, sold her plasma to buy food, and lived in a tent by a river, then came home to find that her boyfriend, who supposedly played guitar like Jimi Hendrix, had offed himself the day before. Then Lizzy lost her voice and was committed to the state mental institution until the words came back four months later. Now she worked there with autistic children.

I met Lizzy and Arlene my second semester, after I'd already decided I had to get all A's. I had a lot to prove because of past life failure, but I also wanted A's because in my first month at Middlesex, I'd overheard a woman in my history class telling her neighbor that she was planning on getting a scholarship to Wesleyan University. I thought she was lying or at least deluded, because although Wesleyan was in the same town as Middlesex, it cost about a hundred times more and was mainly for kids with board scores of 1400 and diplomas from prep schools. I butted into her conversation just to see how far her lying would go. "How can you go to Wesleyan from here?" I asked her.

She said it was easy if you got all A's, because they had this scholarship called Etherington, for community-college students. I had an instantaneous fantasy. I'd get a scholarship. I'd be the only person in the whole school who was on welfare. A bunch of socialists with a severe case of societal guilt would befriend me and make me a working-class hero.

I went home and read the riot act to Jason. "I have to get all A's," I said, "and you have to help. If ever you see me reading a book or writing a paper, don't interrupt no matter what."

"What if I get cut?"

"Well, if you get cut."

"What if Andrew's throwing rocks?"

"Jason, use your own judgment."

"What if Annie's smoking butts?"

"Jason!"

"I don't like it when you study."

"You want me to stay poor and stupid and on welfare forever?"

"No."

"Then don't interrupt."

Silence.

"Okay?"

"I guess."

I developed a talent for pure concentration, which enabled me to hear absolutely nothing when I was reading or writing. In fact if Jason wanted my attention, he had to pull on my sleeve. When Jason had his friends up in his room on winter afternoons and they'd be arguing over who got to go first or accusing each other of cheating or playing hide-and-seek and making the ceiling sound like thunder above me, I'd be trying to figure the value of X, Y, or Z and hearing none of it. I succeeded in getting all A's—which wasn't hard once I figured all I had to do was tell the professor what he or she had already said; or if that was too much of a personal compromise, I simply had to make my own opinion as outrageous as possible. I applied to Wesleyan in the spring of 1975 but would not hear until the summer, because they needed my second-semester grades before they decided.

Finally it was summer, a Wednesday, and I'd gone to my last women's consciousness-raising-group meeting. We were breaking up because we were only five, and one woman was moving while another was leaving for the summer. We had a potluck dinner for the occasion and each of us brought a bottle of wine, which meant by the time we were finished eating, we were pretty loaded. Somebody put Joni Mitchell on the stereo, and one of the women got up and started dancing. Then we all got up. I had my eyes closed and was singing along, "I am on a lonely road and I am traveling traveling traveling, looking for something what can it be," and when I opened my eyes, I saw that my fellow women had taken their shirts off.

Now, the first thing I thought was, What would Fay say? With the exception of one, these women were homely; in high school I would've called them skanks and never given them the time of day. I pictured Fay's face at the window, laughing at me dancing with a bunch of half-naked skanks. Then I decided Fay and her reaction was her problem. I liked these women. They'd listened to my whole story—starting with a father who spied on me at the same time he ignored me, and ending with one feckless no-caring lay after another—and they'd listened with intelligence, good questions ("Why when you talk about making love do you always say *sex*? Do you make no distinction?"), and compassion.

Now I wanted to take my shirt off and join my friends. But it had been a long time since I went shirtless, since the age of eight to be exact, unless you wanted to count bouncing around in bed with a couple of dozen lovers, which I didn't.

I closed my eyes, took a breath, and lifted my shirt off. The air against my skin felt like the opposite of a caress. It was chilling. It was stimulating. To belabor a word, it was liberating. I realized it never would have felt so freeing if it hadn't been so long since I'd done it, and that there is something to be said for deprivation—which is the feeling you get when it's over. .

The next morning, I got the envelope from Wesleyan. I'd been accepted. They were giving me an apartment on campus. My blood pressure dropped. Little sparkles swarmed over the page I was reading. I put my head between my knees to let the blood flow to my brain, and to let the information sink in. This meant I'd leave Wallingford, probably forever. I would leave one life and enter another. I lifted my head, and the sparkles were gone.

CHAPTER 13

SEVEN years after Raymond and I had moved into our mint-green duplex apartment as man and wife, my father, my mother, my brother, Jason, and I loaded two flowered living room chairs, given to me by the woman who'd made my wedding suit, Fay's mother's kitchen set, Jase's and my bedroom furniture, and boxes of everything else into my father's truck early on Labor Day morning 1975. I was to follow the truck in Cupcake. After everybody left, I went back into my house for a last look.

The house had a feeling of about-to-be, like it had already forgotten us and was waiting for its next experience. In my former bedroom, I riveted on some small black smears dotting the walls. They were the stains of dead mosquitoes from our first summer, before we had screens, when the mosquitoes made a feast of my pregnant body every evening, and then every morning as they slept, I whapped them to death with a rolled-up magazine. Looking at the remains of their massacre, which I never washed off, painted over, or hardly noticed for seven years, I wondered if that girl, who suffered through sleepless itchy nights rather than save herself with the purchase of screens, who could ignore her own dried blood on the walls for seven years, could ever be a normal person—and by that I meant could I survive, fit in, resist the urge to fuck up and ruin everything.

The house I'd been assigned on campus was not exactly beautiful. It was covered with haphazard gray shingles and had four small low-ceilinged rooms, with no light except for in the kitchen, plus brown-painted floorboards that slanted toward the middle. I decided to think of this place as my little college cottage. It had a porch and a grill made of rocks out back, bushes, flowers, and trees with squirrels jetting around the branches. It was on a pitted dead-end street at the edge of campus, called Knowles Avenue, and as we pulled up, I noticed a couple of kids riding their bikes down the hill next to the hockey rink across the street and wondered if they'd be friends of Jason's and who my friends would be.

It was still morning when we started unloading. My mother took command. "Your brother will help your father with the heavy stuff. I don't want you hurting your back. . . . Better put the bed there, away from the window or you'll get a draft. . . . If you put your canned foods closer to the stove, it'll be more efficient. . . . I always put the glasses above the sink. . . . What? Aren't you going to put paper on your shelves? . . ." She was out of hand. I was letting her get away with murder. What did she think, I was still that pregnant teenager she moved into the other apartment?

Everything had been moved in. My brother's friend had picked him up, and my father was walking around the hockey rink with Jason. My mother had cleaned the refrigerator, and was finishing the stove, when I sat on my bed, dropped my head into my hands, and thought how it was almost dusk and there might be a beautiful sunset, but how would I know? If

I'd moved in with friends, we might be sitting on the porch, ordering pizza, buying beers, having arguments about anchovies or no anchovies. Why'd I let my parents assume they'd do the moving?

This was my frame of mind when I stepped out of my bedroom and into the kitchen and spotted my mother moving the kitchen table to a different wall from the one I'd placed it against. "What the fuck do you think gives you the right to move that table?" I yelled.

"You'll get too much sun. I just thought . . ."

"You just thought you knew better. You just thought I was an imbecile. Get it straight. This is *my house*."

"Well." She puffed herself up.

I wasn't giving her a chance to talk. As far as I was concerned, she had no defense. "Ma, I know this is hard for you to take, but I'm different from you and I'm going to live a different life. Starting right here and now—with where I put the fucking Campbell's soup." I took a can and moved it from next to the stove to above the sink.

"Then I guess you don't need me anymore. We'd better go."

Now I felt like shit. "Well, we're moved in. You must be tired."

"Sonny," she called outside. She unclasped her cigarette case, took out a Kent, and lit it with a lighter. My father followed Jason in. He wiped his face with his handkerchief, crossed his ankles, and leaned against the stove. "All done?" he said.

"Come here," she said to Jason.

"You going already?" Jason said.

"You're going to miss your Mim, I know," she said.

Jason hugged her hips. She'd be a toll call away now. No way she'd stop by on her way to anywhere ever again. I felt like I was one of those Nazi death camp people shoving Jase into one line and her and my father into another.

She kissed Jase on the cheek, then pressed her pocketbook against her stomach and looked like she might cry as my father put his hand on the middle of her back and guided her out the door. "Don't be strangers now," she said through the car window as they pulled away.

The next morning at nine o'clock, Jase and I were standing in line at the Science Center, the modern building on campus, for registration. I'd been afraid people would stare at me because I'd be the only older person (twenty-five in a few days) and I'd be the only one with a kid. I was the oldest person there and the only one with a kid all right, but I was also the only one who noticed. Since I might as well be invisible, it was safe to take a look around, and what I saw were people cut from a different mold. The guys had over-developed heads and underdeveloped bodies and the girls had frizzy hair, backpacks, and frozen-faced expressions. I felt like the Student from Another Planet.

Jase had put on his *Night of the Living Dead* face and said, "How long do we have to stay here?"

"Until we get to the head of the line."

The line was the length of a football field. "Oh brother," he said, making like he might start crying. I was nervous enough, specifically, that once I got to the head of the line, they'd say, "Beverly Who? I'm sorry. You're not on the list."

"Jason! I don't need it," I said in a yell disguised as a whisper, then a tall lanky guy touched my shoulder and said, "Excuse me, is this the line for registration?"

"I guess," I said. What else would it be?

"Excuse me," he said, turning to the girl behind me. "Is this the line for registration?"

"Quite," she said.

Quite? Who in the world said *quite*? Was this what I'd have to choose from for friends? Why had I been in such a hurry to transfer from community college when I could've stayed there another year before I made this flying leap into whitebreadsville. A chubby guy butted in line in front of me. "Marcy!" he effused. "I can't believe you're going here too."

"Josh! My God. This is so cool," she said.

"I just got here," he said. "I can't tell you how much I miss my baby grand already."

Miss his *baby grand*? These kids were *rich*. Going to a school where a year's tuition could clothe, feed, and put a roof over a family of six's heads had been an expectation, like toilet paper in the bathroom, for most of these people. How could I ever relate? A drop of perspiration dripped from my temple. When the line moved forward, I stepped on the back of the fat kid's shoe.

He turned around.

"Excuse me," I said.

He smiled and turned back to Marcy.

"Ma, you did that on purpose," Jase whispered.

"So?"

"Why?"

"It makes me mad he's so rich."

"Why?"

"Because we're not, I guess."

"We're not poor, though?"

"No. And it's not even important to be rich. It's probably better to be poor. It's just that some people take it for granted and never think about people who aren't."

"I'm going to be rich," Jason said. "If I stepped on his shoe, you'd yell at me."

"What are you, my conscience?"

"What's that?"

"The voice inside your head that tells you when you're wrong."

"No."

"Just remember. You're the kid and I'm the mother."

"Yes, little girl," Jason said.

When I thought about this later, I wondered if I wasn't being as bad as my own mother by not allowing other people to be different—the way she wouldn't allow another place for the Campbell's soup.

Still, I was paralyzed by Fear of the Different and did nothing but study, which I expected would pay off. So when my professor asked me to come see him after I'd worked four days on, then handed in, my first English paper, I thought that maybe, like one of the professors at Middlesex had, he was going to invite me to contribute to the school magazine. Still, I was a bundle of nerves when I entered his office. Professors at Middlesex were regular people, while this professor had a goatee like a devil, an accent like Katharine Hepburn's, and did stuff like turn red in the face and burst forth lines by Wordsworth: "'Great God! I'd rather be a Pagan suckled on a creed outworn . . .'" This he said after storming into class and railing about a gas station attendant who'd just called him Bub. What if I used incorrect grammar? What if he asked me a question using a word I didn't know?

He sat in a leather chair across from me instead of behind his desk and smiled kindly. "You have trouble writing," he said.

I forgot to breathe. "I come from community college," I said by way of explanation.

"Yes," he said by way of saying he could tell.

Then he recommended I take a *remedial* writing course, for *no credit*. I could barely control my trembling lip in his office. I went into the bathroom and cried, sitting on the toilet. I could not flunk out, I simply couldn't. I knew I was the poor relation being let in through the back door of this place, but I'd thought—maybe academically, at least—I'd do all right. The humiliation was even more intense because I'd fantasized that when I graduated from college, I'd move to New York and be a writer. I took a handful of toilet paper and blew my nose. There was another roll of paper still wrapped up. That's Wesleyan for you, I thought as I walked out, extra paper in every stall. Not a speck of dirt or mess anywhere, every window in every ancient building opened with a lift of a finger, every lawn was manicured perfect, and there wasn't a dead branch on a single tree.

I'd only be depressed if I went home, so I wandered through the arts complex, which was a group of square limestone buildings scattered here and there under pine trees. The place was unreal. It looked like a moonscape. I passed a student reading a poem out loud under a tree. They were all over the place—skipping, singing, playing the flute. A woman stood under an arch and played the *bagpipes*. This, I thought, is a far cry from Susan Gerace playing "Taps" in the project.

Susan Gerace, who I'd heard had joined the marines, probably had no idea a place like Wesleyan existed. In Wallingford, if you crossed the street in the middle instead of on a corner, people would beep and you might get arrested. God forbid you should talk to yourself; they might lock you in an attic. One moonless night last week, I'd run as fast as I could with my arms outstretched across the athletic field, leaping across a puddle and splattering myself with mud, and

I'd thought one day I'd follow it up with skipping on a sidewalk. I never wanted to forget where I came from or what it was like there, because places like that were where most of the rest of the world lived—and as far as I could tell, they were populated by much more interesting people—but I didn't want to live there anymore, either.

I headed home finally, and thought of my neighborhood. The first week, the parents on my road had a meeting (three professors, their working wives, another single-mother student, and me) to organize communal day care. This meant I only had to be home one day a week at three o'clock, when our nine kids got out of school. Every other day, I was free until six. Jason had other parents to talk to and their houses to hang out in. He had friends who gave back rubs instead of boxing matches, painted rocks instead of throwing them, and were vegetarians instead of pickers of cigarette butts. They wrote a play and invited us parents. In it, the woman worked, came home exhausted, and then when her husband plopped a grilled-cheese sandwich in front of her for dinner, she said, "What about a vegetable?"

When I got home, I still didn't feel like going into the house and facing my books, so I decided to take a walk to the soccer field at the end of the road. I passed Jase and his friends on a porch rehearsing their new play, *The Martians Invade the White House*. Jason was playing the president. I heard him say, "What's a Martian?" and Brett say, "A Martian is what's in front of you," and I yelled, "Clever line."

"Hi, Ma," he said. "Where're you going?"

"Just for a walk."

"Oh," he said, which made me feel lonely, because he didn't ask if he could come, and envious, because he'd fit right in and I hadn't.

Once on the soccer field, I looked to my right at the school for juvenile delinquents up on the hill. I was looking for a pregnant girl I'd seen pumping on the swing set, but she wasn't there. I wondered, like I had so many times since the first day I'd seen her, if this obsession I had with seeing her wasn't a little unhealthy. Was I hanging on to the past? But her being at a neighboring school and our having so much in common was too much of a coincidence to ignore. Besides, maybe I could help her somehow. Maybe one day I'd get up the courage to talk to her. She had appeared in my dreams once already. She'd been on the hill pumping and pumping, but she was older* and she wasn't pregnant. I wondered if she was me.

I went home finally, opened my *Norton's Anthology*, and forced myself to read.

By the spring, things were different. For one thing, Bub, the professor, had given me an A−, and I'd learned some valuable lessons in my remedial-writing course, such as using connectives like *therefore* and *consequently* in my papers, and never ending them with a firm conclusion, because conclusions were too facile, not to mention fragile. And for another, I hadn't seen the pregnant girl for some time, and had almost forgotten about her, when I spotted a kid tear-assing down the hill and through the field, escaping. I felt exhilarated. It was all I could do to keep myself from shouting, "Go, man, go." I prayed he made it. I prayed the pregnant girl did too. Then, a few days later, Cupcake was stolen. I cursed my rotten luck. I admonished myself for being so cavalier about her, for never locking her and leaving the keys on the floor.

My father put an all-points out on Cupcake, and miraculously, a week later, he got a call from a cop in Bridgeport, seventy miles away, who said he'd recovered Cupcake from a ghetto called Hell's Gate. A key obviously made in metal shop was in her ignition, though her own keys were still on the floor. Then, a couple of weeks later, exactly the same thing happened. Cupcake was stolen, found in Bridgeport, and returned.

I made up a story. Then I believed it. The girl had left the school after she'd had her baby and had been forced by her mean parents to give it up for adoption. But her boyfriend was still locked up. He'd seen Cupcake somehow and had made a key to fit her. Then, when he got his chance, he climbed through the boiler-room window, ran down the hill and across the field, and stole her, driving all the way to Bridgeport, where the girl lived. He got caught, but undaunted, he did the same thing again. This time, Cupcake had been retrieved, but the kid hadn't been caught. He was with the girl, who thought this was the best thing that had happened to her in her life when really it was the worst. In fact, she was probably getting knocked up again that very moment.

I wondered if just as it was Cupcake's destiny to be a vehicle of escape it was mine to be linked with pregnancy and prematurely ended childhoods that last forever because they never were complete. It might be true and it might not. Only time would tell, but meanwhile, I had proof things could change. I'd made friends with people who were different. The first was Sally Dummerston, who became my best friend. She had two daughters and was the other single mother on the block. When I'd met her my first week at school, she'd introduced herself by saying, "Hi. I'm a Woman in Transition, too." Women in Transition was a category the university lumped us dozen or so single mothers into, and at the time I'd thought, anybody who introduces herself as a category is not a person I'm interested in saying two words to. Besides, she had cheerleader written all over her. But then Jason and Sally's oldest daughter, Elizabeth, were best friends and circumstances kept bringing us together, until one night we got drunk and I turned Sally on to pot for the first time in her life and she confessed that she wasn't only a Woman in Transition but a Daughter of the American Revolution and then we giggled for a good ten minutes.

Sally and I made a family with our kids. We cooked dinners together and ate mostly at Sally's, because she had a dining room with a piano on which she played Chopin, a candelabra, and cloth napkins. I learned about WASPs from Sally. I said to her, "But what do you *want?*" and she said, "It doesn't matter," or, "Whatever you like," when whatever it was did matter. Finally, I caught on that I was supposed to ask her four or five times before I could expect the truth, because before that, Sally figured that to tell the truth was impolite. She smiled and was polite to everybody, even the troupes of boring, ugly, single professors who dropped by morning, noon, and night unannounced to get flashed by Sally's smile and soothed by her graciousness. I know for a fact she loathed some of these guys for being smug or pompous or dull, but she offered them wine or beer and put Linda Ronstadt on the stereo and pretended to listen to them anyway. When our kids were acting like idiots, she said, "Now, children," while I said, "Shut up."

When Sally graduated a year before me, Jase and I were sad, but there were compensations: We weren't really losing them because they were only moving to New Haven, and I had asked the university for and had been granted her house, which was much larger and nicer than mine, then I'd invited two men ex-students to join me as roommates.

Their names were both James and they were big and gentle, like golden retrievers. I'd met them in a class called "Toward a Socialist America" and they'd stayed on after their graduation to found a political magazine. They were the type of guys who handed out leaflets and jumped all over the university about this injustice or that discrimination. They'd get drunk with their friends and stay up until dawn debating social democracy versus socialism, throwing words like *hegemony* around and ending by actually singing "We Shall Overcome" at sunrise. They had hundreds of friends who visited our house. Two or three stayed for a couple of months. We had huge dinners and grand dancing parties that spilled onto the street. We sang in the car on trips to the store or laundromat with Jason. We played cowboy family during dinners. Sometimes we read poems by candlelight while we ate dessert; other times we pushed the dining table into a corner, and Jase and I taught them *Saturday Night Fever* dances we'd memorized from seeing the movie five times over.

Like Fay's moving in with me back in 1971, this was a dream come true. There were two guys living in my house, shooting baskets with Jason and reading him stories, which was as good as any father; plus, these guys didn't lionize me, exactly, for being working-class, but they were uncomfortable with their own social advantages and awfully curious about me and my family. "Does your mother vote like your father automatically, or does she make up her own mind? Is her factory unionized? What does your father think of your living with two guys?"

CHAPTER 14

THEY got the answer to that question soon enough. My father came by to hang a spice rack that I'd requested he make me for my birthday, and didn't offer his hand for shaking when I introduced him. Naturally, this pissed me off.

The next Sunday, I showed up at his house wearing a see-through blouse, then struck up a conversation with my mother. "You ever been to a porn shop, Ma?" I said.

"No," she said, glancing nervously at my father, who was pretending not to listen as he watched the Giants game on TV.

"They have this doll. You blow it up human size. It's got a hole . . ."

My father left the room, then slammed into the cellar, where in a moment we heard the screech and drone of his electric saw. This was the first time in memory my father had ever abandoned a Giants game. I considered it a victory.

"Good," I said to my mother. "Want to watch the Bette Davis movie on channel five?"

"Shame on you," she said.

College had not made me your model daughter. Maybe I was worse than ever. I purposely used words they didn't understand, because I refused to curtail my speech to bow to ignorance, and insisted on criticizing my parents' way of life to my mother. "How can you stand to have that television on nonstop? It's like mental Novocain."

"You know your father."

"And you have nothing to say about anything that goes on in your own house?"

"Please, Beverly, don't start."

At Thanksgiving, I suggested my father and brother do the dishes. I got laughed at. I turned on my mother. "You put up with it. What's the matter with you? You must like it. You're a martyr."

"You do what you want in your house and I'll do what I want in mine," she finally said, and I shut up about it.

But that didn't mean my mother shut up about me. One weekend my last semester at college, I dropped Jason off, as I often did on Friday nights, leaving him there until Sunday. This Friday, she said, "Honest to God, Beverly. Don't you ever look at your son? Look at him. Just look at him."

"What? What?" Jase said, looking down at himself.

The kid had dirt under his nails, greasy hair lying like strings on his forehead, and rumpled, obviously worn-too-many-times clothing. Until she'd mentioned it, I hadn't even noticed. I thought back and could not tell you the last time he'd bathed. I felt terrible about this, and on the drive home from my mother's house, it set me thinking. First I thought about Sasha, the woman who lived upstairs from me for a year and a half in the gray shingled house. She had a three-year-old son named Armond, who, if you asked me, she was overprotective of. For this reason she never joined in on our communal day care. Armond hardly left the apartment, even to play in the yard. Periodically, Sasha would go off her rocker and stomp down the stairs with Armond under her arm like a football and knock on my door. When I answered it, her face contorted with anger, she'd say, "I'm taking Armond to the orphanage. He's a very bad boy. I can't stand him anymore." Then Armond would cry and Sasha would make him promise to be good, then end the dramatics. Or if she was really furious, she carried it further, dragging the kid to the car then off to some building she told him was an orphanage. Anyway, one day I'd gone somewhere and not returned until dusk. Maybe Jason had done something to piss her off, like tease Armond, or maybe Sasha was just being a nut, I don't know, but when I came home she was standing in the hallway livid. "You're a terrible mother," she said. "You don't deserve to have a child. How could you leave an eight-year-old for five hours? Five hours unattended?" At the time I thought to say, At least I don't threaten my kid with an orphanage, but instead I just shrugged.

Now I thought of what Sasha had said in light of my mother's pointing out the physical neglect of Jason, and I thought the two of them had something. I was becoming a more terrible mother than ever. I wondered, in fact, if I weren't dissipating altogether.

There was plenty of evidence. For one thing, I was smoking marijuana before class more and more frequently. For another, I had on occasion taken to mixing Kahlúa with milk and substituting it for coffee in the morning. And last semester I'd gone to my dean, sat Jason on my lap as evidence, then asked to drop a class. I said, "It's unfair that at this university there are students who have a maid come in to clean their bathroom when I have to carry the same course load, cook and clean for a kid, plus work part-time at a job (as an editorial assistant, ten hours a week)." The dean had simply agreed and said, "Sure. If you want, drop the class. We understand it's more difficult for you single mothers."

That gave me more time, so what I did was take up with a drug dealer named Sonny Tune, who drove a Lincoln Continental and carried a gun in a briefcase. Half the reason I went with the guy was to be able to tell people and to see the look on the Jameses' faces when I let it drop that Sonny kept his gun under the bed every time he slept over. Sonny didn't last long though. Since he could only call me from phone booths and I could only reach him at the same, he was hard enough to get in touch with, but once a judge put a subpoena out on him, it was impossible.

Next, this final semester, a couple of weeks before, in fact, I went to a bar in Hartford and picked up this muscle-bound ape named Rocky who drove a white Caddy. When we went into his car to snort some cocaine, he rolled up a thousand-dollar bill for the purpose and said, "Do you swing?"

"What do you mean?" I said.

"You know. You and me and my buddy Sal?"

"Sure," I said, "we'll arrange it." Then gave him a fake phone number.

So this day in the car, envisioning the way Jason had looked when I dropped him at my mother's, I thought he resembled a nine-and-a-half-year-old David Copperfield after his mother died, and I decided I should stop this slip-sliding before I got carried away. I figured my dissent was the result of the minor breakdown I might be having due to my imminent graduation from Wesleyan.

Wesleyan had given me an excellent education and paid for it, besides being like a finishing school preparing me for the upper middle class. It had given me a house and shoveled my walks. It had been like the ideal father to me, but in the end it would be just like my father of flesh and blood, who'd said so long ago, "Once you leave, you're not coming back."

Let's face it, I hadn't done such a good job on my own the first time around. I figured it was no coincidence I was using men as a means to disintegrate given what success I'd had using them for the same purpose in the past—conscious or unconscious—starting with Skylar Barrister in the backseat of a car parked by a garbage dump.

I decided to watch out and begin a campaign of good health and better morals. I would begin by instituting bath time every night and by making a date for the movies the next weekend with Jason.

As it happened, the week between my resolve and our date, Cupcake broke down. The mechanic said she needed a new alternator, which would have to wait because I had no money to fix her. Seeing Cupcake covered by a mound of snow in the backyard felt like an omen. It was my last semester. I was about to graduate, and maybe I would leave better off, with a college diploma, but I might also be reduced to the status of carless person. What would that mean?

I was studying a lot of literature and seeing symbolic meanings and foreshadowings in everything. I was being silly. I cheered myself up. There were plenty of students who went four years to college without ever having a car. I could walk to all my classes. I could shop at the little, though more expensive, corner market. I could hitch rides with neighbors. Eventually, I'd save the money to fix her. It would work out.

On Saturday evening, the night of our date, it was freezing out. It had snowed for eight hours and there were mountains of snow bordering all the roads and driveways. Ice covered the paths. Jase and I bundled up and made off to see *Dog Day Afternoon* at the theater on campus, stopping first to buy Jason some penny candy at the corner market.

As soon as we felt the blast of heat in the lobby, Jason took off his mittens and stuck his hand in his pocket to fondle his candy and found there was nothing left but a single, miniature peanut butter cup. "Oh no!" he said. "They fell out the hole." His festive aspect collapsed before my eyes. Immediately, I felt guilty for the hole in his pocket, both because it was there and because I hadn't known it. We sat down. Jason, who'd been chatting lightheartedly with me on our walk, was transformed into a black hole in the seat next to me. I didn't sense him lightening up until midway through the movie, when he laughed at Al Pacino's transvestite girlfriend/boyfriend. Then, as we were exiting the theater, we ran into an acquaintance named Dan who Jason knew to have a car. Jason whispered to me, "Do you think Dan can give us a ride?"

This reminder that once again in my life I was stuck without a car, as well as his suggestion that I rely on a *man* to help us out, irritated me no end. "We're walking," I hissed under my breath. "It's good for you."

Once outside, Jason started chattering his teeth and taking tiny steps like a Chinaman to signify how cold he was. Almost beside myself with loathing by now, I grabbed his shoulder and turned him around to pull his hood up. "Ouch!" he yelled, surprising me.

People stopped and looked at us.

I dropped to my knees in front of him, said, "Hold still," and yanked his hood string so hard it broke in my hand.

"You broke it!" he screamed, which surprised me

again. Next, he yelled, "You're *nuts*! I'm running away." Hysterics were not part of Jason's repertoire. Whining, moping, arguing, yes, but hysterics definitely not. While I stood there kind of dumbfounded, he took off, leaving me in the snow, with half of the school staring, like I was a child beater.

I watched this little black figure gliding along the snow until it disappeared behind a mound and all I could see was his black sailor's cap above it, which turned around every now and then to see if I followed. My chest felt fluttery, like I was on the verge of laughing. But Jason was getting farther and farther away, so I began running. When I was close enough, I alternately ran and walked to keep him no more distant than a hundred yards. With my kid running away from me like I was his enemy, an instance of recent child abuse came to mind. He'd had a friend over from school and they were firing rubber-tipped arrows at me and the Jameses as we prepared a complicated Mexican dinner for one of our socialist professor friends. Jason must've been using us for target practice for about half an hour when my ability to concentrate on what I was doing and ignore kid disturbance reached its threshold and it dawned on me that I did not have to take this. In fact this was ridiculous to allow. So I said to one of the Jameses, "Grab that Indian." He did, and I took an egg and cracked it on Jason's head.

I thought it was a riot. Jason did not get the humor. He was outraged. His face turned red and his eyes bulged from his head and he said, "You're *crazy*!" then he ran upstairs and locked himself in the bathroom. He would not let me in, but eventually he did let the Jameses in. Later, they told me that Jason had cried and said that he was going to become a lawyer and specialize in the rights of children, which I'd heard before.

He also said that now he was afraid his friend would go back and tell his class that his mother had cracked an egg on his head. Which had never occurred to me. Now, as I saw Jason stop at the crossroads—where if he took a left he'd really be running away, but if he took a right he'd be nearly home—I stopped too, thinking that I may have been cursed by being saddled with a kid so young, but that Jason had been just as cursed by being saddled with me. He took a right. My heart stopped pounding in my ears and I walked the rest of the way. I took my time in the house, too. I could see the little puddles left by his boots on his way to the stairs to his room. I put some cider on the stove and smoked a cigarette while waiting for it to warm. I knew we had to talk, but I didn't know what I would say. I looked at the guitar he'd pretended to play earlier in the evening, standing on the hassock and bouncing on his knees. Sometimes when Jason lightened up, we could have a good time. Sometimes he could be a regular ham. We could sing in the kitchen for hours and disco dance like crazy.

He was lying in bed, the covers over his head. I sat next to him. "You're an asshole," I said to make a joke.

"Is that why you chased me all the way home?" he said. "To call me an *asshole*?" He was crying now.

Suddenly, I was mad again. "You made me feel guilty, about not having Cupcake."

"What?"

"You know she's broken and I don't have the money to fix her, yet you had to complain and complain. It's not my fault."

"That's not what it was," he said. "I wanted a ride because I was cold and tired. That's not what it was." Now he was sobbing and choking from not catching his breath. I lifted him onto my lap and rocked him. I'd thought Jason was trying to make me feel guilty when he'd simply been tired. He hadn't been thinking of me at all. Just as I hadn't been thinking of him.

Did I always believe that everything Jason said and did was for the purpose of eliciting some effect in me? Was I that egocentric? Was this a result of my thinking his being born had ruined my life, so I forgot the kid had a life of his own and only thought about how his life affected mine? Had my personality been so unformed when I had him that he simply became a part of it, like a birch grafted onto an elm?

I stroked his back. His face was hot and wet against mine. I hoped that his grandmother's thinking the sun rose and set in him would overcome his having been invisible to me.

In a month or so I got the car fixed, and in May of that year, 1978, I graduated with a bachelor of arts degree in English. In June, I began looking for an apartment in Little Italy—it was cheap and safe—in New York City, where I was determined to make my life and my fortune, whatever that would be. I found my apartment on June 24, on the same evening I totaled Cupcake.

I was alone and exiting Central Park when I didn't see the meridian separating the incoming from the outgoing traffic and sailed right over it, landing splat in the middle of the "in" side. The engine shut off and her lights went black. When I stepped out, I saw that her tires had flattened out to her sides and her belly was flush against the asphalt. I flagged down a Checker cab, which crunched into her rear end as it pushed her against the curb on Fifth Avenue, where I left her. When I returned the next morning for a visit, her doors were flung open, her battery gone, the contents of her glove compartment strewn all over, and the golf ball that had been her gear-shift handle ripped off and gone forever. I sat by her on the bench all day and wept.

I'd planned on giving Cupcake away anyway. She was eighteen years old, not worth much money, and I'd been told I wouldn't need her in New York. She'd be too difficult to park and expensive to keep. Now I wished I'd never driven her to New York at all, that I'd parked her in my parents' backyard, where she'd have been safe, drilled a hole in her roof, and planted a tree through it.

PART
TWO

CHAPTER 15

WHEN we reach my parents', it's nine in the evening, pitch-black out, and no longer pouring rain. We see my mother at the window and in a second she's at the door. She doesn't wait until we've stepped out of the car before she starts talking, "So you finally made it. What weather."

"I bet she's been waiting at the window for three hours," Jason whispers to me.

"Only rain," I say.

"But in all that traffic?"

Jason lopes up the hill to the front door, where my father is now standing behind my mother. My mother kisses Jason while my father shakes his hand and puts his other hand on my son's shoulder, which is taller than his. "The college kid," he says, giving Jase a pat. This trinity in the doorway, a lawn length away, makes me feel strange. Lonely or melancholy, aware, at least, of how nothing stays the same.

We go into the house, and I feel like a clairvoyant. I can predict exactly what will happen in the next half hour. My mother will ask a million questions about the journey, as though we'd come halfway across the world through continents deluged by monsoons when all we did was drive two and a half hours north on the interstate from Manhattan in the rain. Jason will cut himself a piece of whatever she's baked for the occasion, eat it, then go up to the attic recreation room, otherwise known as his room. The Castro convertible will already be made into a bed. He'll take his science-fiction book out of his backpack, lie on the bed with the remote for the cable next to him, and settle in for the night. Since he became a teenager, when he comes to his grandparents', he seeks solitude in corners like a cat. At home in New York, because our apartment is so small, he either shuts the door to his room or goes down to the Polish bar a couple of blocks away, where he plays chess with an old Romanian who wears paper bags for hats, or he plays pool for hours and hours, for as long as he holds the table.

Is this sad?

My kid had no cozy living room with family portraits on the wall, no clan of siblings fighting for space on the couch. No. My son had only me. More to the point of my feelings right now, I had only my son and a cat named Lou to keep me company in my apartment. And now, with his imminent departure to the upstairs room, I am anticipating the grander, deeper, more permanent departure to college that will come the next day. But what's the big deal? Why the moroseness? Hadn't I been shaking my fist at the ceiling, wishing for solitude and an apartment of my own? Hadn't I been chomping at the bit for the day I'd be minus one guilt-inducing kid to take care of? Then, like a flash of lightning, I'm struck with an image of not so long ago. Of his waiting for me to get out of a car so he could walk with me hand in hand. I'm being dramatic. I can't help it. Endings do that to me. Besides, it's in my blood.

Everything goes as predicted, and once Jason has gone off to his room, my father shifts focus back to the

TV and my mother and I sit in the kitchen with cups of tea in front of us. My mother stirs some milk in and says, "My prayers were answered."

"Ma," I say. "Do you actually pray?"

"Of course. What do you think I am? Of course," she says, offended.

"Well, you know, some people use it as a saying. I was just wondering if you really pray or use it as a saying."

"Every night. I prayed for Jason to get all A's and get a scholarship. Then, when he did, I said I'd say so many extra Our Fathers and I forget how many Hail Marys. I pray that you'll do good with your writing. I don't ask for anything for myself. Just give me the strength."

I'm a little shocked by this revelation. I mean, I knew my mother believed in God, if only by the amount of times she'd say, "See? God punished you," when, for example, I'd dropped a gallon of milk on my toe. And her most common curse evoked the Holy Family: "Jesus, Mary, and Joseph, if you kids don't shut up, I'll kill you." But she never went to church, except for baptisms and funerals. She said the priests were mostly Irish and money hungry. But now that I think of it, there's always been that string of mother-of-pearl rosaries hanging on her bedpost, which I'd assumed was for decoration, like the crucifix above her bed.

Now I have the vision of my mother, this short lady (my mother has shrunk about two inches since my childhood) with a big nose and hair that's more pink than brown because the gray refuses to take the dye anymore, lying on her back, clutching her rosary beads to her flat chest, praying for me and Jason and the rest of her family night after night for years and years and years. I figure I'm lucky. How many people have a mother praying for them every night? But knowing my mother, she was probably praying for the wrong thing—like the time I told her I'd be going to college and she said, "I thought you wanted a job." But then, I've been thinking lately that maybe there's a big design, that the end is already there in the beginning and there's nothing we can do about it, not in a lifetime. Nothing we can do about the events, but plenty we can do with them. It all comes down to the way we look at things.

Right now, I'm thinking my mother's looking at me like I'm a heathen. She says, "I bet you don't even remember your prayers."

"I remember," I say.

Now Jason walks through the kitchen on his way to brush his teeth but is bushwhacked by my mother, who has come back down to earth for her role as mother-provider. "I bought you soap, you know, a big pack—economy—shampoo, toothpaste, Q-tips, shaving cream, a couple of notebooks, pens, socks, underwear; can you think of anything else?"

"No," Jason says.

"No," I say.

"You got sheets, towels, a pillow?"

"Yes," Jason says.

"Yes," I say.

"You got a raincoat, boots?"

"No," Jason says, when I was about to say yes. "I don't wear a raincoat or boots," he says. That's the difference between Jason and me. I'll lie 100 percent of the time to get my mother off my back, Jason only 50. Now he's got her going.

"What? You'll catch your death. What're you going to do when it rains?"

"Drown," Jason says, and I laugh.

"And you," my mother says. "I suppose you never make him."

I just shrug. It's the old debate. Good mother, bad mother. Is it worse to have an overprotective one who tries to keep you a kid forever or one who verges on neglecting you and therefore makes you responsible for yourself? Did I neglect Jason out of indifference? I don't think so. It was just our habit. We'd started out as one kid looking after another, and things haven't changed too much, even though I'm now about to turn thirty-six. I went to the source and asked Jason once. We were at a diner in our neighborhood in downtown New York. I was buttering a piece of bread and Jason was sinking an ice cube in his Coke with a straw. He was being moody and uncommunicative, a common state since he had started to sprout pimples a year before. He was fifteen at the time.

"Do you wish you had a real mother?" I said.

He smiled. "We're more like roommates than mother and son, aren't we?"

"Yeah," I said, startled to hear coming out of his mouth what I'd often thought to myself. "But do you ever wish we were more normal?"

"No," he said. "It's better we're this way."

He might've just been trying to shut me up, so I continued with the questions—in search of the truth or, maybe, reassurance. "If I were a regular mother"—I helped him along—"I wouldn't let you play pool at Stella's."

"Right."

"Or stay home from school when you felt like it."

"And you'd probably make me make my bed every day."

"But I'd also cook you breakfast and dinner."

"That's true," he said.

Jason and I grocery shopped together, and he cooked as often as I did, although his repertoire was limited to tacos and hamburgers and frozen dinners (for himself, not for me), while I could be a good cook when I felt like it. Half our meals were eaten at the very diner we were sitting at—an entree of meat, mashed potatoes, and a vegetable for $2.95. Or we ate take-out from the Chinese restaurant around the corner or Pete's A Pizza on 14th Street.

"Still," I said. "You're glad?"

"Ma, you're a good mother," he said.

He might've just said it to spare my feelings, but that was as good as his telling the truth. Jason, I was aware, had become my friend. It started when we moved to New York. Neither of us knew another soul but each other, and for the first time in my life, I couldn't dump Jason on my mother and his loyalty shifted from her to me. Maybe it began when we heard gunshots in the night and talked through the wall dividing our rooms in the darkness. "Did you hear that, Ma?"

"Yeah."

We walked all over the city, going to double-feature movies, shopping in thrift shops, staring at people on the street. We held hands everywhere we went. When I was with Jason, the men with menacing eyes and animal noises coming from their mouths left me alone out of respect for the young man, or maybe respect for motherhood.

When I discovered a great bar a couple of blocks west, with pictures of Al Pacino and Frank Sinatra on the wall, I went there for beers with Jason, who the owner treated to Cokes and chips. Jason learned to play pool and, on Friday nights, at the age of ten, could sometimes hold the table for as long as two hours. But after seven or eight months of camaraderie, I met Nigel. Nigel was eleven years older than I and a painter. He'd been to parties with John and Yoko and lived in the Chelsea Hotel, where Sid murdered Nancy. I was impressed. He carried a camera everywhere and documented my every sigh, dirty look, and burst of laughter with the click of his camera. I made up to cosmetic companies for all those years I had never used their products, because I'd become a twenty-eight-year-old walking, talking, club-hopping Barbie.

Jason hated Nigel. Probably because he was a nut. And looked like it. He had blond hair that stood on end and intense bulging blue eyes that never softened. He was afflicted with severe separation anxiety, which meant he couldn't let me out of his sight. At the time this was fine with me, because it meant he'd support me if I quit my job as a secretary, which I'd taken to feed me and Jason while I continued doggedly writing my short poems, if you can call them that: "I purple my hair my eyes my mouth. My cheeks I paint blue. I make myself into a bruise for you." And I kept a notebook of graffiti for future reference: "Lick me, eat me, make me write bad checks. Lexington Avenue Line, Canal Street, 1979." Maybe I liked that line so much because Nigel could've written it. The guy was a raging alcoholic who threw money around like toilet paper. So once the money ran out from a painting he'd sold, we had to leave the beautiful cathedrallike loft he'd sublet and I got a job typing on a computer three nights a week.

Meanwhile, poor Jase was being ostracized in an all-Chinese school, where he excelled in his schoolwork but had no social life whatsoever, except when he stopped at the post office on his way to school to buy some first-issue stamps that he'd sell to the kids for a profit. Soon, though, after we lost the sublet, we moved to an empty two-hundred-year-old building that was no more than an abandoned construction site. We were planning on renovating it, but in the meantime we slept next to cement bags and walked up stairs made of cinderblocks and washed dishes with a hose poised over a floor drain. Jason met two boys in our new neighborhood, Juno and Amos, kids of sculptor parents who'd lived in a camper on the streets for a couple of months, and for a year in a ditch in New Mexico, so Jase had something in common with his new friends. They began shining shoes in bars for spending money, while I began to seriously dissolute in the same bars with Nigel, making my fear about using men to slip-slide away a reality. Finally, at the bar around the corner, there appeared a gypsy fortune-teller who for five dollars threw three pyramid-shaped dice and told me to ditch Nigel. "And who is the boy?" she said. "The one with light hair and light eyes? He is crying for you. Alone. The man will eat you alive. Leave him, and go with the boy. That is your salvation."

I took her advice and Jason, and I dumped Nigel, who wasn't what you'd call easy to get rid of, because after we moved to our current apartment, a fifth-floor walk-up perched on a corner of Avenue A in the East Village, Nigel called every other minute, then began to appear after midnight, on the corner, calling to my window, "Beverly, Beverly, I love you, you asshole."

Eventually, like a bad dream, he went away, and I decided I had to get back on track. I would enroll one day in graduate school for writing, but right then, typing three nights a week barely paid the rent, so I added nude modeling to my résumé. Which I thought would be good therapy, considering my inhibitions about being nude in front of people unless I'm having sex.

Jason was twelve and disapproved. One night we were walking to the movies and out of the blue he comes up with, "What's a call girl?"

"A high-class whore you make a date with on the phone."

"That's what you are."

"What?"

"Men call you on the phone and ask you to take your clothes off, don't they?"

With the onset of Jason's puberty, it was beginning to feel like Jason was trying to step into the role of my father. He always wanted to know where I was going, what time I'd be home, and then how much money I'd spent. He told me he was planning on becoming a millionaire and then he'd give me an allowance, but no more than a thousand dollars a month, because I'd just squander it.

I'd maintained since the sixties that sex was healthy and good and should not be hidden from children, but I was beginning to think twice. Especially after I left my diaphragm out to dry and Jason said, "Ma. Tell me the truth. Don't you think it's disgusting to leave that thing out, in the kitchen?" We had no bathroom, only a toilet in a closet. The tub was in the kitchen, as well as our one and only sink, so where else to put a diaphragm to dry after washing but on the shelf above the sink? But that was the last time I did that. I began to sleep with men only on weekends, when Jason went to my parents', which he did all the time, taking the two-hour train ride to New Haven, where he was picked up by my father and mother.

Then one year, Jason was almost fifteen, and he

came home from six weeks at camp six inches taller. "I can't believe it," Jase said. "Everything looks so small. I'm taller than you. I bet I can lift you up." Then he did.

The tables were turned. The balance was tipped. He was taller than me. He became the kid and I the parent.

Jason made friends with a twenty-one-year-old carpenter and began hanging out at the Polish bar down the avenue playing pool. I had quit nude modeling, was enrolled in graduate school, and spent most of my time at home writing and reading whenever I wasn't at work. I stopped having sex; Jason started having girlfriends. A whole succession of them. Then one night, when he was a junior in high school, I came home from dinner with a friend and spotted a girl's green leather jacket on a chair in the living room. The door to Jason's room was closed. I went to sleep, and in the morning the jacket was still there. I went out to buy the paper and have a cappuccino. When I came back, the jacket was gone and Jase's door was open. He was reading on his bed. "Who was here last night?" I asked him.

"Carol," he said. "She's cool. She goes to Bard and pays for school by making porn movies. But she's not really the type. You know what I mean?"

Christ, I thought to myself, is my kid going to be fascinated with wild girls because his mother was one? This Carol was the second girl who'd slept over and about the fifth girl Jase had gone out with. Was he heading for a fiasco love life like I had? Would he use women to make a demolition derby of his life, like mine? I figured we were past due for a talk.

"When I was young," I began, feeling like an idiot, uncomfortable with my new role, like I was in a situation comedy or something, "I romanticized creepy people. I was attracted to the seamy side of life. I was very impatient to have experiences. But you know, Jase, you're only innocent once, and when you lose it, it's gone. Gone forever. So don't be in such a hurry, okay?"

"I'm not like you," he said.

I didn't have to reflect much on that one. The kid and I were like night and day, starting with our appearance. I was as dark as he was light. Plus, Jase was a loner. He liked to have one friend and not a group like I had. He got all A's, worked in a bookstore, and never asked me for money.

"Sex should be about love." I changed the subject in order to get to it.

"I know."

"So how can you sleep with all those girls?"

"Who said I had sex with them?"

"Didn't you?"

"Ma, why are you so obsessed with this?"

Was I being obsessed? Did I have a sexual fixation? Was I a maniac about it where my son was concerned, like my father had been with me? This definitely could be a case of generational repeating. This was not the first such conversation I'd had with Jason. I'd told him to always carry rubbers and not to leave it up to the girl to use birth control, because girls had mysterious, unconscious wishes for pregnancy and cannot be trusted. I told him liberated men always shared responsibility. Speaking of which, this would be a good time to put another word in. "I hope you're using birth control."

"Let's drop it, okay?"

"What if you got a girl pregnant? That would be just wonderful."

"I wouldn't mind having a baby."

"*What*? Are you trying to make me crazy? I thought you were going to college."

"I could go to college with a kid. You did."

I felt like grabbing my hair with both hands and pulling, but I got a grip on myself. This called for a modulated voice and sensible words, because obviously, Jason was trying to incite a one-woman riot. "Do you know about the urge to repeat?" I said very slowly and calmly. "People repeat things for generations and generations without being aware. I got pregnant. Mim got pregnant. Grammy got pregnant. Three generations. Don't make it four."

"Grammy was pregnant? Who told you?"

"Mim. A long time ago. Didn't I tell you?"

"I don't remember. I don't think so."

"She got pregnant by a German with blue eyes who took off for the war, so Irene, her mother, got big Matt Donofrio to marry her. He was an Italian immigrant, twenty years older, and a jealous maniac. He had a pizza-parlor business on the corner and a taxi-cab business too, but the phone was at their house. If ever he heard somebody had called and Grammy didn't answer, he'd run home, pull her onto the porch, and smack her. He did it in public, because he thought she was screwing with a neighbor."

"Wow," Jason said.

"Those old Italians were lunatics. Big Matt used to be a bootlegger too, and more than once he got hauled down to the station for fighting. Pop said it took three cops to pin him down and that the old-timers on the force used to say to Pop, 'Your old man would turn in his grave if he could see his son in uniform.' But of course, there's not much difference between cops and criminals. Come to think of it, that's three generations, too: Big Matt, Pop, and Uncle Mike."

I wondered if there was a precedent in our family for born-again virgins like me. Come to think of it, there were only two other college graduates in my family, both elementary-school teachers, and they didn't have the most active sex lives. One, my father's sister, didn't get married until she was over thirty, and had a nose that twitched like a rabbit or like she'd just been shocked by an overdose of carbonation; and the other, my father's cousin, never married. She was so wide that whenever she came for a shower or a wedding, she had to sit on two chairs pushed together. Well, I'd never wanted to marry after Raymond, and I supposed I'd had enough sex to last a lifetime, and fact was, I didn't even miss sex itself that much. Maybe what I missed was love.

Then out of the blue, like a siren, Olivia, the one remaining Italian, besides me, in our mostly Puerto Rican building decided she wanted to be my friend and began telling me her life story in installments. Olivia was the real thing, an authentic old maid. She was in her sixties, short, and shaped like a block. Her hair was dyed blue-black and on the street she wore a dramatic black cape that reached her ankles and a tartan red beret. She inevitably had two shopping bags hanging from her hands, maybe for balance. It was the summer before Jason's senior year, when I was about to turn thirty-five, that Olivia decided to open the door to her apartment every time I tried to pass it on the stairs and invite me in for conversation, which meant to tell me the story of her life.

Her apartment was shiny and white and smelled of gas. She had a plastic ivy creeping up her window and plastic birds stapled to the vine. The last time, she didn't even offer me instant coffee before she started talking, kind of breathless like the air was trapped in her chest, and I knew tonight we would get to the point of her story.

"My life," she said, "was ruined. See these ugly black shoes? Orthopedic. Didn't you ever notice the way I walk? Slow, like the clicking of a clock. The kids teased me on our way to school. I could never keep up. Never got married because of my feet. I know three languages, but I never traveled. I gave up religion because I'm so bitter."

I thought this confession would make her start crying, but apparently she'd given that up a long time ago.

That night in bed, I was awakened by the screech of a bird and the hysterical flapping of wings. A sparrow was flailing around my living room, knocking into walls, whacking its head on the ceiling. I couldn't watch it, let alone try to catch it. I called to Jason.

He trapped the bird in the bottom shelf of the book case, then picked it up and held it in his cupped hands. He looked at it for a moment, petted its head with his finger, then put his hand out the window, and the bird flew off.

When I went back to bed, I couldn't sleep. I kept thinking about birds leaving nests. Flying and getting trapped. Beliefs that cripple and hands out windows. Then I thought of Olivia and how her feet had hobbled her life. No. She had hobbled her life with her belief about her feet.

For half of my life, since the day I got pregnant, in fact, I'd thought I'd been stunted by Jason's birth. But that had only been one way to look at it. Another way to look at it would be that the kid enriched my life, and maybe saved me from getting into even more trouble. With a kid to care for, no matter how haphazardly, I had to keep at least one foot on the ground always. This may have been a good thing. Maybe I never would've been given the opportunity to go to college if I hadn't been a mother on welfare. Maybe I would've been feeling much older right now if I hadn't had a kid, because in the act of being forced to grow up so fast, I rebelled and stayed a kid much longer, which contributed to my bohemian life-style (which was dismally out of sync in the middle of the eighties) and my lack of money (ditto), but it had also kept my perspective fresh, my friends the type of women who decide to buy Harley-Davidsons for themselves at the age of forty-five, and a portion of my interest focused on nothing but joy.

Jason ruined my life or he enriched it. My choice. You're just handed some things in life that you have no control over, so you'd better learn from them rather than letting them get you—like Olivia, stewing in bile and bitterness in a stark-white apartment, alone, with birds stapled to her window.

In the morning, before Jason wakes up, I sit in the kitchen with my parents. My father's eating Special K, my mother and I, rye toast. "You're going to miss him," my mother says.

"Yes," I say, not wanting to have this conversation at the same time I'm grateful that somebody's empathizing.

"I remember when your brother went in the service, I cried. Every day. Then when we couldn't contact him, when he was on that secret mission, remember? And finally I called the Red Cross and he called from a staticky phone on some ship? I thought I'd go out of my mind if I didn't hear from him. But at least you won't have to worry about Jason. You know we'll be here if ever he needs anything. I'll probably end up doing his laundry. You know me."

I wonder, not for the first time, if my wanting Jason to go to Wesleyan so badly had not a little to do with the comfort of knowing my parents would only be miles away. I also wondered if, in a way, I was giving him back to them for a while when he was still almost a kid, because we'd always shared the parenting.

"Knowing Jason," my father says, "he'll be home so often you'll get sick of him."

I honestly didn't know if I'd be happy or sad to have him home all the time. But I did know my father was trying to ease the pain. We have a good relationship now. When he retired from the force, he confessed that he'd hated his job for years. Now that he's retired, he builds things: a shed in the backyard, an extra kitchen in the basement; plus, he crochets afghans of clashing colors. He has trouble following directions from the books, so I teach him new stitches when I visit. And we talk about this and that. I realize that some of that time in the years gone by when he was silent, it wasn't because he was mad at me or critical, it was because he was in a bad mood about the politics in his department or some criminal he'd arrested who'd just gotten off scot-free or his life in general.

Our relationship began to change before he retired, though. It was the Christmas after I turned thirty, the same month John Lennon died, which, at the time, I interpreted as the end of youth and the demise of innocence. Now that I was a bona fide adult, I was even more sick and tired than I'd always been of the repetitious obligation of holidays with my family, so I'd resolved to make this visit short. I was arriving on

Christmas Eve and leaving early the next day, nine o'clock in the morning, to go back to the city and spend Christmas with a boyfriend. My mother protested. I insisted. My whole family was pissed, because for the first time in history, we would open our gifts on Christmas Eve, to accommodate me.

My mother woke me up at seven-thirty Christmas morning. I sat in the kitchen with her and my father and spread some cream cheese on a slice of date-nut bread. My mother poured me a cup of coffee and said, "You have a heart of gold." I was used to her saying I had a big head. This heart-of-gold stuff was new to me and it put me on guard. She was saying it because the night before, I'd given my sister Rose one of my gifts. I'd given it to her because I didn't like it.

"No I don't," I said.

"You'd give anybody the shirt off your back," she insisted.

"No I wouldn't," I insisted back.

"Then you've changed," she said. I could've said, No I haven't, but decided to end the game.

My father got up and started putting on his shoes. I told him I didn't need a ride to the station. I'd rather walk.

"You sure? It's cold out," he said.

"I'm sure," I said, looking forward to the solitude.

I kissed Jase on the forehead without waking him, then I left. At the station, I sat on the bench and smoked a roach I'd found in my pocket. A train flew by in the wrong direction. Then there was no other. It was freezing out and I was beginning to get worried. I sat on my hands and jiggled my body. I moved my feet in circles to get them circulating. I looked up. My father was walking toward me.

The first thing I thought was, Good thing I finished

the roach, and the next thing I thought was, Why's he spying on me?

"Thought I'd check to see you got off all right," he said when he got closer.

I knew it was the truth. He hadn't been spying, just concerned. He was a father looking after his daughter. That was the other side of the story. The story of the man worried about the teenage daughter he'd just spotted ducking in the backseat of a passing vehicle full of drunk teenagers. So simple. But to me it was a revelation. Maybe he loved me after all.

He pulled a schedule from his jacket. There wasn't a train for two hours. He offered to drive me to New Haven. We'd have just enough time to make the next one. On the ride to the station, I wanted to talk. To let him know in some way I knew how he felt. To let him know how I felt. But never past the age of four had we talked. How could I start now, on Christmas, during a twenty-minute car ride? He turned on the radio. "Silent Night" came on. I sang. He sang the harmony.

When Jason and I say goodbye to my parents, there are tears in my mother's eyes and I know they're for me, because definitely, by the weekend my father will drive her to Jason's dorm room. She'll give him a banana bread wrapped in tin foil, remark on what a mess his room is, and start picking up his laundry to take home.

In the car heading for Wesleyan, I say, "What do you remember most about living there?"

"The kids," he said. "They taught me to ride a two-wheeler, remember?"

"Uh-huh. Are you nervous now? Afraid it won't be the same as it was?"

"Yeah. Sometimes I think I should've stayed in New York. Gone to Columbia."

"No." I insist, thinking that he'd live in our apartment for four more years, when it was time to make the break. Time to grow up. For both of us. "It'll be good for you to experience the country. Smell the seasons. Live a different life from subways and bars and traffic fumes for a while."

"But people in Connecticut are stupid."

"What?"

"They are."

"You're saying that if we never moved to New York and we stayed in Connecticut we'd be stupid?"

"Yes."

"Oh God. I never in my life ever dreamed I'd raise a snob. People in New York are maybe more sarcastic and quick, but it doesn't make them smarter. Don't kid yourself." I looked at him then. Black jeans, black T-shirt, sneakers, sunglasses. I wondered if he looked like a city slicker. I wondered how he'd get on. If he'd be expecting it to be one way, the way he remembered, and when he found it different, which he surely would, if he'd hate it. Maybe it had been a mistake to try to go back to utopia, but we'd never questioned it, not for a second. I'd promised him from the day we left for New York, and he'd wanted to stay at Wesleyan, that he could go to school there himself, provided he got all A's in high school. So he got a ninety-two-point-something average, and then came running home the fall of his senior year in a panic. "Ma!" he said. "The lowest average Wesleyan accepted from Stuyvesant last year was ninety-four. They'll never give me a scholarship."

This news threw me into a panic too. I'd just finished graduate school myself the year before. I'd been proofreading and copyediting, mostly at my kitchen table. We had no money, as usual. The only schools he could "afford" to go to were extraordinarily expensive schools like Wesleyan, because they were the ones with big endowments. If he had to go to a state school, I didn't know how we'd swing it. But I acted cool. I said, "Well, then we should consider an alternative. Part of the state university system, Cornell, plus another elite school, Yale or Amherst or someplace."

"You promised I could go to Wesleyan. If I don't get in, I'm joining the air force."

"What?"

"We wouldn't have to pay. Plus, I could wear a uniform. I'd fly a fighter jet. I'd carry a gun."

Now I knew what my mother had meant when she said I was killing my father. I felt like three bullets went straight to my heart. So this is what kids of hippies grow up to be: future four-star generals. The next day I was copyediting at a magazine and had to run into the bathroom for a half-hour weep when I started thinking that maybe this was GI Joe residue. Maybe this air force bullshit was all about his father who, after all, had been in the 101st Airborne Division.

When Jason was eleven, he began asking questions. "What does my father look like? Where do you think he lives? Do you think we could find him if we wanted?" At the time, I thought maybe Jason needed his father because of the approach of puberty. I suggested he make a search. He called the one phone number I had, which was his great-grandmother's, in Bangor, Maine. She gave us the number of his grandmother, who refused to give Jase his father's number, probably because she was afraid we were after back alimony and child support. But she did say she'd give our number to Raymond. Raymond called that same afternoon. Jason talked to his father for a minute, saying, "Fine. Sixth grade. Okay. New York. Good." Then he handed the phone to me.

I'd recognize the voice anywhere.

"I hear you been to college. That's good. You always were smart. I been married again. Fucked that up too. Met her after Nam. We got two girls. Then I left. Don't see them neither. You know what they say: Once a fuck-up . . . I got a job. Loading stuff on trucks. Same old shit. I'm living with a lady. She got a baby. It's not bad. So, how's Jason? He a good kid?"

"Yeah," I said, not elaborating, because I wanted off the phone in the worst way.

"I was wondering. What if Jason came for a visit? We live up at Greenwood Lake. It's only two hours by bus. They got one from the Port Authority."

I took Jason to the bus the next weekend. As we stood on line, he said, "How will I know him?"

I'd shown him a picture. "You saw what he looks like."

"What if he doesn't look like that anymore?"

"Don't worry. You'll recognize each other. I know it."

When he came home, he brought a bag of chocolate-chip cookies baked by Raymond's girlfriend. He didn't say much, except that his father lived with a woman who was nice and had a daughter named Juice because she liked it. He said his father was a little fat and they went to bars, where Jason played pinball and Raymond watched television.

His father had given him twenty dollars and a promise to get in touch.

1 9 9

A year later, Jason said, "How much is Social Security?"

"What do you mean?"

"If my father was dead and I got Social Security, how much would it be?"

"I don't know. Maybe two hundred a month."

"How would we know if he died? We should find out. I could get money."

"Jason," I said. "Which would you rather get, a birthday card or Social Security?"

"A birthday card," he said, diverting his eyes to look out the window.

I blew my nose in the bathroom stall at work. I put on fresh lipstick and went back to my desk to take advantage of the WATS line. I called up the air force academy and asked them to send an application. I asked them questions, then called Jason up and used reverse psychology, like in the old days. I said, "They're sending a catalog. They said we'll have to get a senator from this state to recommend you. Did you know they give you physcial training, like in boot camp? It might be good for you. . . ."

"Ma. I was only saying that. You better get me into Wesleyan."

"I better get you in?"

"You promised. You said if I got A's I could go there."

The subtext was that he'd done his part by being a good student and now it was my part as his parent to provide him with college. Hadn't I been furious at my parents for not being able to afford to send me to college? Wasn't this another skip in the record, another generational repeat? He was right. It was partly my responsibility to get my kid to college, but it still pissed me off. I'd just finished getting myself through college, and then graduate school, with no help from parents. And now, to have my kid threaten me with "you betters" and enlistment in the armed forces was too much.

"Get yourself in. It's your life, not mine. You're acting like an idiot."

"You're an idiot."

"Don't you call me an idiot."

He hung up on me.

We hated each other for a couple of days, then eventually started acting like nothing had happened, which was one of our routines.

I knew a great college essay would do the trick. The requested subject was: Describe the person who had the greatest influence on you in your life.

Jase thought he should write about me. Then I came up with a brilliant idea. "What if," I said, "you wrote about the absence of your father."

"Yeah," he said, barely nodding his head. "They'd like that. But that's harder."

"That's what makes it so great."

Jason's dorm room is a single. He has a bed, a bureau, a desk, and a closet. He also has a balcony, which we stand on first thing. "Smell it," I say, talking about the air.

"Nice," he says.

"Look at your view." It's of a hill with pine trees.

"Um-hm," Jase says.

"Well? Isn't it gorgeous?"

"Yes."

I want him to be more enthusiastic. I want him to set me at ease about leaving him here. When we start unpacking, he opens his suitcase and I see that he's jammed everything in without folding. On the top there's a sweater covered with dust and cat hair. I tell him to shake it over the railing and get a guilt pang because I hadn't helped him pack like a normal mother. Next he begins putting his shirts in a drawer.

"Jase," I tell him. "You hang shirts in a closet." The last closet he had was when we lived at Wesleyan. How would he ever fit in? Across the hall, I see a kid unpacking with his parents and his sister. He's hooking up a complex stereo system. There's a computer on his desk. An Indian rug on the wall. Jason has a clock radio and a portable typewriter. His bottom and top sheets don't match.

"Jase," I say. "Look at that kid's room."

"Nice," he says.

"Do you think you're going to feel deprived?"

"What do you mean?"

"A lot of kids are going to be rich. Most of them are going to have more than you. Do you think it'll make you mad or jealous?"

"I don't care about that stuff, and neither do you."

I wasn't talking only about the things. I was talking about the father and sister in addition to the mother. This I don't tell him.

After his room's set up, we ride over to the hockey rink parking lot, where he's supposed to group with two hundred kids to go on a camping trip for a kind of orientation. Our two old houses across the road appear exactly the same. The hockey rink hasn't changed either except for the parents and students milling around eating cookies and drinking lemonade.

When Jase and I reach for some cookies, he floors me by saying, "I wonder if they think you're my girlfriend. You look young for your age and I look old."

It's not that I hadn't wondered the same thing

about a million times. For the past couple of years, whenever we'd walked together or gone out to eat, people looked at him, then at me, like I was an older woman with a younger man, not a mother with her son. But I'd had no idea Jase had been aware of this too.

"Does it bother you?" I ask him.

"No. I think it's cool."

After he says this, I have to admit to myself I do too.

We take our cookies and lemonade and instead of socializing like we're supposed to, we sit on a hill, our arms touching, watching. In the summer that just passed, Jase and I spent many nights at the Polish bar, sitting on barstools, drinking Cokes or beers, watching. One night, a guy I'd begun seeing surprised me by dropping by. When I introduced him to Jason, Jase stood up and shook his hand, then offered him his stool. When my friend went to the bathroom, Jase said, "He's a nice guy, Mom. I like him. When he comes back, I'll stay for a minute, then leave so you can be alone."

"You don't have to."

"I don't mind."

Jason was being chivalrous. He was being a friend, and he was giving me permission to have a boyfriend. It made me very happy at the same time it made me want to hug him and keep him near. Our days as a couple were coming to a close.

Kids were beginning to form lines near the buses. "Maybe it's time for me to go?" I ask.

"Yeah," he says.

When we get to the car he opens the door for me. I hug him for what seems like a long time but is probably short. I say, "I love you."

"I love you too," he says. His eye kind of twitches and I hope with all my heart he doesn't start crying.

I resist the urge to look for him in the rearview. By the time I reach my first stop sign, I'm sobbing so hard I have to pull to the side of the road. It occurs to me that I have never felt so alone in my life. I make a turn that points me in the direction of Wallingford, and when I see the old reservoir approaching I feel much calmer. I decide to spend the evening at my parents', but once I reach the entrance to the interstate I've changed my mind. I turn south, and go home.